HUSBAND MISSING

BOOKS BY LISA REGAN

HUSBAND MISSING

LISA REGAN

bookouture

Published by Bookouture in 2025

An imprint of Storyfire Ltd.
Carmelite House
50 Victoria Embankment
London EC4Y 0DZ

www.bookouture.com

The authorised representative in the EEA is Hachette Ireland
8 Castlecourt Centre
Dublin 15 D15 XTP3
Ireland
(email: info@hbgi.ie)

ISBN: 978-1-83618-395-2
eBook ISBN: 978-1-83618-394-5

For Kathy Magliane, Bonnie Heintzelman, Harriett Perez, and
Gretchen Oman
for teaching me so much about good mothering

PROLOGUE

TWELVE YEARS AGO

Hunger gnawed at Bug's stomach. The cold from the rock beneath her seeped through her thin pants, numbing her bottom and creeping down her legs until her feet felt like two blocks of ice. She thought about her gloves, bright red like the lipstick her mom let her try sometimes, tucked away in her top dresser drawer at home. If she'd known that she'd be sitting outside all day, she would have brought them. Her boots, too. And her hat. At least she had her coat, though even that wasn't stopping her body from shivering. But there was no way she could have known she'd end up here, tucked away along the side of the road between two huge trees, watching the lights blink on in the house on the hill as evening fell.

Her mother never told her where they were going.

"Life's for adventures," she always said, grinning in that way that was both exciting and kind of scary. Bug's mom had this way of making her feel important, like a best friend. At the same time, there was a shadow in her eyes, flickering behind every smile like the warning light that always came on in their old car.

"It don't mean nothing," her mom would mutter every time

it winked on before slapping her hand violently against the dash.

This didn't mean anything either, right? Her mom wouldn't *leave* her here.

Her mom had never left her behind before. Not forever.

Then again, this was the first time her mom ever went inside the big house. They'd driven past it more times than she could count, her mom always slowing the car, neck craning to stare up at it like it was the first time she'd seen it. It was big. Bigger than any house Bug had ever seen, even on television. It was fancy, too. Pretty like a Barbie Dreamhouse even though it was made of shiny wood, stone, and enormous windows.

The best part was the railing along the big porch. Instead of bars, the black metal had been shaped to show a scene from the woods. Deer running and leaping through trees and over logs. Big deer. Some of them with lots of antlers and others with none. The whole thing was in silhouette, her mom had explained. Bug loved that word. It was one of the most magical words she'd ever learned, to go with one of the most magical things she'd ever seen. She understood why her mother was so obsessed with it. Whenever they drove past, Bug imagined them living there one day. They would always have water from the faucets. The lights would always work. Her mom would always feel happy. It would always be warm on cold days, and there would always be food. All the food they could possibly eat.

Just the thought of food unleashed a growl from deep in her belly. If she'd known they were coming here—that her mom was going inside—she would have brought a snack. There was a crushed two-pack of crackers, like the kind you got in the hospital, in the back of the cabinet over the top of the fridge. Her mom hadn't found it yet. It was all crumbs now but if Bug opened it carefully enough, the plastic would hold them like a little bag while she poured them into her mouth.

She wished she had it now even as guilt needled her. Maybe her mom was hungrier.

But her mom was in the big, beautiful house and she was out here.

"Stay on this rock and don't leave," her mom had told her. "Don't go anywhere until I come back."

Wind whistled through the gnarled tree branches above her. The eyes of a bunch of big, black birds stared down at her. Occasionally, one of them would shriek like someone was stabbing it and all the others would answer until it sounded like they were all being stabbed at once, over and over. She swung her legs, kicking her heels against the stone, trying to force some warmth back into her limbs.

How long until her mom came back? Soon it would be nighttime dark. Black. The soft twinkling lights of the magical house didn't reach this far. Nothing good happened when she disobeyed her mother, but could she really spend the night out here? She'd been here since morning and not a single car had come down the one-lane road. What if she died from starvation? What if she froze to death? What if the black birds pecked her frozen eyes out? What if a wild animal ate her?

The rapid *th-thump th-thump* of her heartbeat filled her ears, almost blocking out the death shrieks of the ugly birds with their dumb, ugly eyes staring at her all the time.

She needed a plan. That was all. Her mom always had a plan.

Before it got dark enough that she couldn't see her hand in front of her face, she'd walk up the long driveway to the house, knock on the door, and ask for her mom. A shiver rattled her teeth. Not from the cold this time. What if the punishment for not doing what her mom said was worse than this?

Before she could think too hard about it, a figure came walking down the long driveway, swaying and stumbling like grown-ups did sometimes when they had too much beer to drink. Fear crawled up the back of Bug's neck like a big spider. She tried to stay very still but her teeth clacked in her mouth and her heart knocked so hard against her ribs, it was difficult not to shake.

Please, please, please be Mom.

She hadn't thought about what she'd do if someone besides her mom came for her.

She clenched her jaw, willing her teeth to stop chattering. Surely, the entire forest could hear it. The figure kept coming down the driveway. Should she stay put, like her mom told her, or hide? Before she could decide, the person reached the bottom. Relief rolled through her small body when she saw it was her mom.

Finally.

Bug didn't even bother looking both ways as she sprinted across the road, clasping her mom's hand. Something hot and wet soaked her fingers. Her mother's head hung down and to the side, making her long hair swing across her face. A weird gurgling, choking noise came from behind it.

"Mom?" Her voice sounded so small and yet, so loud in the dark.

Something warm trickled down from her mom's fingers, over her wrist, and into her coat sleeve. She tried to look at it but there wasn't enough light. A whole mess of fear spiders broke out along the nape of her neck, skittering under her clothes, across her cold skin, making her breath feel funny as it pushed in and out of her body.

The creepy watcher birds were doing their death shriek again.

"Mom?"

Her mother spoke in a broken-sounding voice, the words almost jumbled, like she couldn't get the sounds right.

Bug felt her mom's sticky wet fingers jerk in her hand as they made their way along the side of the road. Hopefully they were going to where her mom had hidden their car. The heater didn't work but it might be warmer than outside.

"Did you spill something?" Bug whispered.

"Shhh." Her mom's legs wobbled. She fell to one knee with a loud grunt. Still, their hands stayed locked, the weird goo holding them together. She'd seen her mom like this before, so she wasn't all that worried.

Not until they got into the car and the sad, yellow light in the ceiling shone on her mom's face. Or what used to be her mom's face. Where her nose had been was something flat and crooked, leaking blood so thick it was almost black. Her bottom lip gaped open, split in two like a slingshot. One of her eyes looked gone, replaced by a big, purple ball. Above her other eye, the skin hung down like a flap, red and pink where her eyebrow had been.

Fear wasn't a thousand spiders anymore. It was a million watcher birds pecking every inch of Bug's skin and bone until there was nothing left and nowhere to hold the air in her body. Turning her hand back and forth, she saw her mom's blood soaked into the folds of her knuckles. Sickness sprouted deep in her belly, like after the time she ate canned soup that turned out to be "expired." A grown-up word for poison.

When she spoke, her voice sounded weird and quiet and shaky. "Mom?"

What happened in the magical house? she wanted to ask. There were so many questions, but she couldn't make her mouth work.

The engine roared to life. "Lissen ah me."

Bug really wanted to look away, but she couldn't. Her mom's lower lip flopped and dangled, revealing teeth that weren't white anymore. Slowly, she reached into her coat pocket and brought out a little cloth bag. Bug wanted to ask what was in it but she couldn't. Suddenly, her mom lunged toward her, making her heart do a little dance in her chest.

Then she stuffed the bag down Bug's shirt. Hard little things pressed through the pouch and poked against Bug's skin. There was a clinking sound, like metal.

She tried again to talk, to ask what was in the little bag and why her mom was giving it to her but her mom kept saying something. Two words. Except they didn't sound like words because her mom's face was not her face anymore. It took Bug some time to turn the sounds back into words in her own brain.

Keep. Hide.

Was it food? No, it didn't feel or sound like food. Her stomach growled loudly but her mom didn't notice. She was making more noises that Bug needed to change into regular words.

"We neber go to thah house again. Neber. Don' talk 'bout it. Don' go."

We never go to that house again. Never. Don't talk about it. Don't go.

Bug's voice came back, tinged with the tears that burned the backs of her eyes. "But we were gonna live there one day. In the magical house. You said—"

Suddenly, her mom's bloodied fingers dug into her cheeks so hard, the pain set Bug's tears free. They rolled down her face.

"Wha' I jus' say? There is no mahhical house. Nah anmore."

What did I just say? There is no magical house. Not anymore.

Bug didn't dare ask why even though she really, really wanted to.

Their faces were so close that she could see into her mother's remaining eye and what she saw there was scarier than a million spiders and a billion watcher birds. It was something she'd never, ever seen before. Her lungs stopped working. Her skin felt gross like she was dead and a bunch of creatures were crawling all over her.

The eye blinked slowly but the thing was still there, shining wetly like broken glass in moonlight.

Fear.

Her mother—who always had a plan, who stood up to people bigger and meaner than her all the time, who responded to bad things with raging fury—was afraid.

Very, very afraid.

ONE

PRESENT DAY

Josie Quinn steadied herself on the ladder and dipped her brush into the can of primer sitting on top of it. With a slow, careful stroke, she cut in from the ceiling, white barely covering the emerald green of the wall. From the floor her husband, Noah Fraley, used a roller to coat the part of the wall she'd already cut in. Music played from an app on Josie's phone, which sat on a nearby windowsill. Noah hummed along with the current song while he worked. He wore jeans and a threadbare black T-shirt and naturally, he didn't have a drop of primer on him. She had had a streak straight down her shirt and white flecks in her black hair within minutes of starting.

She should have let him cut in.

Reading her mind—which he seemed to do often and with ease—Noah said, "You should have let me cut in."

Josie went to coat another section, but she was momentarily distracted by the way the muscles in his arms flexed when he leaned into the roller. "Why didn't you say something?"

He paused, grinning wickedly, and looked pointedly at her ass. "Because the view from down here is so much better."

She didn't even care about the primer dripping from the end of her brush all over the ladder. "Is it really?"

Noah laughed, coating the roller brush again, and covering more of the green. "Stop looking at me like that. We don't have any clean drop cloths left."

Josie arched a brow. "Whose fault is that?"

Noah shook his head, but a playful smile remained on his lips as he moved further down the wall, rapidly covering the old color. "Not mine," he said, feigning innocence. "I was just minding my business, trying to finish the last wall. Now I've got primer in... places."

So did Josie but she wasn't complaining.

From the doorway, their Boston terrier, Trout, whined mournfully. They'd borrowed an old baby gate from their friend, Misty Derossi, to keep him out of the room while they worked. It wasn't going over well. He always wanted to be wherever they were and as close to one or both of them as physically possible. The hall wasn't cutting it. Even though he'd been staring at them intently without blinking for hours, Trout was having major FOMO.

"We're in the home stretch," Noah reminded her. "Let's get this finished."

Josie didn't protest. This guest room had already taken far too long to prime thanks to their inability to focus on anything but one another. They hadn't even picked out a color yet. Josie had bought the house several years ago, when she separated from her first husband, the late Ray Quinn, and she'd never bothered to paint the guest rooms, which was why this one was still green. Even after Noah moved in, there hadn't really been a reason to redecorate the rooms they barely used, but now, they were planning to adopt a baby.

A new song from Josie's playlist came on. Noah didn't know the lyrics. "I'm still thinking beige."

"Boring," said Josie.

"We agreed neutral," he said. "Since we won't know if our baby is a boy or a girl."

"Yeah, but there has to be something better than beige."

After a grueling, months-long application and vetting process, they'd finally been approved to adopt. Two months ago, they'd completed their adoptive parent profile and now, it was just a matter of waiting for the call from the agency that a birth mother had reviewed their file and was willing to give them her child to raise. This particular part of the adoption journey was both exhilarating and nerve-racking. They were as close as they'd ever been to having a child and yet, there was no guarantee that a birth mother would choose them.

They both worked for their city police department as part of its four-person investigative team. Josie was a detective and Noah was a lieutenant. They often worked long, unpredictable hours and danger was built into their jobs. The small city of Denton was located in central Pennsylvania. It was an idyllic college town that sat on the banks of one of the branches of the Susquehanna River. The city limits stretched far into the surrounding mountains. Its scenic views were in stark contrast to some of the crimes that occurred within its confines, especially as the population grew year after year. On more than one occasion, said crimes had personally affected them both in the most tragic of ways.

Josie sometimes wondered at the wisdom of trying to adopt a child while they were employed by the Denton PD, but Noah always said there would never be a right time to become parents. Plenty of couples who both had full-time jobs made it work and being in law enforcement had never stopped anyone from having children before. Whenever she worried, he reminded her that if they had to make adjustments when the baby came, they would. Josie wasn't keen on figuring it out as they went but there was no choice. The call that they'd matched with a child could come in the next five minutes or it could come in the next five years.

"What if we did some kind of theme?" she suggested.

"Like what?"

Carefully, she stepped down off the ladder and moved it a few feet over, then climbed back up. "I don't know. Animals. Like a zoo or a farm. Maybe a forest or something underwater with colorful fish and sea creatures. Or hot-air balloons. Each wall could be a mural painted in that theme."

From the hallway, Trout gave a heavy sigh. He was probably team beige, too. Anything to get them back to his very strict routine of snuggles, walks, Kong-throwing, and over-snacking.

Noah followed the ladder with his roller. "Hmmm. I like the idea of hot-air balloons and the sea creature thing, but Josie, who's going to paint these murals?"

Shit. Neither one of them was particularly artistic. They drew about as well as they cooked, which was to say badly. Sure, Misty had been giving them cooking lessons in anticipation of them adopting a baby—and they had improved—but drawing and painting weren't the same as making a meal. The kind of artistic ability that Josie envisioned gracing the walls of their future child's bedroom wasn't something that could be taught.

She finished cutting in and brought the brush and can of primer down the ladder with her, only splashing a few more drops on her already splattered purple T-shirt. Then she got the ladder out of the way so Noah could complete the final wall. She racked her brain, trying to think of anyone in their lives who might be up to the task.

"How do we not know a single person with artistic skills?"

Noah gave a half-shrug as he primed over more patches of green. "Maybe we should ask around. Someone might know someone."

The next selection on her playlist began. As the first strains of their wedding song filled the room, Noah went rigid. Slowly, he set the roller onto the floor. Without a word, he went to the windowsill and picked up her phone. The music cut off as his fingers flew across the screen. Seconds later, Coldplay's "All My Love" started to play.

"What are you doing?" Josie asked.

Instead of answering, he walked over and pulled her to him. A gasp escaped her lips. One of his large hands splayed across her lower back, while the other brought her sticky palm to his chest. She let him lead, looping her free arm around his neck as they swayed to the soft notes. After all this time, his hazel eyes still had the power to make her heart race.

Trout gave a loud, indignant cry of protest. When neither of them looked his way, he huffed for good measure.

"You love this song, right?" said Noah.

"Yes, but you turned off—"

"We never got to dance at our wedding."

That was true. Their wedding, which they'd planned in such detail and spent so much money on, had been hijacked by a murderer. Instead of exchanging vows and dancing the night away with all their loved ones, Josie had spent the day pursuing a suspect in her wedding dress while Noah ran down other leads. They'd forfeited everything to bring justice to a little girl who'd lost her mother and sister in one horrific act of violence. A few days later, they'd wed in Denton Memorial Hospital, at the bedside of Josie's grandmother, Lisette, with only their closest family members and colleagues present. It had been a somber affair since Lisette was only hours away from her last breath. The killer had taken her, too.

Josie leaned in and rested her cheek against Noah's broad chest. The happiest day of her life was also the worst day of her life.

"We never danced to the song we chose," Noah added, his warm breath caressing her forehead. "Ever."

Oddly enough, they'd roller-skated to it, but he was right. They'd never danced to their own wedding song.

"We should change it," he said. "The first one has a lot of trauma attached to it."

Josie let him guide her around the small room as they spun slowly over dirty drop cloths, content to listen to his heartbeat while the memories of her grandmother's death washed over her. It had been Lisette's final request that they get married. She knew Josie well enough to foresee that if they didn't do it before her death, Josie would never feel right doing it. Lisette also knew that Noah was—more than any other person on the planet—Josie's North Star.

"All My Love" was a perfect fit for their relationship, without the painful reminders of their tragic wedding day. Lisette would never want Josie to associate her marriage to Noah with one of the most horrific memories of her life.

"Let's do it," Josie agreed. "This song is perfect."

"Good." He kissed the top of her head. "I had another idea."

"You're just full of them." She laughed. "Let's hear it."

"We should renew our vows."

Josie lifted her face and met his eyes. "What?"

He gave her a little smile before dipping her, quite gracefully given their surroundings, and bringing her back, flush against him. "Renew our vows. Our fifth wedding anniversary is coming up this spring. Plenty of time to plan something. Nothing big. Just the usual suspects."

"Isn't renewing vows for couples who've been together for decades?" Josie asked but she was already warming to the idea. A lot.

Noah kissed her lightly, continuing to lead her in a slow dance. "I'm pretty sure it's for anyone who wants to do it. Five years is a good milestone. We can make it whatever we want. I think it would be fun."

"The wedding we never had," Josie murmured. "Sort of."

"Exactly."

Their new wedding song concluded. A more up-tempo tune came on, but Noah held her close, their bodies still slow dancing. Trout pawed at the baby gate.

"Was it Trinity's engagement that made you think of this?" Josie asked. "Because I don't want to steal her thunder."

Josie's twin sister, Trinity Payne, a famous television journalist, had just gotten engaged to her FBI boyfriend, Drake Nally. The elaborate proposal that Drake had planned and pulled off—with a lot of help from them and the rest of Josie's family—had gotten under Noah's skin. Though thrilled for Trinity and Drake, he'd expressed regret that he hadn't given Josie something so thoughtful or beautiful. His own planned proposal had taken a back seat to a series of homicides. He'd almost died during that case. Afterward, while in the hospital recovering, he'd declared that plans were stupid and proposed to her while they were both crammed into his bed. Their Chief had held off the aggressive nursing staff long enough for Josie to say yes.

Josie hadn't cared all that much about their plans continually being thwarted in the worst possible ways. She'd gotten what she wanted. Noah was hers forever.

"Trinity and Drake aren't getting married for eighteen months," he said. "There's no way we'd be stealing their thunder. The real issue is going to be stopping your sister from taking over planning every detail."

Josie laughed again. Her sneakered foot slid on a still-wet streak of primer, and she almost fell but Noah caught her expertly.

"Is that a yes?" he asked.

The song on her phone went silent as the ring tone took over. She was close enough to see Detective Gretchen Palmer's name and face flash across the screen. Of all the days to be on call, it had to be the day her husband asked her to marry him again.

Josie looked meaningfully into his eyes. "Yes. Let's renew our vows."

Another quick kiss and he released her. A joyful buzz filled her body as she stabbed at the answer icon on her phone, not even caring about the sticky white fingerprint she left behind.

"Shouldn't Douchebag be on right now?" Josie said without preamble.

Douchebag was Josie's personal nickname for Detective Kyle Turner who had joined their team roughly nine months ago. He'd replaced their beloved colleague, Detective Finn Mettner, who had been killed in the line of duty nearly two years earlier.

"I can't get hold of him," Gretchen grumbled. "As usual."

Turner's blatant disregard for their calls and texts when he was needed, despite the fact that his phone was permanently attached to his palm, as well as his chronic lateness, might have been the two things he was best at. They also had to contend with his bad attitude, sexist remarks, total lack of a filter, and inappropriate comments. Not to mention his shitty reports, always filed late. A smorgasbord of bad qualities.

Working with him had been an adjustment, to say the least.

"It's fine," said Josie. "I'm supposed to be on two hours from now. I'll just come in early."

She didn't miss Noah's scowl. Their jobs didn't allow for much free time with one another, particularly when they had a stretch where they worked opposite shifts. Josie was due home at midnight, so they'd at least get to sleep together before Noah went in the next morning, but starting then, for the next week, their schedule would change again. They'd be coming and going at different times, making it nearly impossible to enjoy their time off together. As if in solidarity, Trout whimpered unhappily.

"I just caught a shooting under the East Bridge," Gretchen said. "Gonna be here awhile. Apparently, there's been an incident at the children's hospital site. Someone needs to get over there ASAP."

Trepidation turned her stomach. "Another one?"

Months ago, developers had started building a children's hospital in southwest Denton. It was meant to rival the larger children's hospitals in Philadelphia and Pittsburgh. City council had been salivating over the idea for nearly a year before the project began, dollar signs flashing obscenely in their eyes at the thought of the new jobs and thousands of visitors it would bring to the area.

Everything had been going well until about three weeks ago when a group of teenage boys snuck into the site during the night hoping to get drunk away from the prying eyes of adults. Naturally, they'd gone to the highest point in the place—what was meant to be the northern wing of the hospital. Seven stories of subfloors and steel beams. No walls. The two security guards on duty had discovered the boys and given chase. Three of them were caught but the fourth fell, plummeting to his death in one of the more gruesome scenes Josie had witnessed during her career. The memory still made her a little nauseated.

Gretchen sighed. "Yes, another one. Some kind of fight. But from what I'm told, this happened out front. Where the protestors were gathered."

The boy who'd died, Nick Gates, happened to be Denton East High School's star football player. He was the top-ranked quarterback among his class in all of Pennsylvania, twenty-seventh in the country, according to his parents, coaches, and everyone who followed his storied high school football career. He'd already secured a full ride to one of the most prestigious universities in the nation. The tragedy had hit the city hard. With nowhere to put their grief, parents and Denton East students had started protesting outside the construction site, demanding that it be shut down altogether. City council had hoped the uproar would die down after a few days but that hadn't happened. The protestors had been loud and persistent but not violent.

"What am I walking into, Gretchen?"

"There's a fatality."

"Shit."

Although Josie had been on-scene the night Nick Gates died, she'd gotten called away to investigate a stabbing near the Denton University campus. Turner had taken the lead on the Gates case. His familiarity with the site and the staff would be useful right about now.

"That's all I know," Gretchen added. "Believe me, I'd be there already if I could. The Chief wants this dealt with immediately."

Josie took one last look at her husband. He'd picked up the roller again, working with easy efficiency. Splotches of wet paint gleamed where he'd held her hand over his heart.

"I'll be there in twenty."

TWO

Cool September air brushed over the exposed skin of Josie's forearms as she emerged from her vehicle. Broken glass crunched under her boots, vestiges of southwest Denton's former life. For as long as she could remember, this particular area of the city had been seedy, rundown, and teeming with criminal activity. Real estate value had fallen so low, you could buy an entire apartment building for a song. The developers of the children's hospital, Phelan Construction, had more or less done that; buying up nearly two city blocks of old, failing buildings—most of them condemned—and demolishing them to make way for the new project. Josie had heard the word "revitalization" on the news so many times, she was wondering if WYEP got some kind of special kickback from city council every time they said it on-air.

Maybe the hospital would be shiny and new when it was finished, but the row of dilapidated buildings across the street from it flew in the face of revitalization. Most of them sported crumbling brick façades marred with graffiti. Several had ground-floor storefronts, their glass cracked and held together with duct tape. Dented rolling metal security grilles shuttered them at night. Despite the city installing public wastebins on every corner, small heaps of trash accumulated along the broken sidewalk. The construction site itself was surrounded by tall, chain-link fencing covered with blue vinyl privacy screens on which bold white letters declared the project was being undertaken by Phelan Construction.

Josie locked her SUV and threaded her way through the rows of police vehicles clustered around the site's main entrance. From every direction, emergency beacons strobed red and blue. The small white pickup truck belonging to the city's medical examiner, Dr. Anya Feist, looked out of place among the marked cruisers, SUVs and ambulances. A low susurrus hum filled the air. Hushed conversations among shocked people. Sorrow, fear, and disbelief quieted the scene like it was a funeral home and not a dirty street in the city's shabbiest neighborhood. Among the vehicles, uniformed Denton PD officers moved from witness to witness, taking statements from each parent and student. Additional officers had separated four hulking security guards from the others, speaking quietly with them one-on-one.

One of the guards waved his hands angrily and raised his voice loud enough for Josie to hear. "These parents and their kids have been itching for a fight ever since that kid died. I don't even know why they're here other than to piss off the company. Those kids had no business being on the site."

He was right. By law, Phelan Construction couldn't be held criminally responsible for loss of life when the victim had broken the law in order to gain access to the premises. The quarterback's parents could sue the company civilly, but they were extremely unlikely to succeed for the same reason. In the aftermath, Phelan had tripled its security, but it hadn't made a public statement. From a legal standpoint, this made sense. Nick Gates's death, while tragic, wasn't the company's fault. Any public statement could potentially be twisted or misconstrued to mean they accepted liability. At this juncture, saying nothing at all was the most prudent course of action.

Unfortunately, that only pissed off the residents of Denton more.

Josie knew better than anyone that grief wasn't rational and often, doing something that made little practical sense held it at bay. Action was better than being smothered by pain. The parents and students who had cared for Nick Gates needed something to do. Here they were.

The Chief had been certain things would blow over soon but now Josie wasn't so sure. Whatever happened today might just be gasoline on a fire.

Josie made her way to where Officer Brennan stood sentry outside a strip of crime scene tape. Behind it was a stretch of ground peppered with pieces of shattered sidewalk, gravel, and dirt where normally construction vehicles lumbered in and out of the building site. The rolling gate was partially open, but she couldn't see much more than a boom lift and a row of porta-potties. The skeleton of the children's hospital towered over everything, the dwindling rays of the day's sunlight slicing through its frame. It was only four in the afternoon, but the evenings were already creeping up earlier than usual.

Just steps from the entrance, Denton's Evidence Response Team had erected a pop-up tent. They only did that when it was necessary to shield a body from onlookers. Several of the ERT officers, dressed head to toe in white Tyvek suits, worked the cordoned-off area outside the tent, making sketches, placing evidence markers, and taking video and photos. Based on the debris, this section was where the fight had taken place. Scattered across the ground was a discarded sneaker, a bottle of water on its side, several empty camping chairs, a crumpled sweater, a walkie-talkie in pieces, and a brown purse turned upside down. A key chain was attached to its zipper. Craning her neck, Josie saw that it was a big pink pompom with a glittery red heart attached to it. Something in her chest tightened. That kind of sweet, colorful whimsy didn't belong at a crime scene.

Then again, death didn't care about the joy it stole. It took blindly.

Josie tore her eyes from the key chain. The crime scene tape stretched for several yards from the site entrance down the sidewalk adjacent to the chain-link fencing. Yellow evidence markers had been placed at uneven intervals. One of the ERT officers followed the trail of them back toward the tent, taking photos as he went.

"We've got a real shitshow," Brennan informed her.

"Gretchen said there was some kind of fight. A fatality."

He dragged a hand down his face. "Yes and yes. There was a brawl. We got a couple of different stories as to what started it, but it seems like the protestors got a little too close to the gate, one of the guards came out to ask them to back up, and that didn't go over so well. They started fighting—four security guys against seventeen protestors. When the crowd cleared, there was a woman on the ground, bleeding. Already dead. Female, mid-fifties. Security tried stepping in to render aid at the same time several of the parents did and there was another scuffle."

Josie shook her head. "None of them rendered aid."

Brennan's features twisted in disgust. "Like I said, a shitshow. By the time 911 was called and the EMTs got here, it was too late."

THREE

Josie gave the scene another quick scan. The security guys stood several feet from one another, two of them being questioned by uniformed officers. All their eyes were locked on the tent. One swayed on his feet, his face taking on an unhealthy green hue. Maybe they were worried about being held liable for the fatality but the twinge of unease in her gut told her it was something more. She scanned the evidence markers on the sidewalk again. The brawl had taken place directly in front of the entrance, but she had a feeling that whatever led to the fatality had started down the street.

"You said the deceased was bleeding."

Brennan glanced back at the tent. "She was stabbed. There's a trail of blood from a half-block away. The perpetrator dropped the knife, left it behind."

The victim had managed to get away from her attacker, fleeing toward the crowd, perhaps hoping for assistance. Or the perpetrator left her on the sidewalk, believing she would die before she could find help.

"Do we have an ID yet?" asked Josie.

Brennan tucked his clipboard under one arm and shifted his

weight from leg to leg. Then he rolled his shoulders as if to loosen tension. He rarely got ruffled. In fact, the last time Josie had seen him flustered was when they'd found an infant abandoned in the city park and he'd been tasked with holding her. "Brennan," she prodded.

"Oh yeah. We got an ID." He scanned the area once more before lowering his voice. "The victim is Gina Phelan."

Josie managed to hold back her "oh shit."

Brennan watched her carefully. As if he'd heard her silent curse, he said, "Total shitshow."

In recent weeks, WYEP had done several profiles on Phelan Construction. It was family-owned. After World War II, a returning veteran, Oren Ellis, had started the company, calling it Ellis Development, headquartered in Wilkes-Barre, Pennsylvania. When he passed away, the business went to his only heir, a daughter named Tilly and her husband, Clint Phelan. Eventually, the couple rebranded the company as Phelan Construction and moved its offices to Harrisburg. Although Josie had seen the elderly couple, now in their eighties, in several interviews and news pieces, she knew that their children were now responsible for the company. Their son, Mace, was the CEO. His older sister, Gina, was the company attorney.

Now she lay stabbed to death in front of their most consequential project in decades.

"Did anyone see anything?" Josie asked.

"We're still getting statements but so far, no one has admitted to seeing anything. We don't even know what she was doing out here. One of the security guys said she drove in through the back entrance this morning."

From the interviews Josie had seen, Gina Phelan was shrewd. She would have known better than anyone that showing up at the front entrance without notifying security while it was packed with angry protestors was potentially unsafe. Then again, maybe she hadn't intended to make contact with the protestors at all. Maybe it was only after she was attacked that she'd turned toward them. Or perhaps one of the protestors had spotted her a half-block away, recognized her, and decided to confront her.

Josie surveyed the witnesses still present at the scene. "You said seventeen protestors."

"That's how many were here when the first units arrived. There might have been more, but we won't know until we get some surveillance footage."

Josie nodded. "There are only thirteen protestors here."

"Four of them had blood on their clothes so they were taken to the station."

Over twenty people at a murder scene was a logistical nightmare. Ideally, all of them would be taken to the stationhouse for interviews but they'd have to be transported separately and kept apart once they were at police headquarters. Denton PD didn't have the manpower or the necessary number of rooms at the stationhouse to accomplish that, which was why only the people with torn clothes, visible injuries, or blood on their person were taken in. The officers on-scene would get IDs and contact information from the rest of the witnesses in case they needed to be contacted at a later date.

"It's Saturday," said Josie. "Did they have a full crew working today?"

Brennan nodded. "Just like any other day. The project never stops, from what I'm told."

"Is there a field administrator on-site?" Josie asked. She glanced up, scanning the top of the fences for cameras. There were two—one on each side of the gate—pointed at the entrance. Denton PD would also be able to narrow the list of people who should be taken for immediate questioning based on the footage from those cameras. More importantly, it would show them whether anyone fled the scene and in which direction.

"We're going to need footage from Phelan and from anyone who was filming with their cell phone," she said. "Plus, any video captured by residents or businesses across the street."

Brennan rubbed a palm over his face again. "Shirley Swenson is the field administrator. She's working on the Phelan footage right now. I'll text you her number. Dougherty's already getting the cell phone footage. Conlen's canvassing the buildings across the street."

"I'll prepare a geofence warrant as soon as possible," she added.

A geofence was a way for police to erect a virtual perimeter around a specific geographic area for a particular time period. Inside those confines, they could track some cell phones, vehicles, and other smart devices. Google had recently changed how it stored users' location history, making it harder for law enforcement to use geofence warrants, but they were still an extremely valuable tool.

Movement near the tent caught Josie's attention. Dr. Feist emerged, her silver-blonde hair tucked beneath her skull cap. A camera hung from her neck. She spotted Josie and gave her a pained smile before beckoning her. Josie held up her index finger to indicate she needed a minute.

"Listen," Brennan said. "Mace Phelan is here too. Security notified him as soon as the fight cleared. The first units had already arrived by the time he came out—through the front here. When he saw Gina, he flipped. Had to be restrained. Conlen convinced him to go back inside the site and call their parents while we got everything processed."

"Their parents? No husband? Children?"

"Her brother said she's divorced," Brennan answered. "No boyfriend. No kids."

Just her elderly parents losing one of their children. Her brother losing his only sibling. All of them members of one of the wealthiest families in the state. A family whose company was already embroiled in scandal after Denton East's star quarterback died on their construction site. A project worth an obscene amount of money. The pride of the city council.

A dull throb started behind Josie's eyes. She used her thumb and forefinger to pinch the bridge of her nose. "You were right, Brennan. This is a giant steaming dump of a shitshow."

He gave her a mirthless smile. "Bet you're glad you caught this one instead of Turner."

"Don't even go there," Josie said. "I'm going to suit up and have a look at the body. Let me know the minute Shirley Swenson has that footage ready."

FOUR

Ten minutes later, Josie was clad in her own Tyvek suit complete with booties and a skull cap. Brennan logged her into the crime scene and she slipped under the tape. Dr. Feist waited at the entrance to the tent. She waved Josie inside. The ERT had set up halogen lamps in the corner, casting the scene in a harsh, unforgiving light. Gina Phelan lay on her back, arms at her sides. Blood coated her hands, drying and flaking on her curled fingers. Her knees were bent, legs twisted to one side. Instead of the high heels Josie had seen her in when she appeared on television, her feet were encased in heavy brown work boots. They were scuffed and worn. Her head was turned, eyes hooded as though she was about to doze off. Silky strands of her long dark hair, threaded with gray, stretched along the asphalt at the back of her head.

She had swapped the feminine power suits she usually wore, with their tasteful blazers and form-fitting skirts, for a well-used pair of jeans, and a long-sleeved flannel shirt that hung open, revealing a white T-shirt underneath. Blood soaked through it, originating from two small, ragged tears in the fabric

on the right side of her abdomen. One was just below the rib
cage. The other was closer to the waistband of her jeans.

"No purse. Hummel said they found her phone on the sidewalk near where he believes the stabbing occurred, but it's
smashed to bits." Anya knelt beside the body. "He also told me
they've got the knife. It's a folding knife. Four-inch blade.
Partially serrated."

The saw-like edges of serrated knives tended to do far more
internal damage than straight-edged knives.

"Let's hope the bastard who did this to her left prints and
enough DNA to help us catch him," Josie said.

She crouched across from Anya, studying the way the blood
streaked down over Gina Phelan's belt to her thighs. Droplets
congealed on the tops of her boots. They wouldn't know the
angle of the attack until Anya completed her examination and
autopsy, but the pattern of the bloodstains fit with Josie's assess-
ment of the scene. Gina was attacked half a block from the site
entrance and somehow, she got away.

"She was bleeding out fast and she still managed to make it
pretty far on foot," said Josie.

Anya peeled the T-shirt up, trying to find the wounds.
There were only two. Each one was no bigger than an inch, tiny
seams split open to show a deeper, darker red than the blood
smeared all around them. "You'd be surprised," she said.
"When I worked in emergency medicine, EMTs brought in a
guy who'd been stabbed in the chest. He was DOA but autopsy
showed the knife had penetrated the left ventricle, left atrium,
and his aorta. Witnesses told police that he pulled the knife out
of his chest and walked up a flight of steps before he collapsed.
He bled out within minutes, but he kept going right to the bitter
end."

Josie wondered if that man had been under the influence
or just desperate. Or both. Her mind conjured an image of
Gina Phelan lurching along the sidewalk, hands pressed to her

abdomen, trying to stem the flow of blood. Had she known that she had only moments left? If someone in the unruly crowd had noticed her immediately, could she have been saved? That wasn't a question Josie needed to answer—her job was to find Gina's killer and make him pay—but it was a question the Phelans would be plagued with for the rest of their lives.

Josie had her own collection of those types of questions. If only there had been one small variation of the scenarios in which her grandmother, or her first husband, or her colleague, Mett, died, they might still be here. That kind of wondering was a sickness. A madness. Under the layers of her professional armor, Josie felt a profound sadness for the Phelan family. Quickly, she pushed it away. She had work to do.

Gently, Anya picked up Gina's wrist, turning it over and opening her hand. "Nothing here."

Josie did the same on her side, finding Gina's other palm empty except for the blood settled deep in the creases of her skin. She wore no rings. Small calluses were visible on the pads of her index and middle fingers, just above the first knuckle. Her fingernails were short and unpainted.

Anya arched a brow. "What is it?"

"Nothing." Josie set Gina's arm back on the ground. "Guess I expected expensive acrylic nails or something."

"You mean a gorgeous manicure to go with the power attorney look? I did, too." Anya looked at Gina's face. "Not that she needed it."

Anya was right. By most standards, Gina Phelan had been an attractive woman. Even the wrinkles creasing her neck and the laugh lines scoring her face—the natural by-products of aging—didn't detract from her beauty.

"What do we have here?" Anya rose up on her knees, gloved fingers probing the skin around Gina's neck. A thin red line marked her skin. The abrasion was fresh.

"She was wearing a necklace," Josie said. "Someone tore it off."

Had Gina's death been the result of a robbery gone wrong? This certainly was the area of Denton in which it was most likely to happen.

Anya must have had the same thought. Shaking her head, she let out a heavy sigh. "So senseless. Why kill someone over something so meaningless?"

This was an almost daily lament in their line of work. It never changed. They fell into silence as Josie helped Anya continue her examination. They rolled Gina's body over. There was nothing beneath her. Anya lifted her shirt to get a look at her back. They checked her pockets, finding one lip gloss and a key fob that Josie assumed was for her car. Then they checked her sleeves, her pantlegs, her waistband, searching for additional injuries or any evidence that hadn't been visible.

"Detective Quinn!" Brennan's voice sounded from outside the crime scene perimeter. "That footage is ready!"

"Go," said Anya. "As soon as I've finished the exam and autopsy, I'll get you my findings, though this looks pretty straightforward."

FIVE

Sweat dampened the back of Josie's neck. The inside of the trailer that served as Shirley Swenson's temporary office was overly warm. Or maybe it just felt that way since Josie had hoofed it all the way around the perimeter of the sprawling construction site to the rear entrance. Keeping outside the crime scene tape, she'd walked past the trail of Gina Phelan's blood to where one of the ERT members was bagging the knife and phone. Then she continued down the sidewalk until the fencing cut to the left, breaking into a jog as night closed in. There were no lights along the fence line. As she went, she tried to figure out why Gina was out here in the first place.

"Would you like to sit down?" Shirley stood behind her desk chair, gesturing toward the open seat. "I've got everything queued up."

Josie didn't miss the small tremor in Shirley's lower lip or the red rimming her eyes. "Did you know Gina well?"

Shirley stepped aside to let Josie sit. A crumpled tissue appeared in her hand, and she used it to dab at her eyes. "Not that well. She doesn't usually have much occasion to visit the sites, but I've met her several times at staff meetings and holiday parties, that kind of thing. She's very sweet. Don't get me wrong, she can be intimidating as hell, but mostly, she's very kind. Funny, too. Really funny. One year, she bought all the supervisors and administrators—basically anyone who spends a lot of time behind a desk or in an on-site trailer—these screaming goat noisemakers."

Josie smiled. "Screaming goats?"

She turned her attention to Shirley's computer screen. The program that Phelan Construction used was a top-of-the-line security system created by Rowland Industries. Josie was familiar with it. She clicked on the thumbnail that brought up the footage from the west-facing camera outside the construction site.

Behind her, Shirley made a noise like she was unsuccessfully holding back a sob. Reaching into the desk drawer on Josie's right, she pulled out a plastic, circular button, about three inches in width and one inch in height. It was a desk toy. From its surface, a dismayed cartoon goat stared up at them.

"I won't press it," Shirley said. "But trust me, it's hilarious. Gina used hers to break the tension during internal meetings sometimes. Well, probably to wake up anyone who dozed off. Sometimes she startled people in elevators. She told us to have fun with them. Find other occasions to use them, like when you felt like screaming yourself but might look crazy doing it."

Josie couldn't help but laugh. "You didn't look crazy pressing a screaming goat button?"

"Well, yeah, we did." Shirley looked at the button in her hand almost lovingly. "But we were having fun looking crazy. It's silly, but Gina liked silly. She said there wasn't enough of it in the world."

The sadness Josie had pushed away earlier returned like a punch to her gut. She had a feeling she would have liked Gina Phelan had she gotten to know her.

"I'm sorry," she told Shirley.

She pressed play on the footage. The camera was in an elevated position, above the fencing. The video started in late afternoon. Two security guards stood outside the gate. A large group of people faced off against them. The angle was such that most of the people were only visible in profile. Josie clicked pause and quickly counted heads. Seventeen against two guards.

"The Phelans will be here soon," Shirley said.

"Great."

Josie hit play again. As the seconds ticked past, the protestors' bodies pressed together, forming a single mass that surged forward. There was no sound, but Josie sensed the growing agitation of the protestors in their stiff shoulders, mouths cracked wide open in what looked like shouts, and fingers pointed toward the security guards. The guards waved, trying to herd them backward. From this angle, at least, a waving sign made it impossible to tell who instigated what came next—one of the guards or one of the protestors—but soon, the entire scene deteriorated into a frenzy of swinging fists, flailing limbs, and aggressive pushes as the protestors attacked the guards. It was difficult to make anything out, especially given how quickly it all happened. The gate slid open, and two more guards joined the fray.

"Did you speak to Gina today?" Josie asked, keeping her eyes on the screen.

"Yes. She arrived around seven this morning. Right after Mr. Phelan—Mace—they were both here to inspect the site. He wanted to make sure the extra security measures he'd ordered had been put into place. She wanted to document them and then assess whether they could do more."

Josie leaned closer to the computer, watching what was visible of the sidewalk beyond the crowd in the direction from which Gina had come. The camera had captured very little of it. Finally, there was movement. A shadow. Then someone barrelled into view.

Not Gina Phelan.

SIX

A blonde woman sprinted into view, her face obscured by a dark blue ballcap. There was no logo on it from what Josie could see. A long ponytail poked through the opening in the back, swishing across her shoulders as she ran toward the brawling mass of people ahead. Her feet were clad in black ballet flats. An oversized gray sweatshirt fell to the middle of her thighs. If she had shorts on beneath it, they weren't visible. Blood smeared and smudged her clothing and bare thighs. She didn't look behind her, instead plunging into the crowd, aggressively muscling her way through to the other side. With so many fists and elbows flailing, cell phones held aloft filming, and bodies jostling to reach the overwhelmed guards, no one noticed her at all.

Emerging from the other side of the skirmish, she fell to her knees, hands breaking her fall. Then she jumped back up and ran, away from everything, disappearing from view. Josie rewound the footage. "Shirley, do you recognize this woman?"

Shirley leaned over Josie's shoulder to watch the seventeen seconds in which the blonde appeared. "No, I'm sorry. I don't."

Josie rewound to when the blonde first came into view and pressed pause. "Do you know why Gina was outside the site?"

"No, I don't."

"Was she grabbing lunch?" Josie asked.

"No. She'd already gone out for lunch around noon, and she took her car for that. Oh, wait. When I saw her this morning, she said something about surveying the fencing to see if there were any places people could slip in. Maybe that's what she was doing? Although..."

Trailing off, Shirley walked over to one of the windows and peered outside. "Her car's not here."

"But she did come back after lunch," Josie clarified. "Could she have parked it elsewhere?"

Shirley turned back toward Josie, frowning. "I suppose."

"What kind of car does Gina own?" As Shirley answered, Josie took out her phone. Dried white flakes of primer skidded across the screen as she punched in her passcode. She sent Brennan a text with the make and model of Gina's car and instructions to have units search the area for it.

Josie beckoned Shirley closer and pointed to the blonde frozen on the computer screen. "I'm going to need stills of this woman. As many as you can get. Fast as you can. Text them to me."

"Sure thing," Shirley said. "I've got a tablet on the table over there. I can grab them from that. I'll also get you copies of all the footage so you can take it with you."

As she shuffled off to the other end of the trailer, Josie fast-forwarded to the point where the blonde fled the scene. Six seconds later, Gina Phelan followed the same path, staggering as though she was drunk. She wasn't carrying a purse of any kind. Blood seeped from the two wounds in her abdomen, forming the streaks on her clothes that Josie had seen on her body. Her hands fumbled at her shirt, palms trying to stem the flow. It took her longer to reach the tussling throng. In the throes

of their attack on the guards, the protestors on the fringe let
Gina slip past without notice. She reached out, trying to touch
the closest person, but soon she was swallowed up by the
writhing bodies, batted around like a pinball until she collapsed.

That was when someone finally saw her.

The rest was just as Brennan had described. Josie closed out
the footage and brought up the video from the east-facing
camera even though she doubted it would offer much. As she
watched, focused on the blonde and Gina Phelan, Josie lifted
her hair and fanned the back of her neck. She was concentrating so hard that she didn't hear the door to the trailer open
and close.

Hot breath cascaded down her neck a moment before she
heard Kyle Turner's voice. "Quinn, is that paint?"

Josie jumped, making the chair creak. As the video
concluded, she looked over her shoulder. He was directly
behind her, his huge frame taking up an unreasonable amount
of space. One of his fingers pointed at the nape of her neck.

Josie quickly let her hair fall. She kept her voice low. "None
of your business. Also, you're standing too close. Again."

With a sigh, Turner stepped back, bumping into a filing
cabinet. In an attempt to look cool and casual, he draped an arm
over the top of it. Matching the volume of Josie's voice so that
Shirley wouldn't overhear them, he said, "I thought we were
getting along."

Josie had warmed up to him somewhat, as nauseated as it
made her to admit, even laughing at a joke he'd made during
their last big case. He had, after all, saved her from being
mauled by a dog and also from plummeting down the shaft of a
crumbling stairwell. There were even a couple of times she'd
swallowed her pride and asked him to do things for her and, in
response, he wasn't a raging asshole at all. She'd been shocked to
find out that her sister had a connection to him, though both of
them had been very close-lipped about it. Trinity would only

say that the Kyle Turner she knew wasn't anything like the douchebag who had joined the Denton PD. Josie often wondered if he was actually human, but she wouldn't go so far as to say they were getting along.

"Debatable," she told him. "Nice of you to show up, by the way."

"Hey, I came in early," Turner protested.

"You left your last shift early."

She shouldn't complain. He would be relieving her at midnight.

"Whatever." His fingers drummed against his thigh as he shifted his attention to Shirley, whose back was to them.

Josie's phone vibrated with the still photos she'd requested. As the pictures came in, she forwarded them to Brennan with a brief explanation. He replied before she'd even sent them all, promising to get units out to search for the mystery woman as well as have officers show her photos to the guards and protestors to find out whether anyone knew her or recognized her. Additional units would check with local residents and businesses.

The blonde was covered in blood, running away from a dying Gina Phelan, and she'd fled the scene without so much as glancing back. Either she had stabbed Gina Phelan, or she had seen the person who did. Maybe she, too, had been wounded. Regardless, she was the key to finding out what the hell happened.

Josie sent the last photo and looked up to see Turner's eyes sweep slowly from Shirley's thick, messy bun to the jeans hugging her ass.

Josie glared at him. Hard. She didn't know whether to be glad or disturbed that he keyed in on it right away. It meant they'd officially worked together so often that they were developing an unspoken language. The thought was like a very sharp stone in her shoe. Or worse, plantar fasciitis. More painful and not fixed by taking off your shoe and shaking it.

What? Turner mouthed.

Josie gave him a look that she hoped he read as "You're disgusting."

Come on, sweetheart.

Josie narrowed her eyes then grinned triumphantly. She held her palm out, keeping it low in case Shirley turned around.

With a barely suppressed groan, Turner fished a dollar bill out of his jacket pocket and discreetly deposited it into her hand. It was all part of Noah's behavior modification program. After Turner joined Denton PD, every third word out of his mouth whenever he addressed Josie was either "honey" or "sweetheart" and he insisted on calling Gretchen "Parker" rather than her actual name, Palmer, no matter how many times he was corrected. Now, whenever he screwed up, he owed them a dollar. It worked both ways. Whenever Josie or Gretchen called him a name to his face, they owed him a dollar. They all had jars on their desks like a bunch of damn kindergartners. Josie was certain that she and Gretchen had already collected at least two paychecks' worth of Turner's money, whereas his own sad jar only held two or three dollars from the times that Gretchen couldn't contain herself. Apparently, nothing brought Gretchen more joy than calling Turner a jackass to his face.

Stop being a creep, Josie mouthed at him.

He rolled his eyes, stopping abruptly when Shirley turned to face them. What Josie was sure Turner thought of as a charming smile spread across his face. He offered his hand. "Shirley, always a pleasure to see you, though I wish it were under different circumstances. Detective Kyle Turner."

To Josie's surprise, Shirley smiled back and shook his hand, her eyes lingering on his face. "I remember you very well."

Good lord.

Turner couldn't resist shooting Josie a wink. A *wink*. Now

her plantar fasciitis had plantar fasciitis. He often claimed that women flirted with him. No one ever believed him. Not that he was unattractive. In his mid-forties, he was actually quite handsome with a full head of dark unruly curls shot through with gray, a neatly trimmed beard, and deep-set blue eyes. He was over six feet, lean, and he always wore a suit like he was headed to court for testimony.

No, it wasn't his physical appearance that made it impossible for Josie to see his appeal. It was the fact that he was so damn obnoxious.

"I found something on the footage," Josie announced. "In case you're interested."

SEVEN

Turner was watching the video on Shirley's tablet when the door to the trailer banged open. Cool air poured into the small space, washing over Josie's sweat-damp skin. For a few seconds, there was nothing beyond the threshold but darkness. Then, Tilly Phelan stepped inside, one of her pale, thin hands gripping the doorframe to pull herself up the last step and inside. Whenever Josie saw her on television, she looked like the wife of a politician. Classy and refined, white hair always twisted into a perfectly styled updo, not a strand out of place. Elegant but modest dresses paired with pearl necklaces and earrings. A serene closed-mouth smile. Tonight, the tip of her nose was bright red. Broken blood vessels mottled the whites of her eyes. Rogue strands of hair framed her face, having escaped her chignon. The buttons on her black and white checkered sweater were fastened unevenly.

Her eyelashes fluttered as she panned the room, taking in Shirley, Josie, and then lingering on Turner. "My daughter," she croaked.

Josie stood up and edged past Turner and Shirley so she could get out from behind the desk.

"Till," a man's voice called from the doorway.

Ignoring it, Tilly stepped closer to them, her steps sure and confident. She regarded the gun at Josie's waist briefly before dragging her blue eyes back up, frowning. "I know you."

"Mrs. Phelan, I'm so sorry for your loss." Josie introduced herself, presenting her credentials.

"Till," the man bellowed from outside.

Tilly Phelan's fists clenched at her sides. Taking a deep breath, as if to marshal all her patience, she yelled over her shoulder, "Mace! Your father needs help!"

"I can do it myself!" Clint Phelan snapped as he appeared in the doorway, even as two large hands materialized at his lower back, giving him a gentle push up the last step.

The patriarch of the Phelan family was tall. Even with hunched shoulders, he was nearly the same height as Turner. He was dressed as Gina had been, in a flannel shirt and jeans cinched by his signature brass belt buckle with its elaborate patterns of leaves and vines surrounding a polished, oval-shaped stone of varying shades of brown. Josie had seen him on television wearing it with his suits. His hair was thick and silver, luxuriant for a man in his eighties. Tears streamed down his face, forming drops along his chin before falling onto his chest. He made no attempt to wipe them away. Josie wondered if he even realized he was crying.

"Till," he said, more quietly, laying a hand on her shoulder. "Where is she? Find out where she is. I want to see her. I need to see my girl."

Tilly was focused on Josie. "I know you."

Turner drew up beside Josie. "Mr. and Mrs. Phelan," he said. "Detective Kyle Turner. I'm so sorry for your loss."

He flashed his credentials. Clint didn't give them a glance. Tilly was still focused on Josie.

Turner nudged Josie's arm with his elbow. "Everyone

knows this one, Mrs. Phelan. She's a local legend. Isn't that right, Quinn?"

Josie ignored him. "You've probably seen me giving press conferences. Or you're thinking of my sister, Trinity Payne. She's got her own show."

Clint said, "I need to see her. I need to see my Gina."

"No," Tilly said to Josie. "It's you. You were on *Dateline*. Some big case. Lots of big cases, I think."

Josie nodded, wondering if it was easier for Tilly to focus on something so trivial rather than the reality that she'd just lost a child.

"Take me to see her," Clint said. "Take me to see my girl."

Tilly reached up to where his fingers dug into her shoulder and patted his hand. "You can't see her now. Not yet."

"Why?" he said, voice tremulous. "Why can't we see her now?"

Tilly ignored him again, focusing on Josie. "Mace didn't know anything. He just said when he saw her on the ground, she was bleeding, and that she didn't make it."

As if conjured by his mother's words, Mace finally stepped into the trailer. Josie knew he was younger than Gina, but his weathered skin made him seem much older. His hair was thick like his father's but still dark although he was grayer than his sister. Like Gina, he'd foregone the expensive suits he wore for media appearances in favor of a fleece with the Phelan logo embroidered on the left side of his chest and a pair of jeans.

Of the three of them, Mace looked the most broken and weary. Locks of his hair stood up in multiple directions like he'd been pulling at it. His shoulders sagged. The skin under his eyes was puffy. He squeezed in beside his mother for another round of condolences and introductions.

There was movement at Josie's back. Shirley squeezed past Turner, mumbling words of sympathy to the Phelans. Tears streamed down her face.

"Thank you, Shirley," Mace said. "Why don't you head on home? I'll handle things from here. If I need anything or if the police want to talk to you again, we'll give you a call, okay?"

With a nod, she raced out the trailer door.

Mace turned back to Josie and Turner. "Please. Tell us what happened to my sister."

Turner delivered the news that Gina had been stabbed while walking along the sidewalk outside the site, half a block from the protests, and that her body had been transported to the morgue for an autopsy. Josie watched as a new, more painful form of grief washed over the Phelans. Clint's breath came in short gasps as more tears fell from his eyes. Tilly's expression went blank momentarily, as if she had mentally shut down, before she, too, cried. Her sobs were silent. Josie could tell from the way her body went completely rigid that she was trying hard to control her emotions. Maybe she didn't like crying in front of other people or maybe she was trying to project strength. Regardless, she let her son gather her against him. With his other arm, Mace pulled his father into the hug. He whispered reassurances into his parents' ears, telling them they would get through this, but Josie could see by the way his lower lip quivered that he was barely holding it together.

Turner tugged at his beard, grimacing. Once the family had composed themselves, stepping apart from one another, he addressed Mace. "Did you check the security footage?"

Tilly looked at her son, waiting for his answer.

Mace pushed a hand through his hair. "No. I just told Shirley to make sure it was ready for you guys as soon as possible, as soon as you were ready for it."

"You didn't check it right away?" Tilly asked.

"Mom," Mace said, exasperated, eyes glassy with unshed tears. "I just found my sister dead on the ground outside, bleeding! I wasn't thinking about footage. Besides, I didn't want to... I couldn't..."

Josie said, "It's often extremely difficult for family members to watch surveillance footage of what might be their loved one's last moments, especially when they're in shock. Detective Turner and I have reviewed it."

Turner explained what they had found while Josie pulled up the clearest photo they had of the blonde woman. Her face was obscured by the hat, but it was the best they could do.

All three Phelans leaned forward to peer at it. Josie watched their faces but saw no flickers of recognition.

"I don't understand," said Clint. "This woman stabbed my Gina?"

"We don't know that," Josie said. "Right now, we're working to locate her so we can question her."

Mace extended his hand and Josie let him have her phone, watching as he zoomed in. His brow furrowed.

"Does she look familiar to you?" Josie asked.

"No," he said. "I can talk to my guys and see if anyone on the site has seen her before. Some of them walk down to the deli a couple of blocks away for lunch. If she's local—"

"We'll interview them," said Turner. "If you don't mind us using this space when we're finished here."

"Of course," said Mace. "Whatever you need."

Josie took her phone back. "What was Gina doing at the site today?"

"Preparing to be sued," he answered honestly. "She wanted to tour the site personally. Document some things. Look over the additional security I put into place. Make her own recommendations."

Clint sniffled. "Maybe you should have let her inspect the sites regularly once they got up and running and that boy wouldn't have died."

Mace rubbed the back of his neck. "Dad, not now."

Turner's fingers tapped against his thigh. "You normally have kids sneaking into your construction sites and dying?"

EIGHT

Josie's skin heated again but this time from anger. This was a new level of douchebaggery, even for him, provoking the family member of a homicide victim. "Turner!" Josie growled in warning.

Tilly sighed.

"No," Mace said through gritted teeth. "This was a first. We have people to ensure the safety of every site—for our own people and the surrounding communities. We abide by all local rules and regulations and we're OSHA-compliant. My dad just thinks—"

Tilly touched Mace's forearm, silencing him. "That's enough."

An awkward silence ensued, filled only with Clint's sniffles. Finally, Josie said, "Do you know why Gina was outside the site?"

Mace shook his head. "Not really, no. I was with her until lunchtime, taking her around. Then I left her to do her own thing. She mentioned wanting to install lights and cameras all along the perimeter fencing. Maybe she was out there to see where they could go."

Clint touched his wife's shoulder again. "Till."

"Not now," she told him.

Josie continued questioning Mace. "Did you go to lunch with her?"

"No."

"Do you know where her car is parked?"

Lines creased Mace's forehead. "Gina's car? Right outside. It's not there?"

"We have units searching for it," said Josie. "Is there somewhere else she might have parked when she returned from lunch? If the spots outside were full?"

"Oh, well I guess out back but..."

"Do you have cameras inside here?" asked Turner. "Inside the site?"

"No," said Mace. "Although now maybe we should get some."

Josie recalled meeting Shirley at the rear entrance. "Do you have any cameras in the back to monitor who comes and goes from that entrance?"

"Not yet," said Mace. "Those were going to be installed this week."

"How about a security guard?" asked Turner.

Again, Tilly looked at her son expectantly.

Mace ignored her hard stare, but Josie could tell by the muscle twitching in his jaw that he knew she was boring a hole right into the side of his face. "We had two guys out back, but I had given instructions that as soon as the protestors arrive each day, they're to go to the front and wait just inside in case a fight breaks out."

That was why the additional two guards had emerged from the entrance so quickly.

"Your security guards," Josie said. "Did you contract with a company for their services or are they Phelan Construction employees?"

"They work for us," Mace answered. "All security is handled in-house."

"When we interview your guys, we'll see if anyone saw Gina exit the site," said Turner. "And if they remember what time."

Clint clutched Tilly's shoulder again. "I want to see my girl, Till. I need to see her."

"You can't see her right now, Dad," Mace snapped.

Red suffused Clint's face. "I'm not talking to you. You're the reason she's dead—"

"Jesus, Dad."

"If she wasn't always cleaning up your messes, if you hadn't run this build so irresponsibly, that kid would be alive, and we wouldn't have protests—"

Mace's voice rose to a shout. "The protestors didn't kill her, Dad! I've run this project just like every other one before it. This isn't on me!"

"Both of you stop this instant," said Tilly icily.

Josie took the break in their family spat to ask another question that was bothering her. "Gina didn't have her purse with her. Do you know where it is?"

Mace turned around and pointed to a row of small lockers at the opposite end of the trailer. "In one of those. That's where she stored it this morning."

"Gina was here to do all this stuff," said Turner. "Did she take notes or photos?"

"She did," said Mace. He walked over to the table Shirley had been using earlier and shuffled some blueprints around until he came up with a clipboard. "She jotted her notes down here. She used her phone to take pictures."

Turner took the clipboard from him and flipped a few pages before setting it onto Shirley's desk. "Was Gina having issues with anyone on the site?" he asked.

"No," Mace answered. "This was the first time she was here."

"We'll need a list of all employees who were on the site today," Josie added. "Any independent contractor. Anyone who might have delivered or picked up materials."

"Anyone who set foot on this site today," Turner added.

Denton PD would interview as many of those people as possible when they were done here but the list would ensure they didn't miss anyone.

Mace's eyes widened. "You think one of my guys did this?"

"We have to look at every possibility," said Josie. "How about Gina's private life? Does she have a boyfriend? An ex who might have been giving her a difficult time?"

"No," Mace and Tilly answered in unison.

Clint cleared his throat. "She divorced her husband ten years ago. They haven't talked since."

Turner fished his phone out of his pocket but didn't look at it. Josie's dirty look went unnoticed. His thumb caressed the power button as if he was itching to bring the screen to life. Was he bored with this case already?

"No one who might have been stalking her?" Josie continued.

All three Phelans shook their heads.

She didn't think Gina had been targeted for personal reasons, but she had to rule it out. Killing an intimate partner and staging the scene to make it look like they were the victim of a random attack was not uncommon.

"Did Gina have any jewelry on today?"

"She knew not to wear jewelry to a build," said Clint.

Behind him, Mace rolled his eyes. "Except that necklace. Remember, Dad? She always wore it. Mom gave it to her for her fortieth birthday."

Tilly met Josie's eyes. "Was it taken?"

"I believe so."

"This was some kind of robbery?" Mace asked. "Gina was mugged?"

"Could be," said Turner. "Was the necklace valuable?"

Tilly answered his question but held eye contact with Josie. "Yes."

"If you've got any photos of it," Josie said, "that would be helpful."

"That's all we have for now. We'll be in touch." Turner dropped his phone back into his pocket and came up with a business card. "In the meantime, if you have any questions or you come up with any of the stuff we asked for, give us a call."

Mace crossed the small space, edging past Tilly to take Turner's card.

"You can also contact me," Josie said, holding out one of hers. Mace reached for it, but Tilly was quicker, snatching it from Josie's hand. Their fingers brushed. Tilly pinned her with that intense stare again. It might have been unnerving to anyone else. Watching the two of them, Turner's fingers started tapping again. Josie could practically hear his thoughts.

This lady is creepy, sweetheart.

But Tilly Phelan didn't unsettle Josie. She wasn't creepy. She was a mother who had just lost her daughter to violence.

"You'll find the person who did this," Tilly said. It wasn't a question.

NINE

Josie leaned back in her desk chair and stretched her arms over her head, trying to loosen muscles grown tense from hours of sitting in the same spot. She'd completed her paperwork on the Gina Phelan case, including a geofence warrant. Hopefully, the results would come in by morning. She and Turner, with the help of many of the uniformed officers, had spent the afternoon and evening interviewing every person involved in the project still on-site. None of them had seen anything. A couple of people saw Gina leave in her car for lunch and return through the back entrance, but no one saw her drive out afterward.

Multiple times, she and Turner had studied the footage from the protestors' cell phones as well as the footage that had been pulled from surrounding residences and businesses. The blonde and Gina Phelan had been caught on some of the phone footage but only for brief, blurred flashes. By the time the two women entered the crowd, the shouting and shoving had become a full-blown brawl. Every video they'd pulled looked as though the owner had tossed the phone violently down a flight of steps. Even pausing it didn't help.

Officers had worked tirelessly for hours canvassing and

taking statements, flashing the stills of the blonde to see if anyone recognized her or had interacted with her in any way. A few locals from the surrounding area had seen her running down their streets shortly after she fled the scene, but they had no information to offer other than that they'd spotted her. Units continued to canvass in the direction the woman had gone but lost the trail. Josie had consulted with Chief Chitwood. Without releasing Gina Phelan's name, she drew up a statement for the press indicating only that an incident at the site had resulted in a fatality and a woman seen fleeing the scene was wanted for questioning as a person of interest. Josie attached the two best photos they had and signed off asking anyone with information to call Denton PD.

Josie had far more questions than answers. They'd located Gina's vehicle parked two blocks away from the site, but even that raised more questions. It wasn't near any restaurants or takeout businesses. None of the homes had security cameras. Neither Shirley nor Mace had any idea why she had left it there. Given the witness statements Josie and Turner had taken, Gina had parked it there approximately an hour before she was stabbed.

Something bounced off Josie's chest, jarring her out of her thoughts. A small foam basketball dropped into her lap. Arching a brow, she lifted her gaze to Turner, who sat across from her. Denton Police headquarters was located in an old building in the city's central district. On the second floor was a large open area filled with desks which were used by uniformed officers to complete paperwork. Only five of the desks had been permanently assigned. One belonged to their press liaison, Amber Watts. The other four belonged to the investigative team: Josie, Noah, Gretchen, and Turner. They'd been pushed together to form a rectangle which meant every time Josie looked up from her computer screen, she saw Turner's irritating face—when he decided to show up.

"Do you mind?" Josie said.

He didn't look remotely sheepish. Instead, he held up a large palm. "Toss it back."

One of the first things Turner had done when he was hired was put a small basketball net on his desk. It was almost as annoying as all the finger-tapping and phone-scrolling. Josie didn't think he'd ever made a basket.

She considered making him work for it, but she wanted to do one more thing before she left for the night and didn't have time to deal with his crap. Aiming wide, she threw it back, watching with satisfaction as it sailed over his head.

"Real mature, Quinn," he muttered as he got up to search for it.

"Have you finished with the warrant for the contents of Gina Phelan's phone?" she asked pointedly.

All she heard in response was indistinct muttering as Turner settled back at his desk.

Josie picked up her phone and started searching for Gina Phelan's social media accounts. There was only one and even though it was set to public, it was fairly sparse. The most recent post was a week old. Many of the posts had to do with an animal shelter near Gina's home where she often volunteered. There were multiple photos of her own rescue dogs, captioned to showcase each dog's unique personality. As Josie scrolled through, she saw that Shirley Swenson was right. Gina was kind of hilarious. Now she was dead.

"Dammit."

"What's that, Quinn?"

She hadn't meant to say that out loud. "Nothing."

Scrolling onward, Josie found Gina's other love—besides rescue dogs and the law—archery. Several photos showed her competing in statewide competitions. From what Josie could tell, she had won several. Josie hadn't expected to learn much about Gina's personal life from social media, but she would have been remiss not to check it. The contents of her phone would tell them a lot more. If Turner finished the warrant this century.

As if he sensed her thoughts, he looked up from his computer. "Stop scowling at me, Quinn. Isn't it time for you to leave?"

She fished her keys from beneath a pile of paperwork. "It's well past time."

Her brain was still working feverishly, building its list of leads to follow up on in the Gina Phelan case, when she pulled into her driveway. She parked beside Noah's car. Her gaze drifted over to it as she tried to switch from work to home mode. It was something she'd been trying to master. If—when—they had a baby, she couldn't be so obsessive about her job when she was home. She'd need to be present for their child.

Her attention lingered on Noah's vehicle for a beat longer than necessary. Something nagged at her consciousness. Too tired to examine it, she hopped out of her SUV and tromped up the front steps. Light glowed from almost every window. Not what she'd typically expect to find arriving home at this hour. It was possible Noah had fallen asleep without turning off some lights but there shouldn't be so many on in the first place. Her tired brain clicked over to high alert before she could even process the thoughts. A frisson of fear ran up the back of her neck. The snap of her holster unlatching barely registered before her fingers curled around the grip of her pistol. When she reached the landing, she realized what was wrong. The eye of one of their security cameras stared down at her but her phone didn't buzz with a notification.

In fact, her security app hadn't chirped in hours.

Not even for Trout's backyard bathroom breaks. A quick glance back at Noah's car and that tiny nagging detail just beyond the grasp of her conscious mind came into focus. When she left for her shift, it had been parked on the other side of the driveway. He'd left and come back, and it hadn't set off the cameras.

Her breath came in small, rapid bursts even as she tried to reason her way through the panic quickly rising in her chest. Maybe Noah had set the app to snooze. They did that sometimes when the other person was home so they weren't bombarded by notifications at work. But he would have turned it back on if he left. The app was down, or the security system itself. That had to be it. Keeping her palm wrapped around the handle of her Glock, she used her free hand to fish her phone out of her pocket. With her thumb she punched in her passcode and pulled up the app. Every square that represented an individual camera was black. Nothing was working. Sometime after five p.m., it had gone dark.

The Wi-Fi was out.

There could very well be a logical explanation for that as there likely was for the lights blazing and yet, she knew, deep down in some visceral place inside her, that something was very, very wrong.

Putting her phone away, she found her house key and inserted it into the lock only to discover the door was cracked open. Her heart thundered in her chest as she pushed her way through it, clocking the total silence within the house. No click-clack of Trout's little claws racing through the foyer to greet her.

She stood just over the threshold, holding her Glock in her hands, tucked up by her chest with the muzzle pointed slightly downward. "Noah?" she called.

No answer.

Her head swiveled to the right, where their living room was situated. An audible gasp dropped from her lips. On autopilot, her body followed her line of sight, pistol sweeping past the mouth of the hallway that led to the kitchen, into the living room. It was completely trashed. The books, framed photos, and other trinkets that normally dotted their entertainment center and the small bookcase diagonal from it lay scattered across the carpet, trampled over. The coffee table was cracked and sagging. Even Trout's toy bin was overturned. There were other details she knew she should be cataloging but her mind was racing too fast, her heart beating too hard.

"Noah?"

TEN

Josie barely heard herself over the roar of blood in her ears.

"Trout?"

Keeping one eye on the foyer, she stepped into the living room. The wooden surface of the coffee table was dark, so it was only when she got closer that she saw blood congealing along one of its edges.

"Fuck."

Some muffled part of her brain—where the professional law enforcement officer lived—screamed for her to step outside and call dispatch to request units. Procedurally, that was the right thing to do. Wait for them to arrive and let them clear the house rather than attempting it herself, alone.

But the blood.

Noah's blood?

The wife in her forced her body to move, Glock high and on point, clearing each room on the first level of their home. It was a minefield. Nowhere to step without disturbing or treading on something. Every cabinet, every drawer had been dumped. Every surface had been violently unburdened. The contents of each shelf had been carelessly strewn onto the floor. All the mundane possessions that made up their daily lives lay at her feet, discarded, destroyed, defiled.

A window had been smashed in at the rear of the house. In the kitchen and dining room, more blood. An uneven trail of droplets. A smear on the wall of the laundry room that led to the garage. She hadn't taken the time to snap on her latex gloves so she used the tail of her shirt to turn the knob. Garish red handprints crept along the now-clear shelving units. All the bins and boxes that they'd stored there after their basement flooded from a burst pipe last year were on their sides, lids torn off or opened, their innards disemboweled. More drops of blood dotted the items that had been cast onto the floor and tramped over.

Still no Noah, no Trout.

No answers to her calls.

After a quick scan of their basement, which was currently only home to their furnace and hot water heater—both untouched—she headed for their second floor.

"Noah! Trout!"

As her feet pounded up the steps, terror gripped her, so dizzyingly potent that her entire body felt like it was being crushed. Her mind threatened to separate from her physical being. Halfway up the stairs, she was no longer eyeing the second-floor landing but floating up on the ceiling, watching herself climb. The Glock trembled in her hands. Her mouth formed the names again.

"Noah! Trout!"

Some other distant part of her that had lived through more trauma than any human should screamed at her to get her shit together. There was no time for panic or fear. If Noah was here, injured or being held by some intruder, she needed to be one hundred percent in control. Calm, cold as ice, steady. Which meant she needed to be present in her body.

The first thing she felt when she reached the second-floor

hall was a tingle along the scar that ran from below her right ear, down her jawline, and under her chin. The most savage memento from her fucked-up childhood. Externally, that was. Her body dropped into the box breathing she'd learned at a retreat for processing trauma which had—in keeping with her own personal brand of bad luck—ended in even more trauma. And murder.

Murder.

Was Noah already dead?

Her soul shoved against the confines of her body once more, demanding release.

This time, it was Trout's muted barks that brought her back. A wave of relief crashed over her, so powerful that her knees nearly gave out. It was brief, though, because she still hadn't laid eyes on her husband. The impulse to race past the doors lining the hall to find their dog was overwhelmingly strong but her tactical training kept her in check.

"Noah!" Her voice shook, telegraphing her weakness.

She kept going, again using her shirttail to open doors. The main bathroom had also been torn apart, towels and toiletries everywhere. In their bedroom was more of the same. Their en suite bathroom was a shambles. Their nightstands overturned. The mattress askew. None of the upstairs closets had doors. Another brutal remnant from her childhood that Ray, and later Noah, had conceded to her. Now, it made her job faster. Nothing was left in their bedroom closet because everything was on the floor.

Trout's barks grew louder and more frenzied as she moved to the first guest room. She'd once used it for an office-slash-home gym but later, they'd converted it to a standard bedroom since they had houseguests so frequently. No one was inside. What little the nightstands, dresser, and closet held had been flung everywhere.

"Noah!"

The contents of the hall closet—more towels, bedding, backup toiletries, new shower liners still in their shiny packaging, and a small handheld vacuum—were heaped on the floor, blocking her way.

"Noah!"

Still no answer. Where was he? Why hadn't he come out or called to her?

He's not dead. He's not dead. He's not dead.

Trout's paws scratching frantically against the final door kept her grounded. His high-pitched barks, now turning to desperate, keening cries were like a thousand tiny knives stabbing her heart.

The nursery. He was shut in what was going to be the nursery.

Leading with her pistol, she eased the door open, nudging against Trout's manic paws as they scratched and clawed at her in an effort to reach her, to lure her down to him for comfort and reassurance. He kept jumping and pawing her, clearly distraught, but she couldn't give him her full attention until she'd checked every corner of the room and the open, empty closet.

No Noah.

The baby gate lay broken in two near her feet. Bunched up in a haphazard pile were the drop cloths in the middle of the room. Nearly empty cans of primer had been opened and tipped on their sides, leaving a viscous white trail along the exposed carpet. The ladder hadn't been disturbed.

Nor had one corner of the room, now markedly different from the way Josie had left it. A standing lamp, now on its side, illuminated a sweet tableau that was perversely at odds with the condition of the rest of their home. A square of soft gray paint had been brushed along the wall with a puffy white cloud crudely painted over it. Two small colorful hot-air balloon mobiles swayed in front of the swath of cloudy sky, dangling from the ceiling on what looked like fishing line.

The idea they'd discussed only hours ago for welcoming the child they hoped to adopt was alive before her, but Noah was gone. Trout's claws slashed the backs of her legs, stinging even through her thick khaki pants. His mewling was even more anguished now that he sensed her horror flaming to life like a five-alarm fire.

A strangled sound worked its way painfully from Josie's chest, past her lips.

Where was her husband?

ELEVEN

ONE WEEK AGO

Bug gripped the hem of her skintight skirt and pulled, trying to cover up more of her thighs. It was no use. The stupid thing snapped right back up, leaving little to the imagination. Even though the point was to show off her legs and her ass, she hated wearing anything this short. With a sigh, she stared at the rickety wooden steps that led up to the second-floor apartment. If anyone walked past while she was climbing them, they'd know the exact color of her lace underwear. Not ideal.

But she'd put too much time into this plan to back off now. In fact, she needed to speed things up. She was exhausted and her anxiety was so bad that her hair was falling out. Absently, she patted it as she climbed the steps. As always, the fifth and the eleventh one creaked and bowed beneath her weight. This place was one paint chip away from collapsing. Bug had lived in some real shitholes growing up, but nothing like this. Every time she spent the night, it took three showers at her own place to feel properly cleansed.

Soon, she'd never have to come here again.

Once she reached the top, she glanced down. Immediately, her stomach clenched. Holden's disgusting old-man neighbor grinned at her from below, one hand shading his eyes. When he licked his lips, Bug almost threw up in her mouth.

Don't pull at the skirt. Don't pull at the skirt. If she tried to cover up, he'd know that he made her uncomfortable. He seemed to enjoy that even more than he enjoyed leering at her. Bug drew her shoulders back, sneered at him, and flipped him off. His hand dropped, giving her a better view of his lined face, now red with anger.

"Don't you have a sex offender registration to complete?" she called, just to twist the knife. She hated old pervs.

He called her a bunch of sexist names which were so predictable, she had to roll her eyes. It was always the same with lecherous pricks. Of all ages, really.

Finished with him, she pounded against the door. "Holden, let me in!"

She would have just walked inside but he had this rule about always knocking "in case I'm in the shower." He really thought she was so stupid. They'd already seen one another naked so who gave a crap if she saw him coming out of the shower? Plus, she already knew about the redhead and the single mom he was messing around with. Holden thought he was smart, but he was about as dumb as a pile of bricks. As much as it annoyed Bug, it worked to her advantage. Him thinking she was a naive little airhead also worked to her advantage.

"Holden!"

The door finally swung open. Holden leaned against the frame like he was oozing sex appeal or something—shirtless with his sweatpants hanging low on his hips. "Hey, college girl," he said in the voice he used when he was trying to be sexy.

She suppressed her eye-roll, forcing a sweet, innocent smile onto her face before stepping forward and wrapping her arms around his neck.

Holden wasn't the worst. In fact, he was pretty hot, but he

was a lying, cheating sack of shit with a bit of a temper. As his hand drifted down toward her ass, she reminded herself this was only temporary. Once she got what she needed, she wouldn't have to see him anymore.

"Wow," he said, dragging her inside. "You look hotter than usual. Trying out a new look?"

He let go of her and she twirled, pretending to be nervous while trying to avoid kicking any piles of trash. Wouldn't want to dislodge the resident roaches. Apparently, Holden had never been acquainted with a garbage bin. The place reeked of stale beer, spoiled food, and some cheap dollar-store body spray he passed off as cologne.

"I'm trying to branch out," Bug told him, fingers twisting her necklace. "You like it?"

One corner of his mouth tipped up in an appreciative smile. "I do. A lot."

She stopped and gazed down at herself, making sure to furrow her brow and pucker her lips like she wasn't convinced. "Do you think it's too much for tonight?"

"Tonight?"

When she looked back up at him, she could see the panic in his eyes. Had he forgotten that he'd invited her? Asked one of his other girls to go with him instead?

No. No way. He wasn't taking anyone else. She'd worked too hard for this. Tonight was the payoff for all her months of hard work. He was not screwing her out of this opportunity.

Bug took a calming breath and concentrated on not flexing her fists. First, she pouted. Then she widened her eyes. So much dewy innocence. Combined with her skimpy clothes, Holden wouldn't be able to resist. With that in mind, she crossed her arms, making sure to push up her boobs enough that he'd be distracted.

Right... there.

It was difficult to hold back her satisfied grin. "You

promised!" she said, pitching her voice an octave higher. "You said you would take me! Holden, you won't introduce me to your family. If you're not willing to let me meet your friends then—"

He held a hand up to silence her. "I never said I wouldn't introduce you to my family. They're a bunch of assholes but if you want to meet them, that's fine. But the people at this party tonight... they're not like my buddies from the bar, you know?"

"Is that your way of saying I'm not good enough to meet them?" Bug demanded, giving a cute little lip quiver. She already knew who they were and exactly why he didn't want her in their company. It was the same reason she needed to meet them.

"Oh no, baby," he cooed, closing the distance between them and rubbing her arms. "That's not it at all. It's just that I want you to be prepared. These people aren't like your college friends, okay?"

She put her hands on his chest. "Holden, I'm tired of being sheltered, okay? I'm tired of being this good little college girl who always does what she's told and only hangs out with people the same as her. You told me you'd show me the world."

It was one of the cheesiest lines she'd ever heard. Bug had used every ounce of self-control she possessed not to burst into laughter when he pulled that one on her. Instead, she'd tucked it away for later—for a moment like this. Holden loved the idea of corrupting her somehow, of feeling like the big, sophisticated man who could rock her safe little world. He was painfully easy to manipulate.

"Oh baby, I didn't say you couldn't go with me. Let me make some calls, okay?"

There was only one call Bug wanted him to make and that was to the redhead he was sneaking around with to tell her to stay home.

Bug smiled, doing her best to look starry-eyed and eager. "I'm so excited!"

Holden's smooth, confident smile faltered for just a heartbeat. One of his hands brushed through his curly brown hair as he appraised her again. "Just, um, tonight when we get there, I need you to stay close to me the whole time, okay?"

Bug gave him another sweet, trusting smile. "Of course," she lied.

TWELVE

Blue and red emergency beacons flashed in front of Josie's home, so similar to the scene she'd found at the children's hospital site only hours ago. The entire street was flooded with police vehicles. Cruisers, two marked SUVs used by their Evidence Response Team, and the personal vehicles of Turner, Gretchen, and their Chief, Bob Chitwood. Josie sat in the back seat of Gretchen's SUV, the door hanging open. The first units to arrive had found blood in the driveway. Josie had been ushered from her own vehicle to the pavement until more of her colleagues arrived.

Trout snoozed in her lap. He was the only thing she'd carried from the house. Finding his leash in the detritus of their home seemed like a herculean task and she hadn't wanted to risk further damaging the integrity of what was clearly a crime scene. She'd already traipsed through the house once to search for Noah and ensure there were no intruders present. In any other circumstances, she would have been far more careful in clearing a structure.

But this wasn't just any crime scene. It was the home she shared with her husband. This was her life.

Numbly, she watched uniformed officers go door to door in both directions, canvassing. She wondered if any of her neighbors had lost their Wi-Fi or only them. Had they been targeted? This was a fairly safe neighborhood. Only one or two of the residents on her street had external cameras. On the sidewalk, Gretchen directed things while the Chief paced beside her, his cell phone pressed to his ear. Josie could hear him barking at someone on the other end, dropping more f-bombs than she'd ever heard him use before.

"I don't fucking care whose ass you have to drag out of bed. Get everyone up. Every person you fucking know. I need your people here an hour ago. Somebody better start breaking some land-speed records right fucking now or I'll crawl so far up your ass, you'll need a root canal to get rid of me."

Josie stroked Trout's warm back, concentrating hard on the weight of him across her legs. She was aware that from the moment she stepped outside with him in her arms, her mind had begun systematically shutting down. Some protective part of her had emerged, an efficient little housekeeper who lived inside her brain, whose sole purpose was to sweep up all the fear, worry, panic, and creeping devastation, and deposit it into Josie's mental vault. Her emotions were locked up tight in a titanium box right next to the place where the bad things lived. All she could feel were physical sensations. It was all she could bear right now.

Where was he?

On their front lawn, Officer Hummel, the head of their ERT, was embroiled in a hushed but heated discussion with Turner. Both men gesticulated wildly. Hummel kept motioning toward the street while Turner stabbed a finger in the direction of the house and then tapped against an imaginary wristwatch.

She knew what was happening. Denton PD couldn't investigate the disappearance of one of their own. They'd had to call the state police. This was their case. In terms of evidence collection, Hummel's team could give them an assist, process the house alongside them, but they couldn't enter the premises until a state police evidence tech arrived. That could take anywhere from thirty minutes to three hours—or longer. Time that could be crucial in terms of locating Noah.

Alive. Locating him alive.

Tick, tock. Tick, tock.

Getting nowhere with Hummel, Turner stalked off. He stopped in front of the open car door and yanked at his beard. It was his nervous tic. Dimly, Josie realized she had worked with him long enough to know his nervous tic. "Quinn," he said. "Are you sure you saw the LT's phone in there?"

For the last hour, she had been replaying every inch of her journey through the house, picking through all the things her subconscious had cataloged for her to examine later, the things her rising panic hadn't allowed her to focus on at the time. "It was in the living room. On the floor."

Everything was on the floor.

They wouldn't be able to ping Noah's location using his cell phone. It had been left behind. The state police would be able to get a geofence warrant to try tracking down whoever had broken into the house.

Turner sighed and yanked at his beard again. "His weapon. Where does he keep it when he's not on duty? Did you see it?"

"We keep them in lockboxes in our bedroom." Josie licked her dry lips. Trout shuddered in his sleep. "His was open. He must have retrieved it. I think he—"

Closing her eyes, she tried to mentally create the scenario as it must have unfolded. Noah was in the nursery, setting up the makeshift mural for her, when he heard something. As a guard dog, Trout was unreliable. If he was sleeping deeply enough, he wouldn't hear a bomb go off in the next room. Sometimes, if someone came to the front door, he'd charge it, barking up a storm, as he had the first time Turner had come to the house.

Other times, he was too lazy to run to the door, instead staying in place and growling to alert Josie and Noah that something was amiss.

But Trout had been inside the nursery, which meant that Noah heard someone in the house and tucked the dog away in the room while he went to check things out. He would have had his phone. She could practically see his path, like she was following him, looking over his shoulder. Emerging from the nursery, whatever he thought he'd heard became clearer. There was definitely someone in the house. Their friend, Misty, and Josie's sister, Trinity, both had keys to their home, but Trinity was in New York City and Misty would have knocked if she knew one of them was home.

Noah did exactly what Josie had done. Instead of calling dispatch and requesting units, he'd held off, getting his pistol from his lockbox in their bedroom and attempting to clear the house on his own. She had a sudden mental flash of her jewelry box on their bedroom floor. Broken and empty. Perhaps Noah encountered the intruder there first. Something had happened in that room that resulted in the perpetrator fleeing downstairs. Noah retrieved his pistol and gave chase, catching up to him in the living room.

She couldn't bear to imagine what happened next. It didn't make sense. Nothing made sense.

"Quinn." Turner's voice drew her out of her thoughts. "Talk to me."

"His Glock is in the living room," she said. "With the phone. Among the... debris. I saw it."

"All right," Turner said. "Good, that's good, but I need to know what else you're working on. I can see your wheels turning."

On any other day, she would have taken a jab at him, telling him she wasn't going to do all of his thinking for him, but he hadn't seen the inside of the house. He had even less context than she did. Trout stretched, his little legs locking and then relaxing. She soothed him back to sleep while she recounted her thought process for Turner.

His eyes narrowed. "Wait a minute. Did you say nursery? Quinn, are you pregnant?"

They knew virtually nothing about one another's personal lives. Josie had never asked him about his and as far as she was concerned, he hadn't earned access to hers. Turner was the only one on the team who didn't know she and Noah were trying to adopt a baby. "No," she said. "We're, um, adopting. Just waiting for a match."

"Huh," Turner said, regarding her with a look she couldn't decipher.

The last thing she wanted to discuss was their adoption plans. "The coffee table in the living room was cracked, broken. There was blood. That's where I saw Noah's phone and his Glock. The foyer—" Her voice nearly cracked as the detail came back to her. She hadn't been able to process it while still inside, searching for Noah. "There's a bullet hole in the foyer wall. The direction... the bullet would have had to come from the living room."

"Which means he confronted someone there," Turner said, picking up her train of thought. "Assuming the bullet came from Noah's weapon. I know you think things started in your bedroom but there was no blood there, right?"

"I don't think so. No. I don't remember seeing any."

Turner nodded rapidly, looking like a bobblehead. His fingers drummed against the side of his leg. "Maybe Noah retrieved his weapon, went downstairs, shit went sideways and then the house got tossed after the fact."

It could have gone either way, but it really didn't matter. Her husband was gone.

One of Turner's feet tapped against the asphalt. She'd never seen him this twitchy. "Whatever happened—the real shit went down in your living room. Noah's a big guy and he was armed but clearly, he wasn't able to subdue the person who broke in."

They wouldn't know if the shot had come from his gun until the evidence was collected and processed. If it had, that meant that Noah had missed, which was unusual for him. He was an excellent shot, cool under pressure. Unless he'd fired more than one and the others had found their mark. If that was the case, where was the wounded intruder? What the hell had happened in there?

Tick, tock. Tick, tock.

"There was more than one guy," Turner said. "Had to be."

That might explain why Noah had missed or only been able to fire a single bullet. She was also fairly certain it took more than one person to cause the unholy mess inside her house. But why had they taken him? It didn't make sense. Assuming he was still alive, holding onto him for any length of time would be dangerous for them. There was no point in that. It wasn't as if they'd try to get a ransom for him. Doing so would be reckless and just plain stupid. Law enforcement didn't make enough money to be targeted for ransom. The most logical explanation was that they'd killed him, in which case the smartest thing would be to remove his body and bury it somewhere no one would ever find him.

No. Josie didn't accept that. She couldn't. Maybe that made her naive since she'd been on the job long enough to know just how slim the odds were that Noah was still alive, but she refused to entertain the thought. Until she knew otherwise, she was going to operate under the assumption—no, the certainty—that her husband was still alive.

"What do you think this was, Quinn?" asked Turner. "A robbery?"

"They didn't take any electronics." She flashed to their bedroom again. Her jewelry box had been looted. "But I had some jewelry. They took all of that. Most of it wasn't valuable but there were some rings and a necklace that were worth a lot."

There was the engagement ring from her first husband, Ray, with its matching wedding band, the diamond pendant he had bought for her, the ring from her failed engagement with Luke Creighton, and the ring Noah had proposed with, which she didn't wear on duty. Those items alone were worth thousands.

"Okay, okay," Turner said, starting to pace before her. One hand continued beating rapidly against his leg while the other tore at his beard. "The string of armed robberies. There was one in Bellewood where they managed to knock out the Wi-Fi. That's what I heard, anyway. The ones here, well, they made a mess, took the jewelry but they also took the electronics."

Josie scratched between Trout's ears. He sighed in his sleep. "Turner," she said softly.

Something about the tone of her voice made him stop pacing, stop moving altogether. It was the weakness. She just knew it. The vulnerability in her tone. She hated it. Turner took a step toward her, hands slack at his sides, and leaned in, bringing his face level with hers. His blue eyes were void of mischief, impatience, of everything. This was him listening. Truly listening.

Josie tried to make her voice stronger, but it still came out a little raspy. "They were looking for something."

Turner glanced at the front lawn where Hummel still waited for his state police counterpart. When he brought his focus back to her, she knew he believed her. Still, he had to ask, "Looking for what? What do you two have, besides your jewelry, that someone wants badly enough to break in, trash everything, and kidnap a grown man? A cop, no less. What do you have that's worth that kind of risk?"

"Nothing," Josie replied. "Absolutely nothing."

THIRTEEN

Josie sat at Gretchen's kitchen table, an untouched cup of chamomile tea in front of her. Trout lay at her feet, his head up, ears pointed, whining softly as he watched her. He'd always been attuned to her moods, keying in on any small shift in her emotional landscape. For the dozenth time, she reached down and scratched between his ears. She wanted to reassure him—in the silly baby-talk voice that she and Noah always used with him—that everything was okay, but he already knew that nothing was right in their world.

Where was Noah?

A glance at the digital clock on the microwave told her it was nearly three thirty in the morning and yet, the house hummed with activity as though it were the middle of the afternoon. In the dining and living rooms, Josie heard the low murmur of voices, the chirps and buzzes of cell phone notifications, and from the foyer, the creak of the front door opening and closing, the soft footfalls of people walking around.

She didn't even remember coming here. One minute she was in front of her house, sitting in the back seat of Gretchen's SUV, and the next, she was here, watching as Gretchen's adult daughter, Paula, made her tea. She kept up a steady stream of one-sided conversation, voice calm and even as she explained everything that was happening. She reminded Josie of a dentist she'd had once who chose to narrate everything he did as he worked so there were no surprises. *You're just going to feel a little pinch here and then some numbness.* Except Paula told her things like, "You and Trout will stay as long as you need. The guest bedroom is already made up. We'll keep the cat in Mom's room while you're here. You probably won't be able to go back inside your house again until sometime tomorrow, but we'll get you anything you need. Mom sent someone to the twenty-four-hour Walmart to get Trout a leash and some food. You can use my phone charger."

On and on she went. The only indication that she wasn't feeling as calm as she sounded was the way she repeatedly twirled a lock of her long, brown hair around her index finger. Josie tried to ignore the tic and only focus on Paula's voice, which was surprisingly soothing.

Trout whimpered and stood up, licking at her fingertips. Absently, she scratched his head again. From the other room there was a shift in the tone of the inaudible conversations. A ripple of some sort, news traveling. Then silence and finally, a slow return to the earlier noise level. Gretchen appeared in the kitchen doorway.

"Keep them out there until I say," she told her daughter. "All of them."

Paula crossed her arms over her chest and nodded resolutely. Though taller than her mother, the resemblance between the two was striking.

Gretchen pushed a hand through her short, spiked brown and gray hair and pulled out a kitchen chair. She sat down and then inched her way as close to Josie as humanly possible, until their knees touched. Trout cried, jumping up and digging his claws into Gretchen's thigh. He was trying to tell her that something was horribly wrong, and she needed to fix it. Someone needed to fix it.

"Hey," Gretchen said, patting his head until he got down. "I called your sister. She's on her way from New York. In the meantime, she got in touch with your parents and your brother. They'll be here soon. Who else do I need to call?"

Josie hadn't let her mind wander that far. The law enforcement officer in her told her that within hours, Noah's face would be plastered all over social media and the news—not just locally but perhaps even nationally. Calls needed to be made. Not just to gather people for moral support but to make sure their loved ones heard the news about Noah's abduction from Josie and not from anywhere else.

"I—" Josie began but her thoughts were too jumbled. How many people did she need to call? There was Noah's older sister and brother. They'd want to know. Should she call his father? They'd been estranged since Noah turned eighteen. Who else needed to know?

"Josie," said Gretchen, "I'll make the calls if you give me the names."

Paula had put her phone on the table next to her untouched tea, plugged into a charger with a cord that reached halfway across the room. Josie brought the screen to life and then tried to log in using her thumbprint but it didn't work. There were still flakes of primer caked and dried on the screen. Instead, she tapped in her passcode, saying it out loud for Gretchen's benefit. Noah's birthday or their anniversary date would have been too obvious, too easy for a hacker or anyone, really, to guess so she'd used the date they'd first had sex. It was silly and a little embarrassing although only she and Noah knew what her passcode referenced. The day was permanently marked in her mind because they'd dated for over six months before becoming physical. Josie had wanted to take things slow, to make sure she was present for Noah and not using his body as a way to blunt feelings she didn't want to face. When it finally happened, it had been transcendent.

Worth the wait. He'd always been worth the wait.

Josie pushed the phone toward Gretchen, rattling off the names of his siblings. She left out his father. She doubted he would care.

"How about Misty?" Gretchen said.

Misty Derossi was one of their best friends. Noah and Josie were so involved in her eight-year-old son Harris's life, that he referred to them as his aunt and uncle. Pain seized her abdomen at the thought of little Harris. He adored Noah. In fact, Noah was the closest thing Harris had to a father. He was going to be so confused and upset. Terrified. It would be up to his mother whether to tell him and if so, how much to divulge. These were the kinds of things parents had to do that Josie hadn't taken into account in their quest to have children. They only ever talked about the fun, positive things. The snuggling, the playing, watching their future baby stand or walk for the first time.

"I'll call Misty," Gretchen said, taking the phone. There were a few beats of silence, Gretchen studying her. "You're really checked out right now, which I get. Believe me, I understand. Better than most people."

It was true. Gretchen was one of the few people in Josie's life who could match her trauma for trauma, starting in childhood. Like Josie, she'd endured unspeakable things. Abuse, tragedy, loss so big that it defied reality. Like Josie, she'd survived most of her life by constructing an impenetrable fortress deep inside her psyche that held all of her feelings so her heart wouldn't have to—even the good ones. Emotions were messy and unpredictable. When you'd lived on the razor's edge of trauma and tragedy for so long, messy and unpredictable became tantamount to death. Better to stay comfortably anesthetized. They'd grown good at it.

"Josie," Gretchen said, "I need you to listen to me right now."

Eight years ago, Josie had become the interim Chief of Police in Denton after she'd exposed a human trafficking ring that left the department with vacancies to fill. She'd hired Gretchen because she had fifteen years of experience as a homicide detective with Philly PD but what she'd brought into Josie's life was a mirror. She understood Josie in ways no other human being ever could.

"Wherever you are right now," Gretchen went on, "you need to come back."

For the first time since returning home from her shift, there was a tiny crack in Josie's mental armor. Emotion, hot and thick, poured through it, filling her body. Saliva clogged her throat. A burning, aching sensation started behind her eyes. The precursor to tears. "I can't," she whispered.

Both she and Gretchen had done a lot of work to process all their trauma, to learn how to feel and manage their emotions, how to communicate and move through crises in healthy ways. Years of therapy, of practicing their newfound skills with those closest to them, had helped but *dead inside* was still a default setting. Any alternative was too damn scary.

Gretchen knew it.

"Then forget about being Noah's wife right now," she said. "Be the investigator who cleared that house tonight. Can you do that?"

Slowly, Josie nodded. She touched her cheek. No tears had escaped.

"Heather Loughlin is here. She caught the case. I'm going to send her in."

Josie gave another mute nod. Heather was a detective with the state police Criminal Investigation Division. She worked with the Denton PD often on cases in which jurisdiction, evidence, or witnesses overlapped. Josie knew her to be thorough, fair, and persistent. As Noah's wife, she was glad Heather was taking point on this.

Trout bumped against Josie's legs, still whining. He didn't even acknowledge Heather when she took Gretchen's place.

"Never thought we'd be meeting like this," Heather sighed. Her trademark blonde ponytail was messier than usual. The skin around her eyes was puffy. She'd been wakened in the middle of the night, like everyone else. A notepad and pen appeared in her hands, along with a pair of reading glasses, which she perched on her nose. "I read your initial statement, but I want you to walk me through what happened tonight anyway."

Josie blinked, willing her brain to come back online. She couldn't work this case herself. Couldn't do anything, really. She'd be on the sidelines, which meant the only thing she could do to help her husband was to answer all of Heather's questions. Her mind needed to be quick and alert. Trout gave a little cry of protest that the second human to appear in the kitchen in the last ten minutes also hadn't fixed Josie, and then he flopped down across her feet. Josie's throat felt dry and scratchy. She took a sip of the tea, now cold, and told Heather everything. Then she waited for the barrage of questions she knew were coming.

The same ones she'd ask if she were in the other chair.

FOURTEEN

Heather scribbled furiously in her notebook, recording Josie's account. Once she finished, she turned to a fresh page. Then she regarded Josie steadily, her expression unreadable. "Was Noah having issues with anyone?"

"No."

"Are you sure? Maybe a coworker? A neighbor? A friend? Someone he arrested in the past?"

"No one," Josie said.

"How about you two?" asked Heather. "Any problems? Marital stress?"

In other words, had their marriage deteriorated to the point that Josie had somehow set into motion a scenario that ended with Noah dead? Had she hired someone to get rid of him? Orchestrated things so that his death would look like a random home invasion? "No problems," Josie answered.

Heather's pen froze over her notepad. "I saw the house, Josie. It looked like you were painting one of the guest rooms. There were mobiles—"

"We're adopting a child," Josie said quickly. "We're just waiting for a match."

Heather leaned back in her chair and tapped her pen against her lower lip. Sympathy shimmered in her amber-colored eyes. Josie tried not to wince. She much preferred Heather to keep things cold and clinical. Josie was barely keeping her own feelings in check. She didn't have the bandwidth to contend with those of others.

"Congratulations," Heather said. "The process of getting approved is long and tedious. That must have been stressful."

"It was, at times, but we handled it."

Heather turned her attention to her notebook again. "I've talked with your chief, but I'll ask you as well. Are there any old cases Noah might have worked where someone he put away would want to come after him?"

Josie had thought about that for the last few hours but come up empty. "No. None."

Heather didn't bother to sugarcoat the next question or to preface it by saying something about her just having to do her job, how these were standard questions she was required to ask. "Is there any chance Noah was having an affair?"

"No," Josie said with certainty.

"Does he have any drug or gambling problems?"

Josie knew these were the correct questions to ask in this scenario. They were exactly the ones she would have asked and yet, it rankled. But wasn't it like that for all spouses in her position? You thought you knew your partner. You were so certain. Then one day you came home to an empty, trashed house, blood everywhere, and the person you thought you knew better than yourself was gone.

Could Noah have been having an affair? Could he have a well-hidden gambling problem? Or a drug problem? They didn't spend every moment together. But wouldn't she have noticed? Suspected? Or, in some sick twist of irony, would she have been the last to suspect? Had she grown too complacent? Given Noah too much trust?

"Josie?"

Or had there been something deeper going on? Something more personal to Noah? His parents had married as teenagers after an unplanned pregnancy. They'd stayed together and had two more children. Noah was the youngest. His childhood had been ideal. A stable home. Two loving parents. Caring older siblings. Youth sports leagues. Holidays filled with fun traditions. Family vacations. Everything Josie always desperately wished her own childhood had held—would have held if she hadn't been abducted at three weeks old by a psychopath, not to be reunited with her biological family until the age of thirty. Then after Noah turned eighteen, his father left to start a new family. He'd been counting down to his youngest child's eighteenth birthday like a man waiting to be released from prison. Noah had been left behind with his devastated mother to pick up the pieces. Everything they thought they knew about their lives felt like a lie.

Trout's head lifted. A small keening noise came from his little body.

Noah had promised Josie he was nothing like his father and that he would never act like his father, but what if it wasn't something he'd been able to control? What if he'd grown tired of their life? What if he didn't want this anymore? Always having to deal with her trauma-informed responses and now the responsibility of adopting a child? What if he had started an affair or developed a drug or gambling problem to avoid facing the fact that he no longer wanted a life with her?

"Josie?"

No. She *knew* him. He wasn't a coward. In fact, his wedding vow to her had been that he'd always run toward the danger with her. If he'd been unhappy, he would have talked with her about it. Not turned to drugs or gambling or the arms of another woman only to have it blow up in his face.

Heather touched Josie's forearm. Trout jumped up, yipping, and swatted his paw at where their skin met. Startled, Heather withdrew her hand. "It's okay, little buddy," she said soothingly. Trout gave her a wary look before dropping back down. With a huff, he flopped across Josie's feet again.

"I'm sorry," Josie said. "What was the question?"

"Does Noah have a drug or gambling problem?"

"No," Josie said. "He doesn't."

"Do you have any idea who might have broken into your house?"

"No."

Heather adjusted her reading glasses. "We found Noah's service pistol in your living room. There was also a bullet lodged in the baseboard of the foyer wall. Same type found in the magazine of his gun. We'll run ballistics, but we're fairly certain it came from Noah's gun since the mag is only missing one round and there's a spent casing near where his weapon was found."

Just as Josie had suspected, he'd fired on someone inside their home and missed.

"How many firearms do the two of you have at your residence?" asked Heather.

"We each have a service pistol, and I have a personal one. A Smith and Wesson M&P, nine-millimeter. It should be in my nightstand vault—if it wasn't taken."

"The lockbox was there," Heather said. "If you give us the code to get into it, we'll make sure your firearm wasn't taken."

Josie told her.

"I know the house was a mess and you weren't in there very long, but did it look like anything was missing?"

"My jewelry. Other than that, I'm not sure. The place was trashed, and I was trying to clear it."

Heather turned to a blank page in her notebook and pushed

it, along with her pen, toward Josie. "Make me a list of what was taken. If you've got photos, send those along to me later. Your laptops, televisions, tablets, all that sort of stuff, those were all still there, weren't they?"

Josie nodded as she quickly jotted down the items she could remember.

"I'll need access to Noah's phone. I'll get a warrant, but—"

"I'll sign a consent form." Josie wrote his passcode at the bottom of her list and pushed the notepad back to Heather. It was the date of their first kiss.

"Did you get a geofence warrant?" Josie asked. "His phone was in the house, but—"

"Yes," Heather said.

Josie waited for her to elaborate, aching for more information. "Did you get the results yet?"

Heather's expression was inscrutable as she studied Josie. Under normal circumstances, as the lead detective, it would be at her discretion as to which details to disclose to the victim's family, but these weren't normal circumstances. A police officer was missing. Josie wasn't just his wife, she was his colleague as well. Heather's supervisor had the ultimate say in what information to share with Noah's family.

Josie knew this. Rules were rules. "Tell me," she demanded anyway.

Heather shook her head. "Josie."

Her palm came down on the table so hard that it stung. The mug jerked, tea sloshing onto the table. Trout jumped up, growling. "Tell me!" she repeated, louder this time.

Heather was unfazed. "I will tell you whatever I'm authorized to tell you as soon as I'm able to do so."

Trout turned and directed his growls at Heather. Josie didn't bother to soothe him. A few seconds ticked by, tense and painfully slow. Finally, Heather sighed. "This should go without saying but we're doing absolutely everything we can to locate him as soon as possible."

Josie had no doubt and yet, it was an empty reassurance.

"Work with me, Josie."

Trout's wet nose nudged Josie's hand. Automatically, she stroked the soft hair under his chin. Choking back the emotion that made her want to scream and rage and destroy everything she could get her hands on, she took a deep breath. Tried to do the box breathing she'd learned in therapy. When that didn't work, she tried the four-seven-eight breathing that she often found helpful. Inhale for four seconds, hold for seven, exhale for eight. She needed to focus. Be the investigator who had cleared their house.

"He went somewhere. Between the time I left and when the house was broken into. I don't know where but if you check the GPS on his car—"

"Already on it," said Heather. "What's his blood type?"

"A positive."

Heather wrote it down but didn't look Josie in the eye. The evidence techs would have been able to type the blood found in the house and in the driveway on-scene very quickly. Josie used the napkin Paula had left next to her mug to sop up the cold tea she'd spilled. "Was it all his?"

Heather shook her head, still scribbling something in her notebook. "You won't be able to get back onto the premises until tomorrow. They're still working. When you do, I need you to go through the house carefully to determine if anything else was taken. A couple of the armed robberies we've been looking at outside of Denton had similarities. The Wi-Fi knocked out, house a mess, valuables taken. Your department has investigated some that are definitely the same perpetrators. I'll review those, see if there's anything that connects to this. Then—"

"Heather." Josie was embarrassed by the way her words came out all hoarse and strangled. "Please."

Heather closed her notebook. She looked down at Trout, who was still standing, watching her warily. Her voice was quiet. "We found two blood types. A positive and O negative. Most of the blood was A positive."

FIFTEEN

"Honey, are you sure this is a good idea?"

"Shan, she has to inventory the house. See if anything else is missing."

"But she hasn't even slept! Christian, this isn't a good idea. Maybe we can do it instead."

Josie tuned out her bickering parents, who stood on the sidewalk beside her, and stared at her house. The mid-morning sun crept across the driveway, where Noah's car and her SUV were still parked. The state police had issued a warrant for the GPS history, but they hadn't needed to impound the vehicle for that. A strip of crime scene tape still hung across the front door. It didn't even look like their home anymore. Josie felt strangely adrift. The house was either going to become a sanctuary again or it was going to be the place where her life was shattered beyond repair.

Either way, she had to go inside.

Her brother, Patrick, appeared halfway down the block, jogging toward them with a tote bag over his arm. "I've got trash bags and latex gloves and some cleaning supplies. Peroxide for the blood."

"Patrick!" Shannon chided.

Christian sighed. "It's fine, Shan. Josie's seen more blood than most doctors, probably. She can handle it."

Josie felt him at her side. When he slid an arm around her, she let her head loll on his shoulder. Almost immediately, her eyes began to droop. Her mother was right. She hadn't slept. How could she? Noah—her Noah—was gone. His blood was all over their house and in their driveway. No one would or could tell her anything.

Since she couldn't be part of the official investigation, she'd spent the night sitting cross-legged on the bed in Gretchen's guest room doing the only things she could do on her own. First, she logged into their Spur Mobile account to review Noah's phone activity for the last two months. There was nothing out of the ordinary. While she couldn't view the contents of his texts, she was able to see all the numbers he exchanged messages with. No surprises. No numbers she didn't recognize. Then she looked at their joint credit and debit accounts. There hadn't been any unusual activity since last she'd checked them. The pending charges from hours ago told her which stores he'd visited while she was at work. She'd passed the information along to Gretchen who said that the state police had already visited the stores and pulled interior and exterior security footage to see if anyone had been following him. Gretchen didn't know what they'd found.

Out of ways to track Noah down or find some evidence of what might have led to the home invasion, Josie spent the rest of her time mentally cataloging all the things she wanted to find out about the investigation as soon as the sun rose. Trout had slept fitfully beside her. Sometime around six, Trinity had arrived, padding silently into the room. Without a word, she'd climbed into the bed, gathered Josie in her arms and held her. Nothing more. No conversation. No questions. No coaxing.

Just connection.

Trinity hadn't left her side. Until they arrived here, though Josie knew she was nearby.

"We're ready whenever you are, kid," Christian said softly into Josie's ear.

"Thanks, Dad."

It was still so strange to call him that and to call Shannon 'Mom' even though they were her biological parents. Josie had grown up what felt like worlds apart from the Payne family. They'd lived two hours from Denton, in a small town named Callowhill. After giving birth to Josie and Trinity, Shannon had hired a nanny to help watch the twins when Christian was at work or when she needed to run errands. When the girls were three weeks old, a young woman from the housecleaning service the Paynes employed, Lila Jensen, had kidnapped Josie. She'd set the house on fire. The nanny, who'd been there alone with the babies, had managed to save Trinity. She'd never even seen Lila that day.

No one had.

The authorities told the Paynes that tiny Josie had perished in the fire. Her family mourned her their entire lives.

"We'll follow your lead," said Patrick, patting Josie's shoulder.

Nodding, she stepped out of Christian's embrace and trudged toward the front door. Her legs felt heavy as she climbed the stairs. She'd had two cups of coffee and choked down a pastry from a tray one of the patrol officers had dropped off at Gretchen's house, but her eyes felt gritty. A wave of dizziness washed over her. It was her body reminding her that it needed rest. But her heart needed her husband more. She was strong enough for this. Strong enough to do what needed to be done to bring him home, even from the sidelines. How many times had Noah come to her rescue? Been strong when she was weak? She was damn well doing the hard things for him now, no matter how her body protested.

With a deep, steadying breath, she pushed inside. Her parents and brother followed. For a long moment, they all stood quietly in the foyer, which was relatively undisturbed. Josie found the bullet hole in the baseboard again. The state police's forensic team would have marked and photographed it, removed the bullet, and then tried to determine the trajectory. It would tell them something about how things unfolded but Josie wouldn't be privy to that. She was just Noah's wife right now.

Josie sensed her parents and brother turning toward the living room and heard their gasps of surprise.

"I tried to tell you it was bad," she said.

"Is the whole house like this?" asked Patrick.

Josie nodded.

Before anyone could speak, Trinity bustled in through the front door. She was dressed in a pair of faded blue jeans and one of her fiancé Drake's FBI sweatshirts. Her glossy black hair was pulled up into a high ponytail. Josie hadn't seen her apply makeup this morning, but she still looked glamorous, like she belonged in the pages of a magazine that showcased fashion and makeup tips.

Trinity clapped her hands together, unbothered by the state of the house. Unless she was freaked out but doing a better job of covering it up. "All right, let's get started. Detective Loughlin needs to know as soon as possible if anything else is missing besides the jewelry. Josie, where do you want everyone?"

Josie pointed at the living room. Because she knew that Shannon would be able to handle it, she said, "Mom, you'll be in charge of cleaning up the blood."

"Also, all this fingerprint powder needs to go," Trinity added. "And someone needs to hose down the driveway."

"Right," said Josie. "Dad and Patrick, start in the kitchen. Put anything that can be salvaged away. If you're not sure where it goes, set it aside."

Trinity put her hands on her hips. "All of you—don't forget to take photos of everything that needs to be replaced. Come on, Josie. We'll start upstairs."

Josie took a garbage bag from Patrick and followed Trinity up the steps to the main bedroom. Her sister pushed open the door and stepped inside. Last night, Josie's senses had been so overloaded, she hadn't noticed just how much it smelled of Noah, of them. Her next breath, full of him, of both of them, nearly put another crack in the shell around her heart that was keeping her from having a breakdown.

"Hardest thing first," Trinity mumbled.

Josie stood in the doorway while Trinity carefully cleared enough room for them to close the door. "How do you know the living room isn't the hardest?"

"Because of the blood?" Trinity shrugged. "Your job revolves around crime scenes. It's easy for you to detach, become clinical. This is where you spend your most intimate moments with Noah. It's harder."

Harder.

Screw breaking down. Josie wanted nothing more than to surround herself with Noah's scent, wrap herself in it. How many times had she buried her face in his neck, against his chest, seeking comfort? There was something left of him in their home. This small thing, fleeting and ephemeral. When the thoughts that it was only a reminder of what she might lose started to creep in, she mentally stomped on them. She refused to let her fear and terror weaponize against her the one piece of Noah she still had. No, she was taking this. Keeping it.

Josie's gaze flickered toward their private bath. She tossed the garbage bag toward Trinity. "I need a minute."

She tried unsuccessfully to close the door behind her. There was too much on the floor. After three tries, she gave up, not caring if Trinity saw, and sank onto her knees, rifling through their belongings until she found the clothes that had been dumped out of their hamper. It was her week to do the laundry, which meant it hadn't yet been done. Emotion pulsed at the edges of her mental shields as her hands closed over a T-shirt Noah had worn earlier in the week. She brought it to her face, pressing her nose against it and inhaling his scent. So familiar, so comforting, and yet, despite her determination to not let this vestige of him upset her, it caused a wave of anguish to crest inside her. Her mental armor held as it crashed against her heart. No tears. No hysteria. No coming apart at the seams, but the pain was so intense it felt physical.

She stood and returned to the bedroom. Trinity was still near the door. She studied Josie carefully. "It's okay, you know. It's just us two right now."

Josie's fingers tightened around the shirt. "I'm not going to cry."

Trinity picked her way across the room and lifted the mattress to peer beneath it before setting it right. "I know. You should, though. It will make you feel better."

"It won't."

"You think it will break the seal and you'll never be able to put all those scary feelings back inside so you can function, but you're wrong." Trinity righted Noah's nightstand, then picked up the drawer and tried to fit it back into its slot. "Think of it as releasing a little bit of tension. Like opening the pressure relief valve on a boiler."

She told herself she was being strong for Noah—and she was—but Trinity was spot-on. Everything she'd said was frighteningly accurate. Also, Josie *hated* crying. She chanced a more thorough look around the room. Exhaustion threatened to overwhelm her. "I know all the things I'm supposed to do," she snapped. "I've been in therapy for ages now."

She was just choosing not to do them. Default settings were hard to undo.

Trinity knelt on the floor and started picking things up,

examining them before putting them either in Noah's drawer or on the bed. Josie should be the one reclaiming the contents of her husband's nightstand, but she couldn't bring herself to move. Not yet.

"Fine," Trinity said. "Then I'll tell you what I found out."

SIXTEEN

Josie's feet moved forward without any conscious instruction. "What are you talking about?"

Trinity held up a book that Noah had been reading. "Still an astronomy buff, I see. The Milky Way, huh?"

"I took him to Cherry Springs to see it last year. He loved it. He's had his eye on a telescope for a long time. A very expensive one." If he came home, she'd buy him one, damn the cost.

Not if. When.

"Trinity, what did you find out?"

She placed the book on top of Noah's nightstand. "None of the neighbors' Wi-Fi was out last night. Only yours."

There was a flutter in Josie's chest. The Wi-Fi outage was one of the things she'd been wondering about all night. Both Turner and Heather said it had happened with some of the recent armed robberies. Josie had only cursory knowledge of them. There'd been three in Denton—which Turner had handled—and a handful more in the surrounding areas. Most of the time, the break-ins were carried out when no one was home. However, on two occasions, the homeowner had been in the residence. Josie remembered hearing that said homeowners had been badly beaten, which meant the perpetrators had no qualms about using violence. Three perpetrators. Enough to subdue a grown man.

If it was the same crew, why had they left the other home-owners behind but taken Noah? Again, the seasoned detective inside her gave a detached and instantaneous answer. The most obvious one. Noah was dead.

No. She rejected the thought just as she had the night before when she spoke with Turner. *He's alive. He has to be alive.*

"It's weird, right?" Trinity said, interrupting her thoughts. "That it was only your Wi-Fi. How is that even possible?"

"There are ways to do it," Josie said. "Not all of them legal."

"It means you guys were targeted though," Trinity said. "Don't you think?"

"Maybe."

Josie thought back to the last couple of weeks, trying to remember if anything or anyone unusual had stood out to her. People she didn't recognize lingering outside. Cars that repeat-edly drove down the block or that slowed in front of her house. There was nothing.

"How do you know about the Wi-Fi?" she asked Trinity.

There was no way the state police were giving out this kind of information to the press, even Josie's sister.

Trinity found Noah's phone charger on the floor and put it on top of the book. "I asked around."

"You went door to door." It wasn't a question.

"Not everyone answered," Trinity said.

"Trin, the investigation. It can't be compromised. You can't—"

She looked up at Josie then, her blue eyes so intense, the words dried up in Josie's throat. "I can. I'm not going to compro-mise the police investigation. I wouldn't do that. But I am a journalist and it's my job to ask questions."

"This isn't a story." Josie's voice came very close to cracking. Control. She had to stay in control.

Trinity surged upright onto her feet and closed the distance between them, clamping her hands over Josie's upper arms. "No, it's not a story. I'm not doing it because I'm a journalist. I'm *getting away* with it because I'm a journalist. People will answer my questions. Most people, anyway. I've built up a lot of goodwill in Denton and a lot of places in this whole country. People trust me. They're comfortable with me, which means they'll talk. You're going to be shut out of this investigation. You're too close. Hell, your department isn't even handling it. But I know you. After the people you love, the most important thing in your life is your work. It's the thing that makes all the bad shit bearable. I've seen you bury yourself in it a hundred times when you were at your lowest points. You don't have that right now and clearly, you're not going to do one damn thing your therapist taught you, so I'm doing this for you."

There was a hairline fracture in Josie's mental shield. "Trin," she choked. "I probably shouldn't be involved in—"

Trinity lowered her arms. "Involved in what? Putting all your stuff back while you listen to me talk? You're not doing anything but what Detective Loughlin asked you to do—see if anything besides the jewelry is missing. Now go to the other side of the bed and start cleaning up."

Clutching Noah's shirt against her stomach, Josie walked around to her side of the bed. Reverently, she placed the shirt on top of her dresser and started picking up its overturned drawers.

Trinity said, "The neighbor across the street, two doors down, saw a young man—maybe mid-twenties—walking down the street a few times around seven thirty. Not someone he's seen on this street before. The reason he noticed the man was because he kept walking back and forth, up the block and then down. Then up again."

Josie slid each dresser drawer home, relieved none of them were damaged beyond repair. "Description?"

"White, brown hoodie, jeans, maybe five-foot eight or nine. Average size. Nothing more than that. The neighbor never saw him approach the house, only walking along the street several times. Another neighbor captured him walking past his house on his home security camera. He turned the footage over to police last night."

Josie froze. "Did you see it?"

Trinity rolled her eyes and picked her way over to where Josie stood. "What do you think?"

SEVENTEEN

Seconds later, Trinity turned her phone toward Josie and pressed play on a video she had gotten from a man who lived across the street, about five houses away. The timestamp was seven thirty-two p.m. Her heart sank as she watched. With his hoodie up and his head angled toward the other side of the street, there was no way to get a clear picture of him. There were four other videos of him walking back and forth between seven thirty-two and seven forty-nine but none of them provided a view of his face.

Trinity must have sensed her disappointment. "I'm sorry, Josie."

"Don't be. This is—it's amazing that you did this for me, for Noah."

Trinity tucked her phone into her pocket and went back to Noah's side of the bed to sort through more of the mess. "Unfortunately, none of the other neighbors' security cameras caught him. Too far from the street. Anyway, the guy might just be a random person, but it seems kind of suspicious to me."

A barrage of questions waited just behind Josie's lips, but

Trinity kept going. "Another neighbor, who lives at the end of the block, said she drove past your house around nine, nine thirty and saw a big, black SUV parked across the driveway. She thought it was one of your colleagues' or something. No idea if it was old or new. She didn't see anyone in it or even near it, no memory of the letters or numbers on the license plate, but she remembered it because it had mud crusted all over the tires and wheel wells."

"She saw that at nine thirty at night?" Josie asked. While her body picked up the clothes at her feet, folded them, and put them back into the dresser, her professional mind whirred to life. Sweet, purposeful relief. This was where she was at her steadiest, her sturdiest. No chaotic emotions sneaking up on her, trying to crack her open.

Trinity found the comforter on the floor and shook it out. "Only because of her headlights. A different neighbor came home from work around ten and he didn't see any vehicles in your driveway except Noah's."

Which meant they'd taken Noah sometime between nine thirty and ten.

"Shit. Heather wouldn't tell me if they'd gotten the results of the geofence or not. If that guy you showed me had a cell phone or the SUV had a working infotainment center in it, if any of the people in it had cell phones, they might be able to find them that way."

Noah had been missing approximately thirteen hours. Shouldn't Heather's team have something by now?

Trinity folded the comforter and put it at the foot of the bed. "These guys were smart enough to jam your Wi-Fi—only yours—would they be dumb enough to show up in a geofence?"

It was a good point. Trinity knew what a geofence was not just from her years of crime reporting but because she spent a lot of time with Josie, Noah, and Drake who were all in law enforcement. The average person might not know what a geofence was but anyone with half a brain would realize that their smart devices were trackable. Come to think of it, Turner's geofence warrants on the armed robberies had turned up nothing.

"You're right," said Josie. "The SUV that woman saw in our driveway—did it have a lot of mud on it?"

"Enough for her to notice."

If the SUV was that dirty, it might have left remnants of the dried mud in the driveway. Josie had pulled right past it, maybe even over it. So had probably a dozen police vehicles. It was a long shot but if any samples could be retrieved, their analysis might tell them something about where the truck had been and possibly, where it had gone.

Another thought occurred to her. The Denton PD also had LPRs, or license plate readers, which scanned the license plates of all moving and parked vehicles nearby and flagged any that had been stolen, had expired tags, or had warrants out on them. The department had installed LPRs on three cruisers. If any of them had been stationed or driving nearby at the time, they might have caught the plate number of the SUV, as well as its owner.

"Did any of the neighbors have video of the SUV?" asked Josie.

"None that I talked to," Trinity said.

Even if no one on their street had caught the SUV on camera, all residential and commercial surveillance cameras within several blocks could be checked to see if any of them had. Denton's responding officers or Heather's team might have been able to follow its path via security footage.

Although wouldn't Josie have heard by now if there were any developments regarding the SUV? Wouldn't one of her colleagues have mentioned it? Let it slip? Wouldn't they have found it by now? She hated not being in charge of the investigation. However, she was sure her department had done all of these things, and if they hadn't, the state police would have. "Do you know if the ERT or the state police lab tried to get samples of the dried mud from the driveway?"

Trinity picked up Noah's pillow and placed it at the head of the bed. "I'm sure they did."

But what if they didn't?

This was exactly the thing Josie did that drove Turner crazy. She always worried that other law enforcement officers would miss something critical. The only way to ensure that didn't happen was to do everything herself or at least double-check everything herself. That wasn't realistic at all, though, and Josie had had to learn to trust her colleagues to do their jobs. It had never been this hard.

As if sensing Josie's internal strife, Trinity said, "I'll ask Kyle to find out."

She felt the familiar twinge of discomfort at her sister's use of Turner's first name. Josie had the feeling that there was much more to the story of the two of them, but all she'd been able to get out of either of them were vague details. At his old department, Turner had solved a famous cold case involving the murders of several high-end escorts. Trinity had interviewed him for a national morning show she was anchoring at the time. After that, they sometimes had lunch when he was in New York City. They both said nothing romantic had happened. Trinity insisted he was a perfect gentleman. It didn't add up, but Josie didn't have the time or the energy to push the issue right now.

"He can't give out information on an ongoing investigation," Josie said. "Even if he was privy to details, which he's not."

But he would find out what he could. She knew he would. Not for Josie, but her sister was another matter.

"He trusts me and I wouldn't screw him over." Trinity

picked her way toward Josie, scanning the floor. "They took your entire jewelry box?"

Josie shook her head. "That was in pieces. The state police took the remnants into evidence. Hopefully they'll get prints or DNA from it. They'll start checking in with pawn shops to see if someone brings any of it in."

That's what Denton PD had been doing with respect to the articles stolen in the armed robberies. As far as Josie knew, nothing had turned up yet.

"I'll get you a new one," Trinity promised.

It wasn't the first time a jewelry box Josie owned had been destroyed. This wasn't even the first time her home had been invaded and trashed, although the last time had been before Noah lived with her and the damage hadn't been so widespread. The last time was to intimidate her.

Lila Jensen, her abductor, the woman she believed was her biological mother for thirty years, had returned to wreak havoc on Josie's adult life. She had almost killed both Josie and Trinity and very nearly destroyed everything Josie had worked to build. Even though Lila had used baby Josie to get back together with an old boyfriend, Eli Matson, she'd hated her. Back then, there were no mail-in paternity or DNA tests. When Lila showed up at Eli's home a year after he dumped her and told him Josie was his daughter, he believed her.

He'd loved Josie fiercely, which wasn't part of Lila's plan. When Josie was six, he'd died, leaving her alone with Lila who was then free to abuse Josie in horrific ways. His mother Lisette, the only grandmother Josie had ever known, had fought doggedly for years to get custody of Josie. Eventually, she paid Lila to leave, and Josie's life had been blessedly free of Lila's wrath for sixteen years. When she returned, like a tornado upending everything about Josie's life, it was, in her words, to "destroy everything you love." Hiring men to break into her home, vandalize it, and steal a few items of jewelry had just been for fun.

But Lila was long dead, and Josie couldn't shake the feeling that this time wasn't only about stealing. Why trash the entire house and only take jewelry but no electronics?

They were looking for something. Josie was certain of it. She just couldn't figure out what.

EIGHTEEN

Putting the main bedroom back together went more quickly than Josie anticipated, though, to be fair, Trinity did most of the work. The shelf in the closet, two of Noah's dresser drawers, and her bedside lamp were total losses. Aside from her jewelry, nothing else was missing. Trinity found a tote bag on the closet floor and stuffed Noah's T-shirt inside so Josie could bring it with her. She could technically stay here since the house had been processed, but she wasn't sure she could handle sleeping in the bed she shared with Noah right now. Gretchen and Paula were happy to host her as long as she needed.

When they finished in the primary bedroom, they moved on to the rest of the second floor, cleaning the mess in the hallway, the bathroom, and the guest room. Trinity took one look inside the nursery and quickly closed the door. No need to go in there and be reminded that their adoption dreams were now most likely on the line. Josie didn't think the agency would give them a pass on this break-in. Assuming they found Noah alive and safe.

As if sensing Josie's thoughts, Trinity herded her back to the stairs. "One crisis at a time."

Downstairs, Shannon was on her knees in the living room, still working on the blood. In the light of day, with no adrenaline pumping through her veins, and time to study the room, Josie saw there was far more of it than she initially thought.

Trinity's fingers curled around her forearm. "Let's check out the other rooms. You can inventory this one when Mom's done."

The dining room was already back in order, though all of their more expensive dinnerware was a total loss. The kitchen was still quite a mess. In the time Josie and Trinity had taken to straighten up the second floor, it appeared as though all Christian and Patrick had accomplished was to put the silverware back in its drawer. Shattered dishes and glasses still littered nearly every tile. Pots, pans, and broken appliances lay among the debris. The cabinets yawned open and empty. Josie hadn't noticed it last night, but the intruders had even cleared out their dry goods and tossed them everywhere. Christian stood in the center of the mess with a box of cereal in his hand while Patrick hopscotched over obstacles, taking photos with his phone.

Trinity scoffed. "How many Payne men does it take to clean up a kitchen? What have you two been doing this whole time?"

"You need a new coffeemaker and a new toaster," said Patrick, leaning over to snap a picture of their now-dented crockpot. "Also, I don't know what the heck that thing is but it looks fine to me."

Josie followed his gesture toward a silver contraption that folded into some kind of press. "I don't recognize that."

Trinity huffed. "It's a panini maker! I bought it for you guys when you moved in together!"

Christian arched a brow and shuffled over to one of the cabinets above the countertop. He placed the box inside it. "I hope that was the last culinary item you gifted them."

Under any other circumstances, Josie would have laughed.

Both at Christian's joke and at the irony that the one appliance that had survived the destruction was one they'd never used.

"It was," Trinity said before turning toward the laundry room, beckoning Josie to follow. "Work faster. We'll be in the garage."

A quick sweep through the laundry room was all it took to get everything back in place. Nothing broken there. Nothing missing. Josie did her best to ignore the smear of blood along the wall. She knew that what was in the garage, on the other side of the laundry room, was so much worse. Trinity flicked on the overhead lights. They weren't very powerful.

"Want me to open the bay door?" asked Trinity. "Get some more light in here?"

"Only if you're prepared to turn away any nosy onlookers," Josie said.

Trinity flashed her a brief grin and rubbed her hands together. "Turn them away? Nosy onlookers are my bread and butter."

Josie bent to pick up the fallen weedwhacker, then a rake, and some gardening tools. She placed them back where they belonged. One side of the garage was for outdoorsy stuff while the other side was for the random personal items they'd initially stored in their basement.

Trinity stopped in the center of the room, ankle-deep in the detritus. "You don't have one of those clicky things for the door?"

Josie nudged their power washer back into its corner. Why in the hell would intruders need to disturb a power washer? "No. It broke a couple of years ago and we never got it fixed. New, automatic garage doors cost thousands. Besides, we've never used this for our vehicles."

"Right. Who would use a garage for cars?" Trinity found the locking mechanism on the door and unlatched it. With a grunt, she heaved the door upward. Bright sunlight flooded the space. The warm golden glow streaming inside would normally make Josie feel happy and energetic but now, all it did was expose just how much worse the garage had been tossed compared to the rest of the house. At least the state police evidence techs had taken away the items on the floor that had been speckled with drops of blood. Still, there were layers upon layers of possessions to comb through and put away.

Trinity pointed to a couple of overturned plastic bins, their contents blanketing the concrete. "What is all this stuff?"

Josie knelt to gather the contents of the one closest to her. Halloween decorations. "A lot of it is holiday stuff but the rest is stuff from my grandmother and Noah's mom. Things we didn't want to part with but don't really know what to do with either."

She stood and hefted the Halloween bin to fit it back onto the shelf but hesitated when she saw the bloody handprints. She'd noticed them last night but that was before she knew that most of the blood in the house belonged to Noah. Had he been out here, injured, searching for something? If the blood belonged to Noah, what had he been looking for?

Or were the handprints from the other person who'd left blood behind? Mr. O Negative. Was the young man her neighbor had seen walking up and down their block Mr. O Negative? Had he come in here after subduing Noah to search for something? Or had he or his accomplices forced a bleeding Noah in here to find whatever it was they wanted? The evidence techs would have typed the blood from each room. Heather's team probably already knew whether the handprints belonged to Noah or Mr. O Negative. Her team would have the partial handprints to work with as well. Whether they could match them to Noah or anyone else was a different question.

"Josie." Trinity held up a metal coffee can with sewing supplies stuffed into it. "Was this Lisette's?"

Josie pushed the Halloween bin onto the shelf. "No. Colette's. Noah's mom."

Trinity fit the lid onto it and picked up what looked like a half-sewn shirt, tucking both into a bin Noah had marked "Mom."

"Are you sure they weren't looking for something in her stuff? No offense, but she spent most of her life hiding a pretty big secret. Who's to say there weren't more?"

That secret had led to her murder. But Josie was pretty sure Denton PD had gotten to the bottom of everything Colette Fraley had been hiding. "I doubt it."

Trinity slid Colette's bin next to the Halloween stuff. Then she looked around until she found the bin labeled "Christmas." Dragging it over, she started packing it with the decorations at her feet. Josie watched, momentarily paralyzed by the overwhelming task ahead of them.

"Oh my God!" Trinity shrieked.

For a moment, Josie wondered if some kind of rodent had gotten into the garage. They occasionally had to deal with mice. One year, a squirrel had set up residence in one of their roof soffits. But at Trinity's feet, nothing moved. Beneath the rolls of Christmas lights, now-cracked ceramic gnomes dressed in Santa outfits, and the pile of holiday-themed outfits they'd bought for Trout, was some sort of file. Pages fanned out from inside its manila folder. Reports so old, they'd been prepared on a typewriter. Black and white crime scene photos.

"Why do you have this?" Trinity asked. "You're not supposed to have police files at home."

"We don't."

Josie picked her way closer, staring down at the photo closest to Trinity's feet. Her exhausted brain was taking a long time to catch up, to process what she was seeing. A splintered wooden floor, its planks peeled away to reveal five tiny skulls, their round white surfaces fractured like cracked eggs. They were all nestled together in a bed of frayed fabric. Each one had its own heap of bones so thin and fragile, they looked as though they belonged to birds.

NINETEEN

Nausea punched through Josie's stomach so forcefully, she had to bend at the waist to keep from collapsing. Unfortunately, that only brought her closer to the photos. What was this? Why was it in her garage? She should know. Except she'd never seen these photos before.

Wanting to see anything but the frail remains, her eyes flicked to one of the reports sticking out.

Commonwealth of Pennsylvania v. Roe Hoyt

There was a docket number. A date going back over fifty years. That name. Roe Hoyt.

"Do you recognize this?" Trinity placed a hand between Josie's shoulder blades. "Why is it in your garage?"

Roe Hoyt. Josie knew the name.

Dropping to her knees, she shuffled through some of the pages until she found something familiar enough to jog her memory. For Trinity's benefit, she tried to push out some sort of explanation but the only words she uttered were, "Lila Jensen."

As if Noah being abducted wasn't enough, now reminders of the worst parts of her past were thrust into her face.

"Did you just say Lila Jensen?" Trinity said. "That file is

about *her*? As in evil, psychotic, conniving, kidnapping, murdering, child-abusing, demon arsonist bitch, Lila Jensen?"

Josie quickly shuffled the contents of the file back into the folder and placed a palm over it, holding it closed. "That's the only Lila I ever knew, yes."

"I don't understand."

A memory burst across Josie's mind: visiting Lila in prison after she'd finally been made to pay for at least a fraction of her crimes. Josie had only gone because she hoped Lila would name some of her accomplices, specifically the ones she'd employed to harass Josie. It was a fool's errand. Josie could have offered Lila freedom and lifetime immunity, and she wouldn't have given Josie what she wanted, just out of spite. Lila had always been an Olympic champion when it came to spite.

She hadn't given Josie the name of a single accomplice. Instead, from the other side of the inches-thick glass partition in the prison waiting room, Lila had offered one tiny scrap of information, scribbling it in the condensation her breath left on the glass.

An inmate number.

"When I saw Lila in prison," Josie said, "not when she was dying. Before that. She was mad I had had a part in putting her there. Of course she blamed me. I was the cause of every bad thing that ever happened to her. I think I blasted her about what she'd done to me. Taking me from you guys. Since everything was always about her, she turned it around, implying her childhood was worse than mine."

It *had* been worse than Josie's. Exponentially worse. Lila had been put into foster care at the age of five. Although she'd blackmailed a judge into destroying her foster care file, there was a social worker who had remembered most of what it said. Because all the things that happened to Lila were so horrific and so disturbing, that information had stuck with the woman for decades.

Trinity folded her arms over her chest. "Lots of people have awful childhoods. That's no excuse for what she did to... well, every person she met!"

"I wanted to know where she came from," Josie said softly. "Where does someone that cruel, that evil, come from?"

"The bowels of hell," Trinity answered even though it was a rhetorical question. "That's where she came from."

"Lila had found out the identity of her biological mother," Josie said. "Roe Hoyt."

It was Roe Hoyt's inmate number Lila had drawn onto the partition glass. Gretchen had tracked down a copy of the case file and given it to Josie, in the event that one day, Josie might be ready to read it. Though Josie had gotten the broad strokes from Gretchen, she'd never actually read the file, never even cracked it open, instead tucking it away in the bottom of some storage bin.

Now, here it was, forcing her to see inside it. She still didn't know why she'd kept it.

"And Roe Hoyt was the Bride of Satan?" Trinity asked.

Josie nodded sadly. "You saw the photos. Roe Hoyt had five babies besides Lila, and she killed them all."

"Oh God." Trinity got down next to Josie and slowly slid the file out from under Josie's hand. "I'm sorry. You shouldn't have to be reminded of all this right now."

Trinity stood and lifted the lid of Colette's bin just enough to slide the file inside. Then she closed it with an audible click. It was enough to settle some of the nausea in Josie's stomach.

But the file wouldn't be the only thing related to Lila they found today.

Josie leaned forward, pawing through the small heap in front of her. Clearing away more Christmas decorations, she saw an old wooden box, flung open, face down. Like the kind her grandmother had used for storing her fancy silverware.

"What's that?" Trinity peered over Josie's shoulder. "Flatware?"

"No, not exactly."

Josie turned the box over. As expected, it wasn't silverware that had spilled from inside. It was decades' worth of Lila Jensen's trophies. Mementos she had kept from the multitude of lives she'd ruined.

TWENTY

The scar along the side of Josie's face tingled. She hadn't thought about this box in years. Not since she buried it on a shelf in the basement. Noah had been the one to move it from there to here after the flood. Naturally, this abomination had survived, taking on no water damage. Even Lila's relics were untouchable. Josie wasn't sure why she'd kept it all this time. Maybe because it had meant something to Lila and having control over something that mattered to that unholy bitch made Josie feel a little powerful. Or maybe it was a physical reminder of the pain she still carried from Lila's abuse that she just wasn't ready to part with because, despite all the therapy, all the "work" she had done over the years to erase the effects of her Lila-inflicted trauma, Josie still wasn't free of it. Maybe her psyche was waiting for the day that this horrid box didn't matter anymore.

"What the hell is all that?" Trinity asked.

The inside of the box was lined with a worn dark red velvet. The fabric along the lid had come loose along one of the edges, revealing a small gap. Had there been something hidden in there? "This is Lila's stuff."

Josie felt the shock that rippled through her sister's body as sure as if they shared the same physical being. Trinity pointed at it like it might grow claws and attack them. "Why in the hell do you have anything that belonged to that monster?"

A few spots darkened the liner. Josie's finger lingered over one of them but she didn't touch it. If it was a recent droplet of blood, she didn't want to disturb it. "After she went to prison, this box was found among her personal things—at the place she was staying."

Trinity put a hand on her hip. "You mean the place she was squatting."

Josie turned her attention to the items that had fallen out of the box. She'd only ever looked inside it once and that was the night Noah had given it to her. She'd taken the items that were personal to her. Some of her cherished jewelry, which Lila had paid to have stolen, a bloodied childhood stuffed animal, and a photo of her father, Eli Matson. At the time, she hadn't had the energy to investigate the origins of the rest of the box's contents. Lila had already taken so much from her, Josie hadn't wanted to give her more time by obsessing over the things Lila had collected.

Josie had made a choice to put Lila where she belonged—in the past.

Now, though, she couldn't be sure what, if anything, was missing from the box. Her brain worked back to the evening Noah had presented her with it. They hadn't even started dating but she'd been staying at his house. She'd been recovering from a broken wrist, courtesy of Lila, sitting on his couch watching television. He'd come home and kissed her on the forehead. Then they'd opened it together.

What was in it? She closed her eyes briefly, trying to put herself back in that moment. The only reason the memory was so accessible, so clear, was because of Noah. He was the first person who ever knew the true extent of what Lila had done to her. Even Ray hadn't known everything. Nor had Lisette, though not from lack of trying to pry it out of her. During the time that Noah had offered up his home as a sanctuary, Josie had told him everything. She'd laid herself bare and he'd wanted her anyway, damage and all. The end of Lila's reign had been the beautiful beginning of them.

Trinity lowered herself to the floor again, across from Josie, pushing Christmas decorations aside so she could get closer to Lila's twisted heirlooms. "I don't understand."

Josie scanned the items on the floor where the box had opened. An ornate, antique pillbox made of silver that had long ago tarnished, a Ziploc bag containing small, black cylinders which Josie didn't recall seeing before. They were metal, their circumference not much bigger than a pen. Some kind of tool? Pieces of drill bits? They were smooth, not fluted, and only about an inch long. Maybe spanner bits? Whatever they were, Lila had undoubtedly used them for nefarious reasons. There was also a gold cigar cutter, a small lock of brown hair tied up with a blue bow, newspaper clippings—including one about the fire Lila had set at the Payne home—and a miniature teacup, like the kind children played with. Josie searched her memory for what else had been in the box that was no longer there.

"There was jewelry," she said. "A brooch, some necklaces, a bracelet, I think." She couldn't remember now. "It's gone."

"Was any of it valuable?"

"I don't know." She couldn't see Lila holding onto anything that had financial value, especially near the end of her life when she was desperate for money. It was usually things that held emotional value for her victims that she enjoyed hoarding.

"I guess if you're breaking into someone's house, you don't stop to examine every little thing to try and figure out how much you might get for it." Trinity sighed and gestured at the mess around them. "All this is about a robbery?"

It was almost the same thing Mace Phelan had said last night when Josie and Turner delivered the news that Gina had been stabbed to death. Had Noah been stabbed? Is that where all the blood came from? Josie's heart went from racing to thundering. Dizziness made her head spin. She wasn't going there. Trying to steady her breath, to force her body back to some kind of equilibrium, she studied the items again.

There were other things that had been there the day she first opened it, but Josie couldn't quite bring them into focus. What else?

"Photos," she mumbled.

"What?"

"There were photos in this box. They were all of men. Not just Eli. A bunch of men. Now they're not here."

Trinity looked around. "You mean photos of all the men she either killed or disfigured?"

"I don't know. I never—no one ever tried to track them down. It wasn't like they were pictures of her torturing them or anything. Denton PD didn't want to waste time and resources trying to find them since there was no evidence that she'd harmed them."

"Oh my God. Really?" Trinity said. "Literally the only thing Lila Jensen ever did was rain death and destruction everywhere she went, and no one wanted to investigate the photos of the men she kept in this little trophy case of terror?"

"There was a public appeal after she was arrested," Josie reminded her. "We did the *Dateline* episodes! The photos weren't shared, but Lila's information was and—"

"There was a tip line," Trinity filled in. "Briefly. For anyone who had information about any additional crimes Lila might have committed."

"No one ever called it."

"Well, are you sure the photos aren't here somewhere? We

should clear more of this stuff out of the way." Trinity went to touch the pillbox that had fallen out of the box, but Josie stopped her.

"I think that's blood." She pointed at the droplets on the liner of the wooden box. "Don't touch anything. I have to call Heather. First, I want to take some pictures with my phone."

TWENTY-ONE

Trinity yanked her hand back as if she'd been burned. "Shit. I'm sorry."

Josie pushed herself to her feet. Her lower back ached. She felt like someone had taken sandpaper to her eyes. Using the heels of her palms, she rubbed at them. Then she blinked several times, trying to clear the gritty feeling. She willed her head to clear as well. Something was needling her from the shadows at the back of her mind. Lila's box had been well-hidden in the garage. Noah had done that on purpose. He knew how Josie hated reminders of Lila, especially when they were unexpected. That's why he'd made sure it was never visible. She'd been in and out of the garage hundreds of times and never seen it. If someone had asked her where to find it, she wouldn't have been able to tell them.

Trinity stood up slowly and started to edge her way around the box and its contents without disturbing anything. Her foot slid on the cover of a cookbook, and she stumbled. Her body teetered, threatening to fall backward as she fought to keep her balance. Before Josie could lunge forward to grab her, Trinity's hands found the edge of the shelf, clutching it so hard, her knuckles blanched.

The thieves had torn the entire house apart. It wasn't surprising that they'd unearthed Lila's creepy cache of souvenirs from all the lives she'd destroyed. They'd taken the jewelry, just like they'd taken it from Josie's bedroom. Yet, they hadn't taken any devices. None of the laptops, tablets, televisions or the gaming system Noah and Harris often used.

Only Lila's old photos.

"Shit." Trinity looked down to see what had nearly sent her on her ass and smiled ruefully. "A cookbook. Why do you guys even have a cookbook? Let me guess. It belonged to Lisette or Noah's mom and since you two culinary geniuses can barely boil water, you thought it belonged out here in storage."

Trinity laughed at her own joke, but the high note in her voice told Josie it was forced. Suddenly, she snatched her hands away from the shelf. "Double shit."

There were those bloody handprints again. They were spread across the shelves. This was the only place in the house they'd been found. Josie mentally replayed arriving home last night and her path as she'd cleared each room. Blood was smeared along the laundry room wall like an arrow pointing to the garage.

The blood, the handprints.

Josie shook her head hard, as if doing so could shake loose the thoughts hidden in the recesses of her brain.

The blood. The handprints. The missing photos.

"Josie?"

She could feel Trinity's gaze on her, but her attention was on the handprints. The *trail* of handprints.

The heavy thud of her heartbeat pounded through her entire body. Without disturbing Lila's things, she inched closer to the shelves. Each print was from a left hand. Finding the most complete print, Josie fit her hand on top of it. Her wedding band gleamed in the sunlight that slanted into the garage.

"Josie, what are you doing?" Trinity's voice was filled with concern.

The print was the right size. She pulled her hand away and leaned in closer. There—two smudges, blurred lines—at the base of the ring finger. The barely visible, indistinct imprint of a wedding band. Her husband's wedding band.

"Josie," said Trinity, drawing closer. "You're kind of freaking me out."

A jolt of awareness hit Josie like an electric shock. A connection made. "These prints belong to Noah. I'm not sure whether he led the intruders in here or they forced him but he left these for me. The wall in the laundry room—these. It's a message. He was trying to tell me something."

Trinity's fingers touched Josie's elbow. "Josie, I think you need more sleep. We can do this later. Or leave it to Mom and Dad."

"I don't need sleep." Josie laid her palm against the print again. "I know my husband, Trin."

And Noah knew how Josie's mind worked.

They were silent. Josie heard the muffled voices of her father and brother from the kitchen. Outside, birds chirped. A car door slammed. The single mom four doors down called for her son to come inside.

Finally, Trinity said, "What's the message?"

"This is about Lila. Whoever did this was looking for something. If all they wanted were things they could sell for a quick buck, they would have taken the most valuable things from the most obvious places. They wouldn't need to destroy the entire house."

"If this was about Lila, why did they take your personal jewelry?" Trinity asked.

Josie shrugged. "They're still criminals. If they're tearing the entire place apart and find something small enough to fit in their pockets that they'll be able to sell, why not take it? But that's not why they were here. They were searching for something. Trin, look at this place. They dumped our holiday decorations, tore everything apart! Why do that unless you were looking for something? Noah knew where to find the box. He could have told them where it was but instead he came out here with them. Maybe they forced him but regardless, he saw a chance to leave me a clue, and he took it. There's blood in the living room—where the initial injury likely happened. Drops in the other rooms. But nothing like this. I'm telling you, he did this on purpose. He wanted me to know that this has to do with Lila."

"But why?" said Trinity. "She's been dead for years. You scattered her ashes."

Josie fished her phone from her back pocket and crouched down next to the box again, snapping pictures, documenting everything before she called Heather. The state police would take all of it into evidence.

"Lila had accomplices. All the shit she did? The crimes she committed? She used to call them her 'projects.' She never did much dirty work herself." Unconsciously, the fingers of Josie's free hand traced her scar. "I mean, some things she took into her own hands but for the most part, she was a master manipulator. When she came for me last time—before she was caught—she had her accomplices help with all the things she did to me. I offered to make her prison stay more comfortable if she gave me their names."

Trinity's nose wrinkled in disgust. "Josie, that's—"

"She didn't accept the offer. Probably because it was more fun for her to know how freaked out I was that her little criminal entourage was still out there and I'd never know who they were."

"You think the photos in this box were of her accomplices?" Trinity said.

"I don't know. I really don't. None of the photos were very recent. By the time I inherited that box, no one printed photos anymore. Everything had already gone digital."

"But maybe one of her accomplices thought there was something in this box that needed to be retrieved?" Trinity suggested. "Even though it's been years since Lila went to prison and died and she clearly never gave up anyone?"

"Maybe." A fresh wave of fatigue hit Josie hard. The lack of sleep, the monumental effort of keeping her panic about Noah's abduction at bay, and now the horrifying possibility that maybe Lila Jensen wasn't done with her yet—even from beyond the grave—was overloading her, clouding her mind again. "I don't know, but I need to call Heather Loughlin."

TWENTY-TWO
ONE WEEK AGO

Holden kept one arm around Bug's waist as they approached the house. It was massive and pretentious as hell. Tall white pillars held up a rounded portico. Statues of roaring lions sat on either side of a pair of heavy double doors. The façade was stone, giving it the appearance of a home built in the late 1700s or early 1800s when, in fact, it had been erected only ten years ago. Bug had done her research. As they reached the door, she could hear music blaring from inside. Two cameras mounted over the doors pointed down at them. Holden's fingers dug into her hip. He was way more nervous than she anticipated. Goosebumps erupted over her arms. For the first time since she'd set her plan in motion, she wondered if she was underestimating the potential risk.

Holden leaned down to whisper in her ear. His breath already stank of beer. "You sure about this?"

Bug turned her head and smiled at him. "Why wouldn't I be sure?"

His usual smirk was gone. Concern blanketed his face. When she realized it was genuine, the feeling of phantom insects crawling all over her skin made her shiver. Since she'd maneuvered her way into his life, he'd gone overboard trying to seduce her, putting on this bad-boy-with-a-secret-heart-of-gold act, always overly charming and confident. Like a used car salesman, except he was trying to sell her a fantasy so he could get into her pants. But she had always known he was using her. That was fine. She was using him, too. It made it easier if there were no real feelings between them.

Bug didn't like these cracks in his veneer.

Before Holden could answer her question, the doors swung open. A man in jeans and a tight black T-shirt nodded a greeting at them. Then his eyes dragged over Bug from head to foot and back again in a slow appraisal that left no doubt about the lewd thoughts churning in his mind. The invisible crawling insects darted over her skin like they were in a race to escape certain doom.

"Hey, Holden," said the man without taking his eyes off Bug's legs. "Who's this?"

Holden pressed her more tightly against his side. "She's with me."

The man smiled like it was some kind of joke. "Right."

"I mean it," Holden said, an edge to his voice. She recognized it as the one he used when he was about to punch a hole into the nearest wall.

"Whatever you say, man." Pervy bouncer guy laughed and held out a box filled with cell phones.

Reluctantly, Bug handed hers over to Holden so he could deposit it inside. He'd told her that guests had to turn in their devices at the door. It was a condition of admittance, ensuring nothing that happened at the parties ended up on the internet. Holden had also insisted she bring the smallest purse possible— it fit only her phone, ID and a lip gloss. He'd checked. She touched her necklace and tried not to think about how powerless she felt without her phone.

Pervy bouncer guy zeroed in on her again, ogling her in a

way that made her feel violated even though there were several feet between them. "Come find me later, honey."

Bug stumbled as Holden pushed her forward, over the threshold and into a foyer bigger than all the apartments she'd ever lived in. Open-mouthed, she took in the details. A sprawling hardwood staircase, marble flooring, a big-ass fancy chandelier, six-figure art that looked like a first-grader painted it, tacky sculptures of half-dressed women. The only thing missing was a fountain.

Her fists flexed involuntarily. Anger chased away the creepy-crawlies, leaving burning hot ash in its wake. She knew what she was walking into and yet, the reality of it felt so much worse. It made her want to tear someone's head off. What she intended to do didn't seem like nearly enough. She deserved more. She deserved blood. There was no getting that tonight, though. Even though she wanted to take a sledgehammer to every person and object in this house, she had to stick to her plan. Through gritted teeth, she sucked in a long breath. If she didn't stay calm, she would blow it.

Forcing an awestruck smile onto her face, Bug leaned into Holden's embrace. "Whose house is this?"

She already knew, of course. When he told her, she asked a question she didn't know the answer to. "Is he here tonight?"

Holden frowned. "Why? You want to meet him?"

Crap. He hadn't answered the question. She'd have to take charge. Now that she was so close to her goal, she just wanted to get it over with. This place gave her the creeps.

Bug knew exactly what kind of evil lurked within its luxurious walls.

"I thought you said he was cool." She stepped away from Holden and tugged at his hand, pulling him in the direction of the music. "It sounds like he throws a pretty awesome party. Come on, I want to meet everyone."

He pushed his hand through his hair. "Sure, yeah. Just remember, stay close."

TWENTY-THREE

Detective Heather Loughlin dipped her chin and peered at Josie over the top of her reading glasses. Her notepad lay on Josie's kitchen table, open to a blank page. The cap of her pen tapped against her bottom lip. In all the time they'd known one another, Josie had never noticed this small habit. Then again, she'd never been on the receiving end of an interview.

In the time it had taken Heather to arrive, Shannon and Trinity had managed to put the kitchen back in some semblance of order. Enough that Josie and Heather could sit at the table like civilized people while the state police evidence techs worked in the garage to photograph and process Lila's trophy box. Shannon had suggested tea, which Josie initially turned down, until she realized she could use another jolt of caffeine if she was going to get through the next hour.

"Here you go." Shannon set two mugs on the table between them. Next, she produced a kettle—an electric one by the look of it—that Josie didn't even know they owned. After pouring steaming water into each cup, Shannon opened a box of tea bags. "All you had was oolong. I hope that's okay."

Heather shot her a smile. "Perfect."

Josie dropped her tea bag into her mug, watching the water slowly turn brown. Shannon fussed a bit more, setting out napkins, spoons, milk, sugar, and honey before bustling out of the room. Josie knew that she was just outside the doorway, along with Trinity. Christian and Patrick had been relegated to the living room after Trinity bluntly told them that their pace was too slow.

"Lila Jensen is dead," Heather said without preamble.

Josie nodded.

"But you think this break-in and Noah's abduction had something to do with her."

"Yes."

The skin at the corners of Heather's eyes tightened. "Because there were photos missing from this box?"

Josie hadn't shared her theory that Noah had meant to leave her a clue. It was one thing to tell Trinity. Her sister was fiercely loyal. They'd been through enough harrowing situations together that Trinity would follow her off a cliff if Josie asked. Heather's job was to deal in facts and tangible evidence, not a wife's intuition. The blood and the stolen photos would be reason enough to investigate Lila's associates in connection with Noah's abduction.

"And jewelry." Josie swirled the tea bag around in her mug. "Which Lila would not have kept if it was truly valuable. She would have sold it instead. Whatever was taken from that box meant something to someone. It was important enough that they were willing to break in here and take my husband in order to retrieve it. It had to be someone who knew Lila, knew about her souvenirs."

Heather tapped her pen against her notepad. "What about your jewelry? Did it have any connection to Lila?"

"No," said Josie. "But I'm thinking they took it for quick cash or to make it look like their intention was to rob the house when really, they were here for something in that box. I never inventoried it so there could have been additional items taken."

"It's a mess in there," Heather said. "Are you sure the photos aren't buried under some other things?"

Josie, Trinity, and Shannon had done a quick but thorough search for the photos before contacting Heather, careful not to disturb Lila's box. "They're not there."

Heather stared over her glasses again. "The photos could have been taken by accident. Swept up along with the jewelry. I don't need to tell you that armed robbers don't spend a lot of time in a home once they've broken in, especially not with an injured homeowner."

Just outside the kitchen doorway, the floor creaked. Shannon or Trinity—or both—shifting their weight while they eavesdropped.

"Don't dismiss this," Josie said through gritted teeth.

"The similarities to some of the armed robberies we've seen outside of Denton are striking, Josie."

"You mean the Wi-Fi being out, the house being trashed, and the homeowner being violently attacked? Are there other similarities I don't know about? Because given the other characteristics of the crime that happened here..." she gestured around them, "there could be more differences than similarities."

Her cheeks were hot with anger. She was aware that her tone was skirting the line between assertiveness and disrespect, but she couldn't seem to modulate it. Noah was missing. If Heather and her team chose to fit the evidence into what they'd already decided had happened instead of letting the evidence guide the investigation, it could cost them precious time. The words slipped out before she could stop them. "Do your damn job, Heather."

"I'm not your adversary here, Josie," Heather said calmly. "I am doing my job. I'm here, aren't I? My team is looking at the

big picture. I'm not dismissing your theory that this has something to do with Lila Jensen."

That's not how it had come off to Josie, but she didn't say
anything.

Heather jotted something on her notepad. Finally. "Let's
talk about Lila. I remember the case that finally put her away. I
know what she did to you and to your family. Never watched
the *Datelines* but I did follow the press coverage. Things
worked their way through the grapevine at work. I'm going to
ask you to go over it with me anyway, so I don't miss anything."

Josie took a deep breath, trying to quiet the anger simmering
inside her. The tea had stopped steaming, but she prepared it
anyway, quickly going through the basics for Heather starting
with Lila kidnapping her and passing her off as Eli Matson's
daughter. In a detached, clinical voice, Josie briefly described
Lila's emotional and physical abuse; her drug addiction; how
she'd finally been persuaded by Lisette to leave Denton when
Josie was fourteen years old; and the details of the case that had
brought her back into Josie's life sixteen years later. The narrative was well-worn, having taken up space in Josie's psyche for
so long that speaking it out loud held no power anymore. There
was no emotion attached to the words. No, the trauma lived
inside her skin, in her sense memories, bubbling up at strange
and unexpected times without warning.

Josie concluded with finding Lila's twisted treasure trove in
the garage, looted.

Scrawling in her notebook, Heather asked all the same
questions that Trinity had. How had Josie ended up with the
box? Had it ever been processed? Were its contents ever
photographed? Had Josie or any agency ever conducted an
investigation into the items or photos inside the box? Did any
calls ever come into the tip line once Lila was in prison?

"I need you to make me a list of the items you remember
from the box," Heather said, pushing her pen and notepad

across the table. "We'll check it against what we find in the garage."

Josie started jotting down the list.

"The men in the photos," Heather said. "You said you're not sure if they're victims or accomplices."

"Or both," said Josie, sipping lukewarm tea.

Heather pulled her own tea toward her and slowly prepared it while Josie finished her list. Then she took the notepad back and flipped it to a new page. "You recognized your father—well, the man Lila Jensen made you believe was your father, Eli Matson. Did any of the other men look familiar to you?"

Josie thought back to the day she'd seen them. "Malcolm Bowen. A judge she blackmailed. He's dead. Cancer. Also, Dexter McMann. He was one of her boyfriends back when she still had custody of me. He lived with us for a while. Last I saw him, he was living in Fairfield and hadn't had any contact with Lila since I was fourteen years old."

Dex's name always brought a twinge of sadness and guilt. He had been one of the bright spots in Josie's childhood. He'd shown her more kindness than she knew how to handle, and he'd paid dearly for it.

"That's it?"

"Those are the only ones I ever recognized."

Heather's pen stopped moving. "Someone she blackmailed and someone she dated. A victim and a lover."

TWENTY-FOUR

"Believe me, her lovers were her victims as well," Josie said. "One night Lila set Dexter McMann's pillow on fire. While he was sleeping."

"Good lord," Heather winced. "Then if you take into account Eli Matson's photo—which you said was also there—the pattern is victims one way or another. That's what the sample size tells us. How many photos in all are we talking about here?"

Again, Josie imagined herself sitting on Noah's couch in his old house, thumbing through them. "A dozen? No more than two dozen."

Heather made a note. "Let's talk about Lila's associates. Not her accomplices, just anyone associated with her. Anyone who had regular or semi-regular contact with her over the years."

"That's going back a long time," Josie said. "Remember, Lila only raised me until I was fourteen years old."

"She had a life before you and during the period of time after she left which you can't fill in because you had no contact with her," Heather agreed. "I get that, but tell me anyway. If we go down this rabbit hole, we'll need a place to start."

Josie took another sip of tea. It suddenly dawned on her that not only was it incredibly strange being here without Noah and with the house in total disarray, but it was odd sitting in their kitchen without Trout. She wished he was here so she could stroke his silky back or feel his warmth over her feet. He was like a drooly, whiny, demanding comfort object and she needed that more than ever. Without Noah, she was rudderless, adrift.

"The only associate I'm aware of is Needle," Josie said without thinking. When she was a kid, she hadn't known the man's name so in her mind, she referred to him as Needle because he was the one who brought Lila the needles she used to shoot up. She corrected herself. "I'm sorry. That's a name I made up for him in my head when I was a kid. His actual name is Larry Ezekiel Fox but he goes by Zeke. When I was growing up, he was her regular drug dealer. She was in contact with him when she came back to Denton seven years ago. He lives under the East Bridge, not near the encampment, though. Further down, along the bank. There's a shed there. That's where you'll find him, but I doubt he has anything to offer."

Then again, Josie hadn't spent much time grilling him on everything he knew about Lila or who she associated with. He may not have told her if she did. Their relationship—if you could call it that—was bizarre and tumultuous to say the least. When she was a little girl, he'd been at their trailer several times a week. He'd stood by and watched Lila do abominable things to Josie, sometimes protesting weakly, but mostly letting it happen. Except for the time Lila tried to cut her face off.

The scar tingled again, and Josie ran her fingers over it.

Apparently, slicing the face off a six-year-old was a bridge too far, even for a degenerate like Needle. As was Lila's attempt to pimp eleven-year-old Josie out to pay for car repairs. He'd stopped that, too. All her life, Josie had lived in a perpetual state of conflict where Needle was concerned. Angry at all he'd let happen but deeply grateful at the things he hadn't. Always, she'd wrestled with the notion that she had expected a man like

Needle—a career criminal with absolutely no regard for the law —to be some noble protector of innocents. Even he had called her out on that.

"You speak to this guy recently?" asked Heather.

"Yeah. I, um, keep tabs on him."

He'd helped Lila hurt Josie seven years ago but then, later, he'd gotten caught up in a case Josie was working and he'd taken a bullet for her. Saved her life. Again. The man literally had no redeeming qualities, and in his lifetime, he'd caused far-reaching damage to those around him and yet, he'd been the fucked-up hero in the tale of Josie's life three times.

"He probably won't talk to you though," Josie said. "He only talks to me. Although he might spill something for a carton of cigarettes. Sometimes a twenty-dollar bill works."

Heather regarded her with a strange look.

Josie sighed. "We have history."

"Okay." Heather flipped to a new page. "Who else?"

"That's it."

"Is there anything else you can tell me about Lila Jensen that we haven't discussed?"

"You could look into anyone Lila might have confided in or grown close with while she was in prison," Josie suggested.

"We'll do that."

The image of those tiny skulls all bunched together pushed its way to the forefront of Josie's mind. She was going to dismiss the file. Lila's biological mother. The woman was probably dead now, and if she wasn't, then she was still in prison. Josie doubted she could offer anything that might help them track down the person or people in Lila's life who had taken Noah. Except that Lila had known that Roe Hoyt was her mother. Lila had known her inmate number. They'd been in the same prison at one point. Whether they ever spoke was another matter, but it was an avenue that couldn't be ignored. Josie always had the sense that Lila had known about her mother long before she, herself, was incarcerated.

The file in Josie's garage was something Gretchen had pulled together and given her in confidence. Heather could get access to anything that was in the file quickly and easily on her own, under her authority as the lead investigator on Noah's case. Keeping the copy Gretchen had given Josie wouldn't affect the investigation in any way. Plus, she really didn't want to betray Gretchen's confidence in case she'd gotten it in a way that wasn't quite aboveboard. Toxic mothers and the need to understand them was something they'd always had in common, and the file was a gift. A nod of recognition from one deeply damaged daughter to another. There was no blood on it. It hadn't been with the silverware box.

Josie said, "Lila's mother was called Roe Hoyt. I'm not sure if she's still alive but last I heard, she was serving five life sentences in SCI Muncy for the murder of her other children."

Heather's pen froze. "The rotten apple didn't fall far from the rotten tree, did it?"

"Sure didn't. Anyway, Lila was the one who told me about her. She knew her inmate number. At one point they were in there together. Might be worth looking into whether they formed a relationship of some sort or if Lila ever told Roe anything that would be useful to know in this case."

TWENTY-FIVE

Josie scrolled through posts on social media devoted to Noah while Trinity drove toward South Denton. With Heather's permission, their press liaison, Amber Watts, had been working nonstop on getting word out to news outlets and across every platform possible. The state police had issued a public information release report about Noah's abduction and Amber had run with it, sharing the information in different types of social media posts, hoping for maximum visibility and engagement alongside the efforts of the state police. The Chief had already held a joint press conference with Heather.

There had been talk of using Noah's official police department photo, but it looked so stiff, so unlike him. It was too formal. To Josie, that wasn't a photo that would make people want to find him or call the tip line if they saw something they thought was important. Instead, she'd provided a candid photo of him that she'd taken two weeks ago in their kitchen. He'd just successfully cooked his first pot roast, going up four whole points in the competition the two of them had come up with for who could cook the most edible meals in a month under Misty's tutelage.

In the photo, he stood, leaning his hip against the kitchen counter, a pot holder in one hand and a gorgeous grin on his face. Josie remembered being pissed that he'd most likely now win September's competition while also thinking that she couldn't wait to give him his very dirty prize.

The absence of him was a deeper cut than Lila had ever made.

He'd been gone almost twenty-one hours.

Josie swallowed down her emotion and swiped over to her text messages. At least her eyes didn't feel so gritty now. After Heather left, Trinity had forced her back to Gretchen's house where she'd managed to get four hours of sleep, much to her surprise. During that time, the number of text messages waiting for her had quadrupled. It seemed like every person they'd ever known had reached out to say they were praying for Noah's safe return and offer any assistance needed.

Misty had decided not to tell Harris yet. She'd keep their television tuned to Disney Plus, and she was confident that it wouldn't be a topic of conversation among the other seven- and eight-year-olds in his class. Josie hoped she was right. She ached to see little Harris, to hold his squirmy little body in her arms and hear his cheery voice calling her "Aunt JoJo" as he prattled on about everything in his world, but she wasn't sure she could keep her shit together in front of him right now.

Noah's older brother, Theo, was flying in from Arizona. His sister, Laura, was making arrangements to leave her little girl with a trusted babysitter for a few days, at least, so she could come to Denton. Nothing from Noah's dad, who had surely seen the news by now. There was, however, a message from his second wife, Andi. She said all the right things and yet, the message sent a hot surge of anger through Josie's veins. She couldn't even say why. It wasn't sunny, much younger Andi's fault that her husband was an asshole. On the other hand, she'd married him, and Josie couldn't quite bring herself to respect

Andi for doing so, especially when she knew exactly why he was estranged from his first three children.

There were no updates from Heather or anyone on Josie's own team. She started to wonder if no updates meant the investigation had stalled. Panic rose like acid at the back of her throat, and she pushed it down, her mind searching frantically for something else to latch onto, if only temporarily. The universe heard her plea. Her phone started ringing.

Trinity glanced over. "Who is it?"

Josie's stomach burned when she saw it wasn't Heather. "I don't recognize the number."

"Answer it," Trinity said.

She swiped the green icon and pressed the phone to her ear, blanching when her "hello" came out small and squeaky. Clearing her throat, she tried again. It was stronger this time.

"Detective Quinn?" It was a woman's voice. "This is Tilly Phelan."

Josie exhaled slowly as a strange sense of relief washed over her. Work. There was always work. Dependable and predictable in its own way with a structure Josie had always found comforting. If Noah hadn't been abducted last night, she'd be working on the Gina Phelan case.

"How can I help you, Mrs. Phelan?" The words were out before she could stop them.

She wasn't in a position to help Tilly Phelan. Noah's abduction had completely eclipsed the Denton PD's pleas for members of the public to come forward with information about the blonde woman's identity. Josie didn't even know if any tips had come in. She was chasing down leads in her husband's case.

"I was hoping you could tell me something," Tilly said. There was a long silence. Josie heard the tiny break in her voice when she added, "Anything."

"I'm sorry, Mrs. Phelan," she answered. "I don't have any updates. I've been... there's another case that I—I'm working on.

Let me get in touch with my colleague, Detective Turner, and find out what's happening."

More silence. A sound that might have been a sniffle. "Yes, okay. That will be fine. I'll be waiting."

The line went dead. From the corner of her eye, Josie could see Trinity sneaking glances at her but she didn't ask questions. Josie tapped in a message to Turner. *Any news on the Gina Phelan case?*

He must have been scrolling because his answer came back in seconds.

Where are you?

With Trinity. Tilly Phelan just called me looking for an update.

I'll get in touch with her.

Is there an update?

I thought you weren't working.

Josie rolled her eyes even though he wasn't there to see it. Technically, there was no reason she couldn't work. She didn't text that to Turner. *Just tell me.* She typed *douchebag* and then erased it before hitting send.

No leads on blondie. Geofence didn't give us anything. GPS on Gina's car shows she moved it from inside the site to the street 38 minutes before she was stabbed. Doc should be finished autopsy tomorrow but there won't be any surprises there. Waiting on some shit from Hummel once he gets done processing the knife.

Josie's eyebrows shot up. She almost hadn't expected him to

answer, just to be a dick. Her fingers flew across the screen. A simple thank you. The moment she hit send, she regretted it. Turner would gloat for days now.

The Great Josie Quinn sending me a thank you? In writing, no less. That's better than any dollar in my jar.

She could visualize the "sweetheart" he'd probably deleted at the end. He was likely screenshotting the exchange right now so he could torture her with it later. Groaning, she put her phone back into her pocket.

"Is that bad news?" Trinity asked.

"If Turner being his normal self is bad news, then yes."

Trinity kept her eyes on the road, but Josie could see the little smile on her sister's face. "You mean a perfect gentleman?"

Josie chose to ignore that. She couldn't look at another social media post about her husband and she couldn't pester Turner for information on the Phelan case since there weren't any new developments. Which left her with nothing to do but run her own shadow investigation and try to convince herself she wasn't doing anything wrong. Hell, even if she was, did it matter? Did anything matter if Noah wasn't in her life?

"Are you sure about this?" asked Trinity.

Outside, southern Denton flashed past. It was the flattest part of the city, industrial lots giving way to rolling farmland as they crossed into the next county. "If I was the one running the investigation, and Lila was my only lead so far, this is the first place I'd go. So yes, I'm sure."

It would take time to track down Needle. Especially for Heather's team. He'd definitely evade them as long as possible. Getting access to Lila's prison records and Roe Hoyt, if she was still alive, would take some time as well.

Which left Dexter McMann, one of Lila's former boyfriends. He'd moved in with Lila and Josie when Josie was thirteen and stayed for a year. Until his kindness toward Josie provoked Lila's wrath.

"Are you having doubts?" asked Josie. "About doing this?"

Trinity laughed. "You're kidding, right? Don't you know me at all? I have zero reservations about doing this. I just want to make sure we're going after the most valuable leads first. I've got your back, Josie."

The hairline fracture in Josie's mental shield stretched, wanting to open wide. She did her best to stitch it up. "Let's just hope that he's already spoken with the state police. If we go in there before they've had a chance to talk with him, it's going to be very bad for me."

Not just professionally. Josie needed this. Sitting around Gretchen's house wasn't going to be enough to keep her from losing her shit.

"We can handle bad," Trinity said.

Josie nodded. She would take all the bad the world had to offer if it meant finding Noah.

TWENTY-SIX

Farms and wooded game land flashed past their windows. Josie knew they were getting close to Fairfield. Dex still lived on a rural road a couple of miles from the heart of the small, sleepy town. Anxiety buzzed under her skin as his one-story house came into view, though she couldn't say why. Dex had never been anything but caring and kind toward her. He was a good man. She had often wondered if they would have been able to have a friendship as adults if what Lila had done to him didn't always hang between them like a poisonous cloud.

Trinity slowed the vehicle in front of a long gravel driveway. "Is this the place?"

The last time Josie was here, the siding of Dex's home had been a dingy white. He'd obviously had some work done; now it was covered in clean tan siding. Even the poorly constructed additions built alongside the house that Josie remembered now looked shored up and newly painted to match the main house. A couple of rocking chairs sat on the front porch. Two bicycles leaned against the railing. The old red pickup she remembered had been replaced by a slightly newer blue one.

But what told her beyond the shadow of a doubt that this

was still Dexter McMann's home were the stunning wooden sculptures carved from tree trunks dotting the two acres of lawn that led to the house. "Look," she said, pointing to a cluster of them. Three dragons stood in a semicircle, their ancient-looking eyes keeping watch on the road. All of them were massive. As Trinity pulled into the driveway and slowly rolled past, Josie was stunned by the breathtaking detail carved into each one. It looked like the figures had lived in the wood all along and finally been unleashed.

"He made those?" Trinity said, awestruck.

"Yes. He sells them. That's how he makes a living."

"This is amazing!" They passed another grouping of carved tree trunks. A mama bear and cub, a hawk, and the grim reaper. An odd combination. "How has no one featured this guy on the news? The national news?"

Josie didn't answer. As they stopped behind the truck, she saw two more, near the porch. A unicorn and a mermaid.

"I just can't believe this," Trinity said. "They're so detailed."

Her eyes were locked on the mermaid as she started to get out of the vehicle. Josie put a hand on her forearm to stop her. "Trin, listen. When you see him—"

Trinity looked back at Josie. "It'll be fine."

Before Josie could say anything more, the front door opened and Dex shuffled out, squinting against the afternoon sun. One hand shielded his eyes, keeping the worst of Lila's fury out of sight for now. "Help you?"

Josie hopped out and walked toward him. "It's me, Dex. JoJo."

She didn't go by JoJo anymore. Only little Harris got to call her that, but that's how Dex had always known her. He stepped forward and smiled. "JoJo? Josie Quinn!"

He ambled down the porch steps and embraced her. As her arms wrapped around him, she realized he was a lot thinner than the last time they'd met, no longer as burly. His jeans and faded flannel shirt hung loose on his tall frame. He smelled like oak and chestnut.

"Good to see you," he said into Josie's hair before releasing her.

Josie turned just as Dex offered Trinity a hand. She sensed her sister's shock, but Trinity gave nothing away, shaking his hand and introducing herself with a perfect television smile.

"The famous reporter," Dex said. "Nice to meet you. I saw the *Datelines*. Long time ago. I was glad to see you were reunited."

Josie noticed that Trinity couldn't help but sneak small glances at the left side of Dex's face where the skin looked as though someone had tried to melt it away. The burn marks were widespread, gnarled in some places and mottled in others. The fire had taken a portion of his hair from behind his temple, leaving an uneven bald patch of thick scar tissue. The glass eye that filled his socket helped diminish some of the horror of his disfigurement, but every time Josie saw him, she felt like Lila was right there, hollowing out her guts with a paring knife.

Handsome Dex with his heart of gold had to bear the marks of Lila's special brand of cruelty for the rest of his life and even after all these years, Josie felt like it was her fault. She should have known better than to accept his kindness. In the year he'd lived with them, he had parented Josie more than Lila ever had. He'd been good at it. Driving her back and forth to school. Helping with her homework. Buying her books he thought she would like. Taking her to the hospital when she needed stitches. Caring for her when she got sick. Making sure she had enough to eat.

When she wanted to go to the freshman formal dance with Ray, Dex had paid for her to buy a dress and asked his cousin, who owned a salon, to do Josie's hair and makeup. He'd even driven them to and from the dance. That was the final straw for Lila. After she set fire to his pillow while he slept, Josie had managed to put out the flames that had engulfed his head, but the damage was done. They'd never been able to prove it to the police, but Josie knew Lila had set the fire. To this day, she could still see the smug, satisfied look on Lila's face as she watched Josie guide Dex outside to get help.

Dex's long sigh brought Josie out of her thoughts. "You can't keep blaming yourself, kiddo. I made my peace with it a long time ago. I don't regret a thing. You needed someone in your life back then and I'm glad I was the one who got to be there."

His words caused another crack in her armor. Dangerous emotion surged forth, so close to the surface she couldn't speak. She'd needed to hear this for such a long time. Or maybe she just hadn't been ready to hear it until now. The last time she saw him, he'd told her it wasn't her fault. The sentiment had bounced off her, never penetrating the thick cloak of blame she wore. This was different. *He* was different.

"I hoped once Lila passed on, you'd maybe make your own peace, but it doesn't seem like she's content to leave us alone, even from the grave, does it?"

Josie shook her head, still unable to speak.

Trinity said, "Do you know why we're here?"

Dex nodded. "I can guess. There's a Denton PD officer missing, and the state police just stopped by asking about my 'association' with Lila."

"That Denton PD officer is Josie's husband," Trinity told him. "My brother-in-law."

"Well, shit." Dex scratched at his neck where the scarring gave way to smooth, unblemished skin. "I'm sorry, Josie. Better come on in then. You're going to want to hear what I told them. I should have just called you when it happened, but I wasn't sure it meant anything."

TWENTY-SEVEN

Josie hadn't been inside Dex's house the last time she visited. The furniture was mismatched, some of it new and some so old it looked antique. It gave the home a quirky, cozy feel, like the aesthetic was a choice, not the result of a single male purchasing things out of practicality with no thought to anything else. What marked the place as unmistakably belonging to Dex were the miniature wood carvings in various stages of completion on every surface. Most were animals or mythical creatures, just like his larger pieces.

There was evidence of someone else living in the house as well. A pair of sneakers too small to belong to him were discarded just inside the door. Scattered across the coffee table was a lip gloss, a paperback book called *Boss Girl* by Emma Tallon, and a pair of silver hoop earrings. Josie was seated next to Trinity on the couch, looking around, wondering if he had a girlfriend and hoping that if he did, she was good to him, when she noticed a mug half-filled with coffee on one of the end tables. It was blue with a picture of a golden trophy on it. Below that were the words: *World's Greatest Dad*.

"You have kids?" Josie blurted out.

Dex took a seat in a wingback chair next to the couch, angling his body so he faced them. He smiled, only the unharmed side of his mouth lifting. "I do. A daughter. She's out with a friend."

"You didn't say anything the last time I was here. I didn't even know you were with someone." She hadn't asked. Too wrapped up in Lila to think about anything or anyone else. Shame poked at the armor around her heart.

"I wasn't," Dex said. "I haven't had a girlfriend in years. In fact, her mother was a one-night stand. She never even told me that she was pregnant or anything. I only found out I had a little girl five years ago. Her mom died in a car accident, and I got a call from the department of health and human services telling me this nine-year-old kid was mine. Paternity test confirmed it."

"Wow," said Trinity. "That must have been a shock."

Dex laughed. "I'll say. It's been an adjustment, but we do okay. Seems all she does is complain about me now that she's a teenager but God, I love her big. Best thing that ever happened to me."

The pride in his eyes was unmistakable. This was exactly the kind of happiness Josie had always wished for him. The kind only love could bring. Love that was steadfast and uncomplicated in its purity and ferocity, in the certainty it brought to every facet of your life. The kind of love that fulfilled you and made you whole, knitting together all the damaged pieces that trauma and loss had ripped from the fabric of your soul. It was exactly what Noah had given her. Exactly what they hoped to give a child one day.

Another rogue wave of emotion washed over Josie, disconcerting her, batting at her mental shields. "I'm happy for you, Dex."

"Thank you."

Trinity must have sensed Josie's internal struggle, the way she was barely hanging onto her composure, because she took charge, trying to move things along. "You said something happened a week ago that made you think of calling Josie?"

He leaned back in his chair and sighed. "This guy showed up out of the blue asking me about Lila."

Josie's spine straightened. "What was his name?"

"He only gave me a first name. Dylan."

It could be a fake name. "How old was he?"

"Not sure. Mid- to late twenties."

Trinity's heel tapped along the floor. "What did he want?"

"He wanted to know if I knew Lila Jensen. I told him if he was here asking me then he knew the answer. I mentioned that she'd passed on years ago but he didn't seem too concerned with that. He asked me when was the last time I saw her. At that point, I wanted to know who the hell he was 'cause he wasn't a cop."

"What did he say?" asked Josie.

"He gave me some story about Lila screwing his dad over when he was a kid. Said she scammed him out of a bunch of money and then took off. He also said she'd stolen his grandmother's jewelry. I think that's what he was after. He told me his dad died recently. When I asked him for a name, he refused to give me one. I asked why he came to me, and he said he thought maybe I might have kept something of Lila's."

The box. The kid, Dylan, was looking for the box. That had to be it. Which made it more likely that he had used a fake name.

Was it Dylan who broke into their home and threatened Noah? Was he the man her neighbor had seen walking up and down the street? Was he Mr. O Negative? Is that why he'd taken the jewelry from Lila's box? Because it belonged to his grandmother? If that was the case, why take the photos? Maybe his father had been in one of the photos but if that was the case, why take them all and not just the one of his dad?

Her thought process snagged on something else. "How did he know about you?"

One of the newspaper clippings in Lila's box of horrors was about the fire at their trailer that had left Dex disfigured but back then, Lila had been going by a completely different name: Belinda Rose. Then again, the kid could have found out her alias from the *Dateline* episodes and investigated from there. Still, Dex's connection to Lila had never been made public.

Dex picked up a small, unfinished wooden owl and ran his fingers over the unsculpted portion. "He claimed he heard her brag about me—what she'd done to me."

"Psycho bitch," Trinity muttered under her breath.

Something about that still didn't sit right with Josie. Lila bragging wasn't implausible but her giving this kid a full name to go by seemed out of character. It was an admission of guilt, her actually explicitly confessing to one of her crimes. Then again, if Dylan was only a child when she said it, he wouldn't understand the legal ramifications. Josie could definitely see Lila telling the story to a young boy with the implication that she might do the same to his father. She always loved to threaten children. It was one of her favorite hobbies.

What made the most sense was that Dylan had seen the box at some point. Maybe Lila showed him the clippings, hinting that she'd been behind the fire.

"Did he say where he was from?" asked Trinity.

"Nah. Didn't answer many of my questions. Something was off about him. My opinion? He was in trouble."

Trinity watched, fascinated, as a small woodworking tool appeared in Dex's hand, and he started whittling at the owl. "What kind of trouble?"

"The kind that makes you desperate," Dex said.

"Someone was coming after him," Josie suggested. "Maybe he was in debt. It makes sense if he was grasping at straws, trying to track down Lila's personal effects to reclaim his grandmother's jewelry."

It also explained why he'd taken her jewelry. Bad people coming after the kid over his debt also lined up with the theory that more than one person had been inside Josie's home and taken Noah. Whoever Dylan had pissed off or owed money to was likely following him. Her heart did a double-tap. "Dex, you need to be careful."

"I always am," he said without looking up from his owl.

Trinity said, "If he wanted something from the box, why didn't he just ask you, Josie? He asked Dex. You probably would have shown him if he'd just been honest with you, right?"

It was a valid question. Had anyone shown up on Josie's doorstep claiming to be a victim of Lila Jensen looking for personal items she'd stolen, Josie would have shared the contents of the box freely. Why would he approach Dex but not her? Why break in and harm her husband?

"I wouldn't have turned him away," Josie answered. "But if he was as squirrely as Dex says, I might have demanded a lot more information from him."

"You're a police officer," Dex said. "That's why he didn't just approach you. Whatever he's got himself into, it ain't legal. He wouldn't want to risk you asking too many questions, given your position."

Or maybe the people he was running from were closing in too quickly for him to try to finesse his way to accessing the box.

"What was he driving?" Josie asked.

Under Dex's quick strokes, the face of a second owl appeared, emerging from the wood, startlingly lifelike. "A beat-up sedan. Blue. When he left, I wrote down the plate number. Pennsylvania tags."

Trinity looked from his hands to his face. "Really?"

He chuckled. "Yeah, really. Kid creeped me the hell out and

I learned my lesson when it comes to Lila Jensen. Pay the hell attention to everything, even if it seems like nothing."

Adrenaline shot through Josie's veins. "You gave it to the state police?"

"Of course. Don't know if anything will come of it."

It wouldn't surprise her at all if the car had been stolen.

Dex kept talking while he carved out the body of the second owl. "He was sitting right here in this room, telling his tall tales, looking as nervous as could be, and you know what I kept thinking about, Josie?"

Her palms were sweaty. "What's that?"

"That old fingerprint kit you used to mess around with when you were a kid."

Josie inched forward in her seat, wiping her hands on her jeans. "Dex, if you're saying what I think you're saying, I'm going to kiss you."

He laughed, hands working at warp speed now, the second owl's talons appearing, as if by magic. "He was a coffee drinker. Put the mug into a paper lunch bag after he left and hid it in the back of one of the kitchen cabinets. That state police detective was just tickled when I handed it over to her this morning."

"Holy shit," said Trinity.

Dex brushed off the sculpture and held it out to Trinity. "Twins."

Josie watched her sister accept it with a look of reverence. The owls were identical, sitting side by side on a branch, majestic and beautiful, their eyes expressive, almost hypnotic. "I can keep this?" Trinity asked.

Dex's half-smile appeared. "Sure can. Josie, you don't have to kiss me. Just find your husband."

TWENTY-EIGHT

Josie didn't even realize she was falling asleep until the sound of Trinity's nails tapping against the table between them startled her awake. She'd never found the booths in Komorrah's Koffee to be particularly comfortable until now. Then again, she was running on four hours of fitful sleep, enough caffeine to keep a horse awake for a month, and fear.

Noah had been gone twenty-four hours.

Blinking the grit from her eyes, Josie straightened her body and looked around. There was only one other occupied table. Two college students across from one another, each of them focused on their laptops. They both had earbuds in and yet, occasionally, they'd bark something out to one another without making eye contact. Playing a video game together, Josie guessed. At the front, the barista leaned against the counter, scrolling on her phone.

"You don't have to be here for this," Trinity said. "Go back to Gretchen's and try to sleep."

"I won't be able to sleep. Besides, I want to see how he acts with you."

Trinity rolled her eyes and took a sip of the caramel macchiato she'd ordered. "You're obsessed."

Josie didn't deny it. "I need a distraction. This is a good one."

Trinity huffed. "I don't know what you're expecting to witness."

"Me neither."

The jangle of a bell announced that someone had come into the shop. Kyle Turner filled the doorway, pulling up short just inside and searching until he spotted them. With a curt nod to the barista, he strode over and muscled his way into the seat next to Josie. His head swiveled in her direction, looking her over. There was something in his eyes Josie had never seen before, and she didn't like it one bit. It nearly killed her when she realized she'd rather see his cocky grin than this.

"Don't," Josie snapped.

His head reared back. "Don't what?"

"She doesn't like pity," Trinity said.

Turner focused his attention on her. The two of them smiled at one another. Genuine smiles. Maybe this was worse than Turner's pity. Josie was going to be sick.

"Miss Payne," he said.

"Kyle, thank you for coming."

There was something between them, for sure. It wasn't flirting or even attraction, but it was something. Mutual respect. That was it. Her sister commanded respect in everything she did, but Turner? Josie still didn't see it and with Noah missing, she didn't have the inclination to interrogate the two of them about their prior connection or whatever the hell they weren't telling her.

He reached into the pocket of his suit jacket and pulled out one of his canned energy drinks. The pop of the tab seemed unusually loud. After guzzling what must have been half of it down, he used the back of his hand to wipe errant piss-yellow drops from his upper lip. "Quinn," he said. "I'm not supposed to feel bad for you?"

"It's a cardinal sin," Trinity explained.

Josie stared straight ahead at her untouched blonde latte. "Pity isn't going to bring Noah back."

Turner sighed. "No, it's not, but you know how much I love to piss you off, and a pissed-off Josie Quinn might be exactly the thing to bring Noah home. So yeah, I feel really fucking bad for you."

That sounded suspiciously like a compliment. Sort of. Maybe. But for the sake of having some normalcy, she said, "Screw you, douchebag."

"Josie!" Trinity admonished.

"You're not getting a dollar for that," Josie added.

"Fine," he said. "I'll take it out of your jar back at the stationhouse. Now, are you ready to hear what I have to say?"

"Please," said Trinity.

"For the record, I was already pissed off before you walked in here."

Ignoring her, Turner started talking. "Wait'll you hear this crazy shit. The prints on the mug from your guy in Fairfield match the prints found in your house, prints found in two of the armed robberies, and..." He paused, blue eyes sparkling, as if listening to a silent drumroll.

"What?" Josie asked irritably.

"They match prints found on the knife that killed Gina Phelan."

Josie's spine snapped straight. "What?"

Her voice was loud enough to draw the attention of the college students. Turner smiled at them and they went back to their laptops.

"That's right," said Turner smugly. "This Dylan, or

whoever the hell he is, was involved in at least two of the armed robberies—the ones over in Bellewood, not in our jurisdiction—then he went to your friend's house last week and yesterday, he stabbed Gina Phelan around two in the afternoon before he hit your house in the evening."

"Were there other prints on the knife used to stab Gina Phelan?" Josie asked.

"One unidentified partial," Turner answered. "Which may or may not belong to blondie."

Josie pictured the blonde woman running away, plunging into the crowd, not looking back. Covered in blood. Gina's or hers? Or both? "When Hummel typed the blood on the blade, how many types did he come up with?"

"Just one," Turner said. "Same blood type as Gina Phelan's. Hummel was able to pull DNA from the knife handle but if this guy isn't in CODIS, that won't help. And before you ask, I've been over everything we've got on the Phelan case twenty times trying to shake something loose now that I know it's connected to the LT. We even managed to grab a couple more videos from some businesses across the street that weren't cooperating the first time they were canvassed. Unfortunately, they don't show us anything more than what we've already got."

Josie's mind labored to slot all of this information into a puzzle that was exponentially bigger than she'd initially thought. From what they knew about the string of armed robberies, there were at least three men involved. The two unlucky residents who had been home when the burglars struck gave statements to that effect. Unfortunately, the perpetrators had worn hoodies and gaiters, making it impossible for those witnesses to give a description that might help locate them. If Dylan was part of the armed robbery crew, that tracked with the theory that more than one person had broken into her home and subdued Noah.

Heather would definitely be focusing more heavily on the armed robbery angle now.

Josie would be taken off the Gina Phelan case. Burglary would be one of the charges filed against the perpetrators in Noah's abduction case which made Josie a victim as well since she lived with him. It put her too close to Gina's murder case and risked tainting that investigation.

Josie mumbled a curse.

Turner must have figured out what she was thinking. He smiled, stoking her irritation. "Looks like you'll have to rely on my exceptional detecting skills to solve Gina Phelan's case 'cause the Chief is going to take you off it."

Josie gave him her best death glare. It wasn't official. Not yet.

"Did you call Tilly Phelan at least?"

Turner drained the rest of his energy drink. "Of course. Couldn't tell her much though. We're not releasing the stuff about the prints. Not yet. I don't think she likes me."

"I can't imagine why," Josie said.

Trinity's nails clicked against the sides of her cup. She changed the subject. "So this Dylan and his friends are on some kind of crime spree? Also, did you say Gina Phelan? As in Phelan Construction?"

"Her name hasn't been released, Trin."

Her sister rolled her eyes. "No shit. I would have heard about it by now."

Without hesitation, Turner launched into a description of what had happened outside of the children's hospital site yesterday afternoon. Josie watched in wonder. He really did trust Trinity. As much as Josie did, evidently. It would be both their jobs if anyone found out they'd talked to her about an open investigation.

"This kid really is in trouble," Trinity said. "He's escalating. I read about the armed robberies. They started by targeting houses where no one was home. From what I gleaned, they stopped caring whether the residences were empty and just assaulted anyone who was inside. Now one of them—this Dylan —killed a woman for... what did you say? A necklace?"

"Seems that way," Turner said.

"Then he broke into the home of a couple of police officers. He's desperate, like Dex said."

Josie wasn't sure where the accomplices fit in. Were they just as desperate as Dylan? Had they all gotten into trouble together? Was someone after them? Had they all found themselves so deeply in debt to someone higher on the criminal food chain that they'd started breaking into homes to try and pay it off? Or was Dylan in debt to the rest of his crew? Whatever the reality, he'd been desperate enough to try to exploit his childhood connection to Lila.

"But his prints aren't in AFIS," Josie blurted out. Dylan had never been arrested or convicted of a crime, so his prints weren't saved in that database, which meant they couldn't locate him that way. He could leave his prints on every damn surface in Denton but without something more, they wouldn't be able to find him.

"What about the tag number Dex gave the state police?" Trinity asked.

Turner said, "Stolen from some accountant in Bellewood. At gunpoint."

Bellewood was the Alcott County seat, located about forty miles south of Denton. There was no way to know where Dylan had come from or where he lived at this point. Josie wondered if he'd stolen the car from Bellewood because he lived there or if he lived somewhere else and drove there to steal a car in order to throw police off. Criminals often started close to home because it was where they were most comfortable. The armed robberies had started in Bellewood.

Turner gripped the empty can in front of him. "There's a

statewide BOLO for the car. They tried tracking it through the infotainment system but evidently that was disabled. Loughlin's doing the usual checks to see if it was flagged going through any tolls or anywhere else between there and Fairfield where he might have been caught on camera."

Josie wondered how he was getting this information, who in the state police CID trusted him enough or owed him something that they'd risk their job to pass things along. Then she decided she didn't want to know. She shifted her body so she could really look at him. Fatigue was sapping her ability to control the words that came out of her mouth. "Why are you helping me?"

Turner smirked. "'Cause your sister asked me to and I actually like *her*."

Josie could count on one hand the number of times Turner had ever answered a question seriously. "It's one thing to update me as your colleague, even if it's frowned upon, but you're sitting across from a journalist, giving out information that she asked you to find out and I'm guessing not all of your inquiries were through official channels."

"So?"

"You could get in trouble."

Turner laughed, long and loud, drawing the attention of the college students again. "Quinn, do I seem like the kind of guy who cares about trouble?"

"You don't seem like you care about anything, actually."

Something flared in his eyes. A momentary blip, gone in a heartbeat. Vulnerability. If Josie hadn't been peering so intently at him, she would have missed it. It was the first chink in Turner's armor she'd ever seen. She let it go.

He said, "Not that I don't trust the powers that be to do their jobs. Loughlin is a fine investigator. If I was missing, I'd be damn happy to have her looking for me. But if whatever you two are cooking up is going to help get the LT back, I don't really care if what I'm doing costs me my job."

Josie's mouth dropped open. It was the nicest thing he'd ever said. He probably realized it because he immediately winked and added, "Because I feel so bad for you, it's keeping me up at night... sweetheart."

Josie rolled her eyes. "We're even. Keep your hands out of my jar. Let's get on with this."

TWENTY-NINE

Turner's fingers drummed against the table. "That's all I've got."

Josie should have been grateful for the information he'd already shared—and she was—but she wanted more. Needed more. Time was slipping away from all of them and Noah was still missing. Assuming he was still alive, these were the most critical hours in the investigation. If they were dealing with the kind of men she thought they were, would they bother keeping a cop alive?

They wouldn't.

Panic batted against her psychological fortress, threatening to demolish it. Shit. This wasn't productive, despite the fact that she'd momentarily dropped into work mode, attempting to analyze the situation as a detached, seasoned investigator and not Noah's wife.

"Josie," said Trinity.

One look at her sister and she knew Trinity was practically reading her thoughts. She was all over the place. Her emotions seemed to shift with each heartbeat and as much as she thought she was in control, that she truly could fall back on her *dead inside* setting, those fractures in her mental armor still bled. She had no damn idea what was going to slip out next. It was unsettling.

Taking a deep breath, she tried to put her thoughts in order. Things were at a standstill for them in terms of their Lila investigation. At least for tonight. The state police would keep working around the clock, following every lead, doing everything they could to bring Noah home to her. The best thing that Josie could do right now was eat and rest and not freak the hell out. But her mind needed something to dig into, even just for the next couple of hours.

"I want to go to the stationhouse and review the new footage from the Phelan case," Josie said to Turner. "And I want to go over the geofence results myself. Also, I need to have a look at whatever we've got on the armed robberies that happened here. Those were your cases, right? I hope you got all your reports in on time. Let's go."

To Trinity, he said, "Is she serious?"

Maybe it was his tone—half irritated, half mocking—that had Josie seething. Or maybe Turner was just an easy mark. She didn't care about his feelings. Shifting in her seat, she looked directly at him.

"She knows she's going to be taken off the case," Turner continued. "When's the last time she slept?"

Something split apart inside Josie. She felt it in her chest. Rage like she hadn't felt in years surged up from where it had been snarling and snapping inside her for the last twenty-four hours, a beast begging to be unleashed. The kind of rage she used to try to numb with Wild Turkey. The kind that made her knock the teeth out of a woman's mouth for attempting to pimp her four-year-old daughter for drugs—her own career be damned. The kind that made her do stupid, stupid things.

Her closed fist slammed down so hard on the table that all their drinks jerked. Turner's can of energy drink tipped over, the few drops left inside scattering. "Don't talk about me like I'm not right here!" Josie shouted.

The college students startled, staring over at her like deer in headlights. She was out of control now, spinning. Whatever they saw in her eyes made them jump from their seats and start throwing their things into bags as fast as possible so they could leave. The barista stood behind the counter, watching warily. Josie glared at her too until she looked away, scrubbing frantically at something on the counter. Then she focused her fury on Turner. Satisfaction rippled beneath the surface of her anger when he inched away from her, eyes wide and surprised in a way she'd never seen.

She stabbed a finger into his arm. "Everyone needs to stop treating me like I'm some fragile little flower that's going to fall apart at any moment. I'm not. Not while my husband is missing. Not while he needs me. Not ever. I'm not weak. I was raised by Lila fucking Jensen."

It wasn't a point of pride. Not at all. But the harsh reality was that for as much as Lila had taken from her, leaving her emotionally broken in ways she still didn't fully comprehend, she had also inadvertently taught Josie how to survive horrible, terrifying, soul-crushing things. Her cruelty had made Josie unbreakable and for the first time in her life, Josie wasn't ashamed of that. Why should she be? None of what Lila had done was her fault. Lila bore responsibility for her own sins. Josie had survived. Made a life. She was here and Lila wasn't.

Trinity watched her, utterly unruffled.

Josie turned her head and traced the indelible scar that Lila had left on her. "I was six years old when she held me down and tried to cut my face off."

That had never been public knowledge. It wasn't part of the *Dateline episodes*. It wasn't information Josie gave out, even when asked about her scar. Turner had never asked, but she'd seen him studying it from time to time.

His blue eyes narrowed, and Josie was happy for him that they flickered with respect and not pity because she was out of control right now. Nothing would have stopped her from punching him in the face.

"No one thinks you're weak, Quinn," he said, clearly measuring his words.

She liked this—Turner off-balance, almost afraid of her.

"I will find Noah even if it means leaving scorched earth in my wake every place I go. I cannot and will not sit around like some sad, meek, helpless wife waiting for my husband to be delivered to me. I'm not built that way."

"I know," Turner said softly.

"I don't need sleep," Josie said firmly. "I need to do something and the Chief hasn't officially removed me from the case yet."

There were a few beats of silence, the defiant thrust of her chin daring him to challenge her.

"Better grab another one of those weird-ass lattes you like," Turner said. "You're gonna need it while you're double- and triple-checking my work."

Josie pushed against his shoulder. "Let's just go."

Turner bristled. "Hey! I put up with that little poke earlier 'cause you were all wound up, but you're the one who's always bitching about me standing too close or being too familiar so stop touching *me*."

He was right. Josie knew she should apologize but the words wouldn't come. Then Turner grinned, and she knew he was just screwing with her. "What is it that you always say to me?" He spoke in a high falsetto voice that sounded nothing like her. "I don't know you that well."

She scowled. "Just get out of my way, douchebag."

Trinity shook her head. "Josie."

Turner's low laughter only aggravated Josie more. He stood

and held out his palm. Grumbling, Josie found a dollar in the pocket of her jeans and shoved it into his hand.

With a sigh, Trinity stood as well. "I assume you two will be at the stationhouse for a bit? There's something I need to do. I'll be back to pick you up later."

"Or," Turner said, gazing down at Josie, "I could give you a lift when you're ready."

"Stop being nice to me!" Josie snapped. "It's weird and I don't like it."

THIRTY

It had only been a day since Josie was back at her desk, but it felt like she'd been gone for years. At first, she took comfort in being in the one place where things always made sense, where there was always a direction to take, where procedure dictated her next move. Then the sight of Noah's desk taunted her. Thoughts of what would happen if they didn't find him alive—if she didn't find him alive—crowded her mind. She shut them down. That wasn't happening. Not while she had breath in her lungs. Life—and Lila's legacy, if that's what was behind this—wasn't taking one more damn thing from her.

A small foam basketball bounced off her shoulder.

"Shit," Turner said. "I missed again."

She thought about teasing him but didn't have the energy. Tossing the ball at his head, she asked, "Did you look over the list of Phelan employees and anyone else who was on the build that day again?"

With a dramatic sigh, he edged his chair closer to his desk and went back to flipping through a document.

Josie had already looked over the armed robbery files, finding nothing of use. Next, she pulled up the geofence results from Gina Phelan's murder. She'd never say it out loud, but Turner had been right. The results gave them nothing. With a sigh, she began reviewing the new surveillance footage the team had gathered from nearby businesses and residences. Most of the videos were useless. The cameras were either too far from the action to record anything of note or they revealed nothing new. Skimming the fourth one, Josie's subconscious whispered, telling her something might be important. Her mind caught the detail but released it just as quickly. She needed to focus. Her eyelids were so heavy. The extra latte she'd bought before leaving Komorrah's was empty.

Back to work. What was it that her brain had just alighted on? It took her three more scans to find it. Turner threw his basketball at her again. This time it glanced off the top of her head. Josie ignored it.

"What are you triple-checking now?" he said. "The additional videos? I already told you, they're worthless."

"No, they're not. Come here."

Turner made a point of hefting himself out of his chair like he weighed a thousand pounds and shuffling around to her desk like it was taking up all of his energy to do so. "What?"

"Here," Josie said, indicating the screen, rewinding to the part of the video that had caught her attention and pausing it. "This car is double-parked here two blocks from the site. It's pointed in the direction of the main entrance. The timestamp is five minutes before Gina was stabbed."

"So?"

The vehicle was only visible from the driver's side, but a small neon-blue glimmer radiated from the dash. Josie lined the cursor up next to it. "See this light? One of the local rideshare companies uses neon dash lights with their logo on it. Blue."

"What's your point, Quinn?"

"A lot of rideshares have dash cameras."

Turner tapped his fingers against his leg. "I'm not kidding, Quinn. Get some sleep."

"It could have driven past the site at the time of the stabbing. It's possible that the dashcam caught something important. You could contact the rideshare company, give them the date and time, and see if they can put you in touch with the driver."

"Rideshares make it their job to avoid giving police anything at all," he countered.

Josie shifted in her chair so she could jam a hand into the pocket of her jeans. She came up with three dollars. As she spoke, she slapped the dollars one by one into Turner's palm. "Stop being a douchebag, you absolute douchebag, and track down this vehicle. Also, you're a jackass."

The ghost of a smile played on his lips. "You done?"

Good God, she really was going to punch him in the throat.

"Probably not," she managed, turning back to the computer.

Laughter trailed behind him as he returned to his desk.

Josie queued up a fifth video offered by a business across the street from the site but in the opposite direction from where Gina Phelan had been attacked. It showed the blonde running past, but there wasn't anything more than what they already had.

Or was there?

Josie rewound and paused, freezing the blonde in profile, center-screen, mid-sprint along the sidewalk. Her cap was still pulled low. This side of her body wasn't covered in so much blood. But what interested Josie the most was the smudge just below her ear. Josie zoomed in. "Turner."

"I'm looking at the list of employees and contractors! Again. A couple of these guys have records. I can track them down tomorrow."

"Blondie has a tattoo."

His chair creaked. Then he was behind her again, leaning over her shoulder to squint at the screen. "That's blood."

"It's a tattoo." Josie found another video taken from a neighboring business and paused it at the point where the tattoo was most visible. The footage was crisper, though the more she zoomed in on the woman's neck, the blurrier the image became. Still, it was enough to prove her point. "Look. It's black. The shape of a star or something."

It was no bigger than a quarter, but Josie counted at least four lines extending out from its center.

"That's not a star, Quinn. The ends aren't even pointy."

She turned her face up toward his. "Then what is it?"

"I don't know," he said irritably, as if this clue was a waste of his time.

People remembered tattoos. A friend or loved one watching the news or scrolling social media might not recognize the woman based on her stature or hair color but those things together with the tattoo could spark something. Even if they couldn't make out the precise nature of the tattoo, its location, color, and size might be just what was needed for someone who knew her to put all the pieces together and contact police.

Josie opened her mouth to lecture Turner on exactly this when he sighed and leaned in closer to her monitor. One of his hands rested on the back of her chair while the other splayed across her desk, caging her in.

He must have sensed her annoyance because he muttered, "Relax. I know. I'm too close. Just give me a second."

Josie turned her attention back to the screen, trying to make sense of the image. Maybe a drawing of the sun with its rays extending outward? Probably not. It pained her to even think it, but Turner was right again. The points weren't pointy enough for that.

"It's an ink splotch," he said. "Or a hand or something."

"It's missing a finger."

Turner tapped against the monitor. "Or that finger is hidden under her earlobe. Take some screenshots. I'll make sure Amber gets this out."

Without another word, he went back to his desk. The whoosh of him tossing his little basketball sounded, followed by curses.

Josie watched him in shock. He was never this easy to work with, even when they agreed.

Clenching the ball in his large hand, he said, "You're off this case, though, so I'm taking credit for the tattoo."

Josie rolled her eyes but didn't argue. It didn't matter to her who got credit as long as the photos got out to the public. She started taking as many screenshots as she could, pausing the footage at different points and zooming in to try to get the clearest picture. Even as her hand manipulated the mouse, her eyelids drifted closed. Somewhere between waking and sleeping, a low hum started in her ears. White noise. The faint sound of Coldplay's "All My Love" joined it. Noah's aftershave drifted over her consciousness. His hands were warm on her hips. They swayed together. He was there, right there, if she could just—

"Quinn!" the Chief's voice boomed, jolting her out of her dreamlike state.

She startled, heart thundering in her chest. With clammy hands, she wiped sweat from her face. The memory of dancing with Noah in what would be their child's nursery slipped away. It felt like another life now.

"Are you listening to me or what?" The Chief stood over her now, his acne-pitted face lobster red. Wisps of his white hair floated over his scalp. "Why the hell are you here? What are you doing?"

"I wouldn't go there, Chief," Turner said without looking up from the packet on his desk. "You're volatile right now, aren't you, Quinn?"

Josie blinked up at the Chief, still slightly dazed.

"You volatile right now, Quinn?" he barked, folding his arms across his thin chest.

Josie nodded, trying to shake off her fatigue. She needed another latte. Hell, she'd be willing to try one of Turner's disgusting energy drinks at this point. Especially for the tirade she was about to endure given the way the Chief glowered at her.

But he didn't yell, didn't berate her. Instead, he said, "Good. Stay that way. You're off the Phelan case. Don't let me catch you snooping or it'll be your ass. Now get the hell out of here."

Then he disappeared into his office.

Josie shook her head, as if that would get rid of her bone-crushing fatigue. Reluctantly, she closed out the open files on her computer.

A gust of air ruffled her hair. Trinity stepped through the door to the stairwell, holding a paper coffee cup from a gas station minimart.

"Miss Payne." Turner greeted her with that stupid conspiratorial smile.

"Kyle." Trinity smiled back.

She set the cup in front of Josie and perched her rear against the edge of the desk. The coffee scalded Josie's tongue, but she gulped it down anyway. It wasn't the blonde latte she'd become so fond of, but it was exactly what she needed, made the way she liked it. She and Trinity took their coffee the same.

"Anything?" asked Trinity.

"Not sure," Josie said. "I've officially been pulled off—"

The ringing of her cell phone interrupted. With trembling hands, Josie took it from her pocket, expecting—hoping—to see Heather's name. It wasn't Heather. She stared dumbly at the caller ID, shock rooting her in place, icing her skin. There was only one reason this call would come so late, but she already knew it wasn't that. The other possibility made her hands shake even more.

"No." The word was barely a whisper.

This wasn't happening. Not now.

Trinity's quick intake of breath snapped Josie from her momentary paralysis. She looked at her sister.

"Are you going to answer it?" Trinity whispered, color high in her cheeks.

Turner said something but Josie didn't hear it. She was only vaguely aware of him pushing away from his desk and sauntering out of the room.

"Josie?" Trinity croaked.

Josie's finger slashed the decline icon. For several seconds, she held her breath, staring as the screen faded to black. Everything was cold and she could feel herself retreating. Default settings. *Dead inside.* She could still get there. Sometimes, it was the only setting that kept her from splintering.

Trinity's palms were warm on her shoulders. "Let's go."

THIRTY-ONE

Even after midnight, Gretchen's house was busy. When this was all over, Josie would have to buy her a really big gift to thank her and Paula for opening their home this way. Noah's siblings had arrived while Trinity and Josie were out. They'd both gotten hotel rooms but, like Josie, they were too worried, too amped up, to rest. Instead, they joined the steadily growing group gathered in Gretchen's living room, everyone crammed together, either sitting down or pacing, their nervous energy palpable. Christian, Shannon, and Patrick were there, engaging Laura and Theo Fraley in small talk that seemed wholly inappropriate given the circumstances. What else was there to talk about? None of them were privy to the details of the investigation.

No one wanted to say what they were all thinking. Noah might not come home, or if he did, it would be in a body bag.

Josie's mind batted the thought away, refused to entertain it for even a millisecond.

Twenty-seven hours.

Paula flitted around, offering food and drinks, the consummate hostess. Trout, who would normally be hot on the trail of any food source or any possible attention from other humans, stayed close to Josie. He whined now and then even though he was fed and walked and had relieved himself plenty of times. Just like her, he wanted Noah.

Numbly, she sat in the corner of Gretchen's loveseat with Trout curled up on her lap, only half listening to the chatter around her. She scrolled through the endless text messages she'd missed through the day. Drake, Misty, Cindy Quinn, Amber. Her former fiancé and Denton PD's current K-9 handler, Luke Creighton. Some of the patrol officers she knew well had reached out, expressing support and offering anything she needed. Gretchen had checked in several times during the day as well. She and Turner were going to be stretched thin now that they were down two investigators.

Even Sawyer Hayes had messaged her. He was another casualty of Lila's evil machinations. A local EMT, he'd come into their lives right before Josie's grandmother Lisette died. A DNA test had proved that he was Lisette's grandson by blood. Evidently, in the year after Eli Matson dumped Lila, he'd started seeing someone else. That woman had gotten pregnant with Sawyer. When she went to Eli's trailer to tell him, she was greeted instead by Lila, who had just returned to town with baby Josie.

Whatever Lila said to Sawyer's mother, it had frightened her enough that she never tried to contact Eli again. Never even told Sawyer who his father was until she was on her deathbed. Poor Sawyer learned of Eli's identity and then, immediately afterward, learned that he'd died years ago. Lisette had embraced him wholeheartedly, but he'd had precious little time with her before she was murdered. Josie had done everything she could to make Sawyer a part of their lives, part of her found family, and he'd resisted at every turn. He resented her for having the place in the Matson family he never had and then, for a long time, he blamed her for Lisette's death. They'd made strides in the past year though. Josie was heartened to see his message. It was the only one she had the energy to answer.

There was a new voicemail from the person who had called while she was at the stationhouse, but Josie couldn't bring herself to listen to it. Wisely, her sister hadn't pressed her about it.

"Okay, okay! I hate to break this up but Josie, you really need to get some sleep." Trinity stood over her as the room went silent.

"But I—"

Shannon said, "Your sister's right, Josie. At least try to get some rest. You've got your phone, but we'll wake you if we hear anything."

Trinity scooped Trout into her arms and headed up the stairs while Josie hugged everyone good night. In the guest room, Trout snoozed in the center of the bed. Trinity sat beside him, cross-legged, her laptop open in front of her. A familiar thick file rested on Josie's side of the bed.

She blinked, dizzy with fatigue. "What are you doing?"

"Getting to the bottom of Lila's shit once and for all." Trinity pointed to the file. "Starting from the very beginning. Come, sit."

Josie knew she should sleep. There was a very good chance that once she was in bed, she'd pass out whether she wanted to or not, but she was too curious to do anything but follow Trinity's instructions. Kicking off her shoes, she picked up the file and sat on the bed. Trout's body twitched and he yipped. Josie placed a palm along his rib cage, feeling him jerk as he dreamt.

Trinity said, "Roe Hoyt is still alive. I searched the Pennsylvania inmate locator site."

Josie looked down at the file in her lap. "You went to the house to get this? I don't—"

"Be honest. After your conversations with Heather and what Kyle told us, do you really think the Lila angle is going to take priority in this investigation? Especially since she's been dead for so long? Don't you think Heather's going to look at the most recent crimes—the armed robberies—as a way to try to find this Dylan person?"

"It's not about what I think. Heather's team has to follow the leads that are there and one of them is Lila."

Doubt needled her, like a splinter under her fingernail. Assuming Heather had very little to go on from the evidence they'd gathered directly related to Noah's abduction, homing in on the robberies might make sense. They were recent and there were several of them—that meant multiple crime scenes which increased the odds of finding something that could lead to the perpetrators. Josie knew for a fact that most of the evidence taken from those scenes hadn't even been processed yet. There was a very good chance Heather could get all the DNA samples expedited. It was possible that one or more of Dylan's co-conspirators would show up in CODIS. If she could find one of the armed robbers, she could find Dylan—and hopefully Noah.

Trinity was right. It was likely a stronger avenue of inquiry. As was the Gina Phelan case. Still, there was no denying the Lila connection. Heather's team had clearly started looking into it but how far had they gotten? How deep would they go? Even in Josie's professional opinion, the Lila lead was weak.

Josie was shut out of the investigation into her husband's abduction and the Gina Phelan case now that they were connected. As wrong as it was, she would have to rely on Turner for information and hope he meant it when he said he didn't care about getting into trouble.

Regardless of which avenue of inquiry Heather's team prioritized, if Josie wanted something to do, all that was left was digging into Lila's past. It was a long shot, but it was the only shot she had. What a cruel twist of fate that even now, years after Lila's death, after Josie had spread her ashes, there was no escaping her. Even in death, Lila was like one of those planet-destroying stars that Noah always talked about. Him and his obsession with astronomy. Lila was the host star—fiery and destructive—and Josie was a tiny, insignificant planet, doomed to remain in her orbit until the day she got too close and fell into a death spiral. The collision would vaporize Josie instantly. There would be nothing of her left.

Wasn't that what Lila had always hoped for?

Trinity laid a hand over Trout's rib cage, right next to Josie's, as he started running in his sleep, little legs working feverishly. "Tell me what you're thinking."

"That I'm stuck with Lila," she muttered. "Like always."

"I know," Trinity sighed. "She's like herpes."

Josie snorted even as her mind descended into the rabbit hole. Would Noah be missing right now if she'd just dug into Lila's past all those years ago when she came into possession of the box? What if she'd laid all of Lila's secrets bare back then? Until there was nothing else to be uncovered. No surprises. What if she'd worked harder to find Lila's accomplices? What if she'd tried to locate the men in the photos or the people Lila had taken the objects from? What if she'd disassembled that sick trophy box of terror before slamming the door on Lila?

Would she be here right now or would she be in bed with Noah, in their own home, with Trout snoring at their feet while they planned their vow-renewal ceremony?

Trinity reached for the nightstand and snatched up a printout of some sort, waving it in front of Josie's face. "You said you never looked inside the Roe Hoyt file. I didn't want to read it without you, but I was curious. I found this newspaper article online."

Josie took the printout. It was from a small Bradford County newspaper that probably didn't exist anymore. The article was dated December 4, 1966.

HUNTERS FIND WOMAN HIDING HUMAN
REMAINS ON STATE GAME LAND

Josie had a vague recollection of Gretchen telling her that Roe had been found in Sullivan County, but she also knew there was a large swath of state game land that stretched across both counties. It was possible that when the case went to trial, the jurisdiction had been found to belong to Bradford County.

She scanned the article, the scant details lining up with what Gretchen had told her years ago when Josie was too exhausted and too chickenshit to open the file herself. It also offered additional information which Josie would probably have known if she'd ever reviewed the file. Roe had been living high in the mountains in a shack that was thought to be an old waystation for game wardens who got caught in bad weather. Her age was indeterminate though she was thought to be in her early to mid-twenties. She was unable to speak, though she could make noises. Dressed in scraps of clothing. With her was a small girl, estimated to be about five years old, naked, unkempt, described as "feral," communicating using only grunts and screams.

Little Lila.

Roe had gotten her name from the noise she made most often. Lila had been given hers by her first foster family. Both of them attacked the hunters who discovered them, and later, the police officers who came to collect them. One of the hunters had been stabbed in the arm with an old hunting knife Roe possessed.

"It's not what I expected," Trinity said. "It's hard for me to muster any sympathy for Lila but..."

"I know," Josie said. The day Gretchen had brought her the file, she remembered thinking poor little Lila never stood a chance. "I have sympathy for the little girl found in the woods.

The one who couldn't speak, who was dumped into foster care and subjected to horrific things."

"That makes sense." Trinity stroked Trout's side as he growled. His little face twitched. Still dreaming. "How did Lila even figure out that Roe Hoyt was her mother?"

"It was probably in her foster care file," Josie replied. "Lila got full access to it before it was destroyed."

Lila had wanted to erase her past, her identity, and yet, she'd tracked down her biological mother. Had she wanted to know where she came from? It was such a human impulse, but Josie had never known Lila to do anything unless there was something in it for her. Had she thought her biological mother might have something that Lila could take from her only to find out Roe was in prison? But why give Josie her inmate number? Why put Roe Hoyt on Josie's radar? To prove once and for all that in the contest of whose childhood was worse, Lila remained victorious?

"I know this isn't likely to lead to Noah," Trinity said, "but it's a place to start. Plus, you said that Lila and Roe were incarcerated together at some point. There might be something to uncover there. But if you think this is a waste of time, we could start with researching the newspaper clippings from the box. You took photos of them before Heather's team took everything into evidence, right?"

Josie nodded. Her fingers traced the edge of the file folder. Even if Noah wasn't missing because of something Lila-related, the specter of Lila would always be hanging over her. If there was even the slimmest chance that she and Noah would still be able to adopt, didn't she owe it to her future child to vanquish all traces of Lila's foul, invasive sins from their lives once and for all? Didn't she owe it to herself?

It would certainly give her something to focus on. Something connected, however tenuously, to the investigation.

She flipped the file open.

"Let's find out why Lila wanted me to know about her mother."

THIRTY-TWO
ONE WEEK AGO

As parties went, this one was a little wilder than Bug expected. As Holden guided her through a maze of hallways and lavishly decorated rooms, introducing her to men whose names she didn't bother to remember, she took in all the sordid details. Music so loud it rattled your bones? Check. Bodies writhing to said music? Check. Couples getting down and dirty on couches and chairs? Check. A vast selection of drugs? Check. Booze? Check. In fact, Bug was carefully sipping the second blue-colored drink that Holden had shoved into her hand. The first had given her a nice buzz, loosening her up enough that she wasn't so apprehensive about what she needed to do.

Holden kept them moving. She met more people. Laughed at jokes that weren't funny. Tried not to recoil at the way some of the men raked their eyes over her. Then there were more rooms. How many living rooms and parlors did one house need?

There were other women here, but she wasn't introduced to any of them. Most of them were too focused on the men they were chatting with to even look at Bug. Some narrowed their eyes at her, assessing her as a threat.

She was a threat, all right, just not to any of them.

Holden found a room where the music wasn't so loud and steered Bug inside. There were only a few groups of people mingling. None of them paid any attention when Holden plopped into a big cushy chair and pulled Bug down onto his lap. Even though her feet were killing her, she didn't want to stop. Her target was here somewhere, and she was afraid the night would be over before she found him.

Swirling the liquor around in her glass, she said, "What are we doing?"

His arms tightened around her waist. "I'm tired of small talk."

She didn't know what to say to that.

"Drink," Holden said, lifting his chin to indicate her glass.

Smiling, she said, "I'm already a little tipsy from the first one. You know I'm not supposed to drink."

It was imperative that she stay alert.

"You'll be fine," Holden said, tipping the glass to her lips.

Bug drank it before it spilled down her front. When she finished, Holden took the glass and set it on the floor next to the chair. Then he kissed her. His hands roamed up and down her body, finding places he definitely shouldn't touch in public. Her heart hammered in her chest, but she let him go on for a while. She needed to act normal. After a couple of minutes, Bug pulled away, trying to put some distance between their bodies. "What are you doing?"

He kept her pinned to his lap. "I told you, I'm tired of small talk."

Bug didn't need to fake her nervous laughter. "Holden, there are people everywhere. I hope you don't think I'm going to let you—"

She broke off as she noticed a man watching them intently from across the room. An involuntary shudder racked her body. Holden laughed and said something, but Bug couldn't hear him. The man sauntered toward them, slugging back a drink as he moved. He didn't stop until his shins knocked into the side of their chair. Bug looked up at him and for a moment, she was eight years old again, hiding in the cupboard under the kitchen sink, and he was there. Ripping the cabinet door off like it was made of paper. Three red welts striped his cheek. He reached for her, and she saw blood on his knuckles.

From another room, her mother screamed, "Run, Bug! Run!"

"Holden, who's your friend?"

That voice, smooth instead of snarly, snapped her back to the present. Her fingers touched the centerpiece of her necklace of their own accord. She couldn't move, couldn't speak. It wasn't supposed to be this hard. The man wasn't supposed to be scary anymore. He wasn't acting scary. He wasn't even being creepy like most of the guys here. In fact, he was bizarrely normal. This time, when he reached out, it was to shake her hand. Holden must have made introductions. As if in a trance, Bug slid her palm against his, surprised by his gentleness. Then again, he didn't know her true identity. Clearly, he didn't recognize her.

Holden's voice seemed to come from very far away. "Sorry, man. She's a lightweight."

Bug blinked, willing the memories away. For now. "I'm so sorry." She forced a doe-eyed smile onto her face. "I didn't mean to be rude. Holden's right. I got buzzed pretty quickly but I'm feeling a lot better now. Your home is absolutely amazing! It's so nice to finally meet you. Holden talks about you all the time."

Holden's fingers dug into her hip. Was that a warning of some kind?

She put a hand to her mouth momentarily. "I'm babbling. Sorry."

The man seemed captivated or amused. Maybe both. That was unexpected. "You're refreshing," he said.

Giggle, she told herself. A silly little giggle would work here. Unfortunately, it came out half a shriek. "Thank you."

From her periphery, she saw Holden shaking his head. The man laughed. Then he extended his hand again. This time, it was easier to take it. Bug let him lift her from Holden's lap. She could do this.

"It's a little crazy up here," the man said. "Has Holden showed you the bar downstairs?"

"Not yet." Holden stood and gripped her waist possessively.

The man winked at her. "It's a lot more than a bar. Come on, we'll have a drink together. I've got the good stuff down there. Food, if you're hungry. Holden, have you fed her at all? No wonder she's buzzed after two drinks."

Bug followed him, studying his wide shoulders, his self-assured walk. For once, she was grateful for Holden's touch. As they descended a carpeted set of stairs into what she assumed was the basement, her legs trembled a little.

Maybe she could use another drink. Liquid courage. Finally, she was going to confront the man from the magical house. The man who had beaten her mother so badly she was unrecognizable, before throwing her out into the cold.

The only man who had ever made her mother feel afraid.

THIRTY-THREE

Josie flipped past the initial reports to the first photo of Roe Hoyt she could find. A gasp slipped past her lips. It was taken at the hospital after she was first found. Josie didn't know how common color photography was in the early sixties but this picture, at least, was in color. The resemblance to Lila was so striking, it sucked Josie right back to her childhood. Mother and daughter shared the same deep-blue eyes, high cheekbones, and defined jawline that would make supermodels jealous. Like Lila, Roe was thin but that could have just been from her circumstances. Someone had clothed her in a hospital gown. She swam in it. One of her gaunt wrists was handcuffed to the metal rail of a bed.

Trinity scooted over, abandoning her laptop and pulling Trout across her lap so she could get closer. Their shoulders brushed. The picture wavered between Josie's thumb and forefinger. "Wow," Trinity whispered. "Lila got all of her mom's genes, didn't she?"

Whereas Lila's hair had been black, like Josie's—a happy coincidence for kidnapper Lila—Roe's was honey brown. It was long, the way Lila had always worn hers, but matted and

tangled with leaves, twigs and substances Josie couldn't identify. Lila's eyes had always gleamed with cunning and malice.
Roe was a different story. Hers looked vacant at first but if Josie
angled the picture a bit, they looked haunted, frightened. It
reminded her of a lenticular photo. Like the kind found on
bookmarks when Josie and Trinity were kids. Holding it flat,
you saw a tiger sitting calmly but if you tipped it slightly, the
tiger threw its claws up and opened its mouth in a roar.

"That's not what she looks like now," Trinity remarked. "At
all."

Josie had forgotten that the inmate locator site provided
pictures of incarcerated individuals. She'd look at it later.
Tucking Roe's photo into the back of the file, she took out a
stack of reports and started reading. Trinity leaned in and read
along with Josie.

What hadn't made it into the initial article Trinity had
found was that law enforcement was never able to find Roe's
family, or anyone who knew her, even after releasing her photo
to the public. Josie wasn't that surprised. Who would want to
come forward and claim the woman living in the woods who
had slaughtered her own children? Months went by, medical
exams and psychological evaluations were performed, the shack
where she'd lived was thoroughly processed—by the standards
that existed in the mid-sixties—and a nationwide search was
conducted for any missing women near her age.

It was as though Roe Hoyt appeared on that mountain one
day by magic with no human connection to anyone in society.
Like she'd stepped through a portal from another dimension. Of
course, that's not what had happened. Someone had given birth
to her. She'd come from somewhere. If she'd been found today,
between modern technology, mail-in DNA tests, and social
media, the police would likely be able to find her relatives in a
short amount of time. DNA wouldn't be used in a criminal case
until 1985, in the UK, nearly twenty years after Roe Hoyt was

discovered. Back then, police hadn't had as much to work with. Although fingerprinting was used in the sixties, it hadn't helped identify her since her prints weren't already on file anywhere.

"No one ever figured out where she came from?" Trinity said.

Josie turned so she could look at her sister's face. A familiar excitement gleamed in Trinity's blue eyes. It was the look she got when a particular story caught her attention and made her want to dig in. They worked in different fields but the one thing they had in common was their obsession with finding answers to questions no one had yet been able to answer. Josie could practically hear Trinity's pitch to her producer despite the fact that Roe Hoyt's case wasn't unsolved.

"If they found any of her relatives, it's not in this file," Josie replied. "You didn't find anything in your online search?"

From Trinity's lap, Trout kicked his back legs out, nudging Josie's thigh. She patted his bottom as he began to snore.

"Not about that," Trinity answered. "Most articles were the same as the one I showed you. Even her conviction wasn't really covered. It was like a footnote. It seems like this would have been a pretty shocking case back then. I'm surprised it didn't get wider coverage. Anyway, let's keep going. If her family was never located, how did she get her last name?"

As Trout's snores increased in volume, they went back to reading the contents of the file.

She'd initially been entered into custody as Roe Doe—a variation of Jane Doe—but the district attorney felt that was too comical given the heinous nature of her crimes. None of the police officers, nurses, doctors, social workers, or prison staff who interacted with her wanted to lend her their last name. Roe viciously attacked every person she came into contact with at the first opportunity in any way that she could. One nurse suffered a concussion. Another received a gash on her forehead that required twenty stitches after Roe slammed her head into the edge of a sink. A social worker's wrist was fractured after Roe tackled her to the ground. Law enforcement and corrections officers frequently reported scratches and bites.

It seemed that no type of restraint was enough to prevent her from attacking people. Even when she was restrained with a straitjacket, she still managed to lash out in the moments before it was first put on or right after it was removed—no matter how many people were there to help. Finally, medication was administered to keep her calm, particularly when she needed to be transported or examined. Eventually someone decided her surname would come from the road nearest where she'd been found.

Trinity took the report Josie had just finished with, running her fingernail along the page until she found what she was searching for. She had to speak louder to be heard over Trout's snores. "They estimated her age to be twenty-five. Based on what?"

Josie spread the pages of the file out on the bed in front of them and thumbed through them until she found a stack of medical reports. "A physical examination, X-rays, and the fact that she'd given birth to at least six children."

That meant Lila's age had also been an estimate though perhaps it had been easier to gauge since she was a child. Looking at the timing of tooth eruption had been a valid method of estimating a child's age long before the sixties.

Trinity jostled Trout as she pawed through more of the reports. "But not based on anything that she was able to communicate to anyone? All of these reports so far say she 'didn't speak' or 'couldn't speak.' Was she able to read and write? Draw pictures?"

"Not sure." Josie flipped through several more pages. If Roe Hoyt was still alive, that meant she'd been incarcerated for over fifty years. This file was thick but not so thick that it would cover that kind of time span. "There are medical reports here and psych evals but I think they only go up to her trial... Oh wait, there are some things from when she was first incarcerated."

Roe Hoyt had had a public defender. Both her attorney and the DA had her examined by medical experts they had chosen themselves. It was common practice for each side to retain their own experts, who would often have differing opinions as to the health and mental state of the defendant. In Roe's case, the physician for the defense believed she had likely suffered some sort of injury to her brain or a stroke that resulted in aphasia, rendering her unable to speak or write. In addition, she had tremors in her dominant hand which made drawing difficult. A copy of one of her hand-drawn pictures had been included. It was crude. Stick figures, one large and one small. Their heads were misshapen. Her and Lila, perhaps? What was possibly intended to be a rectangle hung over their heads, but it, too, was distorted, as though her hand had jerked violently a couple of times while she drew. There was no way to tell what the shape represented. A roof? Josie wondered what else she had drawn.

According to the report from the doctor her attorney had retained, she was able to follow simple directions which led him to believe she understood language and what was happening around her but could not express herself. Tremor aside, most efforts to get her to communicate via the written word or drawings were impossible given her tendency to attack anyone within striking distance. The defense doctor also believed that the brain injury had impaired her judgment and impulse control, causing her propensity for violence.

Roe's attorney had tried to have her deemed incompetent to stand trial. He failed.

Evidently, the judge, and later the jury, found the doctor for the Commonwealth of Pennsylvania more credible. His report opined that Roe Hoyt's failure to communicate verbally may have been attributable to a head injury but could just as likely be intentional on her part. In terms of her right-hand tremor, he dismissed the notion that it was caused by a head injury. Instead, he diagnosed her with an essential tremor, which was often genetic and developed in perfectly healthy people with no known cause. He stated that her tendency toward violence was a result of her having antisocial personality disorder. He believed she knew exactly what she was doing when she attacked people; that her actions were purposeful and malicious, and that she had no remorse for the harm she inflicted on others.

"Good lord," Trinity murmured as she scanned the last pages alongside Josie. "Pretty much the only thing they agree on —sort of—is the possibility of a head injury. Are the X-ray reports there?"

Josie found them. "She had an old skull fracture."

"But they really didn't know the true extent of the injury." Trinity lifted Trout up, interrupting his symphony, and deposited him onto Josie's lap. She retrieved her laptop, doing a quick search. "CT scans and MRIs weren't available then."

"Which means the doctors were more or less guessing as to the seriousness of her brain injury and what effect it had on her."

Trinity put her laptop aside and started riffling through the pages before them. "None of these reports talk about the age of the fracture. Is there a way to tell how old a fracture is?"

"On the skull? I'm sure there is today," Josie said, searching her tired mind for cases she'd worked wherein Dr. Feist had done exactly that. "Based on the stage of healing, I think, and a doctor's clinical experience. I'm not sure it's something that can be pinned down precisely. Were doctors able to do it back when Roe was found? I don't know."

"Which means that she could have sustained the fracture a year or ten years before she was discovered."

Josie understood what Trinity was getting at which was that there was a possibility that Roe hadn't always had aphasia.

Trinity found the radiology report which didn't offer much detail. Josie stroked Trout's side as she went back to the medical reports, rereading. "I wonder what she would have told people if she'd been able to communicate."

THIRTY-FOUR

"We don't even know how long she was living out in the woods." Trinity tossed the radiology report aside. "She *was* living there, right? If she had six children and she was only twenty-five-ish, does that mean she was living out there since she was a kid?"

"I'm not sure she would have survived if that was the case." Josie abandoned the medical reports and used both hands to pet Trout's silky coat. He rewarded her with a contented sigh. "The winters would have killed her, and that's assuming she would have known how to find food and a reliable water source."

Trinity frowned. "Maybe she was coming back and forth from somewhere? Or she went to live out there when she was old enough to survive but someone was helping her?"

Another pass through the file and Josie found the crime scene reports and photos. From the exterior, the shack looked like it might have been quaint at one time with its little porch, complete with a built-in bench and an awning that had sagged from age and decay. By the time Roe was discovered, the wood was the color of ash, faded, splintered in some places and warped in others. The inside consisted of a single room with a crumbling stone fireplace. Along the floor were piles of sleeping bags and blankets, some in fairly good shape but most threadbare, their colors faded. Once removed, they'd been analyzed to see if their origin could be determined. The ones that had tags still on them were sold so widely, there was no way to track down who had purchased them. It appeared that Roe had torn some of them into pieces and tied them together to make a sort of dress for herself.

There were also some camping supplies. A dented green Coleman lantern with no oil to fuel it. Aluminum pans, cups, and battered utensils. Plastic jugs filled with dirty water. A rusty folding shovel that looked like the kind the military used to dig trenches decades ago. Two canteens sporting faded logos from different manufacturers. A thermos. Half a dozen Zippo lighters. A hatchet.

Trinity said, "Did she bring that stuff with her when she went out there or did someone bring it to her?"

"She stole it," Josie said. "Look at this stuff. It's mismatched, in bad shape. Torn. Faded. Dented. Rusted. She was on state game land. Lots of hunters and campers frequented the area almost year-round. I think she scavenged campsites for these supplies. Look at these lighters—Zippos. The Zippo Manufacturing Company is in Bradford County. Plenty of locals would have had these on them out in the woods."

"Okay, she was resourceful," Trinity said. "And somehow managed not to get caught stealing. But what the hell did she eat? What did she feed little Lila?"

Trinity kept reading through the reports while Josie studied the rest of the photos. Among Roe's collection was a worn hunting knife she'd used to stab one of the hunters. Apparently, her hand tremor didn't stop her from trying to kill people. Then again, it probably had the most profound effect on her fine motor skills. Lunging, punching, and other big movements might not have proved as difficult as drawing or writing.

Outside, next to the shack, she had fashioned a crude version of a root cellar and filled it with berries and plants. Nearby was a small ring of stones where she'd had fires. Further from the shack, rudimentary animal traps were found.

"Small game," Josie said. "Squirrels, rabbits."

Trinity wrinkled her nose. "That's gross."

Near the root cellar, Roe had also constructed a lean-to which she'd fortified with a large piece of canvas that likely came from a tent. The fabric was in bad shape. There was no way to know if the tent had been Roe's, if someone had given it to her, or if she'd found it in the woods. Given its condition, Josie guessed she'd found it in the woods like everything else. Inside the lean-to were more blankets.

"What did she need that for when she had the shack?" asked Trinity. "Houseguests? Someone helping her? Or was it to be close to the fire in the winter?"

"She had a source of heat in the shack."

Josie fanned the photos out. Her fingers stilled over a picture of the children's delicate remains hidden in the floor of the shack. Roe had kept them. She'd had a shovel. It would have been easy enough to bury them. Perhaps no one would have known about them if she had. Except that she was in a remote area of the wilderness. Even if she'd buried them fairly deep, it was almost a given that animals would dig them up. The shack was the place where they were least likely to be disturbed. Nausea swirled in Josie's stomach.

"She stayed in the lean-to during the decomposition process. The smell, the insect activity—it would have made the shack uninhabitable for some time."

Trinity sucked in a breath. "Good lord."

Quickly, Josie shoved the photo—and the others like it—into the back of the file, out of sight, and turned her focus back to figuring out how Roe had ended up in the woods and how long she'd suffered from the effects of her head injury.

"Based on all this," Josie said, "she knew how to start a fire, how to forage, to trap, to field dress, prepare and cook what she trapped. I don't think her parents dumped her in the woods at a young age and left her there to survive on her own. However she ended up out there, she already had some knowledge of how to survive."

If she was continuing to do so when she was found, it meant that the skull fracture had left certain parts of her brain intact. Josie made a mental note to research aphasia. She had some rudimentary knowledge of it from when Lisette lived at the nursing home. Several Rockview residents had had it. From what Josie understood, it was a communication disorder that impaired a person's ability to speak and sometimes to write, read, or even to comprehend language. She knew there were different types and that it affected people differently, but she had met residents at Rockview whose minds were completely intact—they remembered and understood every-thing and had no difficulty carrying out their activities of daily living—but simply could not express themselves verbally. Had that been the case for Roe? Or had her type of aphasia or even her brain injury affected more than just speech?

"There's no way for us to even guess if she got that skull fracture before she was in the woods or sometime afterward," Trinity said with a sigh of frustration. "So let's move on. She must have been raised by someone who hunted and trapped regularly. I'm surprised no one ever tried to find her family that way."

Josie thumbed through more pages. Without the benefit of DNA testing, law enforcement could have requested records from the Game Commission listing everyone who had purchased a hunting license in the years before Roe was found, starting in Bradford County, and then expanding outward. It would have been tedious and required a lot of manpower to track each of those people down and interview them, which was probably why no one had done it.

"You don't have to live in the county where your hunting license is issued," Josie said. "Someone in Pittsburgh could conceivably get a tag for Bradford County. A search like that—potentially one that spanned the entire state—was probably beyond the scope of authorities at that time. Plus, you know as well as I do just how many hunters there are in Pennsylvania. Lots of kids grow up doing it alongside their parents."

"But this was the nineteen fifties and sixties," Trinity pointed out. "Did dads really teach their little girls to hunt and trap back then?"

"Not many did, I imagine," Josie conceded. "But if she was living on a ranch or a farm or some fairly remote area then she might have been taught those things out of necessity."

Trinity eyed her. "Isn't it more likely that someone helped Roe Hoyt out in those woods?"

"Sure," Josie replied. "If she was pregnant six times, she clearly had contact with someone, maybe more than one person."

Trinity arched a brow. "I'm hearing a but…"

Josie smiled. "Take Trout again and give me your laptop."

THIRTY-FIVE

Once they made the exchange, Josie pulled up the internet browser and used the information in the file to try to narrow down the approximate location of Roe's shack on a map and added a pushpin. Clicking over to terrain, miles and miles of forest filled the screen. "Here," she said, pointing to a ribbon of road barely visible through the trees. "This is Hoyt Road. If you draw a straight line from the shack to the road, it's about ten miles."

Trinity leaned in closer, eyes dancing from the pin to the road before taking in the entirety of the map. "There's nothing around. No houses. No towns. Nothing. Just that—is that a parking lot?"

"I think so, yeah. The nearest town is..." Josie pinched her fingers together on the screen, zooming out. "Here. Almost twenty miles away. There are other towns but all fifteen to twenty miles from the shack. Trin, this is recent. There are no houses, farms, or residences of any kind for miles. The state game land is protected from development but the land surrounding it isn't."

"You're saying this area is essentially unchanged from the sixties."

"Yeah. Roe Hoyt wouldn't have been able to go back and forth from a town or a house or any semblance of civilization on foot. Not easily, anyway. Even if she routinely hiked out to the road, it's not like she had any way to communicate with people. There wasn't a way for her to call someone to ask them to meet her. She was living out there. If she had help, it wasn't reliable. Also, look at these pictures." Josie set the laptop aside and lined up the photos of Roe's meager supplies. "What don't you see?"

Trinity rolled her lips together. Trout stirred on her lap, lifting his head to look at both of them before dropping it back onto Trinity's leg with a heavy sigh. "No wrappers. No cans. A couple of plastic containers but no store bags of any kind. Nobody was bringing her supplies."

"Right. If she was getting help, it wasn't very much."

"Is that how the first five babies died? The conditions?"

"No. They didn't die from exposure," Josie said, paging through more of the file.

Trinity held a hand up. "I don't want to see the photos again."

"Me either," said Josie. It was already seared into her brain. Plucking another report from the pile, she scanned it, confirming that her conclusion was correct. "They had skull fractures."

"Oh God."

Trout's head popped up again. This time, his eyes were wider, more alert, and his ears formed two perfect steeples.

"From a small, unknown blunt object."

Trinity stroked between Trout's ears, trying to get him to go back to sleep, but he continued to watch them warily. "That's... listen, I'm not a newbie journalist. I've covered a lot of pretty horrific stuff. Gory, nightmarish crimes. Victims of every age."

"But the ones involving children are always the hardest," Josie said softly. "That never changes."

If it did—at least for Josie—then it was time to turn in her badge.

"Yeah." Trinity gave Trout a watery smile, followed by a few saccharine words, and he settled back down. "Okay, so we can agree that no matter where Roe Hoyt came from or when her ability to speak became impaired or when her tremor started or how she ended up in that shack, she was very likely there on her own. Given the condition of the supplies she had on hand, she didn't make it out to civilization often."

"If at all," Josie interjected.

"Not sure I buy that. I mean, who got her pregnant? Six times? I get that she couldn't just stroll out of the forest to go to the nearest grocery store whenever she wanted, but she could have hiked out of there from time to time. It's possible that she did make the journey from the shack back to civilization—it would just be a hell of a long walk. What if this was one of those cases where a family member was abusing her and when she gave birth, she'd take the children to the shack to... dispose of them?"

"Lila was alive," Josie said. "For years."

It still baffled her that Roe had let Lila live. Why? Why her?

"What if..." Trinity shifted her legs under Trout's weight, stretching them out in front of her and depositing him between them again. "What if the babies didn't all have the same father? Let's say this wasn't a case of her being abused by a family member. Think about it. Whether she was having sex with someone she met in a nearby town or someone who came out to her shack, wouldn't that guy wonder what happened to the baby?"

"Unless he was there so infrequently that she was able to hide her pregnancies and the remains," Josie suggested.

"Bullshit," Trinity argued. "That would involve a lot of luck."

"Not if he only came out once a year. A lot of hunters only take one annual hunting trip to a specific area. Let's say this guy was a hunter. Every year he hunts for... let's say deer—antlered and unantlered, regular firearms—which is generally open near the end of November or beginning of December. He treks out to Roe's shack. They have sex and then he leaves. She gets pregnant."

"Huh," Trinity said. "If she delivered full-term, she'd still have three months before he showed up again. So it's possible that he never knew—if she was somehow able to hide the evidence of decomposition. But wait, what about Lila? We don't know the birth order of Roe's children. Lila could have been the baby number three or four. The father would have known about her."

"Maybe Roe was able to hide her," Josie suggested. How, was anyone's guess.

"Why keep Lila?" Trinity asked.

"I don't know."

"What if she killed them because she thought he would get angry or something if he came back and found a baby." Trinity paused. "Hmmm, that still doesn't explain Lila."

Josie didn't think anything in the universe would ever explain Lila's existence. Still, one thought had burrowed its way into her brain while they talked. "Maybe she let Lila live based on who fathered her."

Trinity's top lip curled in disgust. "If we're still considering hunters as potential fathers, that actually makes a lot of sense."

"We're also assuming any sexual encounters Roe Hoyt had were consensual," Josie said. "Even before her brain injury, they may not have been. That could have been a factor in what she did."

"If that's true, does that mean she consented to sex with

Lila's father? That's why she got to live?" Trinity shuddered and rubbed her arms even though it wasn't cold in the room. "All of this is so deeply disturbing. Not to excuse anything that Roe Hoyt did—at all—but there is not one damn thing in any of these reports that even raises the question of who the father or fathers were!"

"If I caught a case like this today," Josie said, "we'd have the tools to find the father—or fathers—even if the mother wasn't able to communicate their identity, but back then? It's not an excuse but without witnesses or an ID from Roe Hoyt or someone coming forward to admit to paternity, that line of inquiry was dead in the water."

Trinity huffed. "Well, after she was arrested for five murders, I'm sure there was no way anyone was going to admit paternity! This reminds me of something my grandmother used to say—shit—I mean, *our* grandmother."

Josie smiled weakly. She'd been reunited with her birth family at the age of thirty. By that time, all of her biological grandparents had passed away. She'd never known any of them. "It's fine. You can say your grandmother. That's what she was. On Mom or Dad's side?"

"Mom's. When I was a teenager, she used to say, 'A man can always pull up his pants and walk away.' I used to think that was her way of telling me not to have sex, but it fits pretty well in this scenario, too. Probably in a lot of different situations."

Josie laughed despite the gravity of their current situation and the heavy things they were talking about. "That's a good one."

"Mom used to say it, too. Seriously, they were trying hard to keep me away from boys. Not that they were lining up back then or anything."

They lapsed into silence. One day, Josie would have to find out what other pearls of wisdom Shannon had frequently shared with her brother and sister. It was just another thing she'd missed out on because of Lila.

Trinity knew it. She squeezed Josie's knee. "I'm sorry."

"Lila had a saying. Not a half bad one, believe it or not."

"Let's hear it."

"She used to say, 'You can't always be all roses and sweetness, that don't get shit done.'"

Trinity pursed her lips momentarily. "That's..."

Josie tried to smile again but she wasn't sure if she did. Her eyeballs felt like they were made of sandpaper. A buzzy feeling settled in her bones. It was like she'd been awake for a week. Her body was shutting down under the stress of the last thirty hours. The effort it took just to regulate her emotions—poorly— had sapped her strength.

Thirty hours.

Where was Noah?

She shook off the questions before they had a chance to crowd in. She was too tired to fight off the storm of emotions they would bring. Blinking, she worked hard to focus on Trinity again. "It's okay. You can say it."

"No. I can't." She started gathering up the reports and photos and tucking them back inside the file. "I think you should go see her."

"What?"

Trinity didn't look at her. "Roe Hoyt. You should go see her. She's very old. I don't know how much longer she'll be around. I think one day you'll regret it if you don't. You can find out if she had any contact with Lila while they were incarcerated together. See if Lila told her anything important— anything that might lead to someone who might know where to find that Dylan kid or how to track him down. There have been lots of medical advances since the late sixties. It's possible she's had therapy for her aphasia by now. The tremor, too. Maybe she can communicate somehow. I know it's not a strong lead in terms of finding Noah, but I think you should go see her."

Josie opened her mouth to say that Heather or someone from her team would do that but thought better of it. This was personal, and not just because of Noah. Besides, what if Lila had told Roe something that only Josie could decipher?

"Wait," Trinity said. "I forgot. There's a three-day waiting period for visiting inmates in Pennsylvania and that's if you're already on the approved list. I could probably get access if I try to do it as a journalist, but it will take longer than three days."

"I can get in tomorrow," Josie said.

"Really?"

It would be cheating, technically, and if her Chief or Heather Loughlin found out, she'd be in deep shit. But she'd throw her career away in a heartbeat if there was even a chance that Roe Hoyt knew something that could get them closer to finding Noah. "I can get in because I'm law enforcement."

"Even if you're not working a specific case?"

Josie grimaced. "That's tricky. As long as no one asks for specifics, I can get in. It's kind of an informal process, especially since I've been there so many times for various investigations. Basically, all I have to do is call the prison to let them know which inmate I want to speak with and tell them what time I'm coming. I'm assuming Roe doesn't have an attorney anymore so that won't be a sticking point."

"No paperwork?"

"I haven't been asked for documents in years. I'll call the superintendent in the morning."

Trinity's look of incredulity turned into a grin. "Perfect."

Josie waved toward the reports and photos spread out before them. "Is there anything there we didn't go over?"

Trinity took her time organizing the contents. Then she pulled out a few more documents. "The appeal her attorney filed which was denied, of course. Records from her admission to SCI Muncy. Oh, and this... this is interesting. It's an approved visitor list. One from just after she was incarcerated in 1968 which lists her lawyer. No one else. But this one..." she thrust the page triumphantly in Josie's face, "is an updated list from 1970."

The words on the page swam. A few hard blinks later, Josie was able to read them. "Who's Eva Owens?"

"I don't know but I'm sure as hell going to find out."

Josie didn't have the energy to change her clothes or brush her teeth or stand up even though Shannon had gone back to her house and packed a bag full of clothes and toiletries for her. But she wanted to stay awake. What if there was news?

Trinity put the reassembled file on her nightstand and pointed at Josie. "You sleep."

"I won't be able to sleep," said Josie. "I shouldn't."

"You will and you should," Trinity assured her. The laptop was back in her lap. The sound of her fingers clacking against the keys filled the room. "Because you'll know that I'm working on leads the whole time from this file. Not one minute will be wasted. When you wake up, we'll be ready to go!"

Josie laid down and turned onto her stomach. Trout rolled over until his back was pressed into her hip. She reached under her pillow for Noah's shirt and brought it to her face, inhaling. Her eyes drifted closed. *I'm coming for you*, she told him silently. *Nothing will stop me.*

"You can say it, Trin," she mumbled as sleep pushed at the edges of her consciousness.

The typing stopped. Josie's body jostled as her sister moved —on or off the bed, she couldn't tell. Her eyelids were too heavy to open. A blanket settled over her. Trinity's fingers were featherlight as she tucked it around Josie's shoulders. With a sigh, she said, "Fine. Lila's saying is kind of badass. All this time, I thought there wasn't a single thing that vile bitch said or did in her life that could be considered remotely positive—besides dying—but I like that saying. Ugh. It feels so wrong to admit that."

"It's fine," Josie said. Sleep was dragging her under fast. "We'll make it ours. Steal it from Lila the way she stole everything from us."

Because the days of Lila Jensen taking things from Josie, even from beyond the grave, were over.

THIRTY-SIX

Josie watched Trout sniff his way around the perimeter of Gretchen's yard, carefully inspecting every inch of ground he'd already smelled and analyzed countless times since their arrival. The morning sun warmed her where she stood. Steam drifted from the mug of coffee in her hand. Voices floated through the screen door that led into the kitchen. The usual suspects. Josie's family. Noah's siblings. Paula. Josie had heard Gretchen somewhere in the house but hadn't seen her yet.

"Any word?" asked Christian.

"Nothing," Paula replied. "But it's all over the news."

"That doesn't seem to be helping," complained Noah's sister, Laura.

"Maybe it will," his brother, Theo, said. "If the right person sees his photo, maybe they'll call in a tip."

Josie sipped at her coffee. She'd slept about four hours and she didn't feel much more rested than she had when she fell asleep. Despite that, her body clamored for a run, for her to push its limits until she was reduced to a sweaty, boneless heap, until there was only room in her psyche for breathing. Just for a few minutes. Anything to quiet the endless thoughts and questions spinning through her brain like an E5 tornado. To drive out the sense of dread skulking in the dark corners of her mind. To exhaust some of the quiet rage simmering in her blood, bringing her closer to going supernova with each hour that passed without any developments.

Thirty-five hours.

Where was he?

It didn't matter. She was coming for him. God help anyone who stood in her way. She'd been shut out of the official investigation, and now the Gina Phelan case, but she'd carve out her own path to Noah. Using the Lila connection.

"Psst." Trinity opened the wooden gate that led to the driveway and stepped into the yard. "You ready to do this?"

The conversation in the kitchen faded, as if everyone had stepped into another room. Josie tapped against where her phone bulged from the back pocket of her jeans. "I talked to the superintendent at Muncy a half hour ago. She agreed to let me meet with Roe Hoyt later this afternoon."

"Oh my God!" Trinity whisper-shouted. "That's great. Did she ask for paperwork? A case name?"

Josie shook her head and downed the rest of her coffee. "No."

Trout waddled over to her sister, wiggling his little body against her shins until she knelt to pet him. "Perfect! Let's go."

Josie frowned, appraising Trinity. There was a familiar fire in her eyes. It was the look of a hungry predator just before it went in for the kill—a kill it was going to savor. "It's too early to leave. What are you not telling me?"

Trinity scratched behind one of Trout's ears and he leaned in to her touch. "I found Eva Owens. She's alive and well and can't wait to talk with us. Even better, she lives close to the prison in Muncy."

Trinity was already gone when Josie woke up, so this was

the first she was hearing about the search for the only approved visitor on Roe Hoyt's list back in the early seventies.

"Who is she to Roe?" Josie asked.

From inside the house came footsteps, rustling, the sound of cabinets opening and closing. The kitchen was filling back up. People spoke. Josie only caught fragments but could deduce that someone had dropped off some kind of food. Paula said something about plates.

"Probably the best way to describe it is that she's an advocate for Roe. Eva Owens joined the Pennsylvania Prison Volunteer Association in 1969 as a volunteer. That's how they met. All she would tell me over the phone was that when she first started volunteering at Muncy, Roe was the only inmate who had absolutely no friends or family to visit or write or check on her. Once Roe's appeal was denied and her attorney was no longer needed, she didn't even have him. Roe wasn't able to speak for herself, so Eva took it upon herself to make sure she received proper medical care and any services available to her."

"How long did she do that?"

Trinity's eyes blazed. "Over fifty years. She's still doing it."

"What did you tell her about why we want to meet with her?"

"The truth. That we knew Roe's only surviving child. That she was called Lila Jensen. I told her all the things Lila had done to you, to our family. What she did to us is already out there for public consumption. Eva hadn't seen the *Dateline* episodes. Doesn't watch much television, evidently. I told her that before Lila died, she wanted you to find Roe Hoyt but you didn't because you weren't in a good place emotionally."

"Did you tell her why I'm interested now?"

"Of course. I also told her that from the standpoint of a journalist, Roe Hoyt's story was of great interest to me."

Josie groaned. "Trin, I know you're interested in this as a story. I don't blame you, but Noah—"

Trinity's glare dried up the words on the tip of Josie's tongue. "Everything I'm doing is for Noah. Truth? Yes, Roe Hoyt's case is fascinating. It would make for great television or even a book. There's no sense in lying about that. You know me too well. But I'm not pursuing her story. I just need Eva Owens to think I am so she'll talk to us. She wasn't receptive to talking to a police detective or even to Lila's kidnap victim—once she found out how evil Lila was—but when I told her what I do, she changed her tune completely. You wanted to know about Roe Hoyt. This is the best way in."

"Okay," Josie said.

She wasn't exactly sure what she hoped to find out from Eva Owens, but her sister had gone to great lengths to set up a meeting. Besides, if Roe Hoyt's communication skills hadn't improved since her arrest, Eva Owens would be the best source of information. Without an official case to link to Roe, Josie couldn't request her prison records. She was lucky the superintendent hadn't asked any questions when she requested the visit.

Before Josie could say anything more, the sound of Laura's strident voice came through the screen door. "Shouldn't there be some kind of press conference? It seems like we should be making a public plea of some kind."

"I'm not sure whose call that would be," Paula answered.

Trinity continued to stroke between Trout's ears, her head canted to the side as she listened.

"I don't see what's stopping us," Laura huffed.

Theo sighed. "His wife should be making that kind of decision."

Josie could practically hear Laura roll her eyes. "Then maybe it's best she doesn't do it."

"What's that supposed to mean?" said Shannon, on the defensive.

Trinity frowned. Trout looked back and forth between the

two of them, ears pointed. He was keying in to the tension now radiating from Josie's body.

"Josie does great on television when she's doing the whole cop thing but she's not exactly warm."

"Because she's usually talking about killers and kidnappers. Heinous crimes," Paula said. "Her affect is completely appropriate in that circumstance."

"Josie's warm," Christian said. "You just don't know her that well."

"She's married to my little brother," Laura said. "And she's been a robot since we got here—when we've seen her. What was she even doing yesterday? Just out driving around?"

Trinity glowered. "Didn't you save this bitch and her baby from being murdered?"

"Yeah." Josie pinched the bridge of her nose between her thumb and forefinger. A headache started to pulse behind her eyes. She couldn't even imagine cracking the seal on her tightly bottled emotions right now for the public to see, but she'd do it for Noah if Heather's team thought it would help. "But Laura's never liked me very much. The important thing is that she's protective of Noah."

Folding her arms across her chest, Trinity started toward the steps. "Well, I'm going to give her a piece of my mind."

"Trin."

As much as Josie would love to see that—or do it herself—starting a war with Noah's sister wouldn't be good for him or anyone.

Gretchen's voice cut through everything, freezing Trinity in place. "It's not really anyone's business how Josie deals with the fact that her husband is missing—or where she goes or what she does while she's trying to navigate this situation. If the lead investigator on the case thinks a public plea will be helpful, they'll ask. There are some situations where it might not be beneficial."

Meaning if Noah had been abducted by men who were chasing someone down for money and had no compunction about kidnapping a law enforcement officer, no public plea, no matter how emotional, was going to convince them to return him alive. If he was still alive at all.

Her brain pushed the thought away immediately.

Laura didn't know any of that.

"Criticizing Noah's wife right now is not only counterproductive," Gretchen added icily, "it's not welcome in my home. If you're not here to support Josie, then you can get out."

No more discussion came from the kitchen. Trinity sighed. Then she walked over and took the coffee mug from Josie's hand. "I'll take Trout inside. Meet me at my car."

Josie didn't bother to ask what her sister would tell the others as to why they'd be MIA today as well. Instead, she peppered Trout's face with kisses, assured him she'd be back as soon as possible, and slipped out of the yard to go find Trinity's vehicle.

THIRTY-SEVEN

Eva Owens waited for them on her front porch, smiling brightly as Josie and Trinity made their way up her front walk. The exterior of her single-story brick home was festively adorned with Halloween decorations. The jack-o'-lanterns lining the steps were intricately carved, reminding Josie of Dex's creations, though not nearly as breathtaking. Eva caught her looking at them.

"I know Halloween is next month, but it's my favorite time of year! I like to get started early. My granddaughter did those for me. She's a teenager now but still comes over and carves them just to make Nana happy."

"They're awesome," Trinity and Josie said at the same time.

Eva laughed, brown eyes twinkling. She was slight, probably over eighty, with thick, short white hair. One of her hands rested on the handle of a cane while the other extended toward them. Josie shook first.

"Twins," Eva said. "You must be the detective."

Josie nodded. They were identical twins and both wearing jeans and sweatshirts, yet, anyone who looked at them could immediately tell that Trinity was the television personality.

Even without the added stress of her husband being missing, Josie had perfected the insomniac, workaholic police officer vibe.

Eva shook Trinity's hand. "The reporter. Come on in."

Sunlight bathed the small living room. Plants sat on every table and windowsill. Piles of paperback books stood in columns beside the couch and recliner as well as along the walls. No television. A wrought-iron plant stand was tucked into one corner. On its surface was a small tabletop fountain that trickled water over faux rocks. The steady sound filled the otherwise silent space.

Josie and Trinity sat side by side on the couch while Eva settled into her recliner. "I'm so sorry for all that your family has been through," she said. "It broke my heart to learn that Roe's little girl turned out... the way she did. For so long, I wondered what became of her. My hope was that she had had a good life. That might have made up for all the tragedy, but life doesn't work like that, does it? It was naive of me to think that way. Anyway, I'm glad you're here. I've tried to draw attention to Roe's case for years. We're both getting up there in age. Time is running out."

Josie's phone chirped. She'd spent the ninety-minute drive to Eva's house answering texts. Tilly Phelan had called her again. She'd let the call go to voicemail and then proceeded to pester Turner, instructing him to call the poor woman back. Then she demanded information about the Gina Phelan case. She knew she had no right to request it, but her control was already in tatters.

"Do you have to get that, dear?" asked Eva.

Josie smiled apologetically. Her heart raced as she punched in her passcode, wondering if it was news about Noah. Then she realized if Heather had anything to report, she'd call instead of text. Josie's pulse slowed as she saw a message from Turner.

Five texts in an hour constitutes harassment.

With a sigh, she tapped out a quick response. *It was 90 minutes. Call Tilly Phelan. Then tell me what I want to know and I'll stop.*

"Sorry," she mumbled to Eva.

Eva waved a hand toward her. "Don't worry. I imagine both of you have urgent things to tend to most of the time."

Trinity rested her hands on her thighs and leaned forward. "Why did you want to bring attention to Roe's case?"

Probably for the same reasons Trinity was so interested in it, even without the Lila connection. Roe's origins were completely unknown, not to mention the identity of the man—or men— who'd fathered her children.

Eva pursed her lips momentarily, considering her words. "I'm getting ahead of myself. Let me start by saying that I don't, in any way, condone what Roe did. I have always believed she should be held accountable for her crimes, and she is serving her time."

Another text from Turner arrived. Josie read it as surreptitiously as she could.

I already called her. Oh, and FYI, you're off the Phelan case. Or did you forget?

"We understand," Trinity told Eva.

Josie pressed her lips tightly together so she didn't curse out loud.

What happened to the guy who doesn't care about getting in trouble?

Got Gina P's phone records. No red flags.

What about calls the day she died?

Really, Quinn?

Josie was aware by the silence in the room that both Trinity and Eva were waiting for her. Luckily, Turner answered without any further coaxing.

About an hour before she was killed, she made 2 calls to an old law school friend who's a DA in Montgomery County. They didn't talk. She left two messages asking the friend to call back. The Phelans think she was preparing for criminal charges in the quarterback case.

With a tight smile, Josie said, "I'm sorry, just a second."

That's all you've got?

Call me later, sweetheart.

That meant he'd found something else and was willing to share it.

Her thumbs typed the words "thank you," even though she really didn't want to give Turner another reason to gloat, but before she could hit send, a new message from him popped up.

Happy?

She erased the "thank you" and replied, *No.*

Shocking. Don't you have something to do besides harass me?

Josie smiled, which felt weird and unsettling. Turner was helping her while still being every bit the asshole she'd come to know and detest. In fact, his infuriating douchebaggery was the only thing in her life that was the same as it had been before Noah was abducted. In a strange and twisted way, it was comforting. This one last vestige of normalcy made it easier for her to hold onto the conviction that Noah's absence was only a temporary crisis. Soon, she'd get him back. She'd put their lives back together.

She texted, *Piss off* along with a smiley face.

Then she put her phone away. "I'm sorry, Mrs. Owens. You were saying you wanted to bring attention to Roe Hoyt's case?"

Eva's smile was strained. The wrinkles at the corners of her eyes deepened. "I want to bring attention to Roe's case because I've always felt that there was so much more to it that got brushed aside in the rush to put her away."

"What do you mean?" asked Josie. "Are you suggesting that she didn't kill those infants?"

Sadness pooled in Eva's eyes. "Oh no. She did it. From what your sister told me this morning, you know quite a bit about the case."

"Only up to the trial," Josie explained.

"Then you know that when she was found, she had an old head injury. That's what caused her aphasia and the tremors in her right hand."

"Have any of the doctors she's seen over the years looked more closely at her head injury?" Trinity asked. "Beyond X-rays?"

"Yes," said Eva. "I saw to it that she had both an MRI and a CT scan when those became available. Those confirmed an injury to her frontal lobe that had caused the tremors and also affected her brain's language centers. Unfortunately, with an injury that causes aphasia, the first year afterward is the most critical in terms of getting treatment. Because of neuroplasticity. That initial time period is when you have the greatest chance of making some kind of recovery. Roe never had that. We don't even know when it occurred. I was only nineteen when I started volunteering at the prison. She was, hands down, the most troublesome and volatile inmate. At first, all volunteers were told we couldn't get near her, for our own safety. But I..."

Her eyes grew glassy as she drifted off. She turned her head toward the fountain. Josie had the sense that she was no longer in the room with them at all. After a long silence, she blinked, shifted in her chair, and returned her focus to them. "Volunteers were restricted to the program area but from the windows, I kept seeing Roe all alone outside during her recreation time, always curled up on the ground. She was unkempt. Any time a guard came to collect her she'd snarl at them, but in her quiet moments, I could tell she was bewildered. Afraid. I knew what she had done but the more I observed her, the more I wondered about what exactly was going on in her head."

"You were curious," Josie said.

"Yes." Eva blew out a long breath, as if it had taken a lot to admit that. "I just wanted to understand where she came from, why she was the way she was, and what would drive her to commit such horrific crimes. She had no family, no friends. As a volunteer, one of my responsibilities was to advocate for inmates who had no one to help them. I wanted to do that for Roe. It gave me a way in, a way to learn more about her."

"The prison let you?" asked Trinity. "Let you get close to her?"

Eva laughed. "Oh no. Not at first. It took a very long time before they'd let me into a visitor's room with her. For months, we were on opposite sides of a glass partition, but it was impossible to communicate with her. I don't believe she ever learned to read before she was incarcerated. With the areas of her brain that are compromised, she hasn't been able to learn, so writing isn't a possibility at all. They did allow her to draw—crayons only because she would stab with pens or pencils—but I never understood her pictures. The tremor made it difficult to figure out what she was trying to get across. Stick figures, I recognized. Always two."

"One small and one large?" asked Josie.

Eva's eyes widened in surprise. "Yes. How did you know?"

"There was a drawing in the file I have. They were standing next to one another."

"That's right, although sometimes the small one was on its side."

"Did she ever draw anything besides the figures?"

"She drew shapes around them, all sizes, above or next to them. At least, I thought that's what they were. Some were hard to identify but from what I could tell, she tried to draw squares, rectangles, and triangles. Her hand would twitch so badly, she often couldn't draw straight lines, so I was left guessing as to what each thing represented. I would say, 'is that the shack where you lived?' 'Is that a tree? A rock?' and of course all she could say was, 'Roe,' so she'd point and repeat her name over and over. Then she would cry when I couldn't understand what she was telling me. We gave up on that after a while."

"That's so sad," Trinity said.

"It is," Eva agreed. "Anyway, I finally convinced the prison to let me meet with her in a regular room. They reluctantly allowed it only because Roe had never been agitated with me. But then..." she pointed to a thin silver scar that went from her left nostril to the top of her upper lip, "she got me good."

Trinity's eyes widened. "You went back?"

Eva shrugged. "I probably had some kind of hero complex but I'm also stubborn. The bigger the challenge, the more I want to tackle it. The best way to get me to do anything is to tell me I can't do it."

Trinity's elbow poked at Josie's ribs. "Oh yeah, I know someone like that, too."

Eva flashed a brief smile. "We went back to meeting with glass between us for years before we were allowed to meet without it again. I think that, to Roe, everyone she'd ever met had either hurt her or tried to hurt her. When she realized I wasn't there for that, she started to trust me. It was a very slow process. I did what I could for her. Her communication skills have only marginally improved since we first met back in 1970, but to get back to your original question, she admitted to me, in the only way she could, that she killed her children."

THIRTY-EIGHT

Josie could feel the excitement rolling off her sister's body. "You *are* able to communicate with her?" said Trinity.

"Yes," Eva answered. "But you must understand, it's extremely limited, given her deficits. She can nod or shake her head to yes or no questions. She can make certain gestures. I lobbied for the use of assistive devices once that technology became available, but Roe gets frustrated very easily and when that happens, even with all the medication the doctors have her on, she becomes violent."

Josie thought of the conflicting medical reports in Roe's file. "She knows what's going on around her? Her mind is fully intact?"

Eva gave another pained smile. "She is most definitely aware of everything happening around her. She understands a lot of things though it's impossible to know just how much."

Trinity said, "What kind of assistive devices has she tried?"

A small laugh bubbled up from Eva's chest. "Oh my. Almost all of them. Well, an alphabet board was out of the question as was anything that depended on her being able to read. She did okay with rating scales—to communicate her preferences and pain. We tried a number of different apps when those became available, all of them reliant on images rather than words. For example, with one app, she could scroll through a whole host of drawings or pictures and if she pressed on one, it would say the name of the object pictured. Table, chair, bowl, tree... basic things. One of the speech pathologists told me that there were similar image-based apps that would allow her to express more complex thoughts as she grew more skilled with them, but we never got that far."

"Because she got frustrated," Josie said.

Eva nodded. "I really think she has it in her to make good use of many of those assistive apps. I'm not sure why she loses her temper so easily. The new technology, maybe? Who knows."

"What exactly happened when she tried them?" Josie asked even though none of this was going to lead to some trail of obscure clues that would result in finding Noah.

"It always starts out well. She scrolls through the pictures, pushing some of them, trying things out. Then, at some point, she just... it's like she's looking for a particular picture and can't find it. She becomes frantic, scrolling faster, aggressively, and she starts screaming her own name over and over. The next thing we know, she's smashing the tablet to pieces against the table or the nearest wall. I suggested using a booklet instead, but the same thing happened, and she just started tearing the pages out and throwing them everywhere."

"Is her name the only thing she can say?" asked Trinity.

"She can make other sounds but nothing coherent. It often seems like she's trying to say words, but they never come."

"What is it exactly about her case that you think was brushed under the carpet?" Josie asked, bringing the conversation back to where Eva started.

"Roe Hoyt exists without context. We know virtually nothing about what kind of home life she had before she was on that mountain. We don't even know her real name! It probably sounds stupid, but I wish I could find out. One day, before one of us passes away—'cause we're not getting any younger—I'd love to walk into the meeting room and call her by her real name. The one she had as a girl before... all this."

"That doesn't sound stupid at all," Trinity said softly.

"She's able to answer yes or no questions," Josie said. "Did you ever ask her about her family? Did she know her mother? Did she know her father? Was he the one who taught her to trap? Did she have siblings? Did someone in her home hurt her? Was it her father? Was it someone else? A brother? A neighbor? Did she go to the shack herself? Did someone leave her there? Was someone helping her? Did she know the person who impregnated her? Was it more than one man? Were any of the encounters consensual?"

She stopped her rapid-fire questioning when she noticed both Eva's and Trinity's mouths hanging open. But the last question blared in her mind, unspoken.

Did she let Lila live because there was something different about her?

"Sorry," Josie said. "It just seems that you could still get a great deal of information from her with simple yes or no answers."

Slowly, Eva nodded, studying Josie with a curious look on her face. "You're right. Over the years, I managed to get answers to many of my questions. The same ones you just asked—well, except for the trapping. I don't know anything about that. She didn't know her mother, but she knew her father. No siblings. Her father hurt her. She went to the shack herself. I asked her if she had been there with her father before and she said yes."

Which meant that her father had been a trapper and a hunter—like practically every other man in that area—and she'd learned some skills from him that enabled her to survive. She must have had a lot of outdoors experience to know how to find the shack on her own.

"She never went to school," Eva continued. "The others, she wouldn't answer. Whether someone helped her and all the questions about the pregnancies. I'm not sure if she wouldn't answer because she was embarrassed or because she couldn't grasp what I was asking her."

Trinity frowned. "What do you mean, couldn't grasp it?"

Eva arched a brow. "My dear, who told you about how babies are made?"

Josie and Trinity stared at her in silence before they both realized it was a serious question. They exchanged a glance and Trinity laughed nervously. "Um, my mom. High school health class."

"Other girls," Josie put in. "Also health class."

She didn't mention the fact that Lila had frequently engaged in sex with slimy, lecherous men in the living room of their trailer with no care at all as to whether Josie witnessed it.

Eva laughed. "In my generation, if you didn't learn about it from other girls at school—the ones mothers referred to as 'loose' and forbade you from hanging out with—you didn't learn about it at all. Thanks to Kathy Glander, I didn't get the shock of my life on my wedding night."

"Roe was isolated. If she didn't go to school, she only saw her father," Josie said.

"Yes," said Eva. "I don't think she ever understood what was happening to her or to her body. All she knew—at least with her father—was that it hurt."

Trinity said, "She must have grown up thinking that it was normal for men to hurt her in that way. There was no such thing as consent. It was just a fact of life."

"So when she came across other men," Josie said, "she wasn't prepared to tell them no. That would explain why she couldn't answer your question as to whether the encounters were consensual or not."

Eva nodded. "I tried to explain things to her. Gave her an anatomy lesson, talked to her about sexual assault. She shut down. I think she did grasp what I told her—and what it meant —and that it deeply upset her. Her father hurt her, and I don't believe that her pregnancies were the result of consensual encounters. How can you consent when you don't understand what's happening and you don't know that you can say no? Listen, nothing can excuse what she did, but we have no idea what drove her to such a dark place. We have no idea if she truly understood the full gravity of her actions. How can you look at the sickening facts of the case and not want the complete story? Those babies certainly deserve a full accounting of everything that led to their terrible ends."

"You want to fill in the blanks," Trinity said.

"Yes," Eva sighed. "I think that Roe feels... remorse. I asked her if she was sorry for what she did and she answered yes. I asked her if she wished she could take it back and she answered yes. As she gets older, I think it bothers her more and more. She cries a lot. Sometimes, she simulates holding a baby in her arms, like she's rocking it to sleep, and she just wails. It's a dreadful sound."

THIRTY-NINE

A chill ran up Josie's spine. Goosebumps erupted all over her skin, despite the fact that her extremities were covered.

"That's more than Lila Jensen ever felt," Trinity remarked.

That was true. Lila was incapable of feeling remorse. Or any human emotion that might have put the brakes on her boundless cruelty.

Eva folded her hands in her lap. "It just bothers me that even with as much as I've been able to learn from Roe, there are so many unanswered questions. It's enough to drive a person mad. I'd like to know where she came from and her father's identity. Really, anyone who hurt her should have been held accountable too."

Men being held accountable for hurting women was challenging in the present day. Josie couldn't imagine how low-priority it would have been back when Roe was arrested. She wouldn't have been able to testify against anyone who had harmed her.

Men.

In the recesses of Josie's mind, a theory took form, pushing its way forward.

"Lila was a girl," she blurted.

Eva and Trinity stilled, waiting for her to say more.

"What if the other children were boys?" Josie said. "Roe might not have understood what sex was or what it meant but she would have known there were differences in anatomy— particularly if she was abused. She would have seen it with her own eyes. If we're right about the things that happened to her, then the one thing she knew without a doubt was that men hurt people."

Trinity sucked in a breath. "You think she let Lila live because she was a girl?"

"By the time the remains were found, the sexes of the babies couldn't be determined," said Eva. "Not back then, anyway. It's possible that you're correct."

Josie and Trinity shuddered at the same time.

"To think," Eva said in disgust. "Her father started a chain reaction with his abhorrent abuse. I'd like to know his name just so I could drag it through the mud!"

"Have you ever tried having her do one of those mail-in DNA tests to try to trace her genealogy?" asked Trinity.

"I've wanted to but the superintendent claims I need a court order and since there's no urgent or pressing legal need for her to take the test, the prison won't allow it. Plus, there is the challenge of getting Roe to do it. I'd need her permission, which means she'd need to understand what I hoped to accomplish by having her do it. I've brought up the idea with her several times and she doesn't seem to grasp it at all. I thought if I could get her to do an at-home DNA test, I could trace her roots that way."

Lila carried Roe's DNA but even if she was still alive, she'd be in prison, subject to the restrictions Eva had mentioned. There would have been no getting a test from her either. Josie wasn't sure it mattered. Given Roe's advanced age, her parents were already dead. If any descendants of their distant relatives were alive today, linking Roe to them would depend entirely on whether any of them had also submitted a mail-in DNA test to one of the many genealogy sites. Josie understood Eva's need to discover Roe's actual name. She also understood Eva's curiosity, shared it even, but at this late stage of Roe's life, finding relatives wouldn't answer the most burning question they all had, which was how she had come to live in the shack in the mountains.

Eva went on, "About fifteen years ago, a reporter contacted the prison and asked to interview Roe. We met for coffee. She said she'd read about the case while looking through old newspapers and wanted to do a story on Roe. After I talked with Roe, she agreed to put the reporter on her approved visitors list so they could meet."

"What happened?" asked Josie.

"I don't know. She went to the prison once. I have no idea what happened during the meeting, but I never heard from her again. Her number was disconnected. Couldn't find her on the internet either although I suppose I should have looked her up when she first tried to contact Roe."

The scar on the side of Josie's face tingled. "What was her name?"

Lila had always used aliases. Josie hadn't known her real name until she was finally arrested. She didn't know all of the aliases Lila had ever used but the two she was aware of had the same initials, B.R.

Belinda Rose and Barbara Rhodes.

Maybe those initials were Lila's calling card, her signature.

"Bea Rowe," Eva answered.

"Can you spell her last name?" Trinity asked, phone in hand, browser open.

"R-o-w-e."

Rowe. Roe.

Josie was probably the only person who knew Lila well enough to see the connections, to follow the crumbs she'd left behind. Her heartbeat sped up, then seemed to skip before racing again. Despite the fact that she'd only been subjected to Lila for the first fourteen years of her life, she might be the one person on the planet who understood Lila best. That was as much from her years living with Lila as it was from all the time spent honing her skills as a detective.

An image of Lila sitting on the other side of the thick prison glass flashed through Josie's mind. Standing up, blowing her hot, moist breath against the glass so she could write Roe Hoyt's inmate number in the condensation. Josie had wanted to know where she came from.

I'll tell you what, JoJo. You're a detective, right? I'll give you a clue. You figure it out before I die, and I'll give you those names.

What if it had never been about giving Josie the names of her accomplices? Josie hadn't believed for a hot second that Lila would disclose them, which was part of the reason she hadn't followed up. Only a fool would trust Lila Jensen to keep a promise. But what if Lila hadn't been trying to one-up her in terms of whose childhood was worse?

Lila had known her end was near. Not only was she in prison but she had stage four ovarian cancer. What if there was something Lila had wanted Josie to piece together? She could have simply told her outright but that wasn't Lila's style. For decades, Josie had been the bane of her existence, the object of her fathomless hatred. There was no way she'd pass up an opportunity to screw with Josie, no matter what the stakes were. She enjoyed taunting her too much to make things easy. She wanted Josie to work for every piece of information.

What had Lila wanted her to figure out? Most importantly, would it somehow help her find Noah? She had to believe that it would. If his abduction was a result of someone searching for Lila's trophy case of carnage, there had to be something in Lila's past that would give them the lead they needed to find him.

Even though the box was now missing crucial items, Josie had to believe she could still piece together Lila's puzzle.

She needed this.

"What media outlet did Bea Rowe say she was with?" Trinity asked.

"Oh," said Eva. "She said she was freelancing but she had a lot of connections and wouldn't have any issues getting it published."

Trinity closed the internet browser on her phone. She locked eyes with Josie for a brief moment and Josie could feel their wispy twin telepathy working. There was no reporter by that name. Until this morning, Eva hadn't even known about Lila. Josie doubted she'd taken to the internet to find out more information before they arrived.

"Show her the photos," said Josie.

During the night, Trinity had tracked down the only two photos of Lila Jensen that they'd been able to find. One, Dex had given Josie seven years ago. He'd kept it from when he lived with them. In it, Lila and thirteen-year-old Josie stood side by side outside their trailer. Lila was very young and still strikingly beautiful, slender but shapely, her long, silky black hair cascading over her shoulders. Her thin face showcased piercing blue eyes and high cheekbones. Men had always found it difficult to resist her. The second photo was her mug shot. In it, she was barely recognizable as the same person. Puffy cheeks swallowed her eyes. Weight gain had stretched her skin taut. Her black hair had turned white and brittle. The contrast was stark.

Trinity had created a digital photo that put them side by side, cropping Josie out of the older one. She turned her phone screen toward Eva. "Any chance Bea Rowe looked like this?"

Eva gasped, pointing an arthritic finger at younger Lila. "That's her, isn't it? Roe's daughter. My God, they look... almost exactly the same. Not now, of course, but when I first met Roe. The hair is different but everything else... Wow." She turned her attention to the mug shot. "This woman—she looks a bit like Bea Rowe except Bea was younger, not so sickly. Do you know her?"

A sad smile stretched across Trinity's face. "I'm sorry to tell you this, Mrs. Owens. That's also Roe's daughter, just several years older."

FORTY

The chill that had enveloped Josie in Eva Owens's living room returned as she stared into the wary, penetrating blue eyes of Roe Hoyt. The cold prickled along every inch of her body. They were Lila's eyes, alert, aware, *intelligent*. They lacked Lila's signature malice, but they were still familiar enough to unleash a barrage of disturbing memories. Josie's scar tingled again. Without her permission, her fingers reached up to rub at the thin, silvered line. Josie wondered what Lila had seen when she sat across from her mother, finally, posing as a reporter. Had Lila told her the truth? Prisons kept recordings of all inmate visits, but Josie wasn't sure for how long.

From the corner of the room, a female corrections officer watched, unable to mask her obvious boredom. Josie had been shocked when she was ushered into a private meeting room usually reserved for when inmates met with their legal counsel. She had expected a non-contact visit with glass separating them.

"She won't hurt you," the guard had said as Roe shuffled over and sat down across the table from Josie.

It seemed like a bold assumption given all Josie had read

about Roe and everything Eva had told them, but looking at her now, Josie believed the guard. Roe's hands and feet were shackled but her body was thin. So thin she looked like a gust of air would knock her down. Crepey skin stretched across her skeletal face and gathered in delicate folds at her neck. Like Lila, her hair had turned completely white, but it was still thick and straight, cascading down her back.

She seemed so inconsequential, so non-threatening. Then again, sometimes the worst murderers were nothing like one expected.

"Miss Hoyt," Josie said. "Thank you for seeing me. My name is Detective Josie Quinn. I work for the Denton Police Department. About two hours from here."

No response. The fingers of her right hand twitched.

"I've just come from speaking with Eva Owens."

A flicker of recognition flashed through her eyes. Her entire face brightened. Eva was right. They definitely had a connection. She was probably the only person Roe had ever encountered who had shown her, if not kindness, civility.

Josie took a deep breath, wondering where to start. She hadn't thought this through. She'd been too focused on driving forward, plowing through the day, doing anything at all to keep her heart from breaking out of its protective shell while she combed through Lila's past in the hopes that something would lead her to Noah. She'd spent the drive to the prison calling Turner and getting his voicemail instead of thinking about what she'd say when she got here.

Thirty-nine hours.

Evidently, Roe grew bored with her silence. The metal of her handcuffs clinked as she awkwardly simulated rocking an infant in her arms, just like Eva described. She dipped her head toward the empty space. Josie wasn't sure if she was lost in memory or if this was some kind of self-soothing behavior. Either way, the creepiness of the tableau brought the fine hairs at the nape of her neck to standing. A stinging sensation sliced down the side of her face, tracing her scar.

She wished Trinity was here but there was no way to make that happen. Besides, Josie knew this was a demon she had to face alone. She was finished running. Finished stuffing the echoes of Lila's imprint on her life into bins and ignoring them. Finished being at the mercy of those old traumas. She would never be completely free of them, but she refused to be cowed by them. Not now. She had a husband to find. No amount of emotional baggage was going to stand in her way. She'd sit across from a thousand murderers while her skin crawled if that's what it took to get to Noah.

"Roe," Josie said. "I knew your little girl. The one—" She broke off, considering how to phrase it. The one you didn't kill? The one who survived?

But she didn't need to finish. Roe's eyes grew wide and filled with tears. Her hands slid across the table, the right one shaking badly, causing the handcuffs to clank against the surface. The guard said, "No touching, Roe. You know that."

Roe froze. Her lips opened and closed. It took Josie a moment to realize she was trying to form a word. It was difficult to watch her struggle. The way her lips almost puckered, flapping against each other, made Josie think whatever she was trying to say began with a P.

"Please?" Josie said. "Are you trying to say please?"

Roe nodded her head vigorously. Her blue eyes filled with something that made Josie's heart pinch. Hope. Had she really waited decades for news of her one surviving child? Did she care? It seemed strange that she did, given what she'd done. Then again, she'd let Lila live.

It seemed Lila hadn't revealed her identity when she met with Roe.

Josie grimaced. She'd told Eva that she intended to see Roe and asked her just how much to tell her about Lila—if anything at all. Without hesitation, Eva insisted Josie tell her everything.

So she did.

Other than the uncontrollable movements of her right hand, Roe hardly moved while Josie matter-of-factly told her everything that she knew about Lila. All her crimes. All her acts of savagery. Josie recited the details without emotion, like a clinician in a research lab presenting her findings without assigning any meaning to them. Tears rolled slowly down Roe's face. Josie watched the storm raging in her eyes. Were they more expressive because she couldn't speak, or was she imagining that? When Josie told her that Lila was dead, they filled with something she had never seen in the depths of Lila's eyes. It was so jarring, a gasp nearly escaped Josie's lips.

Sorrow. Deep sorrow.

Then Roe's mouth worked again, trying to form another word. This time, her lips rolled together before popping open. "Buh." A puff of air. No, a word starting with B.

"Baby?" Josie said.

Roe shook her head and dragged her hands to her chest, beating against it. Each time she tried to say the word, her brows furrowed, face crumpling just a little, like she was in pain. "Buh. Roe, buh."

Josie's stomach felt strange, weightless. "You're trying to say bad."

An energetic nod.

"Bad like you."

Her nod became more subdued.

The next question flew out of Josie's mouth before she could stop it. "Are you sorry?"

Shit. She wasn't here for this. It didn't matter. Nothing could be undone. The damage was irrevocable. The scars permanent.

Roe nodded solemnly, pressing her clenched fists to her chest.

Josie felt her control slipping. Fury slithering through the cracks of her mental shell, tendrils spreading, looking for vulnerable places to root. "Sorry for what she did?" Her voice vibrated with anger. She was aware of the guard's curious eyes on her, but she was beyond caring.

Roe nodded.

"Or are you sorry that you let her live?"

FORTY-ONE

The words, so inappropriate, coated with bitterness, left a strange feeling of relief in their wake. Something hard and impenetrable inside her dissolved, evanescing in a way that almost felt blissful. It was one of those things you didn't even know you felt until it was gone.

Roe stared at her with an odd look in her eyes but she neither nodded nor shook her head.

"Why?" Josie said quietly, still spinning out, unable to stop herself from asking things she knew she shouldn't. "Why the others and not Lila?"

A look of confusion crossed Roe's face.

Yes or no questions, Josie reminded herself.

"Did you kill the other babies because they were boys?"

No response, just that odd, indecipherable look again.

"Did you let Lila live because she was a girl?"

Nothing but the jangle of the cuffs as her right hand shook.

"Because you thought boys would grow up to be a threat, but a girl wouldn't?"

Josie wondered whether Roe was refusing to answer or if she failed to understand the line of questioning. It didn't matter.

Knowing why Lila had survived when her siblings hadn't wouldn't change one damn thing. It was an endless hamster wheel of searching behavior. As if she could undo years of suffering just by finding one shining piece of information that made everything that had happened to her make sense. That wasn't how life worked.

Sometimes, bad things just happened.

Roe's lips formed a circle. An "uh" sound came from her throat. This was an easy one.

"You're trying to say something that starts with O."

This was met with confusion. Then Josie remembered she couldn't read. She knew the word she was trying to say but not how it was spelled. Josie made an "oh" noise. Roe shook her head and tried to form the word again, this time opening her mouth wider. "Uh."

Josie repeated it and was rewarded with an empathic nod. Her earlier guesses had come as much from the context of their conversation as from the shapes Roe's mouth made. This time, she had no idea what the word could be.

Roe lifted her hands and pointed to the guard and then to Josie. "Uh, uh, uh."

The tip of her tongue touched the roof of her mouth, as if she was trying to add to the first sound, but nothing came. Again, she indicated the guard and Josie. Then she brought her hands to her chest and shook her head. Josie watched as she alternated between the two gestures, pushing out the "uh" sound when she came to Josie and the guard. She attempted the second part again, tongue pressed against the roof of her mouth, just behind her front teeth. This time, a "th" noise came out. Air hissed around the sides of her tongue. Spittle flew onto the table.

Josie tried to put the two sounds together with Roe's gestures. Indicating Josie and the guard. Fisting her hands at her chest and shaking her head. "Us three?"

Immediately, Josie felt stupid. The question was if Roe had killed her other children because they were boys and she believed they would grow up to be threats. What did the three of them in this room have to do with anything?

Face flushing, Roe shook her head violently. She repeated the sounds, the motions. Again and again.

"I'm sorry," Josie said. "I don't know what you're trying to say."

Roe slumped in her chair, head lolling against her chest in defeat.

"Try again," Josie told her. "Is there another way that you can... show me what you're trying to tell me?"

Roe's arms returned to the cradling position, rocking and rocking. This time, she looked from the invisible infant to the clock high on the wall to their right. Slowly, she brought her hands up, angled toward the clock. Then she arced them down toward where the crook of her left elbow had been. "Roe," she said. "Roe."

She repeated the pattern. Cradling, pointing to the clock, slashing downward, repeating her name. More tears spilled down her cheeks. Her tremor grew worse. Was the downward motion supposed to represent her bringing a blunt object down on the child's head? But what did the clock have to do with anything?

"Is that how you did it?" Josie asked.

No response, just a repeat of the gestures, her movements becoming jerky.

"Time," Josie tried. "Something about time."

Roe shook her head, even as she thrust her hands up toward the clock once more. She held them there, her cries growing more frantic. "Roe. Roe. Roe. Roe!"

Josie's cell phone vibrated in her pocket with a call.

"Roe," the guard said firmly. "Calm down or this visit is over."

Her cries ceased. She returned her hands to the table, but tears kept streaming down her face.

Josie's phone continued to ring silently, buzzing against her rear end. Every inch of her body hummed with anxiety, but she kept her expression blank, her hands steady, as she took it from her pocket.

Thirty-nine and half hours.

It wasn't Heather. It was the caller from last night. Pain pierced her heart, daggerlike and merciless. Mentally, she caught the arterial bleeding in a jar and locked it away. It had to wait. She couldn't break right now. Wouldn't.

Swiping the decline icon, she took a couple of deep breaths. She needed her four-seven-eight breathing right now but that wasn't going to happen in this room. Last round of questions. The most important ones.

"You met your daughter." Josie pulled up the side-by-side photo of Lila, young and old, and turned her phone toward Roe. "She pretended to be a reporter so that she could meet with you."

Roe's eyes bulged as she took in the photo.

"Did she tell you who she really was?"

She shook her head. No.

The words, "What did she want?" were on the tip of Josie's tongue but she held them back. Yes or no questions. How would she narrow down what Lila came to talk about?

"Did she ask you about the babies?"

Yes.

"Did she ask about herself?"

Yes.

"Did she ask about her father?"

Yes.

"Did you know the father?"

No response.

"Was there more than one? More than one man?"

Nothing.

Josie took another approach. "The man who hurt you before Lila came out of your belly, did you meet him in the woods?"

A nod.

It wasn't Roe's father, then. A hunter, like she and Trinity had thought. "Did he ever meet Lila?"

No.

"Did he know about Lila?"

Roe didn't respond.

"Did he hurt you before the other babies came out of your belly?"

A slow nod. Fear crept into Roe's eyes. That trauma was still alive and well and she was locked inside her mind with it. Anger welled again as Josie imagined Roe, young and alone, isolated from everyone but her father, who had betrayed her in the worst way. She'd worked up the courage to leave, hoping to disappear to a place remote enough that he might not find her, only to fall victim to another monster. Roe had never been given the tools to fight back. Hell, she'd never even been taught basic things in life or anything that might have helped her become more than prey.

Even so, she'd given birth to a predator.

Josie could ask if he'd told her his name but what was the point? Roe wouldn't be able to say it or spell it and even if she could, he had probably given her a fake name. Even if Roe could somehow communicate his real name, he was likely dead by now.

Josie tapped the side of her head. "Did he hurt your head? Take away your words?"

No response.

"Do you remember how your head got hurt?"

No.

That wasn't unusual with traumatic brain injuries.

From the corner of the room, the guard cleared her throat. They were almost out of time. Josie had gotten off track. "When Lila was here pretending to be a reporter, did she tell you anything about herself?"

No.

"Did she talk about anyone besides herself?"

No.

But Lila wouldn't have dished about her myriad crimes or her accomplices at that meeting.

Josie brought up the photos of Lila once more. "Later, she became a prisoner here."

Roe's gaze snapped to Josie's face. She hadn't known. Josie forged ahead anyway, tapping her finger against Lila's mug shot. "This is what she looked like when she became an inmate here. Did you ever see her?"

No.

Josie hadn't asked the superintendent to check but it was likely that Lila and Roe had never crossed paths. Muncy had sixteen housing units and, if Josie remembered correctly, had over fourteen hundred inmates while Lila was incarcerated.

"Did she ever send any kind of message to you through other inmates?"

No.

Josie sighed. She'd known this line of inquiry was a Hail Mary but she felt disappointed nonetheless. Roe Hoyt was a dead end. A sad, twisted, tragic dead end.

She removed her finger from the phone screen. Roe's eyes locked on it. Then she lunged across the table, hands grabbing for Josie's phone. Her voice went up several octaves.

"Roe! Roe! Roe!"

Josie jumped up, backing away as Roe threw herself across the table. The guard yanked her back, lifting her to her feet, shouting for her to calm down. But there was no getting through to her. Straining toward Josie, she flailed as much as she could while the guard dragged her toward the door. Josie's phone had fallen, face-up, onto the floor near her feet. A photo of the contents of Lila's box filled the screen. Had she accidentally swiped to it? Had something in the photo caused Roe's reaction?

Josie snatched up her phone and held it out toward Roe, whose feet kicked in the air as the guard lifted her, carrying her toward the exit.

"Roe," Josie shouted. "Do you recognize something in this photo?"

Roe didn't hear her. Those familiar blue eyes were wild, panic-stricken. Wherever she was, it wasn't in this room.

"Roe! Roe! Roe!"

FORTY-TWO
ONE WEEK AGO

Bug was half expecting some kind of sex dungeon or torture chamber—especially after the man said the bar was "more than a bar." She was relieved to see that his words hadn't been code for something else. At the bottom of the steps, a huge tiled room stretched out before them. Bug couldn't even tell where it ended. The actual bar looked like something out of a movie. Sleek, shiny wood. Taps. Copper-colored cocktail shakers. Behind the bar was a mirror and miles of bottles. Every liquor imaginable. Overhead hung a light fixture that spanned the entire bar. Stained glass wrapped around metal slats that held upside-down wine and martini glasses.

"Cool, right?" said the man, heading straight to the bar.

The rest of the room was filled with pool tables and arcade games. More arcade games than Bug had ever seen in an actual arcade. Taxidermied animals were displayed on stands. Gross. It was a weird combination. A stuffed elk standing next to Dance Dance Revolution. She wondered if they were all animals the man had killed. The dozens of framed photos on shelves across the room answered that question. In each one, he posed proudly with the dead animal, his gun draped casually across his chest.

Bug tried to mask her disgust. She panned the rest of the room. Over a dozen televisions hung from the walls, each turned to a different type of sporting event. They were all muted. It was quiet down here. No music. A handful of people wandered around, testing out the games. The smell of steak and French fries wafted toward them. Holden pulled out a stool for her and she climbed onto it, noticing a set of double doors at the other end of the bar. That must be the kitchen.

The man went behind the bar and started mixing some kind of drink. Holden sat beside her, one hand on her thigh. He seemed more comfortable now than he had upstairs, but a low-level tension still radiated from him. Not surprising. The man's dark side was no secret to Holden. He was always walking a fine line. Everyone in the man's sphere did.

It was getting harder and harder to force smiles. A drink appeared before her. Both men watched as she sipped. It was tangy and dry. Her hand trembled.

"You okay there, kiddo?" the man asked.

A drop of liquid clung to her chin. Holden wiped it away. Breathing felt difficult. This wasn't how she envisioned it. Then again, she'd spent so much time on her speech that she hadn't given much thought to when or under what circumstances she would make her demands. She didn't actually want Holden there to hear any of it but there didn't seem to be any way to get the man alone. Here, in this mostly empty bar, where it was quiet, was probably as good as it was going to get.

It was now or never.

Bug took another sip. Before she finished, the man took the glass from her. "Hey," he said. "Your eyes are kind of big and glassy. Why don't we switch to water for now? We don't want you so drunk that you can't consent."

This time, he winked at Holden who squeezed her leg to the point of pain.

Wait. What?

Alarm bells blared in the back of her mind. She'd known this party would be filled with criminals, but she didn't think it was a *To Catch a Predator* kind of soiree.

"I'm not here for that," she blurted out. "For whatever... for any weird sex stuff. Holden doesn't know but I asked him to bring me here to talk to you."

Holden's hand slid off her leg. The man folded his arms over his chest. A smug smile curved his lips. "Is that right?"

Bug steeled herself, maintaining eye contact with him even though it sent a frisson of fear down her spine. Holden's stare caused a flush to creep up her neck to the roots of her hair.

"You—you hurt my mother. A long time ago. She got away but then you found her. Found us. You tried to kill her and—and me. That's why she had to leave me." Her lungs seized up. Every time she thought about this part, it hurt. No matter how many years went by. "She left me behind so you wouldn't find me. Well, I'm here now and I know. I know, I know..."

She floundered as every last bit of amusement drained from the man's face. There was the monster she remembered. Dangerous. The lines of his face hardened. A muscle in his jaw jumped. "What do you think you know, little girl?" he growled.

Bug touched her necklace, hoping it would give her strength. She'd made it herself, using the last thing her mother had given her as its centerpiece. To this day she had no idea what the small item was or what it meant. All she knew was it had been important to her mom. Now, it was Bug's talisman against anyone who tried to hurt her.

She lifted her chin, staring him down with a confidence she definitely did not feel. "I know who you are. I know what happened."

"I think Holden was right," he said, trying to lighten his tone. "You've had too much to drink. You're talking gibberish."

"I'm not," she insisted.

Then she said the name. From the way all the color left his face, he knew he was screwed. Bug felt high from her victory.

Game on, asshole.

FORTY-THREE

Josie's house felt desolate, stripped of all the energy that had always made it a home. It smelled like bleach, OxiClean, and peroxide. Aside from the items which were beyond repair—now sitting on the curb in a heap for the trash company to pick up—everything was back where it belonged.

It never looked more like a stranger's house than in this moment.

Trinity's palm grazed Josie's shoulder. "We could have just asked Paula to use her printer."

Josie shook her head. "No. I couldn't stay there another hour. I want to try to get hold of Turner again and honestly, I need a break."

It had been difficult to focus on the conversations at Gretchen's. Her head was filled with Roe Hoyt's cries, wondering if it was the photo from Lila's trophy box that had triggered her. It was possible that Josie had accidentally swiped to that photo when she dropped the phone, and Roe hadn't seen it at all. The superintendent told Josie that Roe was prone to these sudden outbursts that seemed to have no discernible trigger. On the way back to Denton, Josie had studied the objects in the photo—the pillbox, the spanner bits or whatever the hell they were, the cigar cutter, the hair, the teacup—but couldn't figure out why any of them would cause such a strong reaction. She wanted to return and question Roe further, but the superintendent said it would have to wait until she was less agitated, which could take days.

Trinity broke through Josie's thoughts. "You mean you couldn't take another hour of that bitch Laura's scrutiny and passive-aggressive bullshit remarks. I don't understand why she even bothered to show up."

Josie didn't respond. Laura had taken Gretchen's advice and no longer openly criticized Josie, but she still managed to get her digs in. Laura was annoying, but Josie had long ago resigned herself to the fact that Noah's sister was never going to warm up to her. With his mom gone, she was his closest family. Despite the fact that she made Josie want to punch her regularly, she loved Noah—and he loved her. Josie didn't want to be a wedge between them.

The current situation was beyond stressful, and everyone dealt with stress differently. For Noah's sake, Josie was trying to extend Laura some grace. "She's hurting, too."

Trinity made a noise of exasperation, shifting the messenger bag with her laptop in it from one shoulder to the other. "The Josie of ten years ago would have cold-cocked her in the face right in the middle of Gretchen's living room."

Josie laughed. Really laughed for the first time since this nightmare began. It felt good and awful and soothing and wrong. "You know," she said, heading toward the stairs. "If I recall, you were one of the many people who insisted I go to therapy. Well, here I am, a bigger, better, more patient person, and now you're complaining."

She could hear Trinity trudging up behind her. "Sometimes I miss that other version of you, that's all."

"Yeah, everyone misses the alcohol abuse and hair-trigger temper, I'm sure."

"Don't get me wrong. You're still a badass but all that therapy still isn't helping you emote properly," Trinity goaded. "Come on, let's have a good cry together."

"No."

She would cry when Noah was back in her arms. Whatever that looked like.

Dread filled Josie's stomach as they reached the second floor. The door to their bedroom hung open. More of his clothes were in the hamper. Trinity had made sure no one washed them.

Forty-five hours.

Mentally, Josie smacked the dread down, visualized grinding it into a million tiny pieces with her boot. She wouldn't sleep in that room again until Noah was with her. She *would* find him. Alive.

The universe would just have to bend to her will.

"Come on," she told Trinity, heading toward the first guest bedroom where she and Noah kept their printer.

On the way back from Muncy, Josie had decided they might have a better chance at finding some link to Noah's whereabouts if they tracked down some of Lila's victims. The only viable lead they had for doing so were the newspaper clippings in Lila's trophy case of terror.

"Don't bother with the ones about Dex or our family," said Josie. "We don't need those."

Trinity booted up her laptop and used the now-restored Wi-Fi to connect with the printer. "That only leaves two."

"Forget the one about the house fire that killed a former foster father," Josie said. "Given the advanced age of that guy, I'm guessing he was one of Lila's foster parents. He likely abused her and killing him was revenge. It happened right after she left me in Lisette's custody. I'm not sure that rabbit hole will lead us anywhere."

"Then we'll look at the other one."

Using the picture of the clipping that Josie snapped before Heather's team took Lila's entire box into evidence, Trinity used a database to locate the full article. The printer whirred to life.

Five minutes later, they sat side by side, cross-legged on the bed, pages spread before them. The article was from a Williamsport newspaper, dated eight years ago. Together, they scanned it.

"This is fairly recent," said Trinity. "I mean, this would have been only a year before Lila came back to Denton to try to ruin your life and kill the two of us. But this doesn't seem like Lila's work, does it?"

Josie took a moment to read the article more closely.

FORMER HOSPITAL ADMINISTRATOR PLEADS GUILTY TO FELONY CHARGES AFTER EMBEZZLEMENT SCANDAL

Alec Slater, former director of Williamsport General Community Hospital, pleaded guilty Friday to embezzling more than $200,000 from a charitable account. He was sentenced to five years' probation with no prison time, according to the Lycoming County District Attorney. Thirty-nine-year-old Slater, a local resident, pled guilty to felony counts of theft by deception, theft by unlawful taking, computer trespass, access device fraud, and forgery, according to court dockets.

Slater initially faced over a year in prison for these offenses but given that he had no previous arrests or criminal records, the judge chose to hand down no prison time. He will also be required to pay back all the money he stole to the Williamsport General Community Hospital Charitable Fund.

Slater acted as the hospital's director for over ten years before embezzling the funds during the last year of his tenure. Shortly after taking over the position of director, he was tasked with overseeing the sizable charitable account which had been put in place decades ago by the hospital's then Medical Executive Board. It was initially created to provide funds for patients in dire need of care who had no insurance and few assets to pay for said care. Donations from private citizens and community leaders funded the account. In the future, it will be managed by a board of directors rather than the hospital administrator.

"It's just a huge betrayal," said a coworker who worked closely with Slater for many years. "I never could have imagined Alec doing something like this, stooping so low to take money from a charity. That's not the Alec I knew. He should have gone to prison."

Josie rubbed her eyes. "Lila wouldn't have this in her little trophy box if she didn't have something to do with it."

"It doesn't even mention her, though."

"Exactly," Josie said. "She always got away with everything. Notice this article says Slater had to pay back the money but it doesn't say what he did with it."

Trinity frowned. "You think she somehow got him to embezzle money for her?"

"Something like that. It definitely fits her pattern—well, one of her patterns."

The driving forces behind Lila's behavior had always been startlingly predictable. Men she could control because they fed her starving ego. Men who might fill the void inside her caused by the circumstances of her birth and a life that repeatedly reinforced the notion that she was nothing. Worthless. That was why she'd always been so jealous of Josie. As an infant, Josie was supposed to be little more than a bargaining chip to win back Eli Matson's affection. When Eli fell in love with Josie—

supposedly his own daughter—Lila went mad. The same thing happened with Dex when he began to care for Josie. Lila had never known love, so she didn't understand it. What had the woman who'd read Lila's foster care file said about it? Everything bad you can imagine happening in a foster home happened to Lila.

If she'd ever stood a chance after being rescued from Roe Hoyt, it had been crushed under the unforgiving boots of the foster care system as it stood in the sixties and seventies.

Beyond trying to fill the void left in her soul with the attention of men, Lila only ever cared about three other things: drugs, money, and revenge. Drugs were plentiful enough that she'd never had an issue getting them. Her revenge tended to be the type that ended in someone's house burning down, as evidenced by the first article. Which meant that she'd somehow ensnared Alec Slater and convinced him to ruin his career and possibly go to prison to provide her with a payoff.

"Slater was either romantically involved with her," Josie said, "or Lila had something on him."

Trinity tapped a nail against the screen, indicating the date on the article. "He was thirty-nine. Lila would have been a lot older and if it was this close to when she returned to Denton, she wouldn't have been looking so great."

Lila had been dying of cancer at that time. Josie hadn't even recognized her after the disease ravaged her body. It wasn't out of the question that she still could have seduced a younger man, but Josie thought this particular scenario involved something darker and more treacherous.

"There's no mention of a wife or family," Trinity added. "But what if this is Dylan's father?"

The same thought had been swirling at the edge of Josie's tired consciousness. Though if that was the case, it meant Alec Slater was dead. Dylan had told Dex that his father passed away. Josie held her hands out for the laptop and Trinity handed it over without protest, watching as Josie opened a new browser tab. For the next twenty minutes, they searched for any information they could find about Alec Slater, eventually discovering that he was married and had a daughter. By all accounts, he was still alive. Disappointment hit Josie hard.

It could never be that easy. Not when her husband's life hung in the balance.

Trinity gave a frustrated sigh. "What do you think? Is it still worth tracking this Slater guy down?"

They had no other leads, no more clues to how Lila had spent her years after leaving Josie with Lisette.

Forty-six hours.

"Yes. Let's do it." Josie stood up and stretched her arms over her head.

Trinity snapped her laptop closed and gathered up the printouts. "I'll find him then. Hopefully he's still in the Williamsport area. We could pay him a visit tomorrow."

Josie's phone rang. Trinity abandoned her messenger bag and climbed off the bed, coming to Josie's side as she pulled it out of her pocket. The two of them stared at it like it was a bomb about to go off.

Not Heather.

"Josie," Trinity said softly. "You have to answer."

"No, I don't." Everything inside her started to shrink, to curl in on itself. An emotional retreat. If she didn't fall back, she wouldn't survive this, and she would be damned if she let herself break.

"You should." Trinity's voice was still gentle.

Josie swiped the decline icon, shocked at the steadiness of her finger. "No," she said firmly. "I have to find Noah."

Trinity opened her mouth as if she was going to say more but then decided against it. She gathered her messenger bag and walked to the door, where she stopped to check her own phone. "Drake will be here soon."

Josie was surprised by just how much she wanted to see Drake. He wasn't just her future brother-in-law. He'd become a good friend to her and Noah. He would be another cool head in this chaos, just like Trinity. Like Gretchen and Paula. Josie knew he'd be there for whatever she needed, making no demands of her.

"Is he getting a hotel?" she asked, following Trinity downstairs.

"Yes, but don't worry, I'm staying with you at Gretchen's house."

Josie's automatic response was to tell her she didn't need to do that, she should go stay with her fiancé, but the truth was that Josie needed her right now. Needing anyone—besides Noah—was a difficult thing for her to admit. She was glad Trinity didn't make her say it.

"Call him back. I'm going to go out front and see if I can get Turner on the phone."

FORTY-FOUR

Josie blinked, trying to clear the haze from her eyes. The phone screen blurred, turning her two dozen unanswered texts to Turner into a jumble of letters. It was too easy to fall asleep now that she was back at Gretchen's, in bed with Trout and Trinity, who were both snoozing. The uncharacteristic quiet of the house didn't help either. Josie didn't want to fall asleep yet. She wanted answers from Turner. Why wasn't he responding to her? At the very least, she would have expected him to accuse her of harassment again. She'd left at least five voicemails for him. He couldn't go ten minutes without scrolling on his phone. Was he even still alive?

Angrily, she typed in a message that was going to cost her ten dollars and hit send before she could overthink it.

"You okay?" Trinity's head lifted from her pillow. Hair stuck to one side of her face, matted with sweat. For once, she didn't look glamorous. She was exhausted. Josie felt guilty for not telling her to leave with Drake.

"Fine, Trin," Josie whispered. "Go back to sleep."

He'd been waiting for them by the time they returned to Gretchen's house. Watching Trinity run into his arms was a punch to the gut. Josie was truly happy for them, but it only drove home how much she missed Noah, how badly she needed to be in his arms.

Later, Drake went with Josie while she walked Trout. She was relieved to see no pity in his eyes, only the same fire she felt burning deep down in her own soul. Drake had been here once, too, searching for Trinity after she went missing. He couldn't help with this investigation. The FBI had to be asked to get involved and even if they had been, Drake's field office wouldn't be the one responding. Still, he asked questions like they were working the case together. No emotion. Only facts. It felt purposeful and meaningful even though they were only covering ground that Josie and Trinity had already been over.

Just like with her sister, Drake's presence and his almost detached calm were oddly comforting.

After he went to his hotel, Josie and Trinity had forced themselves to eat and socialize with everyone who still lingered, waiting for news. At midnight Trinity had insisted they go to bed. Josie had watched her plug her phone into its charger before flopping her head against the pillow and passing out fully clothed. Trout followed suit. Evidently the constant carousel of people coming in and out of Gretchen's house all day, coupled with his anxiety over absolutely nothing being right in his world, had worn him out.

For the last half hour, Josie had been scrolling through her unanswered texts to Turner. Her body craved sleep, but she fought it, hoping he would get back to her with something. Anything. To stay awake, she opened her browser and brought up the WYEP website. Noah's abduction was still the number one story but just beneath it was a piece about Gina Phelan's murder.

Clearly, Denton PD had released her name to the press. Josie clicked on the link and started reading. The circumstances of her death had also been revealed. The photos of the blonde woman were included, along with poor-quality photos of her tattoo, naming her as a person of interest with another plea for the public to come forth with information about her. Josie wondered at the wisdom of making Gina Phelan's name public considering how hated the Phelans were in the city right now.

Someone else must have had the same thought because the second half of the WYEP story was a profile about Gina Phelan that downplayed her role in the family company in favor of more personal details. She'd been volunteering at an animal shelter near her home for a decade. Her three rescue dogs, Siouxsie, Werner, and Goat would miss her but had been taken in by a dear friend.

Goat. Josie smiled, thinking of the story Shirley Swenson had told her about Gina. Then sadness overwhelmed her. More than it should. Usually, she was able to maintain a lot more mental distance from the victims in her cases. Except this wasn't her case anymore and she'd been on the razor's edge of losing control of her emotions since she discovered Noah was missing.

Before they could get away from her again, she kept reading.

> *Ms. Phelan enthusiastically funded scholarships for students at her old high school, not only for college-bound students but also for those who wanted to attend trade school. As a young girl, she took up archery under her father's tutelage. "I didn't even know she was interested in it to begin with," said Clint Phelan, choking up. "She'd been practicing with one of my old traditional bows, sneaking around, trying to get good on her own 'cause that's how she was. Didn't use finger tabs or anything! She's lucky she didn't get nerve damage. First thing I did when I saw she was serious was get her a good glove. Then she moved on to a compound bow. She mastered it, just like she did everything."*

Gina regularly participated in the Pennsylvania State Archery Association's competitions, winning a state championship three times. Fishing was another one of her interests. She'd also been planning a trip to Norway next spring to see the northern lights which had been on her bucket list.

Noah would love the northern lights. Maybe Josie could plan a trip for them. Somewhere less expensive than Norway, if possible. They could go after he came home.

When would that be? He'd been missing approximately fifty-four hours. More than two days.

She abandoned her phone for a moment and took his shirt out from under the pillow again. She huffed it, wondering how long it took for a person's scent to fade from their clothes. Should she keep it in some hermetically sealed bag to make sure it lasted? But then how would she smell it? Would it lose more scent every time she opened and closed it? She'd need to ration it, surely.

No. Not going there. She would find him. Alive.

With a sigh, she picked up her phone again. Along the top of her screen were tiny icons that told her she still had three unheard voicemail messages from the caller she'd been avoiding. She looked over at her sister. Trinity's breathing was smooth and even. Her eyelids fluttered. Josie hadn't answered the calls not just because she didn't want to know what waited on the other end but also because she didn't want to have hers and Noah's dream shattered in front of other people, even Trinity.

This was as alone as she was going to get in the present circumstances. After a long, shuddery exhale, Josie brought up the voicemails. She made sure her volume was low so the message wouldn't wake Trinity or Trout. Then she pressed the phone hard against her ear, listening as the case manager from their adoption agency destroyed what little was left of Josie's world at the moment.

FORTY-FIVE

The first two messages were terse, asking Josie to call back immediately.

The third was longer and right to the point.

"I saw on the news that your husband is missing. They said it was a home invasion and robbery and that he was abducted. My heart goes out to you and I hope he's found safely very soon. However, we cannot make your adoptive profile available to birth parents at the present time. I'm sure you can understand. We weren't even extended the courtesy of a phone call informing us of this change in your circumstances. This isn't the first time you and your husband have had safety issues at your home. Though it pains me deeply, I'm afraid we have to revoke your adoption approval. Please contact me with any questions. I'm praying for your husband's safe return."

Emotion slammed into Josie's chest, nearly knocking the breath out of her. Saliva thickened in her mouth. The backs of her eyes burned. She'd known the calls weren't good, had even known what they were about, but she'd convinced herself the hurt wouldn't touch her. Couldn't touch her. Because this was not the time for it.

But here she was, waves of raw emotion rolling over her, thunderous and destructive, while her traitorous body let them.

"No," she whispered.

Trout's sleepy head lifted at the sound of her voice. His ears pointed straight up. A small whine escaped his mouth. He sensed the shift in her emotions even in slumber.

She wasn't doing this now.

Scratching his head, she soothed him back to sleep and then got the hell out of there. She had no idea where she was going. Just away. As if running down the hall of Gretchen's second floor could carry her away from her feelings. Tears clouded her sight.

This wasn't happening now.

Josie's body collided with something, sending her staggering backward. Not something, someone. Hands gripped her upper arms and spun her. "In," said a voice that sounded like Gretchen's. Josie couldn't be sure. Blood rushed in her ears, distorting everything. Cold tiles touched her bare feet. Light exploded around her. A door clicked closed. Her ass landed on the cool, flimsy plastic lid of a toilet.

She was in Gretchen's bathroom, sobbing.

It was coming out. All of it—the panic, the rage, the pain, the despair, the pressure, the unbearable missing of her other half, and now the death of their shared dream—spilling from her in violent bursts she could no longer contain. Heat stung her wet cheeks. A spasm rocked her abdomen, forcing her to fold over and dip her head between her knees. Snot poured unceremoniously from her face, mixing with saliva, pooling near her feet. Her body always made too much saliva when she cried. It was embarrassing and annoying. Josie *hated* crying.

Noises broke through the roar in her ears. A rustling. The soft tearing of something. Then a hand gently gathered all the fluids leaking from her face onto a wad of toilet paper. Gretchen said, "I promise you, it will lessen. Stop fighting it, Josie."

Her chest constricted. She tried to speak, to tell Gretchen that she couldn't *not* fight it but the sheer strength of the feelings forcing their way out of her body took up too much of her energy, too much of her internal coordination. What did she even have if she couldn't fight? She'd had to fight for her very survival from such a young age, she didn't know anything else. That was what she had, what she did best.

Gretchen knew it. Raised by a mother with Munchausen syndrome by proxy, she still bore the scars of her childhood. They were the same that way. They needed the fight almost as much as they needed oxygen to survive.

Another wad of toilet paper swiped at Josie's face. "This is not a battle you need to win," Gretchen told her matter-of-factly. Josie appreciated her tone and the way she didn't try to soothe. No rubbing of Josie's back, or hugs, or soft, encouraging words. This pain was too raw, too deep and elemental for all that.

The only person who could touch her when she got like this was Noah.

Another dam broke and this time, Josie let it disintegrate. She surrendered, letting her body do what it needed to do until she was completely spent. Lifting her heavy head, she blinked her swollen eyes until Gretchen came into focus, sitting cross-legged on the floor in front of her. She was wearing a pair of sweatpants and a T-shirt that said, *I Like My Cat and Maybe Three People.*

Unexpectedly, Josie laughed. It sounded unhinged and ended in a hiccup.

Gretchen looked down at the shirt and grinned. "Funny, right? 'Cause it's so true. Paula got it for me."

Josie nodded.

"You're one of the three, by the way."

"I know," said Josie, her voice throaty and thick.

FORTY-SIX

Gretchen didn't press, didn't ask her to talk about her feelings. Maybe that was why Josie blurted out, "The adoption agency called. Our approval has been revoked. We can't take care of a baby when one of us has been abducted. This is the second time in the last few months that our home was broken into. I don't think—" A breath lodged in her chest, causing a strange, high-pitched noise to erupt from her throat, her body fighting more sobs. Once she could speak again, she finished, "I don't think we'll get approved again."

Gretchen watched her intently. Josie braced herself for the "I'm so sorry" that she knew would hit like a nail in a goddamn coffin. Instead, Gretchen said, "There's more than one way to expand your family."

She didn't elaborate and Josie didn't ask her to because Gretchen had already given her what she needed. A potential life raft, far off in the distance. Maybe she'd reach it, maybe she wouldn't, but all she needed to get through this moment was that little smudge on the horizon that could be hope. There wasn't the slightest insinuation that they might not get Noah back, that she and Noah wouldn't move toward that horizon together.

"I know you've been asking that jackass for updates on the Gina Phelan case," Gretchen said. "Even though you're off the case."

This was exactly the distraction and the kind of normalcy Josie needed after the meltdown she'd just had. "Don't worry. He's ignoring me."

Gretchen tore more toilet paper from the roll and handed it to Josie. "He's been busy. Lots of other cases. The rest of Denton's criminal element carries on as usual. Also, I think his ass is chapped."

Josie wiped at her nose. "How come?"

Gretchen laughed. "Besides the fact that Tilly Phelan can barely tolerate him and keeps asking for you?"

Josie said nothing.

"You made him look like the jackass he is—he said you spotted a rideshare in one of the videos."

"I did," Josie said.

"Tomorrow on the news there's going to be an update on the Gina Phelan case."

Josie's heart raced. She stayed silent, letting Gretchen continue.

"There was a rideshare that drove down the street around the time Gina Phelan was stabbed. The driver had just dropped someone off. He got another request. He was fiddling with his GPS, trying to find a pickup location, so he didn't see anything, but as his vehicle passed by, the dash camera picked up a male in a brown hoodie and jeans locked in some kind of struggle with Gina Phelan."

Josie swallowed, mouth still overproducing saliva. "Trinity has a still from one of my neighbor's security cameras of a man wearing those same clothes, walking up and down my street about two hours before Noah was abducted."

Gretchen smiled. "I'm going to pretend that you didn't say that. The state police have the same still."

"What about the blonde?"

"She was behind Gina." Gretchen's expression turned serious. "We think Gina was shielding her but like I said, the footage was taken from a moving vehicle and it's only a few seconds long."

Had Gina known the woman or had she seen her being assaulted on the sidewalk and intervened? Questions arose in the back of Josie's mind in rapid fashion, but she kept them to herself. Gretchen was already telling her more than she should.

It physically hurt her to admit it, but the Big Cry had cleared Josie's head a bit. She felt more like her old self than she had since Noah's abduction.

"Tomorrow, Paula's going to suggest that your families start putting up fliers around the city," Gretchen said. "She's afraid if we don't give them something to do, your mother might beat the piss out of your sister-in-law."

Josie smiled weakly. "I'd kind of like to see that, honestly."

Gretchen laughed. "Wouldn't we all."

Josie tore off a length of toilet paper and blew her nose. Her sinuses were going to be on fire tomorrow. Just what she needed.

Gretchen used her foot to nudge Josie's leg. "Go get some sleep, if you can."

"Thank you, Gretchen."

Her friend merely nodded, staying on the floor as Josie left and headed back to the bedroom she was sharing with Trout and Trinity. Both of them were snoring now, their breathing patterns opposite so that when one went quiet, the other filled the momentary silence. It was a symphony. Josie didn't think she'd be able to sleep but the moment she climbed into bed, fatigue hit her like a freight train. She reached up and turned off the lamp on the nightstand. Curling on her side, she found

Noah's shirt and held it against her chest. As sleep dragged her under, her brain cycled through everything she knew about Noah's case, the armed robberies, and now the Phelan case. Clues and leads and questions about all the things she didn't know because they were being held back from her.

Then there was Lila, wandering into Josie's disjointed dreamlike state, beckoning her. What did she want Josie to see?

Her mind wanted to stay awake and sift through all the facts again, but her body had taken over tonight, demanding release earlier and demanding rest now.

FORTY-SEVEN

There wasn't enough ibuprofen on the planet to stop the throbbing inside Josie's sinus cavities. The Big Cry had made room in her brain for a more clinical approach to Noah's abduction and the potential link to Lila's past, but the pain it left in its wake was hard to think clearly through. In addition, her face was puffy and her eyes bloodshot. More reasons she detested crying. When she entered Gretchen's living room at eight thirty in the morning she found Shannon, Christian, Patrick, Theo, and Laura gathered around the coffee table, dividing up the flyers Paula had made.

Laura took one look at her and said, "Getting drunk is not going to help bring my brother back."

Josie hadn't touched a drink in years.

In that moment, she desperately wanted a bottle of Wild Turkey. Not to drink but to bean Laura over the head with. She would have done it, too. There was no doubt, given the way the rage deep inside her woke screaming. A veritable war cry.

But Josie didn't need a bottle.

Shannon saw red, lunging straight over the table for Laura, fists flying. Hundreds of flyers featuring Noah's smiling face danced through the air, scattering. Shannon moved with impressive speed, but Christian and Patrick were faster, scurrying over the surface of the table and hauling her away before she made contact with Laura's shocked face.

"Say one more word about my daughter," Shannon snarled, fighting against the hold of her son and husband. "One more word! You will *not* like the consequences!"

Theo clamped his hands over Laura's shoulders and dragged her toward the kitchen. "That's enough. You need to stop!" he told her. "You're making everything worse."

"Shan, calm down," Christian said.

"Let's get some air, Mom," Patrick suggested, turning her toward the front door.

It was only then that Josie noticed Trinity standing beside her. "Huh," her sister said. "Looks like you got your temper from Mom. Who would have thought?"

Josie pressed her fingers into her aching forehead. "I need to get the hell out of here."

"At least poor Trout didn't have to see that," Trinity said, jangling keys in Josie's face. "I'll text Paula to let her know what just went down and to apologize for the fact that we won't be here to manage the aftermath."

Josie snatched the keys and fled through the front door. The cool morning air calmed her nerves but did little to soothe her headache. Her parents and brother were at the far end of the porch, oblivious to Josie's presence. Shannon paced between Christian and Patrick, her movements stiff and jerky.

"Shan," Christian said. "You can't lose your cool like that."

Josie's mother shoved at Christian's chest, her normally sweet face contorted with rage. "I will defend my daughter in any way I see fit!"

"Mom," Patrick said weakly.

When Shannon turned on him, he jumped back, as if worried she might push him too.

"Josie won't engage with Laura out of respect for Noah," Shannon said. "Because she's a better person than that bitch, but I don't have to stand by and listen to her insult my child. I won't!"

Stunned by the ferocity of Shannon's response to the situation, Josie felt new emotions flood into the place the Big Cry had left vacant. These ones weren't so bad. Warmth. Gratitude. It reminded her of the way her grandmother, Lisette, had been—ruthless in her pursuit to protect Josie from any threats.

There had only ever been one threat. Lila.

Before her parents or brother noticed her, Josie jogged down the steps and toward the street, sliding into the driver's seat of her SUV to wait for Trinity.

Twenty minutes later, they were on the road, headed to Williamsport to find Alec Slater.

Once they arrived, it took an hour to track him down. The address Trinity had found was an old one that led them to a beautiful four-bedroom house in the northern, wooded part of the city where he'd lived with his wife and daughter before he was charged with embezzlement. A neighbor delighted in telling them all about Slater's fall from grace. How his wife had left him and moved on with a college professor. How Slater had somehow gotten nothing from the sale of their massive, fancy home—"wife took him to the cleaners, as she should"—and how he'd had to move into a small apartment in a part of town where all the criminals lived. That area was actually not a criminal hotbed at all, nor was it a place that disgraced ex-cons went to die alone, but Josie saw the point the neighbor had been trying to make.

The embezzlement scheme had resulted in a serious downgrade in Alec Slater's quality of life.

Luckily, Slater's landlord directed them to his current place of employment. Another serious downgrade.

A small, dilapidated building housed the eatery called Burgers. A creative name if Josie ever heard one.

It sat alone on a weed-strewn, cracked asphalt lot on the outskirts of Williamsport, miles from other establishments. A flat roof extended from the rectangular building, sagging over what looked like the remains of an old gas pump. Various paint colors vied for dominance on both the structure and the overhang. Only the neon Burgers sign seemed fairly new, and by new, Josie was thinking the late seventies.

"Are you sure this place is a real place?" Trinity asked as Josie parked along the edge of the lot.

There were three other vehicles, one parked right near the front door. "Looks like people are here."

Josie needed to talk to Alec Slater. She needed him to give her something she could use. The clues to Lila's past were dwindling rapidly—he was potentially the only one left—and she'd been shut out of every other investigation that might lead to Noah.

It still felt like she was racing against a clock.

Sixty-three hours.

It was less than three days, but it felt like an eternity.

"Let's do this then." Trinity's voice jarred Josie back to their present location. Her sister stepped out of the SUV, arching her back and stretching her arms overhead. Her nose wrinkled. "Are you sure the other people here aren't dead? This looks like a place unsuspecting motorists go to get murdered."

The smell of overused fry oil and burger grease hung so heavy in the air, Josie was afraid her clothes would be coated with it in a matter of minutes. Trudging toward the building, she muttered, "We're not getting murdered today. No time for that."

A bell jingled overhead when they entered the restaurant—or whatever Burgers was considered. The odor of grease and oil was even more overpowering inside. A few booths lined one wall, their vinyl seats cracked and mended with duct tape that peeled at the edges. A cleaner, newer-looking set of stools lined a countertop across from the booths. Behind that stood a dark-haired woman who could have been twenty-five or forty-five. She was dressed in all black, scrolling on her phone. As they approached, she nodded to the menu hanging on the wall behind her. This was perhaps the most modern accoutrement in the entire place, its glowing, clean white background peppered with an assortment of offerings. A dozen types of burgers, French fries, and for some reason Josie couldn't wrap her mind around, lobster roll.

"Can I get you?" the woman asked, the first part of her question lost to distraction or maybe the chewing tobacco tucked inside her lower left cheek.

"We're looking for Alec Slater," said Trinity.

"Round back. Tell him his break's almost over."

"Sure," said Josie. "We'll let him know the lunch rush is in full swing."

No reaction.

Trinity added, "After we rob him at gunpoint and steal his car."

Nothing.

Josie was relieved to be back out in the slightly less oily air. Trinity shook her head as they trudged around to the rear of the building. "Do you think if we ordered the lobster roll, she'd just give us a burger? Like the menu is just a list of gentle suggestions but you get what you get because... Burgers?"

Despite the circumstances weighing heavily on Josie's soul, she laughed. She'd never been so grateful for her sister's company as she was now.

As they rounded the back of the building, an old, faded wooden picnic table came into view. Alec Slater sat on top, his booted feet resting on one of the benches. He pinched a cigarette between his thumb and forefinger, puffing away while using his other hand to hold a cell phone against his ear. They'd managed to find a few photos of him at the time of his sentencing. Back then, he'd been clean-shaven with fastidiously cut and styled blond hair. In every picture a neatly pressed suit hugged his slender, muscular frame. He'd looked younger than his thirty-nine years. Josie didn't recognize the man before them at all.

A glance at Trinity told her that her sister was wondering the same thing: had they gotten the wrong Alec Slater?

A small, red paper hat sat on top of a messy, unkempt tangle of gray hair. An uneven gray beard covered his pudgy face but did nothing to hide the ruddiness in his complexion. If Josie had to guess, she'd say that Alec Slater drank a lot. Rolls of excess flesh strained against his stained white T-shirt. His stomach hung over the waist of his faded jeans.

As they drew closer, they could hear his side of the phone conversation. "You're kidding me, right? That phone cost almost a thousand dollars. I'm not—I'm not—Jesus, just listen, would you? I don't care about the phone, okay? Just tell me where you are."

Silence as he listened to the person on the other end.

"Because what if you get kidnapped and I have to tell the police the last place you were! I haven't heard from you in almost two weeks. Your mother is breathing down my neck. You know how she gets... What? What the hell are you doing down there?"

He rolled his eyes as he listened. "What kind of friends are these exactly, making you stay where? Sounds like a sex trafficking den. Just great. Uh-huh, uh-huh. How much money do you need? Okay, okay. I'll see what I can do. Stay the hell in touch, okay?"

He hung up, muttering something under his breath. Josie caught part of it, wondering if she'd heard him correctly.

"Alec Slater?" Trinity said.

He looked over at them, blinking through the cigarette smoke that poured from his nostrils. "Fucking lawyers. Stop bothering me at my job, would you? I know you have my home address. You want to harass me? Do it there. I gotta get back to work but you know what? Since you're already here, you can remind my bitch of an ex-wife that you can't get blood from a stone."

FORTY-EIGHT

Josie and Trinity looked one another over briefly. They were both dressed in jeans and sweatshirts. Josie wore her work boots while Trinity had on sneakers. Nothing about either of them screamed attorneys. Except maybe Trinity's high-gloss hair.

"We're not lawyers," Josie said. "And we've never met your ex-wife."

Squinting, Alec appraised them more thoroughly. He flicked his cigarette butt onto the ground where it rolled toward a large pile of its discarded brethren. "Well, I don't recommend it. She's got her lawyer on speed dial, and if she thinks you jaywalked in front of her, she'll call him."

Josie wondered if his opinion of his wife had been so low before he'd embezzled two hundred grand from a hospital charity. She kept silent though because she needed information from Alec and poking his sore spot wouldn't go a long way to getting it.

"We're here to talk to you about Lila Jensen."

One of his eyebrows kinked. No recognition. "Who?"

Apparently, he hadn't seen the *Dateline* episodes which

meant that if he had ever met Lila Jensen in person, he would have known her by a different name.

"She wouldn't have been going by that name," Josie said. "She would have used an alias."

Trinity pulled up the side-by-side picture of Lila on her phone and turned it toward him. He stared at the photo until the screen went blank. Another cigarette appeared in his hand. Rolling it in his palm, he said, "You're showing me two different people."

"Nope," said Trinity, pulling up the side-by-side comparison again. "It's the same woman. The ugly on the inside finally caught up to the ugly on the outside."

Sighing, Alec looked away and lit his cigarette. In the webbing of his left hand, Josie noticed some kind of mark. Too dark to be a bruise. Ash, maybe.

Ever aware of the ticking clock and Noah's absence, she got right to the point. "This woman, whose real name was Lila Jensen, had a news article about your embezzlement conviction among her personal items when she was arrested for a very long list of crimes. She may have even had a photo of you. Knowing her as I did, that tells me that she had something to do with the embezzlement."

His posture stiffened. Smoke flared from his nostrils. No response.

Josie kept going. "You never publicly said what you did with the funds you stole but I'm guessing by the time you were arrested, they were no longer in your possession. Two hundred thousand dollars is a lot of money."

He chuckled darkly, puffing out smoke in rapid bursts. "Yeah, it is. With the court costs, attorney fees, restitution, and my ex-wife crawling up my ass, I only have to work here until I'm a hundred and seventy-five to pay it all back. Maybe a hundred and seventy, since I do some website design on the side —do not tell her that."

"We won't," Trinity promised, watching him with fascination.

"Living the fucking dream," he added, almost to himself.

"You gave the money to Lila, didn't you?" Josie said. "But you never named her or turned her in which means you were either having an affair with her or she had something on you. Something so bad that you'd rather lose your job and your family and maybe even go to prison than rat her out."

The cigarette burned down to its nub, and he flicked it onto the ground. Still no meaningful response.

Trinity said, "We're not interested in making your life harder than it already is. Anything you tell us will be held in the strictest confidence."

He glanced at her, brow furrowed. Josie wondered if he recognized Trinity from television. "Who are you?"

"Her victims," Trinity answered.

A smile ghosted over his face. "Right. Was there a news article about you in this lady's personal effects?"

"A couple, actually," Josie said. "Some souvenirs, too. She burned our family home to the ground when we were infants. The nanny eventually died from smoke inhalation. Lila Jensen kidnapped me, passed me off as her own. Killed the man I thought was my father. Kept me in the closet for days on end with no food. Year after year. Tried to cut my face off when I was six years old."

Josie turned her head and ran a finger along her scar. The color drained from Alec's face.

"When I was fourteen, she burned our trailer down and disfigured her boyfriend at the time, one of the few people in my childhood who gave a shit about me."

"She came back when we were almost thirty," Trinity said. "Tried to kill us both."

"Where is she?" This time, when Alec took out another cigarette, his hands shook. The mark Josie had seen earlier in the webbing between his thumb and forefinger was visible again. Small, black. A tattoo. She wasn't close enough to see its precise shape but something about it sent up a flare in the recesses of her brain.

"Lila Jensen is dead," Trinity said.

"But she had associates," said Josie. "She kept things that she took from people. I've had them in storage for years."

Weakly, Alec joked, "You happen to find two hundred grand in her things?"

Josie shook her head. "No, but there are people out there after something she had. We're not sure what yet."

"So what is this? Some kind of treasure hunt?"

"My husband is missing," Josie said.

The lighter trembled in Alec's hand as he lit his next smoke. "What's that got to do with this Jensen person?"

"We're not sure," Trinity said.

"Whoever took my husband was looking for something in her personal effects. We think maybe that person was in trouble with someone. The kind of trouble that might get him killed. He was desperate, hoping to find the answer to his problems among the things Lila left behind, and my husband got caught up in a bad situation."

"So we're doing the only thing we can think to do," Trinity added. "Which is to talk to Lila's other victims and try to trace her movements and crimes in the years before her death."

"It's a long shot," Josie admitted. "But I'll turn over every rock on this planet if it means finding him."

Alec held Josie's gaze for a long moment. "Your husband. He a good guy?"

A swift and unexpected surge of emotion clogged Josie's throat. She swallowed it. "The best."

Alec nodded, seeming to consider something.

Josie coughed. "You should know who we are—our names and—"

He raised a palm to silence her. "No. I don't want to know. The less I know, the better. I've spent the last eight years paying for what happened, not just with my job and my family and my financial security. With my soul. You understand that?"

Josie nodded.

"When you leave here, if anyone comes to me asking about things I told you, I will deny this conversation happened. Deny we ever spoke. You got that?"

"Yes."

Alec pocketed his lighter and puffed rapidly, his cigarette burning down to a nub in seconds. He flicked the butt onto the ground with the others. Then his head sank into his hands. Several deep breaths later, he hopped off the picnic table and adjusted the waistband of his jeans.

"The alias she used was Bethany Rounds. I wasn't having an affair with her. She had explicit photos of my eleven-year-old daughter."

FORTY-NINE

Josie shouldn't have been surprised by the depth of Lila's depravity but standing behind the ramshackle restaurant, staring at the broken father before her, shock rippled over her body, making her skin feel cold and clammy.

Trinity said, "Oh God."

Alec sighed and put his hands on his hips. "Video games. My kid wasn't big into them, but she played a couple on her phone. Annoyed the hell out of my wife. I used to see those warnings on the news and on those network shows about people grooming kids using video games. Never gave it a second thought. I mean, how does that even happen? I didn't realize that pretty much every single one has a chat feature. My wife refused to let Erica join any social media platforms. Neither of us thought to keep an eye on the people she played video games with."

Trinity said, "You're saying Lila—through her alias—groomed your daughter using the chat feature in a video game and got her to send explicit photos of herself?"

Alec started pacing in a tight circle, the edges of his boots kicking the cigarette butt pile each time he passed it. "I don't know if it was Lila specifically. The person Erica was in touch with said he was a teenage boy. We didn't do a good job of teaching her how to evaluate people for truthfulness. We didn't do a good job of teaching her anything, I guess. She... she had a lot of mental health issues and as a result, she often sought attention. I don't think she understood that some types of attention are extremely bad. Anyway, this kid never sent her a photo of himself, but Erica believed he was a fifteen-year-old boy who lived nearby. He flirted with her. Made her feel special. It escalated. They took things off the game chat and started texting. His instructions were clear—delete every message immediately after sending or receiving so your parents never see anything."

Josie strongly doubted the fifteen-year-old boy Erica Slater had messaged with was real. Lila might have done the set-up work herself or she might have hired someone else to do it. Regardless, nothing was as it seemed. "What happened?"

"I used to order lunch from this place down the street from the hospital. It was better than the cafeteria food. DoorDash usually delivered it. One day, I opened the bag and in there with my sandwich and chips was a cheap cell phone with a note rubber-banded to it that said, 'Mr. Slater, check your text messages.' It was the weirdest damn thing. I thought it was some kind of joke. A prank or something. But I went along with it. No password needed. No icons on the screen other than the factory-installed shit. There was only one contact programmed into it. Bethany Rounds. The messages were from her. Well, not messages. Just photos of my daughter nearly naked in very suggestive poses."

He squeezed his eyes shut, a full body shudder going through him. "Rounds told me that if I didn't pay her, she would distribute them on the internet. Every pervert in the world would have access to them. I confronted Erica and she told me she'd sent them to this boy. Confessed the whole story."

"Why didn't you go to the police?" asked Trinity.

He laughed bitterly. "I was going to. I went to the restaurant to see if they knew how the phone got into my bag. They didn't. I tracked down the DoorDash driver. He claimed not to know anything either. I thought maybe I could track Rounds down, get ahead of her, but then she said she'd make it look like I was the one who took the photos. Make me look like some kind of pervert. Erica used the timer on her phone to take the pictures so it looked like another person took them. Anyway, I figured it was better to go to prison for embezzling than for... that."

"You didn't think your daughter would back you up?" asked Josie.

"Of course she would but she was terrified. She was... listen... like I told you, Erica always had issues. Major mental health stuff. The truth is that she's my brother's kid. He had lifelong addiction issues. I hadn't seen him since we were in our early twenties. I didn't even know Erica existed until he showed up on my doorstep with this eight-year-old kid. Her mother had overdosed. He was in the end stages of pancreatic cancer. Asked me to adopt her."

"Wow," Trinity said. "That must have been rough. Losing your brother, taking on your niece."

He stopped pacing, eyes cast down at his boots. "Yeah. It was horrible. My brother passed days after the adoption was finalized. Erica was a mess. Very shut down. Extremely fragile. She didn't like to talk about her life before we adopted her. Over time, she confided in me. Told me some stuff about her mom, but I know she held back a lot. I don't think her mom was very good to her but Erica sure did love her. Missed her something awful."

"That's terrible," murmured Trinity.

Alec nodded. "My brother had a good heart, but I can't imagine he was a stable parent. I was afraid that putting Erica through something like that—having to talk to investigators, maybe even testifying at a trial—would break her. She begged me not to tell anyone. Not to mention, if I did go to the police and Rounds made good on her promise to accuse me, my life would be over. Once you're accused of something like that, it doesn't really matter if you're proven innocent, does it? The stain is there forever. I didn't want Erica being teased at school for having a pervert dad. School was hard enough for her as it was."

"What did your wife say?" asked Trinity.

"I didn't tell her. Erica begged me not to. My wife was always tough on her. She wasn't thrilled about adopting her in the first place. She and Erica didn't have a great relationship, and I knew... shit." He rubbed hard at the back of his neck. "I knew my wife would blame Erica. Punish her. She always thought Erica was some master manipulator, but she was a kid! I mean yeah, she had a lying problem. She always did. We worked with a therapist on that. It was like she couldn't stop herself, and the thing was that she lied because she'd tell you what she thought you wanted to hear. It was like she thought we wouldn't love her if she didn't give the right answers."

In Josie's experience, that kind of behavior was often a result of trauma.

"My wife didn't understand." Alec used his thumb to rub at the tattoo on his other hand. "Erica wasn't some Machiavellian supervillain. She was a stupid, scared kid who got screwed over by some piece of garbage, and once she told me the truth, she looked to me to protect her. I promised her I would and that's what I did. Yeah, my life is shit now and yeah, it was embarrassing for my family when I got caught but as far as I know, the photos never got out."

"What did Bethany Rounds offer you by way of assurance?" asked Trinity.

Alec stared down at the tattoo, momentarily lost in thought. Josie took a step closer, finally able to see that it was some kind of animal footprint. A long, silent moment passed. From inside the restaurant came the sound of metal scraping against metal. A spatula over a hot grill, if Josie had to guess.

With a sigh, Alec dropped his hands to his sides. "Bethany Rounds gave me the photos on a flash drive which I destroyed—along with the phone she gave me, even though I'd already deleted the pictures. I'm not naive enough to believe those were the only copies but what else could I do? The bottom line is that I never got accused of being a pervert. My daughter finished school, and no one gave a shit that her dad got convicted of embezzling. Hell, I don't think any of those dumbass kids even knew what the word meant. Since Rounds gave me the burner phone to use, none of the stuff the police seized—my personal devices, phone and email records—implicated her. The investigators hounded me pretty bad about what I did with the money. I told them it was stolen. Gave them some story which they were never able to prove or disprove. One of 'em's probably still keeping tabs on me to see if I suddenly buy a flashy car or something but I'm paying it back, so there's not much they can do."

"You recognized Lila's photo," said Josie. "Which means you met her. You could have called the police when she set up the meeting, had them there waiting."

"Yeah, sure, and risk all hell breaking loose? No fucking way." Alec balled his hands into fists. "And let me tell you something else. About a week before this bitch set up our little meeting, I got jumped by two guys while I was out for a run. Broke my nose and three of my ribs. They told me it was my reminder not to involve the police and if I did, it wouldn't be just me who paid the price. They threatened my kid! What would the police do? They don't offer round-the-clock security. It's not like we could have gone into some witness protection program. No one could stop them if they wanted to come after Erica or my wife. No one. That's the fucking reality."

Leave it to Lila to wage a war of terror to make sure every loose end was tied up and no one would come after her. Josie had known her to manipulate men into doing all kinds of things for her, but she'd never known Lila to have enforcers before. Then again, given that she was coming into two hundred grand, it wouldn't have been difficult to pay a couple of guys to rough up Alec Slater.

"Those guys are still out there," Alec pointed out. "Right before my trial, they came for me again. Had to make sure I wasn't going to rat anyone out. So I took my punishment. I'm still taking it, but my daughter is safe. After all these years, those assholes should know that I'm not about to start talking now."

FIFTY

A deep sadness took hold in Josie's gut. What happened to Alec and Erica Slater was tragic. She'd like to believe that if he simply went to the authorities from the beginning, he could have avoided all of this and brought Lila and her merry band of mercenaries to justice, but she knew better than anyone that sometimes, in spite of all of law enforcement's valiant efforts, the bad guys got away with some of the worst crimes imaginable. Josie certainly couldn't fault Alec for wanting to protect his child the only way he felt he could at the time.

"Did you get a good look at the men who attacked you?" asked Josie. "Could you describe them?"

"Not going there." Alec shook his head. "So don't even bother."

Trinity said, "Once your sentence was handed down, did you have any more encounters with Lila or the men who jumped you?"

He jammed his hand into his back pocket and pulled out his phone to check the time. One-handed, he used his thumb to punch in his passcode, the small footprint undulating. "Nope."

A young woman's smiling face filled the screen, but Josie

caught only a fleeting glimpse of her before Alec angled it away from them. A fragment of a thought tumbled through Josie's mind, too quickly for her to latch onto it. She was too busy staring at the tattoo.

"You never saw Lila on the news?" asked Trinity.

"Nope."

Josie stepped closer to him, eyes following the motions of his hand as he kept scrolling. Four toes. A paw maybe, except it wasn't quite the right shape for that. There was no delineation between the metacarpal pad and the toepads. It was all one solid shape. Long digits, round toes. It looked more like a hand.

Trinity kept the conversation going. "Where is your daughter now?"

Alec gave a bitter laugh before stuffing his phone back into his pocket. "She's supposed to be in college. Lock Haven University—well, I guess it's Commonwealth U, Lock Haven campus now, with that whole state university consolidation thing. Anyway, it's about a half hour from here. I figured it would be easier for me to keep an eye on her if she was close."

"I know where that is," said Trinity. "She's not there?"

It's an ink splotch. Or a hand or something.

It's missing a finger.

Lots of people had similar or even identical tattoos. It was just a coincidence. Josie thought about the conversation Alec was having when they approached him. What she thought she'd heard. Did it mean anything or was she trying to make connections that weren't there out of desperation?

Sixty-three hours and forty-two minutes.

"She still has a bit of a lying problem." Alec sighed and took out another smoke, staring at it as if trying to decide whether he had time for another. Josie wanted to tell him he probably had all day to sit back here given his coworker's finely honed powers of observation.

"I've been paying for her to go to college." At the way Trinity's eyes widened, he barked a laugh. "Yeah. I'm paying for that, too. A portion of it anyway. My ex-wife was paying half. All this time I'm paying my half to my ex-wife and sending Erica spending money and turns out she wasn't even going. That's what my ex-wife's after me for now—she wants me to pay her back for the tuition expenses she put out because she thinks it's my fault Erica blew off school."

"Why did she blow it off?" asked Trinity.

"Guess."

"She met a boy," Josie said.

Alec lit his cigarette. On his first exhale, he said, "Bingo."

"Have you met him?" asked Trinity.

"Hell, no. Besides, they're already broken up. I'm gonna have to help clean up this mess now, I'm sure. Another heartbreak. She's got shit taste in men."

The idea taking shape in Josie's head seemed absurd. Maybe she was cracking under the strain of her husband's abduction. What would Noah say if he were here?

That she should remember that her gut was rarely wrong. He wouldn't think it was absurd because, like Trinity, he'd follow her off a cliff. His faith in her was unshakable. Maybe her inchoate idea wasn't so ridiculous.

She flashed to Lila entering her dream last night, beckoning. What was she trying to show Josie?

"Mr. Slater," said Josie. "Have you watched the news in the last three days? Gone on social media?"

Alec pinched his cigarette between his thumb and index finger, holding it a few inches from his mouth. "What?"

Josie repeated the question.

He laughed humorlessly and gestured toward the building with his cigarette. Ash broke off and fluttered to the ground. "I work at this dump almost seventy hours a week and when I'm not here, I'm trying to earn a little extra designing websites, like I said. What do you think?"

Trinity glanced at Josie briefly. Their eyes met for a heart-beat but it was enough to activate their twin telepathy. Her sister didn't know where Josie was going with her questions, but she played along anyway. "Are you telling me you don't scroll social media when you're on the toilet like a normal person?" she asked Alec.

This time his laughter was deep and genuine. "Not since the trial. Reading all the negative comments about myself put me off social media for life."

Josie pointed toward his hand. "Is that a tattoo?"

Alec took one final exhale before discarding his cigarette butt. Turning his hand over, he rubbed at the tattoo. "Oh yeah. Manly, right?"

Trinity stepped closer, peering at it. "It looks like one of those sticky hand toys."

"I guess it does."

Her sister was right. Except it still only had four fingers. Four points. Round. Sticky. Josie was convinced it was an animal print though, just not a paw. She thought about driving into Williamsport today on Route 15, passing Clyde Peeling's Reptiland. She and Noah had taken little Harris there three times. He loved it.

"It's a frog footprint," Josie blurted out. "A tree frog."

Harris had wanted a tree frog for a pet after the first time they went. Misty was making him wait until he was a little older although Josie suspected she just didn't want live crickets in her house.

Alec stared down at the tattoo, eyes going hazy. "That's right. When we first adopted Erica, she was in bad shape emotionally. I started taking her to Clyde Peeling's, just the two of us. She loved it. Over and over we went until she started talking to me. Really talking. Being herself. Smiling, laughing."

"That's lovely," Trinity whispered.

"The frogs were her favorite. The first time she called me

dad—" his voice broke, "we were watching the orange-eyed tree frogs, and she said it. I almost cried right then and there. Later, when she got older, she told me that was the first time she felt like she had a real dad. Then for her eighteenth birthday, she wanted…"

The words got stuck in his throat. He pressed his palms against his eyes, trying to compose himself, and knocking his red paper hat off in the process. It fluttered to the ground.

"You got matching tattoos." Josie's heart galloped. She felt its heavy beats all the way to her fingertips. "Hers is behind her ear. Her left ear."

Trinity's eyes snapped toward Josie.

Alec dropped his hands, glassy eyes staring at her in shock.

Josie forged ahead, barely able to hear her own words over the blood roaring in her ears. "Was that Erica you were talking on the phone with when we got here?"

His shock turned to suspicion, lines creasing his forehead. "Yeah. Why?"

Josie decided to test out whether she'd heard him right when he muttered under his breath. "She's at the Patio Motel, isn't she? In Denton?"

"How the hell do you know that?"

"Erica might be in danger."

He turned away from her and shouted a curse as he stomped his feet on the ground. Josie took that as a yes.

"You didn't want to know our names, but I have to advise you that I'm a detective for the Denton Police Department."

"Shit," he said, keeping his back to her. "Is this about Bethany Rounds—I mean, Lila Jensen?"

"No," Josie said. "It's something else."

Facing them once more, he said, "I don't understand."

"I'm here as a private citizen. This is my sister, Trinity Payne. She's a television journalist."

The stream of expletives that poured from Alec's mouth was lengthy and impressive, even by a police officer's standards.

Trinity stayed silent, watching their exchange like it was a tennis match.

While Josie explained what had happened in Denton only hours before Noah was abducted, Alec stumbled back to the picnic table and plopped onto the bench. Sweat beaded along his forehead as Josie used her phone to show him the still photos of the mystery blonde. She could tell by the way he fumbled to light his next cigarette that he recognized his daughter.

Smoke shot out of his nostrils. "What happens now?"

"I have to call my colleagues. They'll go get her, bring her to the police station and interview her," said Josie. "Now."

"I'll call her," Alec said.

"No," Josie said. "She might run again. It's better if one of my colleagues just shows up."

"I want to be there. She might not talk to you otherwise."

FIFTY-ONE

Another headache pulsed behind Josie's eyes. The dim light in the small CCTV room had initially helped, causing some of the pain to recede. Now it roared back, a persistent throb. She blinked, trying to focus on the screen that showed Erica Slater sitting alone in the interrogation room down the hall. The girl drew her thin legs up to her chest, pulling the front of her blue sweatshirt over them, cocooning herself. It wasn't the same sweatshirt she was wearing when she fled the scene of Gina Phelan's stabbing. Like the oversized jeans hanging from her small frame, it was clean but worn. Somewhere along the way, she'd also picked up a pair of sneakers. Her blonde hair was clean and loose around her shoulders. Brown eyes scanned the room warily, pausing on the camera. She reminded Josie of a skittish animal. A bird that might let you get close to it but would fly away in a heartbeat.

When Alec and Gretchen confronted her at the Patio Motel, she had tried to get away.

Turner had been off shift when Josie called on the way back from Williamsport with Alec Slater in tow. Gretchen had met them at the motel, alone. Josie knew it was a conscious choice.

Too big a police presence might spook Erica, even with her father there. Then Gretchen had reminded Josie in no uncertain terms that she needed to be as far from this new development in the Phelan case as humanly possible.

To Josie, that was across the road from the parking lot. She and Trinity had watched as Alec knocked on the door to room three.

The moment Erica opened the door, Josie's senses had sharpened. Erica Slater was a runner. Josie knew one when she saw one. There was something about them. A wariness that charged the energy around their bodies. The subtle flickering glances at their surroundings like clockwork. Always searching for the quickest exit even when it wasn't necessary. Erica probably would have run even if she wasn't in some kind of trouble.

It had taken a few minutes for Alec to coax her outside. When she was halfway between him and Gretchen, she had taken off, sprinting down the road in a blur of movement. Alec had given chase but didn't make it very far before doubling over, out of breath. Gretchen had raced ahead with impressive speed. The strict diet and exercise regimen Paula had forced her to maintain was clearly paying off. Still, Josie couldn't risk Erica getting away. She'd driven to the bottom of the hill, turning the SUV to block the girl's path. The urge to get out of her vehicle and end the pursuit had been so strong, it made her hands twitch.

She hadn't missed the look of annoyance on Gretchen's face when she trapped Erica against the driver's side door. Josie knew she shouldn't look but she couldn't help it. Erica's face had been only inches from hers, separated by the glass of the window. Their eyes locked, and Erica's blind panic had transformed into something else. Recognition. Probably from the *Dateline* episodes. It was always those damn *Datelines* Trinity had insisted they do. Before Gretchen had urged Erica away, Josie noticed the fading bruises on her throat, only visible up close, and around her wrists when she brought her hands up, causing her sleeves to slide down.

Now, Josie watched the CCTV monitor as Erica's hands snaked out of those same sleeves. Her fingernails were painted a light purple which Josie had also noticed in their brief, wordless encounter. Erica glanced at the camera again and then used the nail of her thumb to chip away at the nail polish.

Josie pressed the palms of her hands against her eyes, willing the ache to go away. Caffeine would probably help. Drake had come to the station to pick up Trinity and they'd offered to make a Komorrah's run for her but she'd said no. She wasn't even supposed to be here. Trinity had done so much for her already, for Noah. Josie could get her own latte. Besides, the way Drake's hand rested possessively on her sister's hip made Josie feel guilty for keeping them apart even when Drake was in the same zip code. They wouldn't see it that way. Josie knew that but still, she wanted them to have a few hours alone.

She would have wanted that with Noah if the roles were reversed.

Sixty-eight hours and thirteen minutes.

The throbbing in Josie's head intensified. She thought about going to her desk and getting some of the ibuprofen she kept there but before she could, the door swung open.

"Quinn? You've got to be kidding me," Turner said, quickly closing the door behind him.

Just what her headache needed. Josie dropped her hands in time to see him stomping toward her, making the already small space seem impossibly close.

"You can't be here," he told her.

Josie didn't respond.

Turner tugged at his beard. "I'm serious, Quinn. Gretchen's going to talk to this kid, but the state police are on their way. If Loughlin or the Chief catch you in here—"

"I'm not going to talk to her," Josie said. "She'll never see me."

She didn't mention that Erica had already seen her.

If there was anything she could tell them about the man who killed Gina Phelan that might lead them to Noah, Josie needed to hear it for herself.

Turner pulled at his beard again. He got closer, standing beside her. Something bumped her shoulder. A can of his disgusting energy drink poking out from the pocket of his suit jacket. She waited for him to continue his little tirade, but he fell silent. The only sound in the room was his fingertips drumming against the table.

On the screen, Erica's legs slid out from under her sweatshirt as Gretchen entered the room. Straightening her spine, she said, "Where's my dad?"

"He's downstairs. Don't worry, he's not going anywhere." Gretchen set a can of Cherry Coke and a bag of Doritos on the table, sliding them over toward Erica. "He went to the store down the street and got these for you."

Erica stared at the offering wistfully before wiping a tear from her cheek. She took a deep, shuddering breath and said, "You can send him home. Everything's fine. He doesn't need to be here. If he misses work—"

"That's not really our call. If your dad wants to wait, we can't stop him."

Erica's shoulders slumped.

Gretchen sat in the chair closest to her, introduced herself, and read Erica her Miranda rights. The girl mumbled a yes when asked if she understood them. Again, she drew her legs beneath her sweatshirt.

"I don't think everything is fine," Gretchen began softly. "A lot of people have been looking for you. The last you were seen, you were covered in blood. Your dad says you told him you weren't injured. Is that true?"

Erica didn't answer.

"You can tell me," Gretchen said. "I won't report back to him if that's something you'd like to keep private. I do, however, need to get you medical attention if you're injured. We can arrange that without telling your dad all the details."

Erica rested her chin on her knees. Her voice was so small that it hit Josie right in the gut. "I don't want him to worry. That's all he does is worry about me."

Gretchen smiled. "That's kind of what parents are for, and I can tell you that even if your life was perfect and nothing went wrong, he'd still worry 'cause he's your dad and he loves you."

Erica used the sleeve of her sweatshirt to wipe away a few more tears. "I'm not hurt."

It was a lie. Maybe she hadn't been stabbed but someone had hurt her. Given the coloring of her bruises, Josie guessed it happened before the stabbing.

Gretchen knew it too but chose not to push, turning instead to the reason they were there. "Tell me about Monday."

"Monday?"

Repeating the question. Buying time. Josie wondered if she was going to claim it wasn't her in the videos of the protests and stabbing.

"The day you were outside of the construction site for the new children's hospital here in Denton," Gretchen clarified, taking a notepad and pen from the back pocket of her khakis.

Erica kept her eyes downcast. "I, um, was walking down the street and this guy came up behind me. He grabbed me by my shoulder and turned me around. There was a knife in his hand. He said something but I was so freaked out, I didn't hear it. I thought he was going to stab me but then this lady came out of nowhere. She was yelling at him, right in his face. The next thing I know, he's stabbing her. She told me to run so I did."

"Who was the guy?" asked Gretchen.

Erica's eyes snapped to Gretchen's face, her mouth forming

an O for a second before she found her composure. "I don't know."

"You never saw him before he came after you on the street?"

"No."

She was lying. Josie felt a simultaneous surge of excitement and anger. If Erica knew the attacker, it unlocked the entire case—three different cases, in fact—and brought them closer to finding Noah. But if she continued to lie about knowing him, she was effectively standing between Josie and her husband. The thought that the best lead they'd had in almost three days was right there, so close, and still out of reach caused hot rage to pour through the cracks in her emotional armor. This was one of the reasons Josie wasn't allowed in that room. Her fists clenched with the need to stalk in there and shake Erica until she told them what they needed to know.

Noah had been missing for sixty-nine hours.

FIFTY-TWO

"Easy there, killer," Turner murmured. His hand pressed down on Josie's shoulder, keeping her in the chair. The anger rolling off her body must have been palpable. For once, she wasn't annoyed by his uninvited touch. She was on a razor's edge right now, spinning out, self-control a flimsy thread she could no longer catch. Without Turner holding her in place, she didn't know what she might do, but she knew it would blow up her entire world. Some dispassionate, professional part of her pushed through the chaos in her mind, reminding her that with witnesses like Erica Slater, a certain amount of finesse was necessary. It would take as long as it took and there was no guarantee they'd get what they needed from her anyway.

"If this was a domestic dispute that Gina Phelan got in the middle of, you know we'll be able to track this guy down pretty fast," said Turner. "Palmer's got this."

Josie didn't have the mental resources to reflect on the fact that hell had just frozen over. Never in her life did she think she'd see the day Turner complimented Gretchen.

As if sensing her thoughts, he said, "Don't tell her I said that."

Gretchen put on her reading glasses. She flipped a page in her notebook. "Your dad tells me you're from Williamsport, but you were living in Lock Haven. What were you doing in Denton?"

Erica's legs slid down to the floor again. "Don't judge me, okay? I met a guy online. I know, I know, no story that starts like that turns out well, right?" She didn't wait for Gretchen to respond. "We were messaging on Snapchat for a while. He wanted to meet but I was really nervous. I don't trust that sort of thing, you know?"

Given the scheme Lila had hatched to ruin the Slaters' lives, it wasn't surprising.

"That's smart," said Gretchen.

Erica's fingers poked out of her sleeves, thumbnail chipping away at her nail polish once more. "You know how Snapchat has that location feature? Well, his was usually turned off but over the weekend I noticed it was on, and he was in Denton when he told me he was in Williamsport. My plan was to expose him as the big fat liar he was by coming down here and confronting him but when I got here, I couldn't find him and his location was turned off again. He sent me a snap once with a picture of him, but you know those disappear. I wanted to save it but then he'd know I did and if I took a screenshot, he'd be notified."

"This is too practiced," Josie said through gritted teeth. "While my husband is God knows where, she spent the last three days holed up at the Patio Motel concocting this shit and rehearsing it."

Erica had chosen to claim that Snapchat was her mode of communication with this mystery guy because its messages and photos disappeared within twenty-four hours. Most people had no idea that police could retrieve much of that data.

The furor swirling inside Josie's core threatened to blast through her emotional walls and incinerate any restraint she had left. The metal chair quivered under her weight. She was trembling all over and she hated herself for it. Hated her body for betraying her, especially here.

Turner kept gentle pressure on Josie's shoulder, and she despised the fact that it made her feel grounded. "Do some of that weird breathing shit you do, Quinn."

"Piss. Off."

He chuckled. "That's the spirit."

"Why would he care if you saved a photo of him?" asked Gretchen.

Josie dropped into her box breathing, hoping Turner wouldn't notice.

"He wouldn't care," Erica said. "But I didn't want to look desperate. Anyway, my point is that I did look around the last place his location was turned on—down the street from that construction place—but it's not like I had a photo to reference. I mean, I never met the guy. So yeah, I didn't get to do the whole dramatic confrontation thing."

Gretchen peered at Erica from over her reading glasses. "Your dad told us you were seeing someone."

"I wasn't. I just told my dad that because he definitely wouldn't approve of me making contact with anyone I found online."

"What was this guy's name?"

"John Smith," Erica answered easily. Too easily. "It's probably a fake name, though."

Gretchen smiled indulgently, like she was buying Erica's endless stream of bullshit. "Is his profile still accessible to you on Snapchat?"

"I don't know."

"How did you get from Lock Haven to Denton?" asked Gretchen.

Unsurprisingly, Erica had an answer ready. "Rideshare. My car is a clunker. There's no way it would have made it down here and back. Of course, I had to take like three rides since none of those companies go straight from there to here."

"Which rideshare?" asked Gretchen.

"I don't remember."

"Did you intend to stay here for a few days?"

"No. I was going to go home after I made him cry."

Turner smothered a laugh.

"Where did you lose your phone and purse?"

Erica's eyes flitted toward Gretchen and then quickly away. "I, um, I'm not sure. It probably happened when we were attacked."

We.

Gretchen didn't bother to point out that none of her things had been left at the scene. It was pointless. Erica would probably say the attacker took them, and he very likely had. Hopefully.

"Turner," Josie said. "Get her number from Alec Slater. Draw up the warrant to ping her phone. If this guy still has it and it's turned on, we could find him. Even if it's powered down now or he tossed it, we'd be able to see the last place it pinged and go from there."

He squeezed her shoulder. "In a minute."

She was about to argue, but Gretchen spoke again, seizing on the same detail Josie had. The fact that Erica referred to herself and Gina Phelan as "we."

"Had you ever met Gina Phelan before that day?"

"No."

Finally, a truth. Now Josie knew what it looked like when she didn't lie. No prepared answer delivered with a too-transparent attempt at charm. No tightening of the skin around her mouth, no pauses or hesitation before answering, no flitting back and forth of her eyes as she searched for an out. Yet, the "we" implied she and Gina Phelan had formed some type of bond which would not have been possible in the seconds it took for their assailant to stab her.

Gretchen jotted something down in her notebook. "How did you pay for your motel room?"

"I, um, had some cash in my pocket."

Another ready lie or maybe a half-truth. The uncertain pause—the "um"—gave her away. She had to have had cash to rent the room and to buy the burner phone she'd used to contact Alec, but Josie doubted she'd had it on her person. Hardly anyone carried cash anymore, particularly in Erica's generation. Perhaps she'd convinced a stranger to lend it to her or she'd stolen it.

Gretchen used her feet to maneuver her chair closer to Erica. "What happened to the clothes you were wearing when you were attacked?"

"I threw them away in the dumpster behind the motel." She touched the collar of her sweatshirt. "I bought these clothes from a lady a couple rooms down from mine."

Turner kept his hand on Josie's shoulder and used the other to take his cell phone from his pocket. His thumb tapped away at warp speed. Josie hoped he was sending the ERT over to the Patio Motel to see if the clothes were still there.

Gretchen moved even closer, subtly invading Erica's space. "Why did you run?"

"I don't know." Erica's eyelashes fluttered. Her thumb worked harder to dislodge more nail polish. "I was scared. Not thinking straight."

Given her body language, this, too, was true, though Josie suspected there was more to it.

"You ran right into a crowd of twenty people," Gretchen pointed out. "And kept going. Why didn't you stop and ask one of them for help?"

More purple flecks snapped off Erica's fingernails, landing

on the table. "I don't know, okay? It's not like I almost get stabbed all the time, okay? I just ran."

"You kept running," Gretchen said, though her voice was still quiet and free of judgment. "Then you hid. You weren't the aggressor in this situation. Why hide?"

Erica abandoned her nails and reached inside the front of the sweatshirt, coming up with a necklace. Josie hadn't noticed it when she was face to face with the girl. Now her fingers caressed the charm, keeping it covered from Josie's view.

"I don't know, okay?"

"Look at me." Gretchen put her pen down, pushed her reading glasses onto the top of her head and leaned her elbows onto the table.

Slowly, Erica lifted her chin, wincing as she met Gretchen's eyes.

"Given the bruises on your throat and wrists, I'd guess that someone is hurting you."

Erica closed her fist around the charm. "No one is hurting me."

"Where did you get the bruises?"

No response.

Gretchen didn't try to poke holes in Erica's neatly wrapped story. Instead, she got right to the point. "The man who came after you on Monday—you know him, don't you?"

"N-no. I told you, I never saw him before."

"You can tell me the truth, Erica."

"I am! I am telling the truth!"

Rage simmered under Josie's skin with each lie that rolled off Erica's lips. Turner's head stayed bent toward his phone as he scrolled and typed with his thumb. All the while, his other hand rested on her shoulder, steady and—she couldn't believe she was even thinking it—comforting.

"I'm thinking of ordering takeout," he said absently.

Josie lifted her head, glaring at him, and snarled, "I will punch you right in the throat."

He chuckled. "None for you then."

She opened her mouth to tear him a new one, but he squeezed her shoulder again and used his phone to gesture toward the monitor. "Pay attention."

Gretchen's tone was soft. "It can feel confusing—humiliating, even—when someone you care about becomes abusive. It happens more often than you think."

"What?" Erica said incredulously. "Are you serious? That's not what happened."

"There's no reason to be embarrassed."

"I'm not embarrassed!" Her voice went up an octave. "No one treats me like that. I mean it! No one."

Getting nowhere, Gretchen swiftly changed course. "You didn't come to Denton using a rideshare, did you?"

Silence.

"He brought you here, didn't he?"

Erica didn't answer. Her fist flexed around the charm of her necklace.

Gretchen tried another avenue of inquiry, one that Josie had been mulling over. "What happened when you got here? Did he expect you to do things for other men?"

In other words, had this boyfriend tried to traffic her?

Erica's face scrunched up. "What? No! That's—that's horrible!"

"Then it was just him hurting you?"

Erica glowered at her. "I told you, no one hurts me! I never saw that guy before."

"I know this is scary but Erica, I can help you. Keep you safe. But you need to tell me the truth."

"I am telling the truth! You're not listening!"

"You don't need to protect him."

"I'm not trying to protect him!" she shouted. "I don't *want* to protect him!"

FIFTY-THREE

Gretchen let the words hang between them.

Erica's eyes went wide. Her skin turned ashen. The silence stretched on so long, Josie began to wonder if time had stopped. Gretchen waited for Erica to fill it.

When it became clear she wouldn't, Gretchen said, "Tell me his name."

Erica straightened her posture and tilted her chin in what was probably meant to be defiance but the slight tremble in her lower lip told Josie she wasn't as confident as she tried to project. "I don't know his name. I already told you. No one is hurting me. I don't know the person who attacked us, okay?"

Us.

"I can make sure you're safe," Gretchen assured her.

"Stop saying that! I don't need help. I can take care of myself! I've always taken care of myself. I had to."

"I believe you," Gretchen said in that matter-of-fact tone that was uniquely hers. The one that always settled Josie when she was backed into an emotional corner and ready to lash out.

It worked. When she spoke next, Erica's tone wasn't so agitated. "It doesn't seem like you do."

"Then tell me," Gretchen said as if they had all day. As if she wasn't a detective questioning Erica about a murder. They were just two women having a conversation. Two women who recognized the damage in one another, if only for a moment, because there was no mistaking it. Under all her bravado, Erica was damaged. Even if Alec hadn't told them, Josie would have seen it for herself. She had no doubt that Gretchen had let Erica see the same in her own eyes, even if it was just for a moment.

Gretchen was attempting to build trust and then, at some point, she'd circle back to her original avenue of inquiry: the man who had stabbed Gina Phelan. Josie appreciated the strategy but with every minute that passed without his name, her anger threatened to burn her alive. Every inch of her skin was on fire. She tried her four-seven-eight breathing.

Erica released her necklace and reached for the can of Cherry Coke. "My dad? He's not really my dad. I mean, he's my real dad for sure but he's not my bio-dad."

While Josie hadn't shared the story behind Alec's embezzlement, she had briefed Gretchen on the fact that he had adopted Erica. Despite that, Gretchen played along as if she didn't know, letting Erica talk and get comfortable. "Alec isn't your biological father?"

Erica snapped the tab on the soda and took a sip. "He's actually my uncle but he's the best. There is no better person than him. I don't deserve him. His life was ruined all because of me."

"I'm sure that's not true," Gretchen said, probably thinking Erica referred to Alec having to adopt her.

Josie could tell from the way Erica furtively swiped at a tear rolling down her cheek that she was talking about the blackmail and embezzlement scheme. She'd taken the photos that started it all but what she didn't understand was that it wasn't her fault. She'd been an innocent kid. Lila had preyed on her.

"Thanks for saying that." Erica stared at the soda can. "But it's true. What I did to him—I thought I could make it right, but I messed it up. Big."

Josie frowned, her fury tempered momentarily. On the screen, Gretchen did as well.

Erica forced a smile and started speaking again, her words coming out more quickly. "I just never had anyone take care of me like him, so I didn't know how to act. My mom was always... I don't know. I thought she was so great 'cause she was the only thing I ever knew but thinking back, she wasn't the person I thought she was."

"In what way?" asked Gretchen.

Erica shrugged. "She did some messed-up stuff. She could be mean. Scary mean. Not all the time. She also made me feel important and special. I used to think it was because she loved me but now, I wonder if she only treated me that way because I loved *her* so much. I did everything I could to try to make her happy and she didn't even do the things any parent should do. I was always cold and hungry. My clothes never fit right. Neither did my shoes."

"Lots of parents want to provide those things but can't," Gretchen said. "They just don't have the resources."

"That wasn't it," Erica scoffed. "Let me tell you a story that sums up my mom. She had a nickname for me: Bug. My whole life I thought it was short for 'Lovebug.' Then she left me for good and I had to live with my bio-dad. I barely remembered him. He wasn't bad but I was really messed up in the head and he didn't know what to do with a kid. Anyway, one time we were talking and the nickname came up. I said Bug was short for Lovebug—and he laughed at me. He said she started calling me that as soon as I was born because I was ugly, like a bug."

Gretchen remained silent.

"I thought my mom was good." Erica's index finger circled the top of the can. "But she wasn't. The worst part was all the creepy guys coming around constantly. She never even tried to keep them away from me."

Josie flinched involuntarily, that admission hitting too close to home.

"Is that when you learned to take care of yourself?" asked Gretchen. "Not let anyone hurt you?"

"Oh, long before that," Erica smiled, a mischievous gleam in her eyes. "As shitty as my mom was, she taught me well."

Turner's phone chirped. He swore. Then his fingers dug into Josie's shoulder, and he hauled her up out of her chair. She clawed at his hand. "What the hell, douchebag?"

"Heather Loughlin is here," he said, pushing her toward the door. "She's on her way up with the Chief. You need to leave right now."

Josie resisted, trying to free herself from his grip. "Turner, this interview isn't even close to being finished."

"So what? You can't stay for the rest of it."

Noah had been missing for seventy hours. "Erica Slater is lying!"

"No shit, sweetheart."

"You see," said Erica. "All those pervs thought I was so innocent and sweet just because I was a little kid."

"Her phone," Josie protested. "You need to—"

Her words were lost as Turner pushed her roughly behind him. Slowly, he opened the door and peeked into the hallway.

"You weren't innocent and sweet?" Gretchen prodded.

"Douchebag!" Josie hissed.

He spun, towering over her in the cramped room. His glare froze her in place. For the first time since she'd known him, he looked well and truly pissed. His body was completely still, which was bizarre. A non-fidgeting Turner unsettled her.

"With all due respect, sweetheart, shut the hell up. I'm trying to get you out of here before you make a career-ending mistake. It's bad enough that you're the one who tipped us off to this girl. The brass already knows about your little side investigation. Even though you haven't been stripped of your police powers or anything, they're not happy. You are on razor-thin ice right now. If the Chief or Loughlin sees you up here or even in this building, all hell is gonna break loose."

"But—"

"It's not my first day, Quinn," Turner said. "We'll ping the phone. Get the records. Scour this kid's social media. Talk to everyone she knows. We'll go after this hard—just as hard as you would—and so will Heather's team, but right now, I need you out of here."

Erica's voice floated from the monitor behind them. "I wasn't innocent at all. When I couldn't hide or get away, I hurt them. As small as I was, there weren't many options, but I learned. Soft targets. The eyes and the balls. Sometimes bending back a finger worked. 'Cause they weren't the kind of guys who responded to tears or begging and as my mom always said, 'You can't always be all roses and sweetness, that don't get shit done.'"

Josie's world stopped. Everything went still and silent.

She started to turn back toward the screen, wondering if she'd imagined the words but the movement took forever and then Turner's hand closed around hers. He dragged her into the hallway, keeping her behind him. Josie's senses were blunted. She felt like she was underwater. Some muted part of her brain registered the stairwell door swishing open. The Chief's voice floated down the hall, his words unintelligible.

She stumbled as Turner shoved her into the nearest room and slammed the door. Lucky for her it was the file room and not a closet. As Josie leaned against a cabinet, waiting for Turner to sneak her out of the building, she tried to make sense of Erica's words.

No. Not Erica's words.

Lila's words coming out of Erica's mouth.

FIFTY-FOUR

Josie staggered into the municipal parking lot behind the stationhouse. Behind her, Turner said something before pulling the door closed. It was dark. The air was cool and crisp. She tried to get her bearings. Get her legs under her again. Think. A few uniformed officers passed her as they entered the building. Each of them stopped to greet her and offer words of support that she barely registered. She needed to go back inside. She needed to talk to Erica Slater.

Except she would never be granted access to the girl. Even if she managed to get her alone, speaking to her could be a colossal mistake. What Erica knew could be the key not only to finding Noah but to putting his abductors away for a very long time. Any conversation Josie had with her, even one about Lila, could taint that case. No one ever thought about the part that came after a big investigation, after a crime was solved, after arrests were made. That was left to prosecutors and usually carried out with little fanfare, but it was critical. Knowing that perpetrators would be sent to prison was the only thing loved ones had to cling to after their worlds had been shattered.

As desperate as Josie was to find her husband, a realistic

part of her, the seasoned professional buried beneath layers of rage and panic, knew that she might not get Noah back alive. If she didn't, the only thing worth living for would be seeing his killers go to prison. She couldn't jeopardize that despite the fact that with every fiber of her being, she yearned to throw every rule and regulation she'd ever known into the trash.

She looked around, as if coming out of a trance. Her vehicle wasn't in the parking lot. On shaky legs, she walked toward the front of the stationhouse. Where had she parked it? There were too many thoughts whirling in her brain.

You can't always be all roses and sweetness, that don't get shit done.

It was just an expression. Maybe Lila had heard it from someone else. Maybe lots of other people used it and it was just a coincidence that Erica knew it.

Except Josie knew in her gut that wasn't true.

She kept walking, giving a half-hearted wave to a cruiser that passed. Erica had unleashed a tornado inside her head. Snippets of her life with Lila, conversations she'd had over the last seventy hours, and the interview she'd just watched. They batted around in her mind, too fast for her to capture.

It didn't matter anyway. It wouldn't help locate Noah.

That didn't stop her from approaching Alec Slater when she saw him standing beside the front steps of the stationhouse, smoking a cigarette. He wasn't a witness. He had no direct knowledge of anything surrounding Noah's case.

"Hey," he said. "What's going on in there? Is Erica almost done? She's not in trouble, is she?"

Josie tried to organize her thoughts.

Alec's brow furrowed. "You okay?"

The man was disheveled, his stained white T-shirt rumpled and his curly hair in disarray. Large bags hung from under his eyes. The faint smell of grease mixed with the smoke flowing out of his nostrils. Earlier, he'd appeared exhausted and defeated. Now, all Josie could see was a parent's fear in the rigid way he held himself and how his fingers trembled when he flicked his butt to the ground. Josie didn't bother pointing out the standing ashtray nearby.

"Hey," he said. "You, uh, need me to call someone?"

"No," Josie finally managed.

"Is Erica in trouble?"

"Do you have any photos of Erica's mother? Not your wife. Her biological mother."

Alec's head reared back slightly. "What are you—you want photos of Erica's mother? What's going on in there?"

A few people sauntered down the street. Josie moved closer to him. "Erica is still being interviewed. That's all I know. Someone will call you when it's finished. I need to know about her mother. Do you or Erica have photos of her?"

He eyed her skeptically as he lit a new cigarette. "This is weird, you know that, right?"

"Please," said Josie. When he didn't acquiesce, she added, "I think I might have known her."

Alec waited until a woman walking her golden retriever passed. "Does this have anything to do with Lila Jensen?"

Josie nodded.

With a sigh, he said, "I never saw any pictures of her. My brother didn't have any when he brought Erica around. We live in the digital age so it's not like people print them out anymore. He always used those cheap, pay-as-you-go phones. It's not like his shit uploaded to the cloud. There were only a half-dozen pictures of Erica when she was a baby. Always bothered me. But none of her mom."

Lila had rarely let herself be photographed. Before leaving Denton, she'd destroyed every picture she could find. The only photo Josie had of Lila from back then had come from Dex.

"Tell me about her," Josie said.

"You're persistent, I'll give you that." Alec inhaled deeply, holding the smoke in his lungs for several seconds before exhaling. "I'm not sure I should. It's not really my story to tell. Erica doesn't talk about her much, but I can tell it's a sensitive subject."

He had no idea.

"It stays between us," Josie said. "Just like what you told me today."

"Awww shit," he muttered. "My brother—his name was Kiernan, by the way—said they met at a bar. Hit it off, although from the way he talked, the only thing they had in common was drugs."

Lila had struggled with addiction the entire time Josie knew her. That wouldn't have changed after she left Denton.

"The pregnancy was accidental," Alec went on. "They'd only been seeing one another for a few months. Kiernan didn't know what the hell to do but he was ready to step up. As much as he could, given his issues."

Josie did the math. Lila would have been forty-three when she gave birth to Erica. At that age, it was sometimes difficult to get pregnant or to carry to term and complications could occur. Illicit drugs wouldn't have helped. An ugly thought took root. Even at the ideal age and physically healthy, Josie couldn't have a baby, but Lila—older and using drugs—had done it with ease. The unfairness of it felt like a knife in Josie's back. Lila had done nothing but rain destruction over countless lives. Josie had spent her career making her city safer and protecting the most vulnerable.

Lila was the one who'd been rewarded with a child.

"Kiernan said Erica had some problems when she was first born but they seemed to resolve. Doctors didn't think the drug use would have any long-term effects."

"Lucky," Josie muttered.

Alec puffed smoke in little bursts. "No shit. Kiernan tried to make it work with this woman, do the whole family thing, but she got bored or started seeing someone else. Maybe both. He couldn't remember. She took Erica and left. Kiernan was too strung out to notice or even care, apparently."

"How old was Erica?" Josie asked.

"I think he said about a year old, maybe two. He saw her a few times over the years. When Erica's mother needed something. No regular contact."

That also fit Lila's pattern. Still, Josie couldn't imagine Lila wanting to keep a baby, much less care for one. Maybe she'd used Erica as a way to get things or scam people. Who could resist a down-on-her-luck single mother with an adorable little girl? Or was it as Erica had described: Lila had liked being worshiped by her daughter? Perhaps a bit of both.

Josie wondered what it had been like to be parented by a Lila who didn't hate your guts for becoming more than a pawn in her stupid games. Or for unwittingly being competition for a man's attention. By keeping Erica away from Kiernan Slater, Lila had ensured that she never had to compete with her daughter for his affection. There was a difference between Josie and Erica. Eli Matson believed he was Josie's father and, as such, he'd always prioritized her over Lila whereas Erica's biological father didn't appear to have bonded with her. Whether that was because of his struggle with addiction or because Lila kept Erica away, they would never know.

Erica was Lila's biological daughter. Josie couldn't help but wonder if that had made Lila treat her differently. Better, in some small way. Had Lila cared that Erica was her own flesh and blood? Had it mattered to her that she'd carried Erica in her body for nine months?

Josie shook off the thought. "What was Erica's mother's name?"

Alec squinted as he tried to remember. "Bonnie something. Romero, I think."

Bonnie Romero.

B.R. Lila's signature in choosing her aliases.

Belinda Rose, Barbara Rhodes, Bea Rowe, Bethany Rounds.
Bonnie Romero.

Josie massaged her temples with her fingers. The headache
she'd managed to ignore while engrossed in Gretchen's interview with Erica returned with a vengeance. She needed
ibuprofen and more caffeine.

She needed Noah.

This wasn't getting her closer to him, but another question
spilled from her lips anyway. "When did Bonnie Romero die?"

Alec tossed another butt onto the ground. "About six
months before Kiernan turned up on my doorstep with Erica."

Josie tried to recall their conversation from earlier, behind
Burgers. It felt like it had happened decades ago. "How old was
Erica then?"

"Eight, almost nine."

Faking the death of her alias and providing a death certifi-
cate to prove it was certainly not beyond Lila's capabilities.
Someone could always be blackmailed into giving her what she
needed. Bonnie Romero had died so that she could move on.

Then she left me for good and I had to live with my bio-dad.

After almost nine years, Lila had abandoned Erica in a way
that ensured she could not return. Had Erica stopped being
useful, or was that when Lila was first diagnosed with cancer?
When she'd returned to Denton to destroy Josie's life, she'd
been desperate for money so that she could afford some experi-
mental treatment. It was her last chance, she'd said.

Then she left me for good.

"Shit," Alec said, fiddling with his cigarette pack. "I'm out
of smokes."

Erica hadn't said, "then she died." Maybe "left me for good"
could be interpreted that way but Josie was certain that wasn't
what Erica meant.

"How much longer do you think it will be?" Alec asked,

craning his neck to look back and forth along the block, probably searching for a place to buy more cigarettes.

My wife always thought Erica was some master manipulator, but she was a kid! I mean yeah, she had a lying problem. She always did.

Erica had spent eight years trying to make Lila happy. Doing anything she could. Eight years under Lila's influence. Her tutelage.

I don't deserve him. His life was ruined all because of me... What I did to him—

Erica wasn't a master manipulator, but Lila had been. Josie had no doubt that Lila had exploited her sweet, young daughter's desperate need for love and approval for her own selfish ends.

What I did to him.

Alec brushed a hand through his curls. "Do you think they'd let me see her? Just for a few minutes? I'm starting to worry."

Erica grew up watching Lila plot and scheme against unsuspecting people. Watching her lie as easily as she breathed. She'd probably used her daughter in many of her ploys. That was their normal. In her most vulnerable years, Erica had depended on Lila for her very survival, had yearned for any little scrap of affection from her despite her major failings. It was a toxic carousel controlled entirely by Lila's whims. There wasn't a chance in hell Erica would rat out her mother, no matter how low she stooped or who she hurt. In the end, Lila would get what she wanted and Erica would be saddled with the guilt of it all. She would be left behind to witness the wreckage, the ruin of the only person who ever truly loved her.

Alec Slater. Her true dad.

At eleven years old, Erica wouldn't have had any concept of the ramifications of Lila blackmailing him. She probably never anticipated that he would go to such lengths to protect her. No one in her life had ever cared as much as he did. No one had ever shown her what good parenting or unconditional love looked like. By the time she realized what Alec brought to her life, the damage was done.

I don't deserve him.

Alec would forgive her. He would understand. But clearly, Erica didn't believe that.

It was sad. Tragic, even.

"Are you listening to me?" Alec said. "Do you think I can see Erica?"

Pain jackhammered against the inside of Josie's skull. "I don't know if they'll let you see her at this particular moment, but you can certainly ask for an update."

"I guess you're right." He crumpled the empty cigarette pack in his fist and nodded. "Are you going to let me in on why you have this sudden interest in Erica's mom and what it has to do with Lila Jensen?"

It wasn't Josie's place to share her theory that Erica had been in on the blackmail scheme. That was something he should hear from his daughter, if she chose to tell him. Unless he figured it out on his own. She did, however, share her theory about the true identity of Erica's mother. Shock drained all the color from his face. Josie could relate.

Everything she had learned in the last hour was a shock to her already weary system.

But none of it brought her closer to finding Noah.

Seventy-one hours.

FIFTY-FIVE

The muscles in Josie's legs ached. Her chest felt tight. Perspiration poured down her forehead and into her eyes, searing them and blurring her vision. The cool night air did nothing to help her overheated body. All she could hear was her own labored breathing and her sneakers pounding against the asphalt. Light fixtures had recently been installed along the jogging paths in Denton's city park, casting dull circles along the ground every five feet. Ahead of her, Drake's lean form was briefly illuminated as he passed under each one. Soon, he was four lamps ahead of her and her irritation burned worse than the sweat stinging her corneas. This run had been his idea, and he was kicking her ass.

Maybe that was the point.

If he thought he was going to best her, he was out of his damn mind. Her rage was a living, breathing thing now just waiting for an opportunity to be unleashed. With a grunt, Josie willed her body to move faster. She blocked out all the pain—every sensation—and pumped her legs harder. One lamp. Two. Three. Four. As she passed Drake, adrenaline surged through her, propelling her forward more quickly. When she finally looked back, he was gone.

It was almost ten o'clock at night. Josie's earlier headache was a distant memory thanks to a large dose of ibuprofen. Trinity had declined to run with them. She was probably at Gretchen's snoring next to Trout at that very moment. Noah had been missing for seventy-two and a half hours. Three days and thirty minutes. This probably wasn't the ideal time to go for a jog in the city park, but Josie knew that no would-be attacker stood a chance against her. Not when she was so close to her breaking point. Not when the tumult inside her was so desperate for an outlet.

By the time she reached the park entrance where they'd arrived, her T-shirt and shorts were soaked through. Fatigue spread through every inch of her, bone-deep, until she felt like she might collapse. Her muscles felt loose and jelly-like. For a few minutes, she was out of her head, floating over the snarl of questions and messy feelings that had inhabited every moment since Noah was abducted.

She knew she should stretch but all she could do was lie on her back across one of the benches as she tried to catch her breath. From the pocket along the side of her skintight running shorts, the hard shell of her phone case dug into her hip. She didn't bother to adjust it. Minutes later, Drake appeared, looking like he hadn't even broken a sweat.

Bastard.

With one large hand, he tapped her sneaker, and she drew her feet back, bending her knees to make room for him to sit. He leaned forward, elbows on his legs, and rested his chin on steepled fingers.

For a while, they just sat there and breathed. Josie watched moths and other flying bugs dive at the overhead lights that surrounded the little courtyard. The park was eerily quiet. All she could hear was a plane high above them, invisible in the night sky.

"I don't know how to do this," she blurted out.

Drake nodded. "I know."

"I'm even more shut out of the investigations than before. I know why the rule is in place—why I can't be anywhere near the case—any of the cases—but I can't take this."

She wasn't sure if it was her physical and mental exhaustion or Drake's stoicism that made her comfortable talking so honestly, but the words kept coming. There was no stopping them. No energy to stop them.

"We're talking about Noah. My husband! This is my life!"

"I know."

"I just want to punch someone." Josie used her forearm to wipe the moisture from her forehead. "Everyone, actually."

Drake looked at her. One corner of his mouth tipped upward. "That's relatable."

"Lila had a baby. A baby! Erica is a grown woman now, but still. It's... I don't know what it is."

She had told Drake everything. All the things she shouldn't even know because she was supposed to be home waiting for news. He would never breathe a word of it to another soul. Josie knew that beyond the shadow of a doubt.

"After chasing the Lila connection, this Baby Lila thing seems like it should be important but I'm not sure it matters at all."

"Because Erica's relationship to Lila doesn't get you closer to finding Noah," Drake said.

"Right," Josie agreed. "It's her relationship to the guy who stabbed Gina that's most important and I don't even know if she gave up his name."

"If she didn't talk to Gretchen, she's not likely to talk to the state police," Drake pushed a hand through his thick hair. "Like you said, there's something else going on. She's frightened. Whoever this guy is that she's tangled up with, he's got absolutely no qualms about stabbing a woman to death in broad daylight on a city street. He's part of some crew that's brazenly committing armed robberies and didn't even blink at abducting a law enforcement officer."

Josie was glad he said "abducted" and not "killed" even though any seasoned investigator would assume Noah had already been murdered. As far as they knew, he was alive. He had to be alive.

She sighed. "I know. It's not a stretch that this guy could be abusive toward his girlfriend, even one as spunky as Erica."

"This is how it is with domestic violence survivors," Drake continued. "You know this. The most dangerous time for them is when they're trying to leave. From the latest statistics I've seen, it's something like seventy-five percent of women are killed when they attempt it. Clearly, that's what this guy intended to do to Erica. He probably brought her to Denton, she saw an opportunity to escape, so she took it. Gina Phelan paid the price."

All of it made perfect sense. The entire Gina Phelan case wrapped up neatly like a gift with a giant bow on top.

"It doesn't really matter whether she talks or not," Drake added. "Now that her identity is known, Denton PD or Heather Loughlin's team will be able to track this guy down through phone and social media records. It'll solve the Phelan murder, all those armed robberies, and we'll find Noah."

"I hope so."

Everything fit together so perfectly. All the pieces fell into place. Why did every fiber of Josie's being resist this narrative? Was it just her fear that Noah wouldn't be found alive? Or was it easier for her to pick apart the tidy package than to think about her husband and what was going to happen to her life if she didn't get him back?

Those messy feelings strained against the limits of her emotional armor.

"There are loose ends," said Josie quickly, forcing herself to focus on anything besides the ever-widening cracks in that shield.

Drake swatted at a bug hovering near his head. "There always are."

"But this is different. The Lila thing. Erica's boyfriend was one of Lila's victims. What are the odds that her daughter just happened to end up with one of her victims? Well, the son of one of her victims."

Drake held out a hand to Josie and she took it, letting him pull her upright. He said, "Erica's boyfriend was in trouble. That's why he was searching for Lila's trophy box. If Lila targeted his father after she finished ruining Alec Slater's life, it's possible that he tracked down Erica the same way you and Trinity did—using the article. Or maybe Lila told him how she screwed Alec over. She loved to taunt people, especially kids, from what you've said. Maybe he didn't even know about Erica, or that she was Lila's daughter, he was trying to get to Alec because he thought he had something to offer. Meeting Erica was incidental. Or he did know about Erica and thought she had the box?"

Josie thought about the brown lock of hair tied with blue ribbon. Was that Erica's hair? She'd always assumed it was either hers or that of some other unlucky child Lila had victimized.

"Both of those explanations make sense, I guess," she said. "If this kid was that desperate, he might have thought he could get something out of Alec, just like Lila had. Embezzlement is a white-collar crime, and Alec never went to prison. This kid wouldn't have known from the article that he'd lost everything. Or, if Lila told him about Erica, then it stood to reason she would be in possession of the box. He clearly knew about it and its contents."

They lapsed into silence. Moths batted against the park lights, making soft little taps. Fear and frustration oozed from the cracks in Josie's mental shell. The quiet was dangerous now. It let in too many thoughts, too many feelings. She forced her attention back to the loose ends.

"Why was Gina Phelan outside the construction site?" It wasn't a question she expected Drake to answer, and he didn't. She continued, "Maybe she was looking for weaknesses in the perimeter or places they could install more cameras or lights, but she didn't bring her clipboard."

"Maybe she was walking to a nearby corner store for a snack," Drake suggested.

It was plausible but Josie still didn't buy it. She closed her eyes and replayed the day of Gina's murder, from her arrival on the scene to when she left. Something about Gina's actions that day had never sat right with her.

"She moved her car," Josie said. "Drove it off the site to get lunch and parked it back inside near the trailer and then about forty minutes before the stabbing, she took it back out and parked it a few blocks away. Why?"

Drake remained silent, letting her work it out for herself.

"Even if she didn't want her car inside the site for some reason, she could have just parked it on the street that runs behind it where all the other employees do. Not blocks away."

"Maybe she was outside the site because she was walking to her car," he said.

"She left her purse in the trailer. Her ID."

"You said she had her fob. Maybe she was just retrieving something from her car."

Josie thought about Gretchen's interview with Erica and the way she'd used "us" and "we" when she spoke about her and Gina being attacked. Before that, she'd said that she hadn't met

Gina prior to the day of the stabbing. Josie believed she was telling the truth but the "us" and "we" made it sound like they were a unit. Like they'd been walking down the street together. Maybe Josie was reading too much into it, but a voice in the back of her mind whispered that she wasn't.

"I think that Gina and Erica met before the stabbing," she said. "I don't know how or where or in what capacity, but I think they had already talked to one another. They were going somewhere together."

FIFTY-SIX

Drake leaned back, stretching an arm across the top of the bench. "Maybe Gina saw Erica while she was out for lunch, realized Erica was being abused, and decided to come back and help her get away from this guy. Get her into the car and drive her somewhere."

"Maybe," Josie said. "It probably would have been safer to bring Erica inside the site—at least until she figured out her next steps—instead of coming up with some elaborate plan to rescue her."

"If Erica was as scared as you say, she probably wouldn't have gone to the site with Gina."

Drake managed to find a place for every piece of the puzzle that didn't fit. But there were two things that still bothered Josie. An hour before she was stabbed shielding Erica with her body, Gina made two calls to her DA friend in Montgomery County. Not one but two. It was doubtful that any criminal charges would be brought against the company or the Phelans themselves in connection with the quarterback who had died at the build. Even if Gina was concerned about that, discussing it with her prosecutor friend would not have been urgent.

Certainly not pressing enough to make two calls in a short span of time.

Drake took his phone from his running armband and checked it. "We should get back."

The second thing that nagged at Josie was the obviously long-standing tension among the Phelans that revolved around some kind of sibling rivalry between Gina and Mace. It was clear that Tilly and Clint Phelan found their son lacking compared to their daughter. What had Clint said to Mace in the trailer when they were being questioned by Josie and Turner?

If she wasn't always cleaning up your messes.

What messes? Was Clint talking about the football player who had died after sneaking onto the site? That was only one mess. Clint's comment implied that his son had been screwing up for a long time. Josie wasn't well-acquainted with the Phelan company's overall safety record, but she'd never heard of any other builds having problems or "messes" to clean up. Mace himself had said they'd never had any prior issues.

Maybe Josie was grasping at straws because it was the only thing left for her to do, but she felt like she was missing something. Possibly a history in which Mace did stupid things and then Gina swooped in to do damage control, brushing things under the carpet so they never came to light. Protecting both the family and company reputations. If that was the case, did those past incidents have anything to do with why Gina had acted so strangely that day? Anything to do with Erica?

"It's getting late," Drake said. "I'm not going to tell you what you should do, but sleep is your friend."

What if they were wrong about Erica's movements that day? Had she initially shown up at the rear entrance of the site seeking help? Or in an attempt to hide from her boyfriend? If she had, Gina likely wouldn't have wanted to call the police to come there. It would have brought more negative attention than the company was already receiving. Driving Erica to the police station made more sense. But none of the workers that Josie and Turner had interviewed saw her. Then again, any of them could have lied.

"Josie?"

If Gina's intention was to get Erica off the site and somewhere safe, why didn't she notify her brother? Mace ran the company. At the very least, she should have made him aware that someone else had illegally entered the site and that she was handling it. She hadn't told anyone, not even Shirley Swenson, the field administrator. If Gina was just trying to smuggle Erica off-site to avoid bad press, why had she called her friend the district attorney? Why park her car blocks away so they had to walk to it? Why not leave it by the trailer, hidden from the public, and then drive Erica wherever she needed to go?

Because it wasn't the public they were hiding from.

Drake moved to stand up, but Josie gripped his forearm. The sweat on the back of her neck suddenly felt cold. "Gina wasn't just helping Erica escape her abusive boyfriend. She was cleaning up a mess."

"What do you mean?"

"We've been assuming the only possibility is that Gina encountered Erica outside the site, but what if she didn't? What if Gina found her inside? Clint Phelan said Gina was always cleaning up Mace's messes. I thought he meant OSHA violations or something, but what if he was talking about Mace's personal life? We never even checked to see if Mace has a criminal record."

Drake stroked his goatee. "Are you trying to say that Mace Phelan—the owner and CEO of Phelan Construction—was holding Erica Slater against her will on an active construction site with hundreds of workers on the premises and angry protestors just outside the gates?"

When he said it like that, it did sound absurd. Josie forged ahead anyway. "Maybe not him specifically. What if Erica's boyfriend was a Phelan employee? What if he wasn't her boyfriend at all but he abducted her?"

"And he thought bringing her to work was a good idea?"

"I don't know." Josie blew out a frustrated breath. It was far-fetched and she knew it.

"Weren't there still photos of the guy who stabbed Gina Phelan? Wouldn't the inquiry into the employees and subcontractors on the site that day have turned him up?"

"We never got really good photos of him," said Josie. "But Turner would have looked into every employee on shift that day, every subcontractor, everyone who set foot in the place, and he didn't find anyone he thought matched the description. I mean, I assume he didn't. We didn't actually talk about it."

Normally, she would worry that Turner had not done his job but with Noah's abduction, he'd proven himself to be more reliable than ever.

Drake looked at his phone again. Josie was close enough to see that Trinity had sent him a text asking if Josie was still with him. He had changed her name in his contacts to "My Future Wife." It warmed Josie. Those three little words were so adorable and so achingly sweet that she wanted to hug him. She loved how head over heels Drake was for her sister. Trinity deserved it.

Then Josie felt like the worst person ever when a stab of jealousy pierced her heart. It made her think of Noah. If she didn't get him back, would she be destroyed by this feeling every time she saw a couple in love? There wouldn't be anyone else for her after Noah. There couldn't be. She twirled her wedding band around her finger. The vow he'd made to her on their wedding day was engraved inside. To always run toward the danger with her. He'd had to shorten it so it would fit the ring but that was his forever promise to her, and he'd kept it time and again. His ring was inscribed with her vow: that she would always come home to him.

Now everything was turned upside down. She needed him to come home to her.

"Hey."

Josie blinked.

Drake was peering at her, concern etched into his face. "Come back," he said quietly. "Wherever you are in your mind right now, come back."

She blinked again and fisted her left hand in her lap.

"Let's explore this idea of yours," he said. "Erica was inside the site. Since she was in bad shape, we can theorize she was being held against her will. I don't think we have enough information to guess why. Maybe you're right. This kid we thought was her boyfriend wasn't her boyfriend. He runs with a crew that commits robberies, home invasions, and assaults. I doubt they'd turn their noses up at kidnapping women. Hell, maybe this was some attempt at trafficking her. If you want to go really big, maybe they traffic women all the time and Mace Phelan is the mastermind."

Josie arched a brow. "Don't mock me."

"I'm not," Drake said. "Just throwing out possibilities but for right now, we'll put aside the how and why Erica came to be on that site. Let's just start with the basic premise that she was there. Hidden away someplace. That seems like a hell of a ballsy thing for someone to do but we'll go with it anyway."

"It's a big site," Josie said, grateful to get back to a topic that wasn't going to send her off the deep end. "If you knew it well and knew the timing of everything, like which areas were going to be active and when, then I'm sure you could find a place to hide a person. Plus, it's loud as hell. Even if Erica was able to make noise, who's to say anyone would have heard it?"

"Okay," Drake said. "I'll buy that for now but why hide her at an active construction site that's the focus of a huge local scandal? If it's someone who works there, that's pretty risky. Sure, some assholes are dumb enough to do it, but there are a ton of variables that would be impossible to control. Although I suppose if he's there all day, it's easier to keep an eye on things. Logistically, though, it's not a long-term solution to keeping a kidnap victim. She's got to eat and use the bathroom."

"I don't think she was there for any length of time," Josie said. "It makes more sense that she was being held somewhere else and then brought to the site. Maybe even that day. What if Erica Slater was brought there that day so she could be disposed of? If they'd kidnapped her or tried to traffic her, they couldn't let her live. I'm sure there are lots of places to hide a body on a construction site so that it's never found again."

Nausea rocked her stomach as thoughts of Noah broke through. Images of her sweet, gorgeous husband flashed through her mind. This time it wasn't his smile or what waited for her beneath his clothes. It was his lifeless body being dumped into a hole and covered over with dirt. Before she could wonder exactly how that would work with all the excavating and grading that needed to be done on building sites, Drake nudged her ribs with his elbow, bringing her back to the present again. "Keep going."

Josie took a deep breath. "It would have had to happen after hours, so he just had to keep her hidden until then. Gina was inspecting the site. What if when she came back from lunch, she stumbled upon Erica and decided to get her out? Whatever Erica told her made her believe it was too dangerous for her to call the police or to parade Erica around the site. She decided to sneak her out."

Drake nodded along. "She had to get Erica out to her car but to do that, it had to be parked where no one on the site would see them get inside it."

"So she moved her car," said Josie. "Then came back for Erica. They both ran toward the protestors after the attack, but Gina's car was in the opposite direction which makes me think she snuck Erica out along the fence rather than walking her out the back entrance."

"Was there a gap in the fencing when you showed up to the scene?"

Josie shook her head. Someone had covered it up, put everything back into place.

"But that guy caught up with them," Drake said. "Where did he come from? He had to be either working at the site or visiting it for some reason—like independent contractors or truck drivers making deliveries."

Drake was right. How had they missed it though? Josie and Turner had interviewed every employee present when Gina was killed. Just in case some of them had already gone home, they'd been given a list of every person who had set foot on the site that day.

"Son of a bitch," she said, realization dawning.

Mace had given them the list. He'd sent Shirley home. Josie and Turner had taken a cursory look around the site while Mace compiled the list for them and instructed all employees to come to the trailer so they could be interviewed.

Drake arched a brow at her.

"It's Mace," she said. "I'm telling you, he's involved in this somehow."

FIFTY-SEVEN

"We're working on something," Gretchen said. "But I can't talk right now."

Josie's fingers tightened around her cell phone. She heard the guilt in her friend's voice but that didn't make her feel better. Freshly showered and barefoot, she paced at the foot of the bed in Gretchen's guest bedroom. It was one thirty in the morning and Trinity and Trout were sound asleep, giving an encore of their snoring opera. Josie had to speak louder to be heard over it. "Then don't talk to me. Just listen. I think Mace Phelan is involved in his sister's murder and whatever happened to Erica. I don't know how or what his role is in all of this but he's part of it which means, at the very least, he knows one of the guys who was there the night Noah was abducted."

Before Gretchen could protest, Josie launched into her theory, which turned entirely on her other unproven theory that Gina had been trying to smuggle Erica out of the site without alerting Mace. It still sounded a little thin, even to her, but she was beyond caring. If she was a raving lunatic, it was because Noah's absence had made her into one. On the way back from the park, Drake hadn't discouraged her, but he had reminded her that there was no actual evidence to support anything they'd discussed.

By the time Josie walked into Gretchen's house, doubt had crept in. She kept remembering Mace's shocked expression when Turner told the Phelans how Gina had died. He had appeared genuinely surprised and distraught. That didn't necessarily mean anything though. Over the years, she'd met plenty of murderers who were Oscar-worthy actors. Mace could have been faking his reaction, but Josie had a feeling he wasn't.

Whatever he was part of, she didn't think he ever meant for Gina to be harmed.

When Josie finished talking, there was silence on the other end. She thought she heard the voices of several of their colleagues in the background. She was dying to know where they were, what they were doing, but she dared not ask. Thirteen texts to Turner had gone unanswered.

"Josie, I'm just not sure—"

"I know it's a reach. I do." She paused, leaning over to look at Trinity's laptop, which she'd left open on her side of the bed. Before her shower, she'd done some research on Mace Phelan. "Did you know that Mace Phelan was sued civilly four times in the last ten years?"

There was a long pause before Gretchen said, "I'm listening."

Over a dozen tabs were open in the browser, each one containing information Josie had turned up. She clicked through them as she talked. "Three of the lawsuits were brought by the parents of teenagers who attended parties at his residence in Lewisburg where their underage daughters were given alcohol and later had some sort of accident that resulted in injuries. Two of those cases were dismissed. The third—a girl who was found dead on Phelan's property from alcohol poisoning—settled. The last suit was brought by a twenty-five-year-old man who got into a fight at a party at Phelan's Harrisburg residence and sustained injuries. That one was also dismissed."

Mace's big sister had cleaned up a lot of messes.

There hadn't been any criminal charges filed. Other than a couple of DUIs, his record was clean. At fifty-seven, he'd been divorced three times. He had a twenty-eight-year-old son named Ellis. However, Mace's son had changed his last name from Phelan to his mother's maiden name as soon as he turned eighteen. He now lived in Seattle and from what Josie gathered, he was estranged from the entire Phelan family. She couldn't help but wonder what had caused the rift, but it wasn't relevant so she didn't mention it.

"I see where you're going with this," Gretchen said. "Where there's smoke, there's fire but right now there is absolutely nothing linking this guy to any of these cases."

Josie heard what she didn't say, too. Investigators couldn't go after Mace Phelan without those links, without a reason. They were bound to follow the evidence available to them. She knew it. Drake had reminded her of it. In her professional experience, following tangible leads while also listening to your instincts was walking a legal tightrope. Sometimes your instincts were left screaming and there wasn't a damn thing you could do about it. They didn't even have proof that Erica Slater had been inside the construction site, let alone that she'd been involved with Mace. If Josie was the lead on the Gina Phelan case, she'd track Gina's murder suspect first and worry about linking Mace later.

But she wasn't worried about the Gina Phelan case right now. She wanted her husband back. It stood to reason if Mace Phelan was connected to the man who'd stabbed his sister and that man had been part of Noah's abduction, then Mace might know something about what happened to Noah.

There was one other thought that kept rattling around in her head, sending shivers through her body. If Mace and the men he was involved with had brought Erica to the build to make her disappear, they might have done the same to Noah already. Perhaps that was the reason they'd taken him from the house.

No. She wasn't going there.

If there was even the slimmest possibility that he was still alive, Josie had to find him before he became part of a concrete footer on some construction site.

Josie had little doubt that Gretchen knew exactly what she was thinking. On the other end of the phone, the voices of their colleagues faded to nothing. When Gretchen spoke next, her voice was so low that Josie strained to hear her words. "We've got a name."

"Who?"

"I can't tell you that. Not now."

"Did Erica Slater—"

"Erica was released after her interview with Heather. Alec Slater checked them into a local hotel. The DA may want to speak with her tomorrow."

They hadn't gotten the name directly from Erica, then. Perhaps they'd found it in her phone or social media records.

"I can't tell you anything more. I just wanted you to know. They're holding it back from the press for now, hoping to find him quietly so neither him nor his associates get spooked. Everyone's looking for him. There's a statewide BOLO."

It was news Josie had desperately wanted to hear for seventy-six hours but now that she had, she didn't feel much better. How long would it take to find this guy? Would he crack and tell Heather what happened to Noah? Give up the location? If so, how long would that take? What if he refused to say anything? Lawyered up and kept Noah's fate to himself? Heather would have to track down the other guys he'd been working with and try to get one of them to talk. That would take even longer with no guarantee that any of them would tell police where to find her husband.

Her phone beeped with an incoming call but she ignored it.

"Josie," Gretchen said. "The best thing you can do for Noah right now—the only thing you can do for him—is to get some sleep and let the rest of us do our jobs."

She nearly choked on her next words. "I know."

They hung up. Josie sank onto the edge of the bed. Trout's head lifted, his sleepy eyes curious and a little worried. Before she could soothe him, her phone rang again. She swiped answer.

"Miss Quinn?" Alec Slater's voice was strained. "I need help. Erica's gone."

FIFTY-EIGHT

Balancing Trinity's laptop on her knees, Josie slouched down in her seat and watched Officers Brennan and Conlen leave the Woodland Creek Inn. It was a major step up from the Patio Motel. Clean, well-lit, well-managed and properly fitted with very good security cameras. The parking lot was small, but she had managed to find a spot where she wasn't likely to be seen that also gave her a clear view of the entrance. While she waited for them to pull away in their cruisers, she sipped from a paper cup. Bitter gas station coffee scalded her tongue. She tried not to gag. Spewing it all over the computer and the inside of Trinity's rental car would not go over well with her sister. Despite the fact that the sludge was probably a day old and that there had been no sugar or creamer on hand to soften the taste, she needed the caffeine. It was four a.m.

Noah had been missing for seventy-eight and a half hours.

Drake and Gretchen had given her good advice. Sleep. Rest. Once Alec Slater called, there was no way in hell that was happening, no matter how badly her body ached for it or how her eyes burned with exhaustion. After checking into the hotel, Alec had had a long conversation with his daughter. Then he'd taken a drive to a nearby convenience store to buy more cigarettes. When he returned, Erica was gone. Taken. He was certain of it.

Josie dutifully told him to call 911. He'd wanted her to come but she couldn't. Not in a police capacity. Not in any way that would interfere with the job her colleagues had to do. Instead, she promised to be there after he spoke with them. She wasn't even sure why. This wouldn't lead to Noah. It wouldn't give her the name of the man currently being hunted by Denton PD and the state police.

But she didn't know what else to do and the desperation in Alec's voice had called to her like a siren song. He was as terrified of losing his daughter as Josie was of losing her husband.

She choked down the rest of the coffee. The display on the laptop screen was dimmed as much as possible so she didn't draw attention to herself. Between that and Josie's tired eyes, completing her research had been a struggle. Making a list of all current Phelan construction sites as well as all properties owned by Mace had given her something to do while she waited for Alec. She'd come up with a third theory to top off her Tower of Absurdity which was supported by absolutely no evidence and sponsored by her raving lunacy.

But if Josie was right, then Gina had found Erica inside the children's hospital build and tried to sneak her to safety because she knew that Mace was somehow involved in whatever led to Erica being bruised, battered, and held against her will. If Josie was right, Erica had been brought there for the purposes of being killed and buried where no one would ever find her body. The mysterious "Dylan," or Mr. O Negative, had seen the two women escaping together and in the heat of the moment, stabbed Mace's sister to death. Josie wasn't sure how or why he'd gone from that scene to her home, or the role the rest of his crew played in what happened to Noah, but her theories dictated that Mace would have known that the three men had taken a law enforcement officer.

Obviously, they couldn't be trusted to keep a twenty-year-old girl captive. They couldn't be relied on not to kill Mace's sister. They also couldn't retrieve an item from Lila's trophy box without injuring and abducting a law enforcement officer. Josie doubted that Mace would then entrust them with handling Noah—dead or alive.

Alive. He has to be alive.

Between the development projects being handled by the company and Mace's own personal properties, there was a plethora of options for hiding or disposing of a body. Noah was at one of them. She was certain.

Or maybe she was just certifiably insane now.

Josie didn't know what she was going to do with the list at this juncture, but she liked having it.

From her periphery, she saw Alec push through the doors of the hotel, still dressed in the same clothes he'd had on behind Burgers. He paused to light a cigarette, scanning the parking lot. When Josie flashed the headlights, he lumbered in her direction. She stepped out of the car before he reached it and motioned for him to walk with her.

Woodland Creek Inn was adjacent to Denton University's campus. Silently, they made their way out of the parking lot, through an empty plot of land to the crest of a hill that overlooked the stadium. The structure was no more than a hulking shadow, the soft yellow lights along the pavement surrounding it barely piercing the darkness.

"Here," Josie said, stopping before they made their descent. "University police patrol the campus during the night. I don't think either one of us is prepared to deal with that kind of hassle."

Alec snorted. "You got that right."

Between the hotel behind them and the stadium below,

there was enough ambient light for them to see one another, although not very well. The end of Alec's cigarette flared orange, giving Josie a clearer glimpse of his face. He'd been crying. A pit opened up in her stomach.

"The officers you spoke with," she said. "Did they pull the footage from inside the building?"

"And outside, yeah," he said in a scratchy voice. "I was right. They took her. Two men. Grabbed her just down the hall from our room. She'd gone to the vending machines. When I got back from the store, she wasn't in the room so that's where I went looking for her. One of those nasty sneakers she was wearing was on the floor and... I don't know. Father's instinct, I guess. I knew something was wrong."

"I'm sorry," said Josie. "Did the officers say anything about the two men?"

Alec lowered himself to the grass, pulling his knees toward his chest and resting his forearms over them. The cigarette bobbed between his fingers. "No. Wouldn't even let me watch the footage. They were going to get still photos and try to pull a license plate number from the car they were driving."

It was no coincidence that Erica had been kidnapped after she came out of hiding and talked with the police. A shiver ran the length of Josie's body as she settled beside Alec. Entering a hotel and snatching a grown woman in full view of surveillance cameras was incredibly brazen. After the perpetrators had been so careful to avoid getting caught during the numerous armed robberies they'd committed, this seemed out of character.

It was sheer panic.

They were trying to tie up loose ends. This was the most dangerous time for Erica and for Noah, if he was still alive.

Alec stubbed out his cigarette under his boot. "All these years, I never told another soul what really happened with the embezzling. Not until I talked to you and your sister. It felt... good to, uh, let it out."

Josie said nothing.

"Thank you for coming, especially since your husband is still missing."

"You're welcome," she choked out.

There was a moment of silence and then Alec began to sob quietly, his shoulders quaking. His despair hung heavy in the air between them, stoking Josie's own fear. Mentally, she patched the holes where it poked through her protective shell. She laid a palm on Alec's forearm. Staring straight ahead, he nodded and then patted her hand. It was all she could do. There were no words of comfort in this situation. Josie knew that firsthand.

After several minutes, he calmed enough that she withdrew her touch. Lifting the collar of his shirt, he wiped his face. "It shouldn't be this damn hard to protect one kid. I don't even know what the hell kind of trouble she got herself into in the first place."

From everything Josie had learned in the last several hours, she was inclined to believe Erica had been at one of the parties that Mace Phelan liked to throw at his sprawling residences and seen something she shouldn't have. She was certainly in the same age range as the young women whose parents had sued Mace for injuries sustained at or after leaving one of his parties.

"She didn't tell you?" Josie asked, trying not to sound too eager but desperate to know if Erica had told her father anything she hadn't shared with the police. Something that might lead her to Noah.

"Nope," Alec said. "She wouldn't tell me one damn thing. Not about that."

FIFTY-NINE

The concussive boom of the gunshot rattled Erica's teeth. A thunderclap of pain slammed into her head, ripping through her ears. Something hot and wet splattered across her face. The small basement room couldn't contain the vibration. It reverberated all around them. Her and the three men. Except now it was her and two men because the other one collapsed at her feet, and she knew from the way his head looked that he was gone, and he wasn't coming back. Was he one of them or someone completely different? She'd been too busy fighting the assholes who took her from the hotel as they shoved her into the room to realize there was another man already inside. Then he was gone. In a heartbeat.

A scream tore from Erica's throat before she could stop it. It kept going and going. Her entire body was numb except for where the blood and bits of bone and tissue clung to her skin. Then one of the other men—she never did learn their names—stepped forward and slapped her across the face. Her head whipped to the side so hard and fast that she stumbled and fell, catching herself awkwardly on a hand and a knee. If there was pain, she didn't feel it. Cold eyes stared down at her. His lips were moving but she couldn't hear him. The echo of the gunshot was too loud in her brain.

Everything was moving too fast and too slow. Strong fingers dug into her bicep, dragging her body upright. She was pretty sure she was screaming again. Another slap landed on her face and the dim room wavered. Then the barrel of the gun was right there, between her eyes, nearly touching her skin, and she knew this was it.

The end.

SIXTY

Josie was glad it was dark enough that Alec couldn't see the disappointment on her face. What Erica knew would lead her to Noah. She was sure of it and yet, that information remained out of reach—maybe permanently so at this point. Acid roiled in her stomach. Her chest constricted.

No. She would find another way.

"You know," Alec continued, "when I got back to the room and Erica wasn't there, I thought she ran off. Since she wouldn't tell me what the hell was going on, we, uh, talked about some other stuff. You were right about everything. Erica's mom—Bonnie or Bethany or Lila or whatever the hell her name really was—left her with my brother. Everyone thought she was dead, but Erica knew the truth. An eight-year-old kid abandoned by her mom, and having to keep that secret."

Lila didn't always have sensible reasons for the things she did. She couldn't have known that Kiernan would pass away and leave their daughter with Alec and his wife—the perfect targets. There was no end to Lila's scheming but sometimes she just got bored.

"She was in on it, you know? My daughter helped that woman blackmail me."

Josie nodded.

Alec barked a laugh. "You knew that already, didn't you?"

"It was just a theory," said Josie. "It wasn't my place to tell you."

"I figured it out—between all the stuff you told me and Erica confirming her mom wasn't dead when we adopted her. I confronted her tonight and she told me the truth about that, too."

"I'm sorry."

"The only person who should be sorry is that evil woman."

"Did Erica say why Lila left her behind?" Josie asked.

Alec shifted, digging inside one of his pockets. "She wouldn't tell me that, but she did say that a few years later when her mom got back in touch and needed help with this whole blackmail scheme, it was because she was sick. Dying. She told Erica she needed the money for treatment. That probably wasn't even true."

"I don't know if that's what she used the money for but she did have cancer."

He found what he was looking for in his pants pocket, curling a fist around it. "Imagine using an eleven-year-old kid like that. Manipulating her into taking those photos. Makes me sick. Erica held onto the secret for so long. Until now I had no idea the guilt was eating away at her. She thought if I found out, I'd hate her. I never saw her so scared, so upset as I did tonight when she told me that she thought I'd stop loving her, stop being her dad."

Josie looked over at him. "It's because of the way Lila raised her. Unconditional love is a myth to someone like Erica. You always worry that you'll do something wrong or that the person who loves you will find out that you're broken and leave."

"I tried to tell her that's not how this works." Alec opened his fist and let a thin chain fall through his fingers. A necklace. He rolled the charm around in his palm. "You know, I never thought about kids before my brother showed up with Erica. My life seemed fine. Wife, career, nice house. It was boring but I figured that's what adulthood was supposed to be like. Then this little person showed up and sure, she was fragile and damaged and shut down, but she was also smart and funny and kind and just a really cool kid. She needed us. Needed me. All of a sudden, I had a purpose. It was so clear. My job was to be her dad. I *wanted* to be her dad. It was easy. Even the hard shit was easy because I loved her in this completely selfless way that I didn't even know was possible."

Now emotion battered against Josie's shield. What Alec described was exactly what she and Noah hoped to give a child one day. Listening to him, she liked the idea of giving that kind of love to a child who might not have grown up with it otherwise. But that dream was dead, and her husband might be as well.

Seventy-nine hours.

"I don't regret it," Alec said, his voice low and throaty. "Not one fucking thing. Not the embezzling or the way people treated me when I got caught. Not losing my career, my marriage, my house. I'd do it again and again. I tried to tell her that. You wanna know the worst part?"

SIXTY-ONE

When the barrel touched her skin, Erica felt its heat. She expected it to be cold. Cold metal. Instead, it was hot. Probably because it had just been fired. The singe, the pressure of it against her flesh was just a reminder that she was out of time, out of ways to stall. There were no more tricks up her sleeve. No more lies or fast-talking that might buy her more time or get her out of this. Her fingers scrabbled against her chest, searching for her necklace, but it wasn't there.

Maybe it was foolish to believe that it would protect her. It hadn't so far. Her brilliant plan had gone horribly wrong. Every time she thought things couldn't get worse, some fresh new hell was unleashed, and she realized that her worst mistake was a failure of imagination. Never did she think that things could get so bad. She wasn't as savvy as she liked to believe. Wasn't as cunning or calculating as her mother.

An irritated voice broke through the ringing in Erica's ears. It was faint, as if it came from another room, but she knew it was the other man, standing near the door. "Come on, man. I'm tired of this shit. Shut her up, once and for all."

Erica closed her eyes and touched the little frog foot tattoo under her ear, conjuring an image of her dad. Even though she'd let him down time and again and ruined his life, he still loved her. He'd told her as much at the hotel, after she came clean about her part in the blackmail scheme. She wanted her last thoughts to be of him.

SIXTY-TWO

Josie nodded in answer to Alec's question because she couldn't speak just then.

He bounced the charm in his hand, and she got a better look at it. Her scar tingled. A jolt of realization cut through the emotion of the moment, making her heart pound.

"Erica still loves her mother," Alec said. "Even after all the bad stuff she did, Erica's still trying to gain her approval. Trying to get acceptance from a ghost."

Josie considered explaining how the whole toxic mother thing worked. Every little girl yearned for her mother's love. When that mother was too toxic or evil to give it, a void formed in the little girl's soul, leaving her incomplete and desperate to fill it because if she didn't—if she couldn't—that meant she was irreparably broken. Damaged. Worthless. Even when the little girl grew up and understood that the failing was with her mother and not her, the longing for something that never existed in the first place never went away. Neither did the void, and from time to time—against all logic—attempts to fill it had to be made.

Except Josie couldn't tear her attention away from the necklace. "That's Erica's."

"Yeah. She rarely takes it off, but she got into the shower as soon as we settled in the room. Left it on the bathroom counter." He pinched the charm between his thumb and forefinger. "This was the only thing she had from her mother when she came to us. Not the chain or even the setting, just this weird-ass thing. Her mom gave it to her before she left. Erica doesn't even know what the hell it is or what it means but she's always been obsessed with it. I don't know what it is either, except weird. When she was about fourteen, she got this idea to make it into a necklace. Got all this fancy wire and tiny beads from the craft store and she made it into this."

It was almost as if the object generated its own energy, drawing Josie toward it, urging her to touch it. "May I?"

Alec shrugged and dumped the necklace into Josie's open palm. Then he fished his lighter and another cigarette from a back pocket. He lit up, mumbled something, but Josie wasn't listening anymore. She used the flashlight app on her phone to get a closer look at the small, black, cylindrical object. A half-dozen tiny red beads sparkled from the ornately patterned copper wire that hugged its smooth surface. It was metal, about an inch long, and surprisingly heavy. Solid. Its circumference was no bigger than that of a pencil. One end was flat. The other flared out slightly, a bit thicker than the rest of the shaft. Its surface was concave enough that she could fit the tip of her pinky finger into it.

It wasn't a spanner bit. Not a tool or part of a tool, either. Deep in the recesses of Josie's brain, something fought to break free from the shadows but failed. She didn't know what the object was but she knew there were five others exactly like it in Lila's twisted trophy box.

SIXTY-THREE

The bullet didn't come. After what felt like an eternity, Erica opened her eyes. The man looming over her lowered his pistol, sending her heart into an erratic rhythm. His smile unleashed an army of invisible insects over every inch of her skin. Predators like him were a dime a dozen and she knew exactly what waited behind that creepy-ass smirk. He was going to prolong her demise and enjoy the hell out of it. Make her wish that he'd simply shot her and called it a day.

Despite the terror invading every cell of her body, she couldn't let the moment pass without lashing out at this skeevy bastard. It wasn't even a conscious choice. If it was, she'd probably keep her mouth shut. But submission wasn't an option. She wasn't built that way.

"Keep your nasty, rapey, Neanderthal hands off me, you piece of trash."

Laughter came from behind him, but he wasn't amused. Not even a little bit. Shocker. With one fluid movement, he flipped the pistol in his hand and brought the grip down on her head, turning her world black.

Erica had no idea how long she was out. Time didn't exist in this crap hole. All she knew was that her brain had its own drum section now and every beat was like a skewer straight through her skull. The events of the night came back to her in fragments, each one more horrifying than the last. Patting her body, she was relieved to find herself fully clothed. She didn't think these guys were the types to mess with an unconscious girl. No, they'd much rather get off watching her die inside while they took whatever they wanted.

The weird, coppery smell of blood filled her sinus cavities. Turning her head, she saw the shadowed corpse they'd left her with and scrambled to her feet. Blood pooled around his head. She must have fallen onto her side when she was knocked out because half her body was soaked in his blood. One of her sneakers had come off at the hotel and now her sock was wet. So was her hair. Blood, blood, and more blood.

"Oh God."

Dizziness hit her so hard, she almost passed out. She held onto the wall as she waited for it to abate.

A bang from above startled her, followed by heavy thuds, and then male voices. She couldn't make out the words over the pounding in her head. Drawing in several deep breaths, she tried to pull her shit together. This was a second chance—or a third or fourth depending on how she viewed it—and she wasn't about to waste it. She used the sleeve of her sweatshirt to wipe the death remnants from her face and realized some had gotten on her lips, into her mouth. Dry heaves doubled her over.

"Did you take care of him?" Through the ceiling, Erica heard Mace's voice, slightly muffled.

"Downstairs."

"What?" Mace shouted and even through the floorboards, Erica could hear the anger and incredulity in his tone.

"You told us to tie up all the loose ends."

"Not inside my fucking house! Do you have any idea how hard it's going to be to clean up a mess like that?"

Erica managed to quash her nausea. Survival mode. That's where she needed to be. She'd done it as a child, she could do it now. Shoring herself up, she took a good look around her. The man crumpled at her feet didn't have a face anymore. Was it Holden? She hadn't seen him or heard his voice this time. Did she care if he was dead? The last time they brought her here, he'd been the only thing standing between her and the other men. Apparently, holding her captive with the intent to kill her was just fine by him but letting some other guy touch her wasn't. That was his only redeeming quality. The way he'd stabbed Gina Phelan so viciously was permanently imprinted on Erica's mind. That knife had been meant for her. Tears stung the backs of her eyes at the memory of Gina. They'd had only moments together, but it was obvious that Gina was the best one among them. A good person. Erica hadn't deserved her heroics, and she hadn't deserved to die.

Maybe it made Erica a shitty person but no, she wouldn't be upset if Holden was dead.

"At least tell me you got the girl," Mace said.

"We got her. She's downstairs. Out cold."

The dumbasses left the door open this time. They probably figured the blow to the head would knock her out until they came back. Or maybe they weren't worried about her getting away. Wherever this place was located, it was surrounded by forest and she had the feeling that even if she made it outside, there would be no Gina to save her this time.

Erica stepped over the body and crept toward the door. The first time they brought her here, she'd been hogtied in the back of an SUV but once inside the garage, they'd untied her and marched her inside the house. Although most of her time had been spent in this dank concrete cell, they had let her into other parts of the house when she needed to eat or use the bathroom. That was how she knew that turning left led to a flight of steps that went to the first floor and turning right took her to the garage.

"Don't kill her in the house," Mace said. "But if you want to have a little fun with her before you do it, that can stay indoors."

"That was the plan."

Erica's stomach lurched. No way was she risking those degenerates getting their sick, filthy hands on her. She ran. There wasn't a strategy, only two words screeching inside her mind on repeat: *get out.*

SIXTY-FOUR

Josie's hands clenched the steering wheel of Trinity's rental car. On the horizon, the first rays of sunlight bled through an array of striated clouds, painting them pastel pink edged in fiery orange. A soft ding came from the dash, indicating that she had forty-five miles before she had to fill the gas tank. She'd been driving for hours, ever since she left Alec Slater at his hotel, both of them bewildered and hopeless. The smart thing to do would have been to return to Gretchen's and get some sleep, but she couldn't. It was as though her body was keeping vigil, like she wouldn't sleep again until Noah was found.

Calls and texts to Gretchen and Turner had gone unanswered. With nothing left to do but wait, Josie started driving, visiting each place on the list of properties she'd made, starting with the closest one and working outward in an ever-expanding circle. It was pointless, since she couldn't actually search any of them. She didn't know what she expected. Noah trying to squeeze through a gap in the fencing around one of the construction sites? Or escaping through the window of one of Mace Phelan's residences? Maybe some inexplicable psychic pull when she drove past the place they were keeping him?

She'd been blindly following her instincts for days, counting on them to steer her in the right direction. If she was being honest with herself, she was counting on them to provide that psychic pull.

Obsessing over Erica Slater's necklace kept her awake more effectively than any cup of coffee. She kept feeling the weight of it in her palm. The smooth metal against her fingertip. That flicker of recognition, too fleeting to pin down. The more she thought about it, she felt certain that she hadn't seen the five in Lila's box before she and Trinity had found them in her garage. Recalling the way the liner had separated—or been torn—from the inside of the lid, Josie wondered if Lila had hidden them there. But why? They were unremarkable. Even the men who'd broken into their house hadn't taken them.

They weren't valuable. Nothing in that box held any monetary value. Lila kept things because they meant something to her. Each object was a memento from one of her evil conquests. A symbol of the damage she'd so gleefully inflicted. Yet, she'd hidden these. Kept them but secreted them away in a hidden compartment. Were they a reminder of a failed conquest? Was that why she didn't want to look at them every time she opened her trophy box? Then why give one to her daughter as a parting gift? According to Alec, even Erica didn't know what it was. Or were they so precious to Lila that she didn't want to risk losing them should someone access her collection?

Regardless, Josie couldn't shake the feeling that the small, confounding items were the key to unlocking a crucial question that she hadn't even articulated yet. She also had the sense that both question and answer were tantalizingly close, hovering just out of reach of her consciousness.

The chime of Josie's cell phone jarred her from her thoughts. She'd connected it to the in-vehicle infotainment center so she could use the hands-free feature. Trinity's name flashed across the console. When Josie answered, her voice filled the car.

"Where are you?"

"I'm..." she glanced at the GPS, "near Lewisburg. On my way to the state game lands in Clinton County."

"What?" Her sister was not pleased. "Why in God's name are you driving around in my rental car, with my laptop, in Lewisburg? And why are you going to Clinton County?"

She'd just circled Mace Phelan's sprawling Lewisburg mansion a dozen times, her only takeaway that it was gaudy and not remote enough to effectively dispose of a body. It was, however, only a half hour from Williamsport and roughly an hour from Lock Haven. Erica could easily have been invited to one of Mace's infamous parties. Now Josie was heading to his hunting lodge.

None of those things seemed like a sane answer to the question but she was talking to Trinity, so that's exactly what Josie told her.

There was a long silence, followed by a sigh. "You made that list, didn't you?"

Josie had shared all her crazy theories right before Trinity passed out in bed next to Trout.

"Forget it. I already know the answer and clearly the sleep deprivation has fried your brain because you didn't wake me up and take me with you."

"Trin, I don't want you in danger. This could—"

"Josie, we both know you can't enter any of those properties without causing a series of events that could, at best, mess up your career, and at worst, give the men who took Noah a get-out-of-jail-free card."

"At best, find him, Trin."

Because Noah had been gone for eighty-one hours, and Josie was approaching the point of no return. What she didn't say out loud, what she hadn't even admitted to herself, was that if she found a property that seemed remote enough for Mace and his associates to do their dirty work, no rule, no threat to her career, not even the possibility of justice not being served, was going to stop her from searching for her husband.

"You're right," Trinity conceded. "But you still should have brought me. There's no reason I can't go onto these properties and start knocking on doors. I'm just a little old civilian journalist."

Sleep deprivation really had gotten Josie's wires crossed. "I'm turning around now to come get you."

SIXTY-FIVE

A single door connected the basement to the garage. Erica closed it behind her as quietly as possible. The air was cooler, not so thick, and she sucked it into her lungs greedily. An SUV and an old pickup truck greeted her. From where she stood, the voices of the men were garbled but she kept attuned to their low murmur. As long as she could hear that, she knew they were still in the kitchen.

All three of the bays were closed. There were two other doors just like the one she'd come through. In front of the vehicles, at the top of a short flight of stairs, was the first door. It led to the kitchen, where Mace and his meathead minions were presently discussing their perverted, murdery plans. The other was along the opposite wall from where she stood. It had to lead outside. Her feet carried her toward it. As she passed each vehicle, she peered through the windows. Was it too much to ask for one of them to have left the keys behind? After all, they were dumbasses.

Footsteps rumbled from the direction of the kitchen, receding. Erica's heart thrashed wildly against her rib cage. How long did she have before they made it to the death room and realized she wasn't there?

No keys in the vehicles. That would have been too easy.

She couldn't hear them at all now and she knew they were probably entering the basement. An idea formed in her mind a split second before their voices drew closer. She'd go in the direction they least expected. Bonus if she found something she could use to get the hell out of here. First, she threw open the door that led outside. Then she turned back, racing up the steps and pushing her way into the kitchen. Just as the door closed behind her, shouts erupted from the garage.

"Where the hell did she go?"

"Shit. She got out."

Every part of Erica's body shook, adrenaline shooting through her veins like fire and ice at the same time. All she had were seconds, heartbeats to find a way out and the percussion section in her skull was reaching an agonizing crescendo. She nearly collapsed when she saw the phone one of them had left on the kitchen table.

Dumbassery was on her side today. It might just save her.

Snatching it up, she chanced a look out the windows. Dawn was breaking. The men poured from the garage and ran across the driveway. The meathead minions disappeared into the woods alongside the house. Mace jogged toward the rear. By the time she found the back door, she was hyperventilating.

She knew she should stop to think about her next move, to strategize, but fear overruled logic. Get out. All she had to do was get out. The locks on the door turned easily. As she gripped the knob, a strange sensation descended on her, like the heat of someone standing directly behind her, brushing lightly against her back. Terror strangled the scream rocketing up her throat. All that came out was a weird little gurgle. When she whipped around, she was alone.

Get out. Just get out.

She pulled the door open and froze, quickly closing it again. A second later, she cracked it, peering through a tiny sliver. Mace stalked across the backyard and stopped at a small shed. He disappeared inside. Ten seconds later he emerged, face lashed with fury, and went back the way he'd come. She waited until he was out of sight and then took several deep breaths before stepping outside. Her mind begged her to cross the yard slowly in case Mace returned, but her body wouldn't listen. Twigs and leaves crunched beneath her feet. The noise seemed almost as loud as the gunshot from earlier even though she knew that wasn't possible.

The yard wasn't so much a yard as a huge clearing hemmed in by even more trees. There was a wooden apparatus, like an arch, with hooks and other weird stuff dangling from it that she knew had something to do with hunting. Several crudely built plywood tables dotted the area, each one facing a different target. Big blocks with bullseyes painted on them. Some were riddled with bullet holes while others were impaled with long, thin shafts adorned with brightly colored fletching. Erica did a double take when she saw a rabbit sitting on top of the archery target. No, not a real one. It was fake, made of some kind of foam. There were two more on the ground near the target. Of course these sickos would get off practicing shooting arrows into defenseless little rabbits.

Someone had been getting ready to use the archery target recently because scattered across the surface of one of the tables was a mess of arrows and other materials as well as a bow. It looked just like the kind Jennifer Lawrence used when she played that badass girl boss character in those movies about food and killing games. Erica made a beeline for that table. Just before she reached it, the foot still wearing a sneaker caught on something—a rock, maybe—and she crashed into the table. The materials went flying every which way, some landing in dirt and others landing in grass.

"Shit, shit, shit."

Surely that was loud and she was near the edge where the yard met the driveway. Random items had rolled onto the asphalt. There was no time to clean up or put everything back into place. If someone had heard that, they'd be on her in no time. She plucked an arrow off the ground. One with a deadly-looking broadhead on it. Her thundering heart filled with joy as she imagined plunging its sleek, silver, razor-sharp point into the flesh of the men pursuing her.

A shout came from nearby. Too close. Clutching the phone in one hand and the arrow in the other, Erica started moving again. Another bout of dizziness assailed her. The spikes driving into her head rose to a new level of pain. She had to keep going. Plunging into the forest seemed like an exercise in futility. What if it went on forever? They'd hear her. Be able to track her. She'd have no sense of direction. What if she walked for hours only to end up right back here? Could she walk for hours with the entire cast of *Stomp* giving the performance of a lifetime behind her eyes? Her gaze flitted to the shed again. They'd expect her to flee into the trees. That's where they were already searching.

Hopefully they'd be gone long enough for her to make a call.

She sprinted toward the small structure. A cry of relief escaped her when the door opened with no resistance. Laboring for breath, she sealed herself inside. Hazy light filtered through a single, small, grime-covered window near the back. One-handed, she brought up the phone's lock screen.

"Holy shit."

Her own face stared back at her. There she was, blowing the camera a kiss. Holden had taken this stupid picture. Whenever they were together, he made sure it was on his home and lock screens. One time, he'd forgotten, and left a photo of the redhead on the display. Erica didn't need a passcode to make an emergency call, but she entered his anyway. Within the first week of knowing him, she'd surreptitiously obtained it.

Deep down, she knew he was the guy they'd killed in front of her in their creepy little death room but this confirmed it.

The hours-old memory of his brain splattering across her face made her hands tremble. She stumbled forward, needing to sit, needing to breathe before she could call 911, and tripped over another body.

SIXTY-SIX

"I'll be ready," Trinity said. "By the way, have you been listening to the radio?"

Josie's heart thumped. "No, why?"

"The state police released the name of the suspect in Noah's case, the armed robberies, and the Gina Phelan stabbing. There's a bona fide manhunt going on right now."

Other motorists beeped their horns as Josie made a three-point turn in the middle of traffic. "Tell me."

"Holden Doyle. Get this. He's employed by Phelan Construction as a security guard. Mace is unavailable for comment."

Which meant that Trinity had put on her journalism hat and started poking around. Josie floored it, whizzing around other cars, trying to calculate how long it would take to retrieve Trinity and get back here. "Just be ready," she told her sister.

The call disconnected. Josie was so focused on not getting T-boned as she blew through red lights that when her phone rang again, she stabbed blindly at the console until her finger found the answer button. She assumed it was Trinity again.

Except the voice that filled the car didn't belong to her sister. "Hello? Is this… is this Josie Quinn?"

It took a moment for Josie to place it. "Erica? Erica Slater?"

There was some rustling. Her next words were fainter. "I called 911. I'm—some guys took me. They work for Mace Phelan. He's here. They're all looking for me but I'm hiding in a shed behind the house. Waiting for the police. There's someone else here, with me. He… he gave me this number and asked me to call. He, um, he's in bad shape. They must have thought he was already dead. I thought he was dead at first with the way he —" She broke off, a high-pitched sob ripping through the line and right through Josie's frayed heart. "They just left him out here and I don't know what's wrong with him. I don't know if he's going to make it."

The car screeched to a halt on the shoulder of the road. Josie swallowed down the emotion that threatened to spill over and consume her. Her mouth was dry. It felt like there were razor blades in her throat. She didn't even sound like herself when she said, "Put him on."

And then. Then.

Noah's voice. Strained and raspy but audible, the sound-track of her very soul. "Josie."

Oh God. It was too much. She needed to be with him. Right now. Needed to put her hands on him.

"Where are you?"

"I'm sorry," he said. "I couldn't stop them. There were three… they wanted something from Lila's stuff. It was about Lila—"

"I know," Josie said. "Noah, where are you?"

"Whatever they were looking for wasn't there," he went on. "They took me. Thought I knew something, that I was hiding something of Lila's. Tried to beat it out of me, but I didn't know what they were talking about… they kept talking about some kind of statement…"

He drifted off and Josie could hear him trying to catch his breath. "It doesn't matter," she told him. "I don't care about that. Where *are* you?"

In the background, Erica whimpered.

"Listen," Noah said. "I love you. I've always loved you."

"Noah." Her voice cracked. All the messy feelings she'd been pushing down exploded inside her, demolishing her emotional armor. Tears streamed down her face. Unstoppable rivers. "I love you, too."

"You're perfect," he said, voice falling to a whisper. "Exactly the way you are. Remember that."

"No," she choked out.

"I love you."

This was not happening. She was not losing him.

"Tell me to my face," Josie said, her voice strange and squeaky. "Because I'm coming to get you. Put Erica back on."

More rustling and then some sniffles. "It's me. The 911 dispatcher said the police and ambulance will be here in fifteen minutes. They said to stay put. I'm worried about Mace and his goons finding us before the police come—"

"They won't," Josie croaked, as if saying it would make it true. "The property—where is it?"

"I don't know," said Erica, crying softly. "There's nothing but trees and—"

"It's fine." Josie cleared her throat and tried to sound like herself, like she wasn't melting down in a rental car on the side of the road while her husband might be dying. "Open Google Maps and pin your location, then share it with me. I'm on my way."

SIXTY-SEVEN

Erica shivered as the phone screen faded to black. Stupid tears leaked from her eyes. She used the hem of her tank top to wipe them away, hoping Noah wouldn't notice. Her sweatshirt was turned inside out and folded under his head. She'd nearly gotten the dry heaves again when her fingers brushed the open gash along the side of his head, hidden by his matted, blood-stained hair. At least the blood underneath him, staining the shed floor, had dried and congealed. Some of it peeled away from the concrete like strips of plastic. This was not a tidbit about blood that Erica had ever wanted to know. In fact, if she never saw blood again, that would be cool.

She really had thought he was dead when she tripped over him. The smell alone was enough to convince her. Copper and dirt and piss. Then she saw him, curled onto his side, unmoving, the blood from his head wound spread across almost the entire shed floor. Bruises covered his bare forearms, some the perfect imprints of boot treads. And his face. Good lord, his face. Nose so crooked it almost made an L, dried rivulets of blood staining his lips, his chin, and his throat. The skin around his eyes was black and puffy. One of his eyelids had swelled so badly that he couldn't open it. It reminded her of the day her mother had gone inside the magical house.

If this wasn't full circle, she didn't know what was.

"Hey," Noah whispered.

She could tell it took a lot of effort for him to hold up his hands. He'd kept telling her he was fine but how could he not be dying?

"Erica."

Even as jacked up as he was, he had some kind of weird calming effect on her.

Scuttling closer to him, she picked up the arrow and used the broadhead to saw through the duct tape around his wrists. He dropped his arms to his sides, hissing in pain. Every movement seemed to cause him pain. Without prompting, she freed his ankles next. That took longer. Sweat poured down her face while she worked, mixing with the tears that just wouldn't stop.

"Thank you," he said.

There were more gasps of pain as he tried to move his legs.

"Stop," she said, placing a palm over one of his knees. "Just be still. Rescue will be here any minute."

"Yeah," said Noah. "But they won't get to us for hours."

SIXTY-EIGHT

An invisible vise tightened around Josie's chest as she stood along the road among dozens of emergency vehicles, staring up at Mace Phelan's hunting lodge. It was the only house in the area for miles and miles. It sat adjacent to State Game Land 89 in Clinton County. Josie had been nearly ninety minutes away when Erica shared the location. She'd made it in forty-five. On the way, she'd called Heather Loughlin, Gretchen, Chief Chitwood, Trinity, and even Turner. Talking to them kept her panic at bay. It grew exponentially with every mile she traveled because she knew that, based on what Erica had told her, getting to Noah would be no simple task.

Given the remote location of the lodge, three armed suspects on the loose in a large wooded area and two innocents at risk, the local borough police department would need an assist from the state police. Their Special Emergency Response Team would be called in. SERT was equivalent to SWAT. In this situation, their vast resources would be critical to apprehending the suspects and securing the scene. Drones would be deployed as well as helicopters equipped with FLIR or forward-looking infrared cameras, which could locate the suspects via their heat signatures. No medics would be able to retrieve Noah until that happened, no matter how badly he was injured. It simply wasn't safe.

It had been two hours since she arrived on-scene. She was only allowed to stay if she followed Heather's directions to the letter, which were for her to remain in the exact spot where she currently stood until told otherwise. SERT had made contact with Erica on the phone she'd been using. Josie had broken and texted a few times for updates on Noah. He was hanging in there. She wouldn't believe it until she saw for herself and put her hands on him.

Overhead, the steady *thwip thwip thwip* of the state police helicopter grew louder as it made another pass over the house, searching the wooded area behind it. Josie scanned the scene again. The driveway was long and steep. The house was as huge as it was beautiful. White pine accented its rustic fieldstone veneer. Tall, sleek windows gleamed in the morning sun. Across the front was an expansive deck with what appeared to be an ornate metal balustrade depicting the silhouettes of deer and elk running through a forest. It looked more like a resort than a hunting lodge—an unlikely place for the horrors Josie knew had taken place there in the last several days.

A burst of chatter squawked over the police radios around her. Tactical teams moved up the hill, through the woods. A sense of urgency and frenetic energy rolled through the officers gathered around her and Josie knew this nightmare was close to being over. The rest happened in a blur. Two men she'd never seen before and Mace Phelan, secured with zip ties, were marched down the driveway and put into vehicles. An ambulance raced toward the house. Then Heather was pushing her into a car, and they were following it, and the stricture around Josie's chest was so tight she could barely draw in air.

A trooper cordoned off the backyard with crime scene tape in anticipation of the forensic team. Only the paramedics were allowed past it. Josie's chest pressed against it as she watched them leave their stretcher outside and enter the shed, bags in hand.

Minutes ticked by but no one emerged. They weren't coming out. Why weren't they coming out? Maybe she asked the question out loud because Heather said, "I'll find out what's going on."

People moved all around Josie. Evidence techs in Tyvek suits swarmed the yard and still no one came out of the shed. Maybe she was overreacting. Maybe only a reasonable amount of time had passed but it felt like a thousand years, and she was so close. So damn close.

What if they were too late? She couldn't do this. Couldn't handle it.

Her heart. Her heart was going so fast and now she felt everything and the pressure on her chest was so much worse, crushing, crushing, and she was pretty sure her rib cage was cracking because the crushing was too much. It was too much. Someone was next to her, talking, but she couldn't look at them because no one was coming out of the shed and she wasn't going to survive this. She knew it. She wouldn't. This was the worst one. Worse than Ray or Lisette or Mettner. This was worse than anything Lila ever did to her, and she wouldn't be able to take this. She wouldn't.

An arm curled around her shoulders. Chief Chitwood's voice broke through her silent hysteria. "Quinn."

She couldn't remember him ever being affectionate toward her, even in her lowest moments, but she sagged into him, nonetheless. At that moment, one of the paramedics came out and started gathering equipment.

"Look," said the Chief. "Spine board. Cervical collar. Not a body bag."

Noah was carried out moments later, secured to the spine board, and placed onto the stretcher. When they finally cleared the crime scene tape, the Chief gave her a gentle push and there he was, finally, within reach. The air whooshed out of her lungs when she saw the damage to his face, the head wound, the dried blood everywhere, the bruising on every inch of exposed skin. The Chief gripped her shoulders, steadying her again. Despite the paramedics scolding her, she laid her hands on Noah, touching him lightly everywhere she could, avoiding his face, while she walked alongside the stretcher.

"Josie."

His voice again. Faint, broken, but *his* voice.

"I'm here," she said. "Oh God, I'm here."

"You came."

She rested a palm gently on his chest, feeling his heartbeat, strong and steady despite how he looked. "I'll always run toward the danger with you."

"That's my line." A smile stretched across his battered face. It was the most beautiful thing she'd ever seen.

The paramedics paused when they reached the back of the ambulance. The cervical collar wouldn't allow Noah to turn toward her so she leaned over his face, grinning so wide, her cheeks hurt. "Promise to always come home to me."

"I promise," he answered, voice still strained. "But let's stop at the hospital first. I might want to try out their CT scanner."

SIXTY-NINE

Laughter burst from Josie's lips and the weight of the past three days lifted. The paramedics chuckled, too. Even the Chief cracked a smile.

Then Josie was shooed aside as Noah was loaded into the back of the ambulance. "You can ride with him but just give us a minute."

She took a step back while they performed their checks and readied Noah for the journey. The fear and anxiety that had consumed her until this moment drained away. It felt like coming back to herself. Everything was quiet inside her brain. Taking a deep breath, she turned back toward the scene in time to see Heather guiding Erica out of the shed.

This was not the plucky woman who had lied to Gretchen in the Denton PD interrogation room with forced confidence. The woman trudging toward her was bedraggled. Her blonde hair was matted, much of it stained varying shades of reddish-brown. Dried blood streaked her pale skin. A bruise darkened one of her temples. Her rumpled, dirty tank top fully exposed the bruises on her throat and wrists. Blood-covered sweatpants sagged on her thin hips. Her gait was wonky, one foot in only a sock while the other wore a sneaker.

Her eyes found Josie and flickered with the same recognition they had the day Gretchen had taken her into custody. They were more haunted now, sorrowful, making it hard to find a resemblance to Lila. It was there though, in the high cheekbones, the fullness of her lips and the black roots peeking from her scalp.

They didn't speak as Heather walked her past. It wasn't the time for that. Josie backed up to give them room. Her heel came down on something. It rolled under her boot, sending her off-balance. Flailing her arms, she shifted her weight to her other foot, avoiding an embarrassing tumble. The shaft of an arrow rolled along the asphalt of the driveway. Its green fletching was shredded and its broadhead had either broken off or never been attached.

It was outside the crime scene tape, but Josie didn't dare touch it. Had Gina practiced here? The lodge was in Mace's name though it had been transferred to him from their father, Clint.

Where the driveway met the thin grass of the yard, a trail of related items led to a plywood table. A single glove sat in its center. A traditional bow teetered on the edge, its smooth, light maple finish in stark contrast to the rough surface of the table. Beyond that was a large square target and three additional small, foam targets in the shape of rabbits.

Rabbits.

Josie's heart did a double-tap. She stepped right up to the crime scene tape again, letting it graze her chest. Craning her neck, she studied the items scattered along the patchy grass. Searching, searching. Question and answer.

Josie's knowledge of archery was based almost entirely on things she'd learned from coworkers who were lifelong hunters. There were two types of bows. One was the traditional bow which was just what it sounded like—the kind humans had been using for thousands of years. She knew those came in two different shapes. The longbow formed a D, its limbs curving toward the archer, whereas the limbs of the recurve bow curled toward the target. Josie had always thought of the recurve as the longbow in a fancier font.

Behind her, one of the paramedics spoke. "UPMC Williamsport will take him. They're a level-two trauma center."

The second type of bow was the compound bow which was so elaborate that Josie had never been able to make sense of its complex network of cables, rods, cams, sights, and wheels. She only knew that it was more powerful, more accurate and easier to shoot. In the profile that WYEP had run about Gina, she'd been pictured using both a traditional and a compound bow.

"Quinn?" Chief Chitwood drew up beside her. "Something wrong?"

Josie shook her head. The ambulance was going to leave soon. She kept cataloging the fallen archery items. Shiny silver broadheads. Edged, penetrating. They were ideal for hunting large game like deer and elk, sometimes even bear.

"I can see you working on something," the Chief said.

Two kinds of bows. Broadheads. Large game. Rabbits.

Question and answer.

It was right there. A hair's breadth away. Mettner would know this.

"Rabbits are small game," she muttered, crouching and scanning the ground. "Two different kinds of bows. Two..."

"We'll get you checked out at the hospital, too," said the Chief.

"There!" she said, more loudly than she expected. As she pointed to the handful of small, black, metal cylinders no more than an inch long, their circumference no wider than a pencil, flared and concave at one end, the pieces clicked into place.

Just as there were two types of bows, there were two types

of arrowheads. The broadhead was pointy and sharp. The blunt-tipped arrowhead was non-pointed, sometimes rounded, sometimes flat or even concave. It was made from rubber, plastic, and even steel and used to hunt small game. Rabbits, squirrels, grouse, pheasants.

"Are you going to tell me what's happening right now?" asked the Chief.

The items in the baggie in Lila's box and the charm on Erica's necklace were blunt-tipped arrowheads.

"We're just about ready here," called one of the paramedics.

Josie took out her phone and snapped a few pictures of the ones in the grass before hurrying toward the ambulance. She settled in on the bench next to Noah and covered his hand with one of her own. He was asleep, his chest rising and falling evenly.

Chief Chitwood stood just outside the back, one bushy eyebrow kinked. "Glad we had this talk, Quinn. I'll see you two at the hospital."

The paramedic tending to Noah shut the doors and they were off. Josie kept her focus on her husband's mangled face, ready to reassure him if he woke while her mind kept spinning.

Why would Lila keep blunt-tipped arrows in her morbid box of mementos? To Josie's knowledge, she'd never picked up a bow, which meant they hadn't belonged to her. She'd taken them from someone. The Phelans? Why had she given one to Erica, though, without ever explaining its significance?

Blunt-tipped arrows weren't unique. There were probably tens of thousands of the very same kind circulating all over the country. But it would be foolish to discount the Phelans. Lila had led her to them.

Everything was about Lila.

She'd wanted Josie to see something.

A memory flashed across Josie's mind. Visiting Lila in

prison the day she'd traced Roe Hoyt's inmate number into the condensation left by her breath.

"Oh, you want to play that game? Who had the worse childhood? You don't want to know what happened to me."

Josie leaned forward. "You're wrong. I do want to know. Your foster care file was destroyed. There is nothing left. I don't even know where you came from."

Lila considered this for a moment. Then her hand tightened around the receiver. "I'll tell you what, JoJo. You're a detective, right? Big-time chief of police and all that. I'll give you a clue. You figure it out before I die, and I'll give you those names."

Lila had wanted Josie to see Roe Hoyt, her mother.

The items in her box had led Josie to Erica Slater, her daughter.

That only left one other player. Her father.

Clint Phelan was the right age, a lifelong hunter, and an accomplished archer. He'd mentored Gina and she'd gone on to win state championships. Josie didn't know if he'd ever had a hunting cabin or been part of a camp in Bradford County but that wouldn't be difficult to check.

How had Lila known? Had she done a mail-in DNA test? Or did she remember him from her time with Roe? She wouldn't have known his name—she didn't even have language skills when she was found. But the Phelans often appeared on local television. Would she have recognized his face? Maybe not, but she might have remembered the brass belt buckle he always wore.

Noah stirred, groaning. His good eye opened. "Josie?"

She stood up and leaned over so he could see her. "I'm right here. We're almost to the hospital. I'm not going anywhere."

His arms and legs were strapped down. There was no way for him to reach for her, but she felt his fingers twitch under her palm and she squeezed them.

When he drifted off again, she resumed her seat but kept

her hand on top of his. She never wanted to break contact with him again.

"Forty minutes out," shouted the driver.

Josie's brain went back to work. Lila must have made contact with Clint Phelan at some point. Obviously, he hadn't welcomed her with open arms. Why would he? She was living, breathing proof of his greatest sin. Forcing himself on a troubled young woman who wanted so badly to be free from her father's abuse that she chose to live alone in the woods, stealing from campers and hunters to clothe herself and trapping small game to eat.

Small game.

Another flicker in the recesses of her brain. She let it lie.

Even if Clint Phelan had wanted to acknowledge Lila—even if he believed his encounters with Roe Hoyt had been consensual—admitting his paternity would tie him to one of the state's most disturbing criminal cases. It wouldn't have been a good look for the public face of one of the biggest construction and development companies in Pennsylvania. He would be the man whose mistress turned out to be a violent, feral woman who killed her own children. Five of them.

It was more likely that Lila had tried to blackmail him. That was her specialty, after all. Maybe she had succeeded, but why take blunt-tipped arrowheads for a souvenir?

Five of them.

No. Six. Lila was the sixth.

Clint was an accomplished hunter and archer. Blunt-tipped arrows were used to hunt small game. Squirrels, rabbits, grouse, pheasants. A sharper broadhead would obliterate a creature that tiny and delicate. Blunt-tipped arrowheads did just enough damage to kill.

Her stomach lurched. She hadn't eaten in hours but bile threatened to come back up.

Five tiny skulls, their round white surfaces fractured like cracked eggs.

"They had skull fractures. From a small, unknown blunt object."

"Oh God."

The paramedic looked up from the clipboard he was scribbling on. "You okay, miss?"

Josie forced her nausea down. "Fine," she replied with a stiff smile.

Roe's arms returned to the cradling position, rocking and rocking. This time, she looked from the invisible infant to the clock high on the wall to their right.

It hadn't been about time at all. She'd been trying to indicate something in the distance, maybe someone in an elevated position, on the top of a hill. The clock just happened to be there.

Slowly, she brought her hands up, angled toward the clock. Then she arced them down toward where the crook of her left elbow had been. "Roe," she said. "Roe."

Roe.

Arrow.

It wasn't a random sound. It wasn't meant to be her name. She'd been trying to tell everyone. For over sixty years, she'd been trying to tell everyone that an arrow had killed her children.

SEVENTY

Erica's ass hurt from sitting in what had to be the hardest and most uncomfortable chair on the planet for hours, maybe days. As interrogation rooms went, this one was pretty clean and it had an actual carpet, but it still smelled weird. Like body odor and onions. She wondered what kind of fat-ass perverts sat in this chair before her, sweating while the pretty blonde detective tricked them into confessing to their disgusting crimes. As police detectives went, Heather Loughlin was pretty savvy but Erica would have preferred the one from Denton with the short, spiked brown and gray hair.

"Erica? We're almost finished here." Heather had her notepad out again. "You've told me how you started dating Holden Doyle. He took you to one of Mace Phelan's parties at his Lewisburg residence. Holden, Mr. Phelan, and two of his associates held you against your will for one week, during which they kept you at the hunting lodge. They later transported you to the children's hospital construction site. As you understood it, they were going to kill you and dispose of your body there. Gina Phelan found you while she was inspecting the site and tried to get you off the site without anyone noticing. Holden saw you two fleeing and pursued you. He tried to stab you but Gina Phelan put herself in front of you and told you to run, which you did, hiding out until Denton PD located you."

As recaps went, it was pretty good. "Can we take a break?" Erica asked. "I'm hungry and I want to see my dad."

She thought they'd arrest her as soon as they rescued her but instead, they'd had her checked out at the hospital, put her and her dad up in a hotel, provided clean clothes, and some takeout, all so she would be cooperative in this never-ending interview.

"I'll order a pizza," Heather answered. "Your dad went back to the hotel to get some sleep."

Erica tried not to think about how much work he'd missed. He'd told her it didn't matter but she knew it was going to put him deeper in debt. "I like pepperoni," she told Heather. "And can we get some Cherry Coke?"

She thought Heather would leave to put in the order, but she merely nodded toward the camera on the wall above them and kept on asking questions. The ones Erica really didn't want to answer.

"I just want to fill in some blanks. What happened at Mace Phelan's party that led to you being held against your will?"

Erica squirmed in the chair again. "Can I at least get a cushion for this thing? Or a sweatshirt or something I can fold up and sit on?"

Heather looked like she was fighting a smile. Then she ignored the request. "Why didn't Gina just call 911 when she found you? I know you told her that her brother was involved but if she'd just called the police, they could have shown up before Mace or the others had a chance to cover anything up."

"I told you." Erica sighed. "I don't know."

"Why didn't you call the police after you escaped?"

Round and round they went. "I told you. I panicked."

Heather placed her notepad on the table and took off her reading glasses. Oh boy. Shit was getting serious now. "I talked with Josie Quinn. Noah's wife?"

Erica drew her knees to her chest, balancing on the chair. "How is he?"

"Fine. I'm not sure if you're aware but Detective Quinn has some history with your biological mom, Lila Jensen."

She knew, all right. From the time she was old enough to be curious about her mom's special box, she'd been told all about how Josie ruined her mom's life. It was only when Erica got older and had some distance from her mom that she wondered how Josie could possibly have ruined her life when she was only three weeks old. It took Erica a long time to figure out that her mom was seriously deranged and kind of evil.

"I didn't know her as Lila Jensen," Erica said. "I found out her real name when she went to prison and the *Datelines* aired, the same time as the rest of the world did."

Heather blew right past that. "Detective Quinn told me that your mom blackmailed a lot of people. Most of those activities aren't documented. She was never charged, but I'm inclined to believe it's true."

Erica's body rocked back and forth.

"Did your mom ever tell you about her biological parents?"

Holy whiplash. "Yeah. I know about them."

"She told you that Clint Phelan was her father?"

Her eyes bulged. Walked right into that one. Did it matter though? DNA wasn't illegal. "She thought he was, yes. I don't know if she had a DNA test, or what. My whole life she said she didn't know her bio-dad but one day she saw him on TV and she was sure it was him."

"Did she ever make contact with him?"

Erica hadn't understood what her mother had been doing at

the magical house right away. She was young and scared. It wasn't until she got older that she asked what had happened that day. "She went to his house—the lodge—when I was eight. I don't know who was in there or what happened. She made me wait outside. When she came out, she was all bloody and messed up. I didn't know who owned the house until later. She had taken this bag of these weird little metal things. I don't know why. They were important to her. I don't even know what they are but about a week after she was there, Mace Phelan showed up at our apartment and tried to kill us both. We got away. She left me with my dad because she said it was too dangerous for me to stay with her."

"Why was it too dangerous?"

"At first I thought it was because she stole those metal things but later she told me that Mace wanted her dead because she was his sister and with her mother being a baby-killer and all, he didn't want that kind of scandal for his old man."

Heather arched a brow. "It wasn't also because your mom tried to blackmail the Phelans? Convince them to give her a large sum of money and she'd keep her identity secret?"

When Erica didn't answer, Heather said, "Lila Jensen is dead. You don't need to keep her secrets anymore."

For as obvious as that fact was, it hit her like a slap to the face. Why was she keeping her mom's secrets still? She'd loved her mom so much but nothing good had ever come from her or their relationship. Even now, years after her mom died in prison, Erica's dad was still paying the price for her crime. He'd be paying it for the rest of his life because he'd taken responsibility for his actions, even though he hadn't wanted to embezzle money. What kind of person was she that she couldn't take responsibility for crimes she had committed? That made her just like her mom, and Erica didn't want that. She wanted to be like her dad.

"Fine," she said, voice trembling. "You're right. My mom

did try to blackmail her dad except that she couldn't get access to him. Mace handled it and he beat the shit out of her and made her afraid. He brutalized her. Broke her in a way I didn't think was possible. I still don't understand it but blackmailing her bio-dad was the one thing she never went through with. She even warned me off. I was never to have anything to do with the Phelans."

Heather leaned forward. "Then how did you end up at Mace's party?"

She rocked so fast that the chair creaked. Maybe it would break. No chair this uncomfortable deserved to live. "I tracked him down. Researched him. Spied on him. Figured out who his people were, asked around certain places." Her mother had taught her well. "Mace hired guys to work security on his sites, but he kept a handful of guys on the payroll who were security guards on paper but in reality they just did whatever illegal shit he wanted done. Score drugs. Lure young girls to his parties. Shut people up when necessary. Did you know that after that football player in Denton died on the children's hospital site, Mace told Holden and two of the other guys to cause a distraction? That's why they were doing the armed robberies."

She could tell Heather hadn't known this. The reading glasses went back on. She scribbled on her notepad as Erica continued.

"I tricked Holden into dating me so that I could get access to Mace. It took a few months, but I finally got him to invite me to one of the parties."

Heather looked up. "For what purpose?"

"You really can't tell where this is going?" Erica said dryly.

Now Heather gave her a real-deal smile. "It's better if you tell it."

"Right. I went to the party to blackmail Mace. The same exact way my mom tried to do it. Pay me three hundred thousand dollars or I'll tell the whole world that I'm your niece and that your dad knocked up my grandmom six times while she was living out in the woods like she was raised by wolves or some shit. Oh, and I'll also tell the whole world how she hated having his babies so much that she killed them all—except for my mom."

"I don't want to encourage you to follow in Lila Jensen's footsteps," said Heather. "But you're an impressive young woman."

Erica's posture straightened. She couldn't remember the last time anyone besides her dad gave her a compliment. Especially a badass female detective with a big gun. "Um, thanks."

"You should use your powers for good."

Wait. Did telling the truth unlock some kind of alternate dimension?

"That's the plan," she said, infusing her voice with as much confidence as she could muster.

"Mace didn't take your ultimatum very well, did he?" asked Heather.

Erica scoffed. "That's an understatement. I knew he was violent but I just thought... I don't know what I thought. That somehow it would be different when I did it than when my mom tried, but he was going to kill me right in the basement of his house. Well, not him. One of his meathead minions."

"You talked him out of it?"

"I told him to forget about the blackmail thing. I'd keep the secret and in exchange for him not killing me, I'd give him something in return. Then I told him that my mom had this box of stuff she kept from people she screwed over and that she had something incriminating inside. Something that would be very bad for his dad and if he wanted it, I could get it for him."

Heather made another note on her pad. "What was in the box?"

Erica smiled. "Nothing. I made that part up. I was trying to get the hell out of that house."

"Lila never had anything incriminating on Clint Phelan?"

"No. I mean, the worst thing she had on him was his DNA but that's not illegal."

Heather tapped the end of her pen against her lip, staring at her for a moment that stretched out a little too long. Erica got the feeling that Heather knew something she didn't.

"Mace Phelan believed you though."

"Yeah. I had to make something up so I said that my mom had tracked down a hunter who'd witnessed Clint Phelan raping my grandmom and gotten a written statement from him. I told him that it was hidden in that box and if anyone ever found it, they would know the truth. It was pretty weak but Mace is pretty dumb, so he believed me."

Erica could see Heather trying hard not to smile again.

"Anyway," she continued. "He wanted the guy's name, tried to choke it out of me, but I told him I didn't remember it. Said it was some old dude my mom found in a nursing home and if he wanted the name, he'd have to let me go and I'd bring him the signed statement."

"He didn't let you go," Heather said.

Erica sighed. "Guess he isn't a complete dumbass. No, he wouldn't let me retrieve it. Instead, he made me tell Holden where to look for the box. I had no idea what happened to it but I had to send him somewhere. I could only remember two names of the people my mom used to talk about a lot: Dexter McMann and Josie Quinn. I told Holden that one of them probably had it. I was just trying to stall—to stay alive. I told him what to say—the sob story about being one of Lila Jensen's victims looking for his grandmother's jewelry."

Heather wrote something on her pad. "Holden and his associates took photos from the box. They also took the jewelry. Do you know why?"

"There was a photo of Clint Phelan in the box. Mace, too, I think. That's probably why they took those." Erica used a thumbnail to scrape off the last of the purple nail polish on her pinky. It had taken tons of hand-washing to get the blood out of her cuticles. "I'm sure they took the jewelry because they thought they could sell it. They would steal anything if they thought they could make money from it. I had no idea what was happening. A week passed and it became pretty clear that regardless of whether Holden found the box, Mace was going to have me killed. I figured that out when they brought me to the construction site. All hell broke loose from there."

Heather nodded. "Gina Phelan?"

Tears pricked Erica's eyes. Gina's death was her biggest regret in all this, and she would carry the guilt of it for the rest of her life. "I told her the truth. Everything. She wanted to hide me until she could figure out how to handle everything without Mace finding out right away. She told me he got away with a lot of stuff and she was tired of cleaning up his messes."

"Thank you for being honest with me," Heather said.

"That's it?" Erica put her feet back on the floor. "You're not going to arrest me or send me to prison?"

Heather grimaced. "That's not entirely up to me. What happened involved multiple jurisdictions. The investigations will take a long time, and then the facts will be reviewed by prosecutors who will decide whether or not to bring charges, but given all you went through, and your assistance in rescuing Lieutenant Fraley, I doubt you'll be charged with anything."

Erica felt a sense of relief so profound, she thought she might start floating.

"I'm just curious about one more thing," said Heather. "Why did you ask for three hundred thousand dollars?"

More tears. She blinked them back and looked at her lap. "I wanted to help my dad. It's what he has to pay back from the embezzlement thing. I know everyone thinks he's a horrible person because he stole money from a hospital charity and he should reap the consequences—and he is, gladly, but... well, I can't tell you more than that."

Erica had thought about telling the police the truth about that, too, but it wouldn't change anything. Regardless of the circumstances, her dad had still embezzled the money. His motivation didn't matter to anyone but her.

"Just know that he did what he did to protect me."

SEVENTY-ONE

Josie woke to the slow, rhythmic symphony of beeps that told her Noah was stable. How she loved the sound. The lights in his hospital room had been turned off but outside, the sun was rising. The morning light filtered in slowly. They'd been here for two days. Josie shifted in the so-called sleep chair the nursing staff had provided. The way her neck, shoulders, and back ached, it was more like a torture device. She'd tried slipping into bed with Noah but even with the heavy-duty painkillers being pumped into his system every few hours, he was too sore for that.

She struggled to her feet and stretched her arms before going to the side of the bed so she could watch him sleep. Surgery had fixed his nose. The beatings he took had broken several of his ribs and left a lot of bruising but he would recover well. Lots of fluids had taken care of his severe dehydration. Anti-inflammatories had reduced the swelling in his injured eye. The scary gash on the side of his head had been stapled. He'd have a scar but his hair would cover it. There was no long-term neurological damage, but every time Josie looked at it, her world felt like it was tipping. A fraction of an inch to the left and she'd be standing over his grave right now.

Lucky for them both, the late Holden Doyle had been a terrible shot. When Noah's attackers failed to get the information they wanted from him—whether he and Josie were hiding additional items that could land Clint Phelan in trouble—Mace had instructed Holden to take Noah out to the shed and kill him. The bullet had grazed the side of Noah's head but bled profusely enough to convince Holden that he'd gotten the job done. They'd left him there, intending to dispose of his body at some point. Noah had been too injured and too weak to remove his bindings and escape. Josie wondered how long it would have taken her colleagues to find him if it hadn't been for Erica Slater.

"Stop doing that." Noah's hand found hers. His smile looked so much better now that his face was healing.

"Doing what?" said Josie.

"Thinking about all the ways I could have died. I'm right here."

Clearly, his mind-reading ability was still firmly intact.

She wanted to kiss him so badly, but she wouldn't risk bumping his nose. Everything would have to wait, including breaking the news to him about the adoption.

"Hey, what is it?" Even heavily medicated, he didn't miss a thing.

A knock at the door saved her from answering. Heather Loughlin poked her head inside. "Looking good," she told Noah. "I've got to steal your wife for a bit."

Josie hated leaving him for even a few minutes, but she needed to talk with Heather. In silence they made their way to the cafeteria, grabbing coffees and pastries before settling across from one another at a table.

"We released Erica Slater," said Heather. "She can go back

to her life. At least until it's time to testify against Mace Phelan and his accomplices."

"Was I right about the blackmail?" asked Josie. "First Lila and then her?"

Heather took a long sip of coffee and smiled. "You were exactly right, though I still don't know how you figured it out."

"I was raised by Lila Jensen, that's how," Josie said. "Have you talked to anyone about Clint Phelan and Roe Hoyt? What I told you?"

"Roe Hoyt's original conviction took place in Bradford County. I spoke with a DA there who is willing to look into it, but Josie, unless Clint confesses to killing those children, Roe will die in prison."

Heather was right. Josie was under no delusion that the arrowheads Lila had kept were the ones Clint Phelan had used. Lila had taken them for what they represented to her and nothing more. She must have been fifth in the birth order and old enough to witness what happened to at least one of her infant siblings to know that Roe wasn't a murderer and remember what the arrowheads looked like. Even if they were the ones used in the murders, six decades after the fact there wouldn't be any way to prove that they were. Without witnesses or any circumstantial or physical evidence proving Clint's guilt, there was nothing anyone could do to change Roe's fate.

"The DA will do some research, build up a file, and try for the confession," Heather said.

It was cold comfort. Clint Phelan wouldn't have any motivation to confess. He'd kept the secret all this time. Josie didn't think he was about to grow a conscience now.

"I'll give you the prosecutor's number," said Heather. "You can follow up."

SEVENTY-TWO

TWO MONTHS LATER

Josie pulled her jacket more tightly around her body and jammed her hands into her pockets. October and most of November had been mild with spring- and summer-like weather. Naturally, the one day that she decided to drive up to meet with the Bradford County DA who'd agreed to review Roe Hoyt's case, it was freezing. The temperature hadn't mattered much during lunch, but it was seriously hampering Josie's tour.

As it turned out, Oren Ellis, Clint Phelan's father-in-law, had owned a home about eight miles from Roe's shack. Although Oren and Clint had used it for hunting, once Mrs. Ellis died, Oren and Tilly had lived there full-time. The house had changed hands a half-dozen times since. Now it was owned by a hunting club comprised of six men. Josie had been shocked when all six of them gave her permission to explore the premises. She wasn't even sure what she expected to find. The new owners had given her a list of renovations made to the house. At this point, all that remained of the home Oren and Tilly Ellis shared was the foundation.

She just needed to see it for herself. On a warmer day she'd bring Noah back with her and they'd hike out to where Roe's shack used to be. For now, she circled the small house that had been renovated to look like a log cabin on the outside. An acre of land separated it from Hoyt Road. There was no driveway, just a dirt lot next to it large enough to accommodate four vehicles.

Around the back were all the things Josie would expect to find at a hunting camp. A blue barrel half-filled with empty beer cans. A couple of archery targets in the shape of deer. A firepit. Shoddy lawn chairs. A meatpole. A four-wheeler parked beside a small firewood rack shaped like a house—three walls and a roof. Josie lingered under the meatpole. She'd seen plenty in and around Denton but none like this one. High above her head, a sturdy wooden beam, at least six feet long, connected two ash trees. Thick metal hooks hung from it at regular intervals. From one of them dangled a hanging gambrel —a heavy-duty steel instrument that resembled a clothes hanger but was used by hunters to suspend deer by their feet. The practice allowed rigor mortis to run its course while blood drained from the carcass. Josie looked at the ground beneath the beam. No fresh blood. Only tufts of coarse brown and white hair from unlucky deer. She looked back up and realized that the beam was what made this meatpole different than others she had seen. It was old, very old, its wood dark and weathered.

"It belonged to my father."

Josie whipped around, heart thumping. It wasn't often that someone was able to sneak up on her, much less a woman in her eighties. Josie hadn't heard her footfalls, even with the smat-tering of fallen autumn leaves on the ground. Tilly Phelan moved like a ghost. Today, she looked more like the woman Josie had seen on television multiple times, though she was dressed casually for their current environment in boots, a pair of jeans, and a flannel shirt. Her white hair was tied back in a neat bun, not one strand out of place. She looked sad but serene. Stately and solemn.

"Mrs. Phelan, what are you doing here?"

"My husband was asked to meet with the district attorney to give a statement. Now that Erica Slater's relationship to him has come to light, they wanted to talk to him about Roe Hoyt. From what I understand, they're hoping he'll know her real name."

It was all a ploy by the prosecutor to open discussions with Clint Phelan in a non-threatening way. At lunch, the DA had informed Josie that the first interview was taking place today. She just hadn't expected to run into Clint, much less Tilly. Especially not here.

"Does he know Roe Hoyt's real name?" Josie couldn't help asking.

"Yes."

Shock and anger rattled Josie's insides, but she kept her expression neutral. Clint Phelan had repeatedly raped Roe Hoyt, killed the children she'd borne, and let her take the fall for five murders but somehow, keeping her name from the world, especially when she could never speak it herself, seemed especially egregious.

"Did he tell you?"

Rather than answer, Tilly lifted her chin in the direction of the beam. "My husband wanted to bring that with us when we sold this property—after my dad died—but I thought the past should stay in the past."

"Well," said Josie, "some things shouldn't be left behind."

She turned away and walked around the meatpole toward the four-wheeler and fire rack. Tilly followed. Along one of the outer walls of the fire rack, she noticed three nails, all in a row, protruding from the wood at eye-level. A piece of fabric was snagged on one of them. It was old and faded. It might have been yellow at one point but now there was no way to tell.

Tilly drew up beside her. "In hunting camps, there's usually a wall like this. Whoever takes a shot and misses has to put a piece of their shirttail on the wall. It's tradition."

Josie knew that already, but she didn't bother telling Tilly. The woman had an agenda and she'd make it known in her own time. Or maybe she'd just follow Josie around all day, talking in code.

"Tell me," said Tilly, her blue eyes like lasers burning straight through to Josie's soul. "Have you ever missed a shot?"

The question hung between them for a beat too long.

"Not often," Josie said coolly.

Tilly nodded.

"I shot my husband once," said Josie, feeling a small sense of satisfaction at the surprise on Tilly's face.

It was a well-placed shot into a part of his shoulder that wouldn't leave him with permanent deficits. .22 caliber. Not very much of a wallop. She'd done it to save a young girl in jeopardy. They were only colleagues then and Josie didn't know if she could trust him. Noah had proven that he wasn't corrupt and that he was fiercely loyal to her. He'd forgiven her instantly, but guilt still weighed on her. Yet, she'd run her fingers over the puckered scar at least a hundred times since he came home just because she could.

Tilly maintained her unnerving stare. "Was it the dishes, then? I hate when Clint leaves dirty dishes in the sink."

Josie laughed unexpectedly. "Nope. Not that."

Tilly offered a small smile. Then the wrinkles at the corners of her eyes tightened. "Well, we all do what we think we must."

"Not all of us."

"You're wrong about that. It was good to see you again, Detective. Time for me to go. I've set up my own little meeting with the DA."

Tilly extended her hand. With a frown, Josie shook it. As

she withdrew, she felt hard little calluses on the pads of her index and middle fingers. Just like the ones Gina had. Tilly paused, staring at Josie with a knowing look.

Blood roared in her ears as the final piece of the twisted Phelan family puzzle fell into place. She recalled the article she'd read after Gina's death.

As a young girl, she took up archery under her father's tutelage. "First thing I did when I saw she was serious was get her a good glove."

All archers used gloves or finger tabs when they shot their bows. Without them, the repetitive pressure of the string each time it was drawn back caused blisters and calluses, and sometimes, nerve damage.

Gina had been shooting behind her father's back long enough to get calluses. Because she was a girl? It was perfectly acceptable today for women to take up archery. Sixty years ago, when Tilly was a young woman, things were likely different.

Where their fingers touched, Josie felt an uncomfortable tingle, but she couldn't tear her hand away. Couldn't look away from Tilly.

"No one noticed you," she said.

Tilly laughed. "Of course they didn't. I was just a girl. Well, old enough to get married and bear children, but still considered a girl. I was a better shot than any man though, I'll tell you that. Stealthy, too. She never even saw me hiding in the trees. Never knew it was me. All I had to do was wait for her to come outside, holding a baby. After... I collected the arrows when I knew she wouldn't see. I was exceptional. I only missed that one time."

The scar along the side of her face blazed with heat. "Why?" she choked out.

Tilly released Josie's fingers and shrugged. "Everyone misses eventually."

"No." Josie shook her head. "Why did you do it?"

"I wish I could give you some profound reason, but it all comes down to one thing. A tale as old as time. Jealousy."

Recoiling, Josie took a step back. Unconsciously, her fingers stroked her scar. "Jealousy? Then why not kill her? Or him? They were babies."

"And the one I didn't get turned out just fine, did she?" Tilly laughed and the sound was colder than the most frigid Pennsylvania winter.

"Lila never stood a chance. You and your husband doomed her before she was even born! No matter what she did, none of those babies deserved what you did to them."

Tilly pursed her lips and nodded. "No, they didn't. It took me this long to see that. It took losing Gina. I think I always knew there would be a reckoning. I just didn't think it would come at such a cost."

Josie shook her head. "Roe Hoyt has paid a higher cost than you could if you lived to be two hundred years old."

Tilly nodded solemnly before turning away. She was almost out of sight when she looked over her shoulder. "I knew her when we were girls. Roe. She was about four years younger than me. Her father was transient. Moved around from place to place, making a living by doing work for anyone who would give it to him. Lived in the woods if he couldn't talk someone into sheltering them for a night or two. He dragged her along everywhere. Wouldn't let her speak to anyone. Told her what to do and she'd scurry off to do it because she was afraid of him. He was cruel. Sick. Roe was beautiful. Truly ethereal. Her father took a job at the farm next door to Clint's family and oh, did my Clint take a liking to her even though we were already going to be married. She didn't want attention from any man, but Clint couldn't see that. Through our entire courtship, on our wedding night, and our first anniversary I lived under the shadow of his fixation with her. Imagine finding out that he'd been visiting her at some hovel in the woods for years. Putting babies into her."

"What's her name?" Josie asked through gritted teeth.

"Now I'll set her free."

"Her name," said Josie. "What's her name?"

SEVENTY-THREE
ONE MONTH LATER

Josie reached under the metal table and set her hand on Erica's knee. It had been bobbing furiously for the last five minutes. "You don't need to be nervous. We're here to deliver good news."

From Erica's other side, Eva Owens laughed. "Oh, I think if you're not nervous visiting a prison then you need a reality check."

Erica snorted. "She's not wrong."

"You know what I meant," said Josie.

It had taken a lot for them to convince the superintendent to let the three of them visit Roe together with no glass partition between them, but ever since Josie had met with her privately to tell her about Tilly Phelan's confession, Roe had been, in the super's words, "remarkably docile."

They were sending her in with two guards just in case.

Erica drew in a shaky breath as the door to the private room swung open. Roe loped inside, her bright blue eyes catching on each one of them, lingering on her granddaughter.

The knee bobbing began again in earnest. "Oh God," Erica mumbled. "This is crazy. I can't believe we're doing this."

The guards flanked Roe as she shuffled over and sat down across the table. Her cuffs clinked against the table as her right hand twitched.

Before Josie or Eva could speak, Erica blurted out, "I'm your granddaughter."

Roe's eyes went saucer-wide and a moment later, fat tears rolled down her cheeks. She clasped her hands together and held them to her heart. "Roe," she said softly. "Roe."

"I don't understand why I can't hug her," Erica whispered into Josie's ear.

"Because she used to give people concussions just for looking at her," Eva said quietly, her smile never faltering. "I think she's past all that now, but the protocols will be in place as long as she's here."

Frenetic energy rolled off Erica's body in waves, filling the entire room. It was obvious how badly she wanted to get on with this, but Josie had a couple more questions she needed answered—for herself. So did Eva. They'd discussed the matter several times.

"Roe," she said. "Remember when we first met and you told me that Lila was bad like you?"

A nod. Yes.

Eva sat up straighter in her chair. "Remember all the times that you indicated that you killed the babies?"

Yes.

"Why?" Eva blurted out. "Why would you... let people believe that?"

"Yes or no questions, only," Josie murmured. She had her own theory as to why Roe had accepted responsibility for the deaths of her children. "Roe, you thought you were guilty because you couldn't protect them. Is that right?"

An emphatic yes this time.

"Bad because of what your father and Clint did to you?" Josie asked.

She looked at the table and nodded slowly.

Erica said, "That's bullshit. It's not your fault that they hurt you."

Roe's head snapped up. Her mouth hung open.

"It's true." Erica pushed her hands across the table, as close to Roe's as she could reach. "But I want to talk about the real reason we came to see you. We're breaking you out of here, Grandma."

Roe's eyelashes fluttered. She looked to Eva for an explanation.

"You've been exonerated. The judge will be handing down an order for your release in the new year. In a couple of weeks. You'll have to be moved to a skilled nursing facility that has a behavioral health unit, but Josie and I are working on it."

Roe sobbed, mournful and primal all at the same time. Decades of pain encapsulated in that singular sound. Instantly, it brought tears to Josie's eyes. She blinked them back because someone in this room had to hold it together.

Eva and Erica cried quietly for a few minutes, both of them staring at Roe. Josie knew they wanted to embrace her. One day they would. Very soon.

"There's one more thing," Josie said. "Your name."

Roe shook her head. "Roe, Roe."

"It's true," said Eva.

"I want to say it," Erica whispered. "Let me say it."

Her whisper wasn't quiet. Roe stilled when she heard the words and then, a huge smile broke across her face. Eva gasped. The transformation was breathtaking. For a brief moment, Josie saw the ethereal beauty that Tilly had described, and her heart broke at the realization that Roe probably hadn't smiled in six decades.

Erica grinned back at her grandmother and there, there was the resemblance.

Clearing her throat, Erica squared her shoulders and

announced the words like she was casting a spell. "Miranda Lawson."

Roe nodded and patted the table. The fingers of her right hand jerked. The smile never left her face, no matter how many tears she shed.

The rest of the visit was mostly Erica blurting out random things in a very high-pitched voice. Roe hung on every word. When the guards told her their time was up, she stood without protest, and, with a quavering hand, blew a kiss at the three of them.

For the love of God. Josie was going to have to have a Big Cry in the car on her way home.

Roe was almost to the door when Erica leapt from her seat and flew around the table. Before any of them could stop her, she threw her arms around Roe's neck in an awkward side hug that only lasted long enough for Roe to pat her arm before the guards pried them apart.

Josie looked back and forth between Erica and Eva, noticing the way their faces glowed with excitement and joy and she thought maybe, just maybe, something good had come from Lila Jensen's legacy after all.

SEVENTY-FOUR

From the bathroom on the second floor, Josie could hear the laughter and chatter of their friends and family as though they were right outside the door. It was only eight in the evening but their New Year's party was in full swing. They'd never had so many people crammed into their house before, but Josie had never been happier to have everyone they loved under one roof along with some new faces.

Her entire family was there, including Drake, and Brenna, her brother Patrick's girlfriend. Noah's brother and sister had turned up. Laura was on her best behavior, although Josie put that down to Shannon's repeated warning glares. Misty and Harris had brought food and a karaoke machine. Cindy Quinn —Harris's grandmother and Josie's former mother-in-law—had brought a collection of glittery hats and noisemakers.

Gretchen and Turner were working, but Gretchen had popped in. Josie refused to admit, even silently, that part of her hoped Turner would as well. She already knew he wouldn't, what with the way he'd balked at her invitation and said something offensive. Maybe normalcy was a good thing. Chief Chitwood, his sister Daisy, Amber, Dr. Feist, and Paula were there for the duration. Luke Creighton, Josie's former fiancé and the police department's K-9 unit, had brought his bloodhound, Blue. Trout had given him a chilly reception at first but later decided to share his Kong, which was a peace offering if Josie ever saw one. Even Sawyer had come. So far, he'd spent most of the evening chatting with Alec and Erica Slater.

It was perfect.

As she checked her makeup in the mirror, she tried to ignore the tiny voice in the back of her head that wanted to add, "except for us not having a child." It still stung. Noah had taken the news far better than she did but there were days she could tell it bothered him as well. They hadn't talked about next steps or options or if there even were any. Not yet. Everything was too raw. Noah still had nightmares about his ordeal and the two of them were wrapped up in one another, trying to make up for the days Noah had been missing. Every single one had felt like a year.

The door creaked open.

"Occupied," Josie called.

"Exactly what I was hoping for." The door clicked shut and Noah's hands gripped her hips. She had a brief glimpse of his mischievous smile before he dipped his head and started planting kisses along her jaw.

"In case you hadn't noticed," Josie said as she tipped her head to the side to give him access to her neck. "We have guests."

"They won't miss us," he said against her skin.

She turned in his arms as he slid his warm palms beneath her shirt. "What if someone has a question?"

The clasp of her bra snapped open. "Misty knows where everything is," he breathed. "I just want to see my wife naked one last time this year."

Josie's hands tangled in his thick, dark hair, the tip of her index finger brushing the scar from the graze wound. The reminder of how close she'd come to losing him made her think his crazy idea wasn't so crazy after all. But for good measure, she reminded him, "You saw your wife naked this morning. Twice."

"The third time—"

His words were cut off by the sound of a doorbell chiming from the back pocket of Josie's jeans.

Noah pulled back and waited as she took out her phone and checked the camera app. "Who would ring the doorbell?" he asked. "Is it Turner?"

Josie's brow furrowed. Something about the person standing on their doorstep was vaguely familiar. "No. I'm not sure who it is."

"Turn around."

She did. He refastened her bra and straightened her shirt. Then they walked hand in hand out of the bathroom, crossed the hall, and headed down the stairs. The bell rang again just as they reached the door. Josie opened it.

The girl couldn't have been more than fourteen years old. Black hair, dyed bright red at the ends, hung to her shoulders. Her frame was swallowed up by a hoodie three sizes too big for her. Under that was a pair of black leggings that disappeared into large men's work boots that had probably seen their best days five years ago. On the ground next to those was a duffel bag. Two curly wood shavings clung to its surface.

Josie's heart began to pound, each beat its own little earthquake. Noah squeezed her hand. "Can I help you?" he said to the girl.

"Yeah," she said, addressing Josie, voice quavering. "My dad just died and left custody of me to you."

A LETTER FROM LISA

Thank you so much for choosing to read *Husband Missing*. If you enjoyed the book and want to keep up to date with all my latest releases, just sign up at the following link. Your email address will never be shared, and you can unsubscribe at any time.

www.bookouture.com/lisa-regan

Each book presents its own unique challenges. Some are more difficult to write than others. *Husband Missing* may just be the toughest in the series to date. It's always hard to put Josie in a position where she doesn't have the benefit of her police powers or resources. Through this entire series, I've always tried to strike a balance between keeping things entertaining while also making the procedural aspects as authentic as possible. Even though Josie was in the most desperate situation possible, I still wanted her to be true to her character and true to real life insomuch as it was possible. That meant keeping her "rogue" behaviour to a minimum. This posed a lot of problems in terms of developing the plot. I hope readers will respect the choices I've made here. With every book, it is my fervent hope to bring you a story that will transport you to Denton and keep you glued to the pages until the very last word. This is a story I've wanted to tell since Book 3, *Her Mother's Grave*, and so the book you hold in your hands truly is a labor of love.

As you know, I take my research very seriously. I consult as many experts as possible through every aspect of each book. I do a lot of reading, relying on various sources: the internet, professional journals, textbooks. I take online courses or seminars whenever I can. My favorite sources, however, are people with lived experience in whatever field I'm researching. I strive to make sure I find and talk to those people with each and every book and each and every field I represent. Unfortunately, with this book, I did not receive any responses to the requests I made to speak with someone on the staff at the Pennsylvania Department of Corrections, SCI Muncy, and a reputable prison volunteer organization. I was fortunate to speak to some experts in positions adjacent to these types of organizations who provided valuable information. That said, if the scenes involving correctional facilities don't ring true, please know that I did my best. Also the Williamsport General Community Hospital doesn't exist. I made it up.

Again, thank you so much for reading. I truly can't believe I'm still getting to write this series for all you amazing readers. I'm so grateful that you still show up for Josie. I love hearing your thoughts and questions. You can get in touch with me through my website or any of the social media outlets below, as well as my Goodreads page. Also, I'd really appreciate it if you'd leave a review and recommend *Husband Missing*, or perhaps other books in the series, to other readers. Reviews and word-of-mouth recommendations go such a long way toward helping new readers discover my books. Thank you so much for your loyalty to this series and your passion for all things Josie. I hope to see you next time!

Thanks,

Lisa Regan

KEEP IN TOUCH WITH LISA

www.lisaregan.com

 facebook.com/LisaReganCrimeAuthor
x.com/LisalRegan

ACKNOWLEDGMENTS

Amazing readers: Thank you for your patience. This book took longer than usual but I hope it will be worth it. As always, I am blown away by your love and excitement for this series and how deeply invested you are in the characters of Denton. I can't say it enough: it is my privilege and pleasure to write these stories for all of you. No other readers in the world compare to you! Thank you from the bottom of my heart! Thank you, as always, to the members of my Reader Lounge. Your enthusiasm, passion, good humor, and kindness bring me so much joy!

Thank you, as always, to my husband, Fred. Let's face it. At this point, you deserve your very own superhero cape and probably a vacation after holding my hand through the whole, ugly, torturous, but also beautiful (sort of) process of writing this book. Thank you for reminding me at all the right times and in all the right ways that I really can do this. Thank you for knowing I've got this even when I don't. Also thank you so much for all your help with the archery and hunting camp research. It ended up being the thing the whole book turned on and it was very useful to be able to wake you up at three in the morning to ask things like, "What's a cam?"

Thank you to my daughter, Morgan, for always coming into my office at exactly the right time to hug me and make me laugh so that I'm refreshed and happy when I return to the page. You always know the right thing to say!

Thank you to my rock star multimedia coordinator, friend and first reader, and apparently now one-woman support group and hostage negotiator, Maureen Downey, for talking me off so many ledges. Seriously, it's got to be a record. Thank you for always reminding me of all the best reasons why I do this awesome job and, as always, for making the world go round while I disappear to Denton. Thank you to my first readers and friends: Katie Mettner, Dana Mason, Nancy S. Thompson, and Torese Hummel. As always, your input is invaluable! Thank you to Matty Dalrymple and Jane Kelly for always being on standby for plot emergencies!

Thank you to my grandmothers: Helen Conlen and Marilyn House; my parents: Donna House, Joyce Regan, the late Billy Regan, Rusty House, and Julie House; my brothers and sisters-in-law: Sean and Cassie House, Kevin and Christine Brock and Andy Brock; as well as my lovely sisters: Ava McKittrick and Melissia McKittrick. Thank you as well to all of the people who continue to spread the word about my books— Debbie Tralies, Jean and Dennis Regan, Tracy Dauphin, Jeanne Cassidy, the Regans, the Conlens, and the Houses. I appreciate you! I am deeply grateful to all the fantastic bloggers and reviewers who take the time to read and review every JQ book. I'm also thankful for the reviewers and bloggers who picked up *Husband Missing* as their first Josie Quinn story.

Thank you, as always, to Chief Jason Jay for all your prompt, patient, enthusiastic and detailed answers to my endless stream of inane questions delivered at all hours of the day and night! I can never repay you for your generous assistance! Thank you to Stephanie Kelley, my amazing law enforcement consultant, for all your insight and expertise, for reminding me what this series has always been rooted in and for always being willing to hop on a call and entertain every single bizarre and complicated scenario my crazy little writer brain can whip up! Also, thank you for not making fun of me. Thank you to Dr. Kimberlee Moran for taking so much time to discuss so many complicated topics. Your generosity astounds me!

Thank you to Kevin Brock for helping with my EMS questions. Thank you to Amy Quinn for the very detailed primer on prison protocol. Thank you to Lisa Dopp for your assistance with questions concerning visiting inmates. Thank you so much to Leanne Kale Sparks for answering all of my legal questions so thoroughly and patiently. Thank you so much to Annie Lannan for your assistance with all things related to aphasia.

Thank you to Jessie Botterill for your boundless patience, and for convincing me time and again that this was a story worth telling. Thank you for all the spontaneous calls to help work out tricky plot points again and again and again! Thank you for reading every sad, panicked email and responding so kindly and compassionately. Thank you for talking me off all those ledges. Thank you to Jenny Geras for everything, including see above, also panicked emails and ledges, as well as your insight and your perfect advice. Thank you for pushing me across the finish line after so many failed attempts that I was beginning to think the finish line was a myth. We made it! Woo-hoo! Finally, thank you to Noelle Holten, Kim Nash, Liz Hatherell, and Jenny Page, as well as the entire team at Bookouture.

PUBLISHING TEAM

Turning a manuscript into a book requires the efforts of many people. The publishing team at Bookouture would like to acknowledge everyone who contributed to this publication.

Audio
Alba Proko
Melissa Tran
Sinead O'Connor

Commercial
Lauren Morrissette
Hannah Richmond
Imogen Allport

Cover design
Head Design Ltd

Data and analysis
Mark Alder
Mohamed Bussuri

Editorial
Jenny Geras
Lizzie Brien

Made in the USA
Middletown, DE
01 April 2025